And Silently Falls the Snow

(UND LEISE RIESELT DER SCHNEE)

A NOVEL

Klaus M. Schwarzenholz

Melbourne, Australia

A catalogue record for this book is available from the National Library of Australia.

ISBN: 978-1-7637042-7-5 (Paperback)
978-1-7637042-6-8 (E-book)

Produced by Putting Words
Putting Words
PO Box 5062
Wonga Park, Victoria, 3115
Australia.
www.puttingwords.com

To Doris Leadbetter, poet, writer, mentor and friend.

May you rest in peace.

Reproduced in Memory of Klaus Schwarzenholz

To Klaus,

Whose storytelling ensures that the past is not lost to time. Your family's journey from Silesia is now woven into history through these pages, a testament to resilience, survival, and the enduring power of love.

With all our love, Robyn and Ruth.

Silently falls the snow...
Quiet are sorrow and pain...
Muted the misery of life...

(Leise rieselt der Schnee...
Still schweigt Kummer und Harm...
Sorge des Lebens verhallt...)

From: Leise rieselt der Schnee.
German Christmas song
by Eduard Ebel (1839-1905)

Chapter 1

They waited for the end to come.

The sunlight reflecting off the fresh snow highlighted the brightly painted eaves of the lodges. Icicles hung like large daggers from the roofs, sometimes breaking off with a sharp click, sometimes without any sound, coming down like an assassin's knife.

The blanket of snow covering the road was undisturbed except for a few animal tracks. No people were in sight but the doors of their houses were wide open to discourage intruders forcing their way in.

Krummhübel, the old coal mining town which transformed itself into a winter sport resort, had survived the war without any damage, or even loss of business. After the Nazi takeover in 1933 the town had become very popular with NSDAP hierarchy. Until mid-1944 the lodges and Bauden were crowded with bureaucrats and their families, among them the black uniformed SS acting like overlords. But when the Russian winter offensive started, none of the Nazi customers remained. Then the invasion of Silesia started and the battle for Breslau, Silesia's capital.

Krummhübel waited fearfully for its turn.

The sound of the Russian artillery's rolling thunder in the distance was, in a strange way, reassuring. They were still safe. Only when there was a pause did people look up and try to reassure each other in fearful whispers.

Rolf stood at the open window and listened—nothing but silence, as if the town was holding its breath. He combed his hair with his hands. His hair was dripping wet; he was perspiring despite the coldness of the winter morning.

He had listened many times before, waiting for the resumption of the artillery, but this time the silence continued.

There! Movement. Someone walked past the window in the house on the other side.

Only his neighbour. He shivered and closed the window. The waiting continued.

Krummhübel was a small ski resort at the foothills of the Schneekoppe, the highest peak of the Sudeten Mountains, bordering Czechoslovakia and Germany. The town was at the end of the road from Hirschberg, the district administration centre.

There was no other way in or out of the town. Only old men were left. The young ones were at the eastern front and the women and children were hiding in the caves and mines. The rumour was that the invaders only burned down unoccupied houses.

The waiting continued.

There was a sound in the house. He tried to identify it. Like running water—but that was impossible, the plumbing was frozen. Puzzled, he followed the sound down the hallway to the kitchen.

The sun through the kitchen window framed a huge, bear-like figure pissing into the sink. He turned his head as Rolf drew near.

'*Stoi! Stoi!* You SS?'

The leathery Mongol face distorted into a ferocious snarl, as the man spun around and punched his gun into Rolf's stomach. Rolf collapsed to the floor. The Russian pulled his clothing over his genitals. He wore a *Wehrmacht* officer's overcoat with the insignias ripped off. His bloodied boots were mismatched; looted from different bodies. His only clean clothing was his fur cap with a bright red Soviet star. He stank.

'You SS! *Stoi!*'

His shout was more of a statement than a question. Rolf struggled to sit up, trying not to vomit. He knew that only incredible luck had saved him from being instantly shot. He shouldn't have sneaked up on the man.

He raised both arms so that the Russian could see that he didn't have the SS blood-group tattoo on the inside of his upper arms. The Russian seemed to accept that Rolf was not an SS man; his demands changed.

'Uri? Uri!' He pointed to Rolf's wrist.

Rolf took off his watch, and like a gleeful child the Russian grabbed it and held it against his ear. His face lit up. Countless cracks and wrinkles proved that he was used to smiling and laughter.

'Tick, tock,' he said, moving his head from side to side like a pendulum.

Rolf lowered his aching arms but the Russian's face became a snarling mask and he slammed his gun into Rolf's stomach again. Rolf saw, through a red haze of pain, the Russian's grin as he went back to the sink to finish his piss. He turned frequently to check on Rolf, not bothering where his urine stream was going. Why did he bother to piss into the sink in the first place? Rolf thought.

The Russian started to search the kitchen. He said something to Rolf, pointing to his mouth. Bad luck, Rolf thought, there is no food left in this place. He shook his head. More shouting and kicks to his legs was the instantaneous response.

A sound came from the lounge room. The Russian froze, shouted something and fired his gun towards the sound. Bullets ricocheted through the kitchen; plaster walls exploded until his magazine was empty. He carried something to Rolf.

'Uri?' he said. Rolf recognised the remains of his cuckoo clock. 'Uri!' Rolf said.

The Russian frowned, gave Rolf a few hearty kicks in the ribs and left. Rolf passed out. As he was regaining consciousness, he could hear new voices.

'Uri? Uri?' Then a different voice, but more demanding 'Uri! Uri!'

We could have won the war if we had enough watches to hand out, Rolf thought. They would do anything for watches. He kept his eyes closed, desperately trying not to groan when the newcomers kicked him again. At last, they left and he slipped into painless darkness.

It was night when he woke. The cold numbed the pain but he was shaking violently. He stumbled to the bedroom. The feather duvets were untouched. He cried out when he saw someone standing in his bedroom.

When he realized it was only his reflection in the bedside mirror he was horrified. He was a tall man with broad shoulders and a muscular physique, looking ten years younger then his fifty-eight years, but the reflection staring back at him looked like a badly bruised seventy-year-old. His sandy coloured hair had suddenly developed large grey patches. Dried blood around his mouth gave his face the expression of a permanent snarl. He collapsed onto the bed. It seemed to take hours before he was warm enough to drift into sleep.

When he woke the next morning, bright sunlight blinded him for a few moments. His body hurt but it didn't seem to be serious, only bruises. Then he heard something which made his skin crawl.

Tanks!

The low rumble grew louder and louder. The building and his body were vibrating as the first steel monsters passed the house. The screeching from the tanks' chains, hungry for lubrication, jarred his teeth and screamed through his brain. He slumped to the ground panting, shivering, hoping to die fast.

The house continued to vibrate. There was something different; he looked up. The ceiling had developed a network of cracks and had begun to disintegrate. He rubbed burning plaster dust out of his eyes and forced himself up.

From behind the curtains he saw an endless column of tanks. His heart stopped for a moment when he became aware of infantry soldiers jumping from the tanks and entering houses.

He wouldn't survive another beating. He had to hide, but where? The soldiers were systematically combing through the houses,

occasional shots confirming that they were not only looting. Where to hide?

The attic? No, too much junk that would interest looters.

The coalbunker? No, it would take hours to create a hiding space in the neatly stacked briquettes.

Ah, yes, the well! It was deep and a casual glance wouldn't find him. He dashed out to the back of the house, lifted the wooden lid of the well, and hesitated. There was fresh snow everywhere. He swore: the well as a hiding place was out because he had just shifted the snow cover off the lid. They wouldn't even bother to look. A grenade would assure them that no one was alive down there.

Shots came from a house nearby. The sharp pain in his stomach urged him to find a solution. He looked around. Of course! There in front of him was the answer. The lavatory!

The path to the lavatory was well used, snow-free. It wouldn't give him away.

As he closed the door he heard someone coming into the backyard. The Russians were searching his house. He lifted the wooden seat, hesitated at the stink from the hole, and jumped in.

The cesspit had been in use for years and was nearly filled. He expected the surface to be frozen solid, but he was wrong. Slowly he sank down until the excrement was up to his chest. The smell was so overbearing he thought he would vomit, or pass out.

Above his head he could feel the wooden frame of the seat. He squeezed his hand under the lid and tried to pull himself out, but the suction of the icy sludge was too strong. He strained against the drag, despite his fear that the Russians would hear his panting over the noise of the tanks.

Russian voices! People coming down the path.

He let go and splashed back, sinking deeper than before.

It doesn't matter if they find me, he thought. I'll drown in my own shit anyway.

The toilet door creaked.

Oh *mein Gott*!

The Russian lifted the lid and for a moment Rolf's face was bathed in light, only to be plunged into darkness when the man placed his arse over the opening. For a moment Rolf felt lucky that the Russian didn't peer into the hole, until warm faeces began raining down.

Rolf stayed in the hole until the sounds of the tanks faded and were gone. After a few panicky moments fighting the sludge, which was trying to hold him back, he forced the lid open and climbed out.

The tanks were gone. There were no soldiers anywhere in sight.

The sun was still shining and in its warming rays he suddenly became aware that the stinking shit he was covered in was steaming and the stench was increasing by the second. He ripped his putrid clothes off and rolled his naked body in the snow. There was no water, the pump was frozen, but there was plenty of snow. He rubbed himself with snow until his body turned blue and numb.

He ran into the house. The blankets and duvets were gone and he had to cover himself in the curtains and rags that the Russians didn't think worth looting.

It was too dangerous to light a fire; the smoke would have been visible for kilometres. Slowly his body warmed up, and with the warmth came shrieking pain, as each limb's nerves came alive again.

Most of his clothes were gone. Dressed in his Sunday suit, the only one left, he searched for his friend Hans and any others who had stayed in their houses and survived.

Hans had hidden in his coalbunker. His bright smile was even brighter through the coal dust.

'Nice suit,' he said and gave Rolf a hug and jumped back. '*Herr im Himmel! What* is that stink?'

'Shit', Rolf said.

Some of the unoccupied houses were on fire or smashed by tanks, but most of Krummhübel was relatively untouched.

The town had paid a price.

Of the sixty men who stayed behind twelve had been shot. Either they didn't give the Russian looters what they demanded, usually watches, or the Russians didn't believe that there were no women in the town.

Some were shot for no reason.

But now the tanks were gone and no troops had been left behind. 'Twelve dead, we should have had prevented that.' Hans looked at

Rolf as if he had murdered the men.

'They chose to stay, like you, but didn't hide like you. You are lucky they didn't burn your house down.'

'If they had hidden, they would be alive.'

'Maybe, but they chose to stay and make the Russians believe that everyone else left. Would you have preferred four hundred raped women?'

Chapter 2

The whole town attended the funeral of the twelve murdered men.

Day-by-day the population was shrinking. Every day, loaded wagons headed down the main road, as those left behind looked on without waving goodbye. They stay with us, but they want to go, Elli thought.

Hans and Rolf pleaded with people to wait until they could all leave together. The exodus went on, some leaving in the middle of the night, as if they were ashamed.

It was a week since their ordeal in the caves and they were still recovering, especially the children. Elli's daughter Anna woke up crying every night and did not settle unless her mother lit a candle in her room and stayed until she fell asleep again. But candles were getting scarce.

One night Elli was woken early by banging and shouting coming from their neighbour's house. They were loading their wagon. She rushed out.

'Hannelore, what are you doing? Wait! It's too dangerous to go on your own.' Hannelore, a young-looking woman in her forties, and her three young daughters, stopped packing for a moment.

'Heike, get the mattress, and Lotte, don't stand around, there is more kitchen stuff to be loaded. Help Elke. *Schnell!*' The two girls looked at their mother, perplexed, but then rushed back into the house.

'Hannelore, are you listening?'

Hannelore spun around and raised her arms as if she wanted to push Elli out of her way. For a moment she stood there, tense and shaking, trying to stare Elli down. Elli forced herself to smile and reached out to her. Hannelore resisted at first but then crumbled into her arms. Sobbing, she asked Elli if she didn't know that the Poles were coming and they would all be murdered.

'The Poles? The Prisoners of War here in town?' Elli asked. She knew what Hannelore was talking about. The news was impossible to ignore, as the *Reichsradio* repeated several times a day that Polish settlers would follow the Red Army and evict the remaining German population. There were also reports that the Poles were dealing with the Germans in an even more barbaric way than the Russians.

'They said on the BBC that the Russians are giving Silesia to the Poles, and if we don't get out we'll all be killed!' Hannelore looked up, tears streaming down her face. 'I have to protect my daughters. Hans and your father are wrong to wait.'

Elli was shaken; she hadn't heard that there was any truth to the propaganda of the German or English radio broadcasts and still did not believe it. She tried to convince her neighbour. Everyone was just panicking. Hannelore stopped crying. Elli was amazed when the woman, who a moment ago was falling apart, straightened up and looked her in the eyes.

'If only half of what I've heard is true there is very good reason to be scared.'

The *Reichshof*, Krummhübel's leading hotel where Elli was employed as a chef had, like many other businesses, allocated POWs as workers for menial and dirty work in and around the hotel. Every morning three trucks arrived from Hirschberg's POW camp. The prisoners were guarded by *Wehrmacht* soldiers who accompanied the men to their designated work places. A black car carrying several SS men always escorted the men. The POWs, mainly Poles, looked starved and were often covered in bruises.

Some were so weak they were unable to work. One day Elli said jokingly to a guard that she had to feed two of the men before they were able to work. She never complained again when one of her kitchen hands told her that two SS men escorted the prisoners to their car and left with them.

'They took them back to the camps?'

'No they were back twenty minutes later—without the prisoners.'

Elli knew that her careless remark had cost the two men their lives. She expected soon to be interrogated by the Gestapo to see if she had complaints about any other POWs, or anyone else. Denunciation was a part of life in the Third Reich. Everyone spied on everyone else and people disappeared. Every German citizen listened for the sharp knock on the door in the early hours, and hid under their blankets, hoping it didn't mean them. When they heard the pleading and screaming, they held their hands over their ears wanting it to stop. After the Gestapo and their victims left, doors opened and white faces appeared, trying to identify who was taken, and who had denounced them. Maybe tomorrow it was their turn. It didn't need much—only someone telling the block-warden their neighbours listened to the BBC. Very few of the people taken away came back and if they did, they had changed. Terror was etched in their faces. Their neighbours kept away, knowing that the Gestapo would visit them again.

Elli never complained or joked again and made sure no one observed her when she fed prisoners.

'They treated them badly in the concentration camps,' Hannelore said. 'They said on the BBC that many were starved to death or even murdered. Don't expect gratitude because you treated some well. They hate us with good reason.'

'Hannelore, you can't believe everything you hear on the BBC. That's just propaganda to create fear and disunity among the population.' Elli could see by Hannelore's expression that she wasn't convinced, so she tried appealing to the woman's fear for her family. They would be safer in a convoy than on their own. A broken wheel or a lame horse could be the end of them if they travelled alone.

'I'll take my chances. I don't think we have days to spare,' Hannelore spoke with determination. 'Here Elli, I want you to have this,' she said, and handed Elli a thin, silver necklace with a zodiac pendent of Scorpio. 'Remember us. You were a good friend and neighbour.' Elli felt embarrassed; Hannelore had never before expressed herself like that.

'Wait Hannelore. Here take mine.' Elli took off her golden necklace with a single large pearl that her father had given her at the completion of her Abitur. Hannelore blushed.

'Elli, that is very expensive. I can't take that.'

'Sure you can,' Elli smiled. 'Remember us too.'

When the wagon rolled slowly down the road, Elli felt her eyes burning and asked herself if it was really wise to stay.

Two days later, a small convoy of Polish soldiers arrived in Krummhübel.

Except for the Lutheran church, the *Rathaus* was the largest building in Krummhübel. The buildings faced each other across the cobblestone street. In 1933 the Nazis replaced the council with Nazi party appointees and the SA made the town hall its headquarters. In 1941, with the increase in holidaying party officials, the Gestapo also established itself in the building. The *Rathaus*'s locally mined granite facade was in stark contrast to the church's light sandstone structure and contributed to the building's sinister impression.

The *Rathaushalle* was bursting with people. Laid out as a multipurpose room, there was no fixed seating. Flimsy fold-up chairs strained under the weight of people sharing them. The whole population of Krummhübel was squashed into the room, built for a maximum of three hundred people. In the aisles there was jostling as people tried to see the stage.

The freezing hall's central-heating boiler was shut down for lack of coal and the room's icy air mingled with heat from the densely packed crowd. Tobacco smoke and breath produced a choking fog in which the crowd was barely visible and only the brightly lit stage stood out.

Like most others, Elli was dressed in layer upon layer of clothes, restricting her movements, and barely allowing her to fit into the narrow space her chair occupied. To her left was Elfriede Schulze, the local butcher's wife, a large woman dressed in a moth-eaten fur coat with a blanket wrapped around her legs, forcing her to share part of Elli's seat. To the right Elli was squashed against Irmgard Kopetz, one of her children's teachers. Irmgard was dressed in a worn-out coat, with a thin scarf covering her head. Hunched in her chair, she shivered.

'Elfriede, please share your blanket with us. Irmgard is freezing.'

Elfriede looked at her, annoyed, but then spread the blanket out over Elli and Irmgard's laps. 'Irmgard, swap seats with me; you'll be warmer between us.' Elli manoeuvred the small woman between her and Elfriede.

'*Danke*, Elli.' Irmgard spoke softly. 'How silly of me not to dress properly.' Elli smiled at her. She knew the widowed teacher had barely enough clothes and blankets for her daughters.

'Who do these Polacks think they are?' Elfriede said to Elli, ignoring Irmgard between them. 'We were ordered to come to this meeting. How come Hans Kruse let them tell us what to do? When your father was the *Bürgermeister* no one told him what to do. Kruse is so weak.' Elli didn't answer. Elfriede Schulze looked even more annoyed and turned to others for support.

'What will they do to us Elli?' Irmgard Kopetz's whispery voice was only just audible.

'Who, Irmgard?'

'The Poles! I heard terrible things. They rape and murder women and children.'

'Everyone is scared. There are so many rumours. We survived the Russians and we'll cope with the Poles. Hans and my father will know what to do.' Irmgard stared at her for a moment. The fear in her face was undiminished as she shrank back into her seat.

The walls were still plastered with large posters alerting the German population to be suspicious, not only of strangers, but anyone. Spies could be everywhere. In the centre above the stage, some thoughtful soul had hung a painting over the faded official photograph of the *Führer*.

Much better, Elli thought, but rather silly to leave the swastika flags on each side.

She looked around and shivered when she saw several small round holes in the cracked plaster wall, surrounded by brown discolorations. Bullet holes and blood. Maybe someone was shot against that wall. She felt sick in her stomach but still tried to see if there were more. The smoky atmosphere in the hall deflected the light and made it impossible.

'Irmgard, what do you think those holes in the wall are?' Irmgard looked at the wall beside her. When she turned back to Elli, her white face showed Elli that she had drawn the same conclusion.

'*Oh mein lieber Gott*, someone was shot here.'

Elli remembered her terror when, in the middle of the night, the Gestapo arrested her father and every other member of the council and took them to the Rathaus. Had it not been for Hans, Rolf would have disappeared like so many others. Hans, the newly appointed administrator, used his connections to have Rolf freed, at great risk to himself.

The hall had been a cause of anxiety for Elli since her childhood. It was where her mother directed the local amateur theatre group. Elli did not remember the stage being so small. It had seemed a huge space with nowhere to hide and with an invisible audience hanging on her every movement and word. She hated it, even though she had participated in only two plays. The first time she had forgotten her lines and Ruth had saved her with several prompts. The second time she forgot her lines again, and Ruth was not around to rescue her, so she improvised. She ignored the bewildered looks of the other performers and her mother's gestures and continued to demolish the play. The audience responded with howling laughter. They loved it, but

Elli never went on stage again— unlike Ruth, who loved to perform, never forgot a line, had impeccable timing and always looked striking.

If Ruth had not become a successful painter, Elli knew she could have been a famous actress.

Suddenly there was a commotion. Elli's thoughts jolted back to the Rathaus. Hans was coming through the back door, followed by four men in Russian uniforms. No, not Russian, Polish!

Hans went on to the stage and raised both arms. The noise died down.

'Friends and neighbours, the purpose of this meeting is to decide whether to stay in Krummhübel, or to leave.'

His voice was low, barely audible. Angry hisses from all sides finally silenced those who had continued to talk.

'By now, all of you are aware that Polish settlers are coming into Silesia. These officers have told us that the first group of settlers is only two days away and that we have to decide now if we want to stay or leave. The settlers will have their choice of our houses, our business, our property.'

There was silence in the hall.

A falling chair sounded like an explosion. People jumped off their chairs, yelling and hurling abuse at the men on the stage. Hans stumbled back from the onslaught. The four soldiers made attempts to unbutton their pistol holsters. Hans lifted his arms, and gestured at one of the Polish officers to step forward.

The Pole, his face ablaze, started to yell, slapping his hands together, emphasising each word.

'This is not your town anymore! In the future it will be called by its Polish name, Karpacz. Karpacz!' he said again. 'Germany has lost the war. Now the German people will pay for it. We take back what is ours. Silesia was, and is now again, West Poland. You can stay, but if you do you will have to work for us.'

The room exploded, everyone shouting at the same time. 'Please friends, settle down and let me talk!' Hans tried to cut in. He had to repeat himself a few times but slowly the crowd quietened. 'Friends, we have to face reality. Silesia is no longer German and the Poles will settle here.'

The crowd was restless. This was not what they wanted to hear.

Several people interjected but Hans took no notice of them.

'Don't expect any sympathy or understanding from the Poles. As they see it, we are still their enemies. We invaded their land and now it's their turn. They give us one choice only—to stay or leave. And we have to decide here and now.'

The Polish officer stepped forward again.

'We will allow you to stay if you want to. You destroyed our country and murdered our people, but we will forgive the past. You can help to rebuild Silesia.' He stopped for a moment and looked around at his audience. 'You won't be allowed to own property; only Polish people can do that. You will work and you will earn your living.'

'What, stay as your slaves?' Elfriede, who until now had been talking to others around her, jumped up. To Elli's horror, she shook her fists at the stage.

'Sit down Elfriede! Are you totally mad?' Elli forced her down. The Polish officer didn't see from where the interjection had come, but responded to it.

'We were your slaves; you used us and killed us, but we are not like you. You may stay, but you will have to work. You can stay in your houses if Polish people don't need them, but you'll have to pay rent to the Polish government. Should you decide to leave, you must be gone within two days. You must not take anything with you, except clothes, pots and pans. No animals, with the exception of one horse for each wagon. This is a very generous offer from the Polish people. We expect you to be grateful.'

With a formal smile, he stepped back.

Elli was not sure if the Poles really expected the Germans to stay.

What the speech certainly achieved was a decision.

When Hans called for a show of hands in favour of leaving, there were no abstentions.

Chapter 3

Two weeks earlier.

'We can't leave now,' Rolf said. 'It's too dangerous. Look.' He spread out a map of the area around Krummhübel.

Both his daughters, Ruth and Elli and four of his five grandchildren were in the kitchen.

Elli, 34 years old, blond, tall and slim, the mother of three children, represented the perfect Arian woman for the Nazis. Like a highly regarded breeding cow, as a jovial SS man dining in her restaurant highlighted, by offering to sire two more children for her so she would be awarded the 'Mother Cross' medal. Furious she slapped him and walked out. Moments later a pale, shivering restaurant manager asked her if she was insane and warned her that she would be visited by the Gestapo, but nothing happened.

Elli's sister Ruth, 38 years, was a brunette with the petite figure of a ballet dancer. The sisters were so different that Rolf often had to field questions about how sure he was of their paternity. The joke went sour when Ruth was first refused her Aryan certificate, a written confirmation that none of her ancestors, going back to great-grandparents, were Jewish. She had studied painting in Breslau and Berlin and many of her teachers had a Jewish background, which was also held against her.

Ruth's two children were playing with pots and pans they had dragged out of the cupboards, utterly unaffected by the tension between the adults.

'Elfi, Hubert, stop that noise. Put the pots back.' The two-year-old boy and his four-year-old sister ignored their mother. Fritz, Elli's son, stood between the women and stared at the map his grandfather hammered at with both fists. Anna, his sister, sat on her grandfather's lap, looking up at the old man as if she expected a goodnight story.

'It's not a question of if we can leave.' Elli said, her voice rising as she continued. 'We have no choice, father. We have to leave.'

'Look at the map,' he said, stabbing it with his index finger. 'Look. The area we have to go through is under deep snow and more is coming. We would never make it. We would get stuck, freeze to death. We have to wait as long as we can.'

Elli and Ruth looked at each other. Elli tried again. 'Papa, the Russians could be here in a few days.'

'I know, I know, and we will leave, but not right now. We have to wait until the weather improves. I think it may even be safer to leave after the Russians get here. There is nothing for them in Krummhübel.'

Rolf hoped that the Russians would even bypass Krummhübel. Not only was there nothing of strategic interest in the town, it was at the end of the road to the foothills of the Schneekoppe. If troops came to the town, they would have to back track to Arnsdorf to get out of the cul-de-sac. There were only footpaths leading over the mountain to the Czech border.

'That is crazy!' Elli said. 'Have you heard what the Russians did in Eastern Prussia?'

With the fall of Eastern Prussia, the most eastern of the German provinces, rumours were spreading of large-scale slaughter and rape by the Russian troops. Radio Greater Germany, whose announcements had to be listened to by every citizen who didn't want to risk arrest and a concentration camp, went into great details. The Red Army shot all males, even young boys, and every female they found was raped, sometimes many times over by gangs of soldiers.

'Of course, it's on every one of Goebbels's radio stations—if you believe them.' Rolf said, with a dismissive wave of hand.

'I wish to God that it was nothing but propaganda.' Elli grabbed Rolf's face with both hands. Her eyes were red, and tears streamed down her face. 'Papa, the refugees have told us stories so horrible they are hard to believe, but we have heard them again and again. They are animals. No woman, no girl escapes.'

'I've heard the stories.' Rolf said.

'Papa, we have to leave! I don't want my daughter to...' She slumped on the chair, sobbing. 'Oh God, help us.'

Ruth crouched down, enclosed her sister in her arms, and rocked her.

'I know what is happening in Eastern Prussia.' Rolf hesitated. 'Of course I do. I just didn't want to scare you even more.' He took both his daughters in his arms and gently kissed them on their heads. 'In the last few days Hans and I have worked hard to prepare places where all our women and children can hide.'

'Hide?' Ruth and Elli looked at him. 'How can you hide five hundred women and three times as many children? Where can we go?'

Rolf explained that Hans Kruse, the town mayor, and the town committee of which Rolf was a member had developed an emergency plan.

Krummhübel was honeycombed with old mine shafts as well as limestone caves. The idea was to hide all women and children for as long as the Russian troops were in town. After the Russians left, the men who had chosen to stay in their houses would retrieve their families.

'It's not only women and children we'll have to hide; each family will have to take a horse with them.' Rolf looked at the disbelief mirrored in his daughters' faces.

'Papa, have you any idea how strange that sounds? Papa you...' Elli spoke gently as if he was a child.

'Let me see if I've got this right,' Ruth interrupted. 'Not only do you want to hide about two thousand women and children but also....' She tried to calculate the number of horses.

'One hundred and seventy-eight horses—Clydesdales,' Rolf said.

Two years ago, the local brewery closed down, unable to keep production going when all their brewers were drafted to the eastern front and their supply of hops and malt dried up. The breweries'

Clydesdales, which had pulled the wagons delivering beer barrels to the local pubs, were unsuccessfully offered for sale. The town rallied to adopt the animals to prevent them ending up at the knackers.

'But they are Clydesdales! They are as big as elephants—and you want to hide them too?' Ruth said. 'And why do you want to hide the horses?'

'Because refugees from Eastern Prussia have told me that the Russians are slaughtering domestic animals for food, or just for revenge. The Clydesdales are our only form of transport. Without them we'll be walking, which would be suicide in January's cold and snow.'

'It's impossible,' Elli said. 'There is no way you could hide all these people and those big animals. Not even for a few hours.'

Rolf explained how the town committee had prepared some of the old coalmines and a large limestone cave. They had made sure the places were safe, and intended to allocate the families over several mines and the cave. The cave was large enough for thousands, but when the Russians come the Krummhübel people won't have time to get to just one place and therefore would have to go to the nearest hiding place. Rolf calculated that they would have to hide for one or two days at the most.

'I don't want to hide like a rat in a hole but we don't seem to have any choice,' Elli said.

'None!' Ruth said. 'I don't see how hiding all these people and horses in the mines will work, but I can't come up with another idea.'

Three days later a single *Wehrmacht* truck, with loudspeakers mounted on the roof, stopped in the market square.

'People of Krummhübel, the Russian Army will come through your town within the next few hours. The *Führer* orders you to fight. Every German must resist the Bolshevik hordes. Anyone who runs away will be shot as deserter.' The truck's engine started up and it turned and rolled slowly out of the town.

There was no way to follow the truck or the next SS or Field-Gendarmerie would stop them. They would recruit all the boys, even those as young as twelve. The older men without any discharge papers from the army, or those who were sick, would be dealt with as deserters and shot on the spot. They had to activate their plan and hide—from the Germans and the Russians. Rolf's family would hide in the limestone caves only a few hundred metres from their house.

'Papa, everyone knows about the limestone caves, have you thought of that? You can't seriously call them a hiding place,' Elli said.

'I have my doubts that the Russians know our tourist attractions. Two days ago, to make sure, we pulled down all the signs pointing to the caves.'

During the last few weeks, the men had feverishly prepared the hideouts by storing food, water, blankets, and hay for the horses and for the families to use as bedding material.

'But the caves have been closed for years. They can't be safe anymore.'

'They are safe,' Rolf said. 'Don't you remember? At one stage during the war they were being prepared as bomb shelters. Totally stupid of course. Why on earth should anyone waste a single bomb on a little tourist town and what...?' He stopped in mid sentence. 'Herman where are you going?' His grandson froze and let go of the kitchen door handle.

'I have to report to my group. We are ordered to defend the bridge at the entrance to the town, *Opa*.'

'Defend the bridge? Your group? You are not even Hitler Youth.

Since when do they send children to defend a town?' 'We have five Bazookas. We'll stop the tanks.'

Rolf shuddered, seeing the enthusiasm on his grandson's face. The boy really believed that his group of twelve-year-olds could defend the town. If the boys were even allowed to try, not only would they be killed, but the Russians would flatten the town.

Despite his age Herman was also in pre-military, the preparation for the paramilitary Hitler Youth, the Youth Folk. All German boys were compulsory members in these organisations. From the age of ten to fourteen all boys had to participate in the Young-Folk and from fourteen to eighteen in the pre-military Hitler Youth. Herman was drafted two years earlier into the Youth-Folk and was recently promoted from a *Pimpf* to *Jungenschaftsführer,* a group leader of over fifteen other boys. He was very proud of his new rank. His unquestioning loyalty to the group, and adoration of Hitler, scared Rolf. He knew how effective the Nazis were in turning children against their families, encouraging them to report any deviation against the state. Elli tried to tell him her son would never do that but how could a twelve-year-old resist when to do so would make him an outsider? Ten-year-old Fritz was nearly drafted into the Hitler Youth but his asthma saved him. Only healthy Arians were real Arians besides, with the invasion of the eastern provinces, the authorities were not drafting boys into the Pre-Hitler Youth organisation.

Herman's mother made a decisive move to resolve the situation.

Elli stepped up to her son and hit him with her flat hand, left and right across the face.

'You are not going anywhere, my boy. You are my son and twelve years old. You won't run out of here and play soldier and neglect your duties. You know that you are needed here to look after your brother and sister.'

'But, but...' tears were running down Herman's face. 'My *Führer* needs me.'

Elli enclosed her son in her arms. 'We need you more. Beside *Opa* you are the only man in the family. You have to look after us. Didn't they teach you that?'

'But I've sworn an oath to the *Führer*, I...' Elli held her crying son as tight as she could.

They had only a few candles left and the carbide lantern had run out of fuel. Darkness was closing in, holding the families in its paralysing grip. They were deep underground, but still everyone whispered as if the Russians were close. From somewhere out of the darkness Elli could hear dripping water. The cave used to be a tourist attraction but in 1943, when the guides were drafted and sent to the Eastern Front, it was shut down.

The worsening war situation prevented any maintenance, and the constant humidity and occasional flooding had destroyed the internal wooden structures, so the families had to stay close together.

Elli had no idea how many people were in the cave but she knew there were at least twenty families. Each family had taken a horse into the cave, their only hope to make it westwards when they were able to leave the cave. With each extinguishing light, people and horses moved closer together, seeking warmth and reassurance from each other.

'Elli, are you awake?'

'Shhhh! Not so loud, Ruth, you'll wake the children.' 'I need the candle. Elfi has to go to the lavatory.'

'It's the only one we have left. If you take it, it'll be pitch dark.' 'I've got to have it,' Ruth said. 'There's too much shit close

by. It's disgusting, everyone crapped where they sleep. We should have organised toilet pits.'

'*Ja*, you're right, but who knew we would have to stay here for

days?'

'We'll be back in a moment,' Ruth took the candle. The erratic movement of the light looked like a firefly disappearing into the darkness.

Elli waited. She could hear Ruth and Elfi but the cave distorted sounds, making it impossible to know how far away they were.

The only light came from candles reflecting on the large bulk of a few horses. Nothing interrupted the silence but the horses' gentle snorting and the occasional scraping of hooves.

With the sense of sight and sound reduced, Elli's other senses were on alert.

The cave's humidity had penetrated their clothes. Everything was clammy and smelled as if their clothes and their bodies were rotting.

The smell of human faeces was powerful but outstripped by the horses' excrement and urine.

If we stay here much longer, we'll rot or go insane, Elli thought. Feverishly, she tried to think of something pleasant, clean, without these assaulting smells. She saw herself as a child, her mother gently soaping her in the bathtub. The image was filled with warmth, the perfume of soap, the gentle touch of her mother's hands. Something slowly penetrated the picture: a clearer, urgent question. Where were Ruth and Elfi?

'Ruth? Elfi? Ruth, answer please.' There was no reply. Oh God, what did she do now? Too dark to search. She couldn't leave her children. If she screamed, others would panic. She had to do something! 'Ruth?' She pulled back in horror as someone touched her.

'What is it? You'll wake the children,' Ruth said.

'Don't do that again.' Elli could barely control her anger. 'Sneaking up on me like that.'

'Calm down. You were asleep when we came back.'

Elli tried to relax, but the darkness closed in on any chance of comfort.

'Ruth?'

'*Ja*.'

'We have to get out of here. The stink, the cold and damp, I can't stand it anymore.'

'We must wait until Papa and the others come to get us,' Ruth said. 'We wouldn't find the way out of here. We have to wait.'

'How much longer? It's been three days.'

'If we left too early, and if we did find the way out, the Russians could be still there.'

'Better them than slowly dying or going insane.' 'Just a little longer, *Liebling*. Papa will come soon.'

Elli did not mention her greatest fear: that their father had been killed and no one would come for them.

When she tried to move Anna into a more comfortable position, her daughter felt like a limp doll. She was unconsciousness, not asleep.

'Anna! Wake up! Anna?' She shook her. Her panic increased as the girl's head rolled from side to side. 'Anna!'

'What's the matter?' Ruth said. 'She won't wake up.'

Ruth held the candle close to Anna's face. 'She's sleeping, deep asleep.'

'I have to get her out.'

Suddenly, voices came out of the darkness.

'Papa! Ruth, Papa is coming to get us out!'

'Be quiet.' Ruth extinguished the candle. '*Schnell*, everyone, put the candles out.' Elli saw a light flashing in the distance as soon as it was dark.

'What are you doing?' she whispered.

'They don't sound like Papa and Hans,' Ruth said. 'Oh God, the Russians have found us.'

The voices came closer. Elli tried to understand them, but the cave's echo made it impossible. It sounded like German—but she wasn't sure. Suddenly a beam of light hit one of the horses.

'They are here! We've found them!' It was Hans' voice.

Chapter 4

The heavy snowfall diminished the scarcely present daylight to a twilight of swirling shadows.

The convoy—one hundred and eighty-six horse-drawn wagons and more than eighteen hundred people, stretching nearly two kilometres along the main road—waited for inspection by the Polish troops.

The majority of the wagons were converted hay carriers. They were solid but basic: a two-metre-wide platform with four wheels and a driver's bench. The high sides were solid latticework to support hay-bales. The front and back were open. Some people had fitted a second floor for sleeping space and left the narrow base for storage. Tarpaulins, blankets, whatever could be found, had been used to make the wagons weatherproof.

From time to time Elli could hear horses snort as they blew snow off their nostrils.

All the animals were well looked after and covered with blankets.

Without the horses they would have been stranded.

Elli and Ruth had agonised all night over what to take and what to leave behind, only to conclude that there was no space to take anything other than the minimum they were allowed: clothes, bedding, cooking utensils, food, and fodder for the horse. Elli's wagon had to sleep Elli and her children, Herman, Fritz and Anna, and after everything was loaded, and the children squeezed in between the luggage, the wagon was packed tight. Luckily Ruth and her two children, Elfi and Hubert could travel with Otto and Erica Schlichte who had no children and a larger wagon.

It was ten o'clock. They had been in the queue for more than four hours. Elli and Elfriede tried to keep warm by stomping around their wagons, visiting neighboring rigs and making litres of hot tea on Elli's small carbide-stove.

As the adults waited, cursed the Poles and exchanged news and gossip, their children built snowmen. Soon, an army of snowmen, like frozen soldiers, surrounded the wagons.

Still no sign of the Poles.

Rolf was travelling in the leading wagon with Hans and Ulricke Kruse. Elli's rig was in the twelfth position and Ruth was at the back of the convoy. Ruth could have travelled with Elfriede but her dislike of the feisty butcher's wife made her choose the Schlichte's offer.

As the elected convoy leader, Rolf had been up all night, checking rigs and reassuring people. Grimfaced, he finally arrived at Elli's wagon.

'Here, Papa, you need this.' Elli handed him a cup of steaming tea. Gratefully he sipped the hot fluid, and coughed as it took his breath away.

'Is there any tea in this schnapps?'

'Only a drop,' Elli smiled.' You not only look frozen but very worried. Trouble?'

'I just hope the Poles aren't inspecting the houses first,' Rolf said, wiping his mouth.

'Why do you say that?' Elfriede said.

Rolf told them that many families had sabotaged their houses. Floorboards were partially cut; staircases had nails and screws removed, so it wouldn't take much for someone to enter a house and find they were in the cellar. Some homeowners were more ingenious and had cut or removed power cables, cut pipes, and damaged roofs. Many houses could be death-traps.

'Well, let's hope we are far away before the Polish settlers move in.' Rolf walked off to continue his inspection.

'What fantastic ideas!' Elfriede smiled at Elli. 'Compared to that, I hardly did anything.'

'What? You damaged your own home? It never occurred to me to sabotage my family's home.'

Elli shuddered at the thought of damaging her parents' house to disrupt a Polish family settling in. Two years ago, her husband Claus, the father of her three children, had left for the Russian front and had not returned. Her mother had died at the same time so it seemed common sense to move back into her parents' house. Damaging the home that she and her sister had grown up in would be a sacrilege for Elli. She only hoped that the Polish family moving into the house would find it as much a home as she had.

'Elli! Come on, girl! That's not your parent's house any more.

A Polish family is going to move in, and into my place. I wanted to make sure that they didn't get it totally for free, I just shredded the linen, damaged the rugs and a few other things. Nothing like what Rolf just described. More an annoyance than danger. I wouldn't like to have a dead woman or child on my conscience.'

For Elfriede leaving her home was less traumatic. Married for only two years, without children, and her husband also somewhere in Russia, her house was an empty shell without many emotions or memories attached to it.

'But it's your and your husband's home and he is still alive. You told me you got a letter from him only two weeks ago.'

'*Ja*, two weeks ago. But every day they are dying at the front.'

Elli knew that this was Elfriede's way of dealing with the possibility of her husband being killed at any time, by being prepared for the worst in the hope of reducing the grief should it really happen.

'Elfriede, he is alive. As long you don't get one of the dreadful letters that Ruth and I got, you must believe that he is alive. He needs that, and so do you.'

'I'm sorry Elli. I sometimes forget that Claus is missing. That must be even harder than definitely knowing, like Ruth, that her husband won't come back.'

'No! Horst is dead. I at least have the hope that Claus is alive, even though not knowing is tearing me apart.'

'At least you have the children,' Elfriede said.

'*Ja*, the children, children who have only their mother to whom they are a constant reminder of their father. Maybe you are the lucky one Elfriede.'

Elli saw Herman disappear into one of the houses nearby. She remembered being in that house. Herman's old teacher lived there. She had been to his place many times after Herr Schneider had sent her letters about Herman's school performance.

'Anna, why is Herman going into Herr Schneider's house?' 'I don't know, Mama. Maybe Herman and Fritz are collecting things for their stupid snowmen.'

'But they can't just go into other people's houses.' 'But all the people are here. The houses are empty.' 'That doesn't matter. Wait here, I'll get him.'

By habit she knocked at the door and instantly realised the futility of doing so. She pushed the unlocked door open and went inside. The house was dark and cold. In the kitchen stood a container full of coal briquettes. The spilled coals and the coal-dust handprints on the kitchen bench suggested that Herman had found eyes for his snowman. But where was he?

'Herman.' First, she whispered but as no answer came back, she shouted. 'Herman, you come here at once! Herman, do you hear me?'

'Yes, Mama.'

'Let's go, young man. You can't just go into other people's houses.'

'But Mama, I haven't ...' 'Out, now.'

Herman dashed out, avoiding the slap his mother tried to land on his bottom. Elli followed him. As she passed one of the bedrooms, she saw light coming from under the door. She knocked but there was no answer. She knocked again and as there was still no answer, she opened the door.

'Herr Schneider? Are you in here? Herr Schneider are you...oh my God!'

The light came from a candle. The candle had melted into a pool of wax and the wick was slowly drowning. The flickering light shone on the head of the old man. Elli touched his face. It was stiff and cold. He was dead.

The children called Herr Schneider 'The Pea', because of a dominant wart on his nose. She saw the wart on the cold face. On the bedside table was an empty box of sleeping tablets.

The Pea had decided to stay.

Outside, Elli saw Herman running over to a faceless and noseless snowman. Herman's face was red with excitement as one hand held out a couple of carrots and the other clutched some briquettes against his chest. His snowman would be perfect.

Her daughter relieved the boredom by throwing snowballs at the teacher's house. Wrapped in Elli's fur coat and with an equally oversized fur hat, she looked like a fur ball. Her blonde hair cascaded from under the hat and with squeals of delight, the little girl was systematically smashing the teacher's windows.

'Anna! You horrible child! Come here!' But before she was able to grab her daughter, Fritz came over, triumphantly holding up a large carrot.

'Look what I found. The biggest snowman nose in the world.'

His triumph was immediately shattered when he saw his brother's bundle of carrots.

'Mine is bigger,' he said, defiantly.

Fritz rushed to the snowman, fell over his long coat and disappeared into the deep snow. When he surfaced, he screamed with anger. The carrot was gone, lost into the unfathomable snowdrift. The howling laughter of his brother and sister ended in screams when Fritz hurled well-aimed snowballs at them.

The waiting continued.

'What is that noise?' Elfriede said. 'It sounds like people screaming—and something else.' The sounds came from the front of the convoy.

'Dogs?' Elli said.

'No, it sounds like someone is shouting commands,' Elfriede said. 'Look, over there, two wagons ahead. Someone is coming!'

'*Ja*, you are right. It's a group, but I can't identify them. The snow—wait a second. Uniforms! They're in uniforms, and they've got guns. Poles!'

The inspection had started.

The news travelled rapidly from wagon to wagon. People hurried back to their rigs, shooed the children back inside the flimsy safety of the wagons, and waited.

Elli herded her children into the wagon and told them to lie down. They protested but the urgency in their mother's voice quickly settled them down.

And they waited. The sounds from the front of the convoy where the inspection had begun came closer.

Elli's wagon was the next to be searched. Elli was scared. What would happen if they found the family jewellery? Was it well enough hidden?

Elli stayed on the driver's bench, trying to look busy, by tying the tarpaulin down. From behind her back she heard voices and the squeaking sound of snow compressing; someone was walking towards her.

'You, woman, off wagon, *robota, robota, schnell, schnell*!'

One of the two approaching soldiers shouted at her in a mixture of German and Polish. He was a young man wearing a dirty, long, army overcoat. A Kalashnikov sub-machine gun hung over his shoulder. There was no doubt that he took his job very seriously.

'Please sir, be careful. My children are in the wagon and my little daughter is ill.'

The boys' white faces appeared from under the tarpaulin at the back. Elli frantically gestured them to duck down but they continued to stare wide eyed at the approaching soldier. The soldier stared back, then moved to the side of the wagon and lifted the tarpaulin. Among all the clothing, pots, pans and other household items the light fell on Anna, pretending to be sleeping. The soldier bent over the sleeping girl. A faint smile lit up his face and tenderly he adjusted her blanket, stood back and dropped the tarpaulin.

'Your wagon right, woman,' he grunted, and left.

Elli realised that she had held her breath during the whole episode. She opened the tarpaulin again and moved her daughter from the hidden items.

'It's was lumpy,' Anna said. 'Is the bad man gone, Mama?' '*Ja*, he is gone, but he wasn't really a bad man.'

By now, there were Polish soldiers everywhere and from the frustrated shouts and yelling Elli concluded that the Poles were helping themselves to whatever they wanted.

'Polack swine.' Elli heard Elfriede's loud voice. 'Go away, or I'll break your scrawny neck, you thieving dog.'

Moments later, Elli saw two Poles hastily climb out of the wagon, trying to avoid pots and pans being thrown at them, as they moved out of range. Elfriede appeared in the tarp opening, waving a butcher's hatchet.

'*Dreckige, verfluchte, verkommene, Schweine!* Come back so I can bash in your heads!'

Amazingly, the soldiers did not retaliate, but disappeared down the convoy.

Elli was impressed.

From one of the wagons further up came a woman's high-pitched screams. Household items were ejected and then a woman fell out, picked herself up again and came running towards Elli. She fell down, struggled to her feet and continued to run. As she came closer, Elli could see that she was naked except for a torn skirt. She left a trail of blood in the snow. Behind her, a Polish soldier climbed out of her wagon and stumbled after her, occasionally falling down but laughing and waving a gun. Elli rushed forward and wrapped her coat around the sobbing, shaking woman. The left side of her face was swollen, bite marks were visible on her neck and breasts, and blood was running down her legs.

'Help me to get her into our wagon,' Elli shouted at Elfriede. She turned to a stunned neighbour. 'Susie, get Dr. Schreiber.'

Schreiber was not a real doctor, but a vet.

The soldier finally caught up. His face was flushed, his hands covered with blood, and there was the sour smell of Slivovitz on his breath.

He grinned as he tried to push Elli out of his way to follow Elfriede and the woman into the wagon. She must have seen him. She screamed.

'Don't let him in! Keep him away! He hurt me, oh, please don't...' Her pleas drowned in hysterical sobs.

The soldier grabbed Elli by the arm, trying to pull her way. Elli bent over and sunk her teeth into his hand. He howled in pain and tried to pull his hand away. Elli hung on. She wouldn't let him enter the wagon. She felt a sharp pain below her ribcage. Without letting go, she saw his gun pressed against her body and the soldier fumble for the trigger. She heard voices shouting.

'Elli, let go! Don't shoot! Don't shoot!'

There was a violent jerk. Four arms ripped her away from the Pole. Elfriede with the help of another woman pushed her down in the snow, and then Elfriede stood up and faced the man, who was shaking his bleeding hand.

'Try to do that with me, you Schwein. Come on, try it.' She stepped towards him. He stumbled back in surprise, dropped his gun and bent down to retrieve it. Elfriede's slammed her foot into his groin. With a long, deep groan he fell on his side hugging himself as Elfriede stood over him with a malicious grin. The soldier recovered fast, groped with both hands in the snow and came up with his gun.

He stood up, his face distorted by pain and anger. He lifted the gun to his hip, aiming at the women. Oh God, who will look after our children, Elli thought. That bastard will kill us. I don't want to die!

A ring of people closed around them. The soldier looked around like a trapped animal, his eyes wide open, his body trembling.

'Halt! I'll shoot.' His hoarse voice was only just comprehensible. Sweat ran off his face and steamed in the cold air. He lifted his gun as the crowd closed in.

He fired a burst over their heads, shouted something in Polish, and then pointed the gun directly at the crowd and pulled the trigger.

Nothing happened, only a click.

Feverishly, he ripped out the magazine and tried to load another one. Shots rang out from behind the crowd. A Polish officer ran towards them, a revolver in his hand. He shouted at the soldier, slapped his face and ripped his gun away.

There was silence as everyone stared at the soldier and the officer.

Suddenly, an older man pushed his way through the ring of people. With a swift movement, he lifted a pitchfork and thrust it into the rapist's chest. As he pulled the pitchfork out, the man's shirt turned red. The old man lifted his weapon again for another blow. The officer fired. The old man stumbled, fell back, still holding the pitchfork. The soldier fell forward onto it and impaled himself. With a gurgling sound, the soldier rolled sideways. A large pool of blood stained the snow around his body.

The old man had a small round hole in his forehead. He continued to convulse for a few moments and then was still.

'My God, they are both dead,' Elfriede gasped. 'Who is that man?' Elli said.

'Peter Braun, Lara's father, the woman in your wagon,' Elfriede said.

More soldiers arrived. They moved slowly toward the crowd, their guns aimed at the people.

The officer shouted in Polish. The soldiers hesitated, stopped.

They shouldered their weapons and four of them picked up their comrade and carried him away.

The officer turned to the crowd.

'He was a good man but war makes people bad. Bury the old man and then go back to your families.' He walked off.

The inspection continued without further incident.

Chapter 5

Strange: no legs. She tried to move them, but there was nothing. Panic, and then pain. It came as a biting, stabbing sensation up from her toes. She opened her eyes but what she saw did not make sense. Brilliant white light followed by darkness and white again. And what was that flapping sound? Someone must have left a window open. Slowly her eyesight adjusted and she stared with disbelief at her legs. A thick layer of snow covered them and more snow was drifting in through the flapping tarpaulin.

She forced herself to get up despite the disobedience of her legs and the biting pain in her toes.

The tarpaulin was as stiff as a board. Only where it bent to the movement of air could Elli push it open and slide out of the wagon. The landing was soft as she submerged in the powdery snow. The pain in her toes forced her up, hopping from foot to foot.

'Elli what are you doing, dancing?' Ulrich was in a neighbouring wagon. He laughed as Elli desperately tried to get some circulation back into her frozen feet.

'*Schweinehund!* My feet are dead and all you can do is laugh.' 'Do they hurt?'

'Yes, they hurt, you miserable bastard.'

'Temper, temper, what language for a fine young lady. If they hurt they are not dead. Keep on dancing.'

Elli farewelled him with some of the best names she could come up with, but he was right. The pain subsided.

More people emerged. The camp was waking up.

Rolf had divided the convoy into groups of four or five wagons.

Each group in the camp shared resources and supported each other in caring for their horses, wagon maintenance, food preparation and guard duties.

It was Elli and Lara's turn to make breakfast. Despite their primitive facilities Elli knew that her camp expected something special. Open fire cooking was a far cry from the restaurant kitchens she had worked in, but she was determined to prove that a trained chef could produce a tasty dish under any conditions.

Elli remembered her mother's horror when she learned that her daughter intended to become a chef.

'That is impossible, *Liebling*! You can't do that,' Helene said. 'You have excelled in your Abitur, better then any other girl, and most of the boys. You could choose any career.'

After Ruth finished her Abitur she went to the Academy of Fine Art in Breslau to study painting, a course her mother considered proper for a young lady. Elli's idea of becoming a chef seemed preposterous to her. Cooking was for servants, not for a daughter of Krummhübel's mayor.

'How ridiculous! Cooking!'

'Not cooking, Mama. I want to become a chef.'

'Cook, chef, what is the difference? Both are servants. You have the talent for so much more! These days a woman can do anything. You could even become a doctor.'

'I don't want to be a doctor. I want to be a chef. Only a few women have become famous chefs, but I will.'

So Elli became a chef, and returned to Krummhübel when she finished her trade course in Hirschberg. In the Reichshof, Krummhübel's leading hotel, she worked with Claus Hirsch, married him and had three children. Life was good, until the war started, and Claus was drafted.

Ruth also came back to Krummhübel. After her studies she had rapidly established herself as an expressionist painter. However, the Nazi's concept of what constituted good art and their relentless oppression of 'Degenerate Art' and artists like Ruth, forced her to stop painting. At thirty-three, she married Horst Bredien, an engineer, and had two children. In 1943 Horst died at the Russian front.

Even though they had been on the road now for seven days, there was still plenty of food, except for breakfast. Eggs were rare and bacon only a faint memory. All the farms they passed were deserted and totally cleaned out. Breakfast was mostly porridge and toast.

Elli hated porridge. Her mother had force-fed it to her when she was a child because it was 'good for her'. Each time she saw the white slime, which now was even gooier as they were short of milk, she wanted to throw up. She desperately avoided looking at the cereal and concentrated instead on the toast browning on the piece of tin over the open fire.

'How is Lara coping?' Elfriede said.

'Considering all she's been through, well. She cries a lot, but otherwise she's very quiet. I think being with us helps.'

By now, everyone had gathered around the fire.

'Mama, Anna isn't sharing the *ja*m!' Herman screamed his anger.

The *ja*m on her son's toast was finger thick and both his hands and his mouth were covered with the sticky, strawberry delight. Well, there goes the treat I hid, she thought.

As it was also her turn to organise the main meal together with Elfriede, she took advantage of the roaring fire to make a large pot of Klopse. The little meatballs in a creamy white caper sauce were her speciality, simple but delicious.

They still had plenty of cream, and Elfriede supplied the minced meat. She seemed to have brought along a large supply from her butcher shop. Luckily, nothing could go off in the freezing cold; getting food warm was the problem.

'Who is scrubbing the potatoes? *Faule Hunde*, do I have to do everything myself?'

Elli approached the job of meal preparation in her own fashion, with lots of energy and swearing. The few people who did not know her cringed. That kind of language was unusual coming from an attractive woman.

'Helmut, you *Arschloch*, don't just stand around, make yourself useful—peel potatoes.'

'No, let him prepare the horses. Yesterday he cut himself so often that I thought I was making blood soup,' Elfriede said.

'Okay, do something for the horses, you useless shit, and don't expect too much food for lunch.'

The frazzled teenager stumbled over to the horses where most of the men were taking refuge from Elli.

'She is a tough little bitch, our Elli, isn't she?' Ulrich grinned.

Slowly they dismantled the overnight camp and readied the horses and wagons for departure. Elli heard the engine of the snowplough starting up. The converted tractor was the only motorised vehicle in the convoy and vital to clearing a path. Without it, the leading horses would have to push through deep snow and would tire very quickly.

They were travelling through a countryside of whiteness. The fog had lifted and even though it was still snowing, they had a majestic view from the elevated road.

Except for the huffing and snorting of the horses, and the clanging of their gear, it was quiet. The dense snowfall absorbed all sounds.

With an enormous crack, a massive pine tree collapsed under the weight of its snow.

'*Scheisse*, that was close!' Elli said. If the tree had been on the other side of the road, it would have fallen right on top of them.

As they slowly moved on, they had to stop often to shift fallen trees and rocks from their path.

The convoy stopped abruptly but this time it didn't start moving again. Some people became impatient and started the difficult walk to the lead vehicle. Still nothing moved, and none of the people who had gone to investigate came back.

'I'll see what is going on,' Elli told Lara.

As Elli drew closer to her father's wagon, she saw a crowd standing around the snowplough.

'What's going on, Papa? We have to keep moving. The horses are too warm to let them cool down now.'

'Look,' Rolf said, pointing at the front of the snowplough. Despite Rolf's attempts to hold her back, Elli moved over to the pile of debris in front of the blade. She stepped on something in the snow. It felt like a log but when it moved under her weight, a child's arm lifted out of the snow.

Elli froze. She stared down. She was standing on the body of a child. 'Oh, Papa!' She rushed into her father's arms.

'There are more, look.'

He pointed at what seemed like a pile of timber and debris. But what looked like branches coming out of tree trunks were arms. She stepped closer—white eye balls in frozen faces stared back at her above black cavities of mouths frozen in final screams of fear and pain.

'Oh Lord, they are people,' she said. 'What happened here?' Rolf pointed at the red, crystalline blotches on the bodies. 'They were all shot. It looks like a refugee convoy.'

A few metres away, Hans knelt in the snow. He looked up and waved them over.

'These murderous bastards. Why are they doing this?'

'What is it?' Rolf took something out of Hans's trembling hands. 'Oh my God. We have to get off this road,' Rolf said.

What he held in his palm was an empty 9mm cartridge from an SS officer's side arm. This group of refugees must have run into an SS patrol.

Among the eighteen bodies they found four children. Their heads were smashed in. The SS had killed them like feral dogs by crushing their heads to avoid wasting any ammunition. A woman with a bullet hole in her forehead, cradling the broken body of her dead child, must have stared straight at her executioner. Her frozen face still showed the terror she experienced. Most of the other adults had been slain with a single shot through the back of the head—the trademark of an SS execution.

After a short prayer, they covered the bodies with snow as the frozen ground prevented the digging of graves. The people in the convoy were terrified when they heard that the SS was behind the massacre. Some of the refugees wanted to go back to Krummhübel.

'We can't go back.' Rolf said bluntly. 'Polish settlers will be living in our houses by now. Do you really think they would let us come back? We have no choice but to continue westwards. Look we have to get off this road—quickly—and use a less direct route to the Neisse River, or this will happen to us too. And we have another problem. The snowplough has had it; the blade's falling apart. We are very low on diesel too, but it will make it to the next junction, I think. A rural road goes from there to Ostritz where we can cross the river.'

Up to this point, the people of the convoy had been relatively content and handled the hardship of their situation with stoic determination. The frozen corpses changed that. The bodies they just had buried were refugees like themselves. Fear of what was ahead paralysed them. Most were convinced, that with SS troops near by, it didn't matter what road they took.

'We'll all die. The SS troops are in the vicinity and who says we will be safer on the other road?' Ludwig Rotenbaum, a small man, a tailor, was still holding the pickaxe with which he had dug out graves in the snow. He spoke quietly, and his voice trembled as much as his body.

'You are right,' Rolf said. 'There is no guarantee that we'll be safer on the detour road, but I'm calculating that the SS vehicles will be too heavy for a narrow road. Look there.' Rolf pointed at an imprint in the snow, almost covered by the shifting snow. 'German Tiger tanks, see how far apart the tracks are? They are wide and weigh more than fifty tons.

They can't follow us.'

They stared at the tracks, even more fearful than before. Not only were SS troops close by but they were also in these steel monsters.

'We have to get off this road,' Rotenbaum said.

❄

The iced over street sign was twisted and bullet holes riddled the words 'Ostritz-Neisse, 50Km'.

They had made it to the junction. The rural road was hidden under an undisturbed layer of snow. The only indications that there was a road were the snow-posts every ten metres. Most of them were barely poking out of the snow. As they reached the sign, the snowplough broke down.

Rolf came up with a solution. 'We'll change the lead unit every hour and send a group of people to trample the snow down in front of the horses. It will be hard and slow but we can do it. There are about five

hundred adults here. If we swap the leading group every hour it will work.

Anyway, we don't have much choice. It has to work.'

No one objected, even though moving through fresh, powdery snow, in some places shoulder high, was not an appealing thought.

Elli volunteered to be in the first group of 'tramplers', together with her father and about fifty others.

'Papa, how did you come up with the figure of five hundred tramplers?

You included everyone, didn't you? Crippled, sick, old-everyone, *ja*? I mean there aren't enough people able to deal with the snow, are there?'

'Let's be a bit optimistic, Elli. Anyway, everyone can contribute, even if only for a few minutes. We haven't any choice and it will keep people warm and distracted. They won't be as frightened—stomping through this bloody snow will keep them too busy for that.'

For the first half hour, Elli actually enjoyed pushing her body through the powdery snow. The snow was so cold that it behaved like dry sand.

They did not really trample it down, but shifted it with their feet. Because of its powdery consistency it was relatively easy to move through, but slowly fatigue and the cold were getting the better of them.

Although Elli felt warm, with her face covered in perspiration, her feet were a different matter. They hurt as they had in the morning when she woke up.

'Papa, I have to stop. I can't feel my feet anymore, just pain,' she moaned.

'Just a bit more. Our hour is nearly over. We have to set a good example for the others. Stamp harder. That will increase your circulation.'

'Curse the others and curse you, you slave driver!' She screamed at him, but continued to work.

It was slow progress, but by the late afternoon they were halfway to Ostritz. It was getting dark. Rolf walked down the convoy and told the exhausted people to break up into their support groups. Soon large fires illuminated the evening and the smell of food hung in the cold air.

After Elli got some feeling back in her feet, she quickly prepared her pre-cooked Klopse. Boiling the potatoes took longer but eventually everyone had a generous helping. The caper sauce compensated for the simplicity of the meal.

The temperature dropped rapidly and soon people disappeared into their wagons.

Elli and Lara fed Karla and covered her with several blankets. When they were satisfied that the horse was comfortable, they joined the children at the fire.

'Mama, I want to walk in front tomorrow, like all the others,' Herman said.

'Maybe, darling, we'll see tomorrow?'

'You are too short, you *Zwerg*,' Anna said. 'When you move through the snow we will only see your *Mütze*. You will be a snow U-boat!' She laughed as her brother went red.

'Yeah, and with your fat arse you'll make a good snowplough,' he shot back. Elli did not interfere; as long as they could fight they were healthy.

'Can I join you tomorrow?' Lara spoke quietly.

'Of course, you can, but are you sure it's a good idea?'

'I want to. Sitting all day on the wagon makes me think too much.

Karla steers herself. I'm not doing anything. She knows where to go better than I do. Please.'

'Sure, but look after yourself. Go back to the wagon when you need a rest; you have been through a lot. Promise?

'Promise. It wasn't my fault, Elli. I didn't lead him on, believe me.'

Elli closed her arms around the shaking young woman and held her until she calmed down.

'Don't you ever think that again. Of course, I believe you. Even if you had flirted with him, there is no excuse for what that animal did.'

Elli continued to reassure Lara until she stopped shuddering. 'Elli, I'm so glad to be with you. You remind me of my mum.' 'What happened to your mum?'

'She died. The enemy bombed the ammunition factory she had to work in.'

'Oh, my God, I'm sorry.'

'I had to identify her. She didn't have any hands or legs. Her body was ripped open. Only her beautiful face was unscratched. Now I'm alone. I can't be pregnant. He was so drunk that he couldn't do it so he pushed a bottle into me. That can't make me pregnant, can't it?'

'No, of course not. Lara, let it go. You are not alone. You are with us.'

'I'm okay.'

Suddenly Lara screamed. Out of the darkness, there were people—men—walking towards their fire. Three soldiers! Their long coats, boots and woollen gloves were ice encrusted. Their heads were only partially covered with thin scarves. They looked frozen.

'Please, we don't want to do you any harm, please!' One of them said, his voice more trembling than his body. 'Could we just warm ourselves? Maybe you could spare a bit of food, we haven't eaten for days?'

As they came closer, Elli saw that they had no weapons and wore grey *Wehrmacht* uniforms, not the black of the SS. People emerged from the wagons, fearfully looking at the newcomers. They became bolder when they saw that the soldiers were unarmed. Slowly a crowd surrounded the soldiers and gently manoeuvred them towards the fire.

Someone filled bowls with Klopse and steaming hot gravy. For the next few minutes, the only thing that mattered to the three men was the food. They wolfed it down as if this were their first meal for weeks.

'How come you are here?' Rolf said. 'I thought all the *Wehrmacht* units had withdrawn from Silesia.'

The oldest of the three, a tall gangly man, his unshaven face covered in bruises, told them they had been separated from their unit, the 306th Infantry Battalion.

'You aren't separated son, you are overrun. The Russians are moving through Saxony towards the Elbe River. You are far behind the German lines. How come?'

'We stayed back to look after two injured men. When they died we tried to get back to our unit, but we soon realised we were behind the lines,' the speaker said.

'What's your name?'

'Oh, I'm sorry.' Despite the dirt and beard stubble he visibly blushed. 'I'm *Unteroffizier* Jochen Pohl, and these are *Gefreite* Wilfried Meyer and Heinrich Schnabel.' Meyer and Schnabel just stared with blank expressions.

'Well, there's not much use trying to get to your unit, too many Russians between here and there. Good chance that your unit doesn't even exist any more. You'd better stay with us,' Rolf said. 'God knows, we certainly could use three strong men. How about it?'

'You don't have to twist our arms, we'll stay,' Jochen said.

He spoke softly in a deep voice. His mousy brown hair stuck to his scalp and his face was dirt caked. Still he looked handsome, arousing something in Elli she had nearly forgotten. Guilt rose up—too young, wrong man, what was the matter with her? She was a married woman!

She felt herself blushing, rescued from her confusion by Rolf.

'Good. Why don't you stay with this group, Jochen? The women need some help.'

'You're welcome Jochen,' said Elli. 'But my dear father should have asked us first. It's not just me.' She pointed to Lara who watched the three soldiers with wide, fearful eyes.

Rolf understood at once. 'I'm sorry, Lara. Sometimes I'm absent minded,' he said.

'Sometimes?' Elli said. Her voice was cold and angry.

'Well, I'd better get a place for the other two, and I'll ask the people first.' He mumbled apologetically. 'Get rid of your uniforms, boys, you don't need them any more and they could be a danger if we pass any Russians. Come with me then, you two. What were your names again?' They disappeared down the convoy.

'Great,' Elli said. 'Me and my big mouth. Where do we sleep you, young man?' She hoped her patronising attitude would cover up her attraction to him. 'There are three children and the two of us, and now you.' She looked Jochen up and down. 'There is no space for him,' she said to Lara.

'I could sleep in a tent,' Jochen said. 'I'm used to that.' 'We haven't got a tent,' Elli said.

'We can't let him sleep outside,' Lara said quietly. 'Isn't there enough space with the luggage in the lower part of the wagon? If we shift a few things around he would fit in.'

'*Ja*, as much space as in a coffin,' Elli said. 'But Lara is right, and it will be warm enough.'

Three days later, in the evening, they reached the Neisse River. Hans was right, at this point the river was frozen solid and only about fifty metres wide, but its steep banks were ice covered.

Crossing the river at this spot would be difficult and they decided to look for a better place in the morning.

The smooth surface of the river reflected the pale moonlight.

Dozens of campfires spread their warm, calming glow through the night. Elli sat on a log beside the wagon and for a moment succeeded in pushing away the horrors of the day. There was something black sticking out of the snow. Her heart stopped. Please, not another one. She forced herself to bend down to look at it but it was too dark to see. She had to touch it. It felt stiff and cold but rough, not like the dead child's hand.

It was a piece of wood, the dead branch of a broken tree.

Elli was relieved but the feeling of peace had dissolved and now the white river under the pale moonlight felt threatening.

'Elli?' She heard her father's voice. 'Elli, I forgot to give you something I found. I think it belongs to you.' He opened his hand and Elli saw her pearl necklace. She felt her knees giving way. 'Careful, *Liebling*.' Rolf grabbed her and gently sat her down. 'It's your necklace, isn't it? The one I gave you?'

'*Ja*, it's mine. I gave it to Hannelore,' Elli said.

'Hannelore?'

'*Ja*. Where did you find it, Papa?'

In this moment of silence, Elli remembered the way Hannelore, her neighbour for so long, had set off bravely with the earlier group of refugees.

'Oh my God.' Elli saw the distress in his face. 'Oh my God.' Elli knew the answer but still she asked.

'Papa, where did you find it?'

'Among the debris around those murdered people.' He cleared his throat. 'I'm so sorry darling. That poor woman and her children. Why didn't she wait?'

'She wanted to do the best for her children. I should have stopped her. Oh Papa, I should have stopped her.'

They cried together into the night.

Chapter 6

Elli was cold, and the blanket she shared with Lara and the children warmed her only for moments before it was yanked away. Annoyed, she retrieved it, only to feel it ripped off her again. She sat up. In the dim light, she saw Lara glaring at her.

'I'm freezing my tits off, Lara,' Elli said.

'Well, mine aren't in much better condition,' Lara said. They looked at the children, blissfully asleep with satisfied smiles on their faces.

'How come the blanket covered all of us before?' Elli said. 'The children are moving around too much, squeezing us out.'

They looked at each other, speculatively.

'Let's do it,' Elli said. Quickly they rolled the two boys apart and slipped in between them. Anna was now between the two adults and the boys were on the outsides.

'Are the boys covered?' Elli said.

'As long as they don't roll away from us. But they won't. They wouldn't want to get cold. Are you warmer now?

'*Ja, ja*. Ah, beautiful!' Elli purred like a cat in front of the fire. Finally, she was warm and drowsy. She felt herself slipping into sleep.

She must have slept for hours. She could see daylight through the cracks in the tarpaulins.

'Elli?' 'What now?'

'It's so quiet,' Lara said. '*Ja*. Isn't it beautiful?'

'It is, but where are the boys?'

In the silence, it took a few moments for Lara's question to sink in.

'*Scheisse*.' Elli felt around but could feel only Anna between them. The boys were gone. 'Where are the boys?' 'That's what I asked you,' Lara said. 'The little devils must have sneaked out.'

Elli jumped up, stepped on Lara, who yelped, and climbed out of the wagon.

It was like walking into a white fog. The sunlight reflecting from fresh snow created a merciless glare. She closed her eyes until they adjusted and tried again. Slowly, white shadows became the shapes of trees, wagons, and horses. Odd: no people. She looked around, but couldn't see anyone.

'Can you see them?' she heard Lara ask from the wagon.

'No, can't see anyone, but wait a minute, I can hear something. You could come out and help me.'

'I'm convinced that you can handle it. Just call me if you can't find them,'

Lara said. 'I'll look after Anna.'

There were voices in the distance. Elli stumbled through the snow towards the sound until she was balancing on the edge of the riverbank's steep slope. Down on the ice the scene was like Krummhübel's skating pond as parents watched their children ice skating, and tobogganing down the slopes.

'Watch out, Mama,' she heard, seconds before Herman shot past her on his toboggan. Still not fully awake, she tried to hold on to a small tree but fell on her back and slid down the riverbank, faster and faster until she hit the ice with a loud thud. Pain rattled her spine. Screams of laughter from the people on the ice greeted her.

'Very impressive, darling, but wouldn't it be more comfortable on a toboggan than on your Popo? Although yours is solid enough for such a ride.'

Rolf ducked to avoid the snowball hurtling towards him but he was too slow for the second one.

'Ouch! I give up, just kidding! Come over and join us, Elli. We are discussing how we'll make the crossing,' he said, laughing, and turned back to the group of people standing beside him. 'Let's go through this again,' he said and they walked off.

Herman and Fritz fussed over Elli, brushing off the snow and sticks she had collected on her wild ride down. She was touched but suddenly became aware that Herman was wearing the Hitler Youth uniform she had hidden. She bit her tongue to prevent lashing out at him.

'Heinrich it's too cold to wear your Pimpf uniform. It's too cold for a thin shirt and shorts. Go and change into long pants and a woollen jumper. Clear?'

'Yes Mama.' She was amazed that he went back to the wagon without any protest, obviously relieved for not getting the expected lecture on sneaking out.

She had to make sure the uniform disappeared permanently.

She walked over to the group standing around Rolf as he gave them a speech.

'So, where do we cross?' Elli interrupted. 'Here, at this spot,' Rolf said.

'Why here? Isn't the riverbank too steep?'

Rolf explained that where they were standing was the site of an old bridge. The road which went over the bridge continued on the other side of the river. After the old bridge fell into disrepair a new one was built in Ostritz, 15 kilometres down river. Rolf was sure that it would be extremely dangerous for them to use the Ostritz Bridge. As it was the only crossing point for many kilometres in every direction the bridge would be guarded either by the *Wehrmacht* or enemy troops. Neither would let a refugee convoy use the bridge and slow down their respective troop movements.

'But how can we cross here? The horses might break their legs going down that slope and the wagons would arrive on the ice as firewood,' Elli said.

'Well now, that's where your new travelling companion comes in.

Jochen came up with a plan.' Hans said, turning to Jochen. Elli had not noticed Jochen before. She had assumed he was still sleeping in his space among their luggage.

Jochen's plan was simple, but labour intensive. They would use rope hoists to lower two horses down onto the ice and use the same method to get them up the other side. After they had horses on both sides they would lower the wagons and, with the help of the horses, pull them up on the other side. Three teams would be needed for the task, one team lowering horses and wagons, a second team on the ice making the transfer to the other side, and the third team pulling the horses and wagons up.

'How does that sound?' Jochen said proudly

There was silence for a moment, then everyone talked at once. 'Meschugge! The Clydesdales are as heavy as elephants!' 'Why don't we let the wagons slide down?'

'The horses will need some protection over their hooves, or they'll slip.'

Hans lifted both arms and whistled until he had everyone's attention.

'Okay! Now let's organise this a bit, *ja*? Who has good horse skills?' Several dozen hands came up. Rolf stepped in and addressed one of the volunteers.

'Herr Leber, weren't you the brewery's stable master?'

The short man in his fifties, who looked more like a council clerk than a horse expert, nodded.

'Manfred, I didn't know that you were back,' Elli said. 'Didn't you leave Krummhübel?'

'Hello, Elli. *Ja*, I came back from Hirschberg three weeks ago. Just got out before the Russians came through.'

Elli turned to Jochen. 'Manfred was not only the stable master; he's a wizard with horses and knows every one of them. When our brewery closed, Manfred allocated the horses to families who wanted to adopt them. He was very careful to match each horse to a family.' The former stable master blushed. 'Manfred never stopped caring for them. He visited each horse at least once a week and didn't hesitate to tell us off if we did something wrong.'

'Elli is very kind,' Manfred said, smiling. 'Not that Elli ever did anything wrong, she's a natural with horses—I just like to see them. I worked with them most of my life.' He fumbled for his handkerchief. 'I miss them, all of them,' he said, and blew his nose.

'I'm glad you're back with us,' Rolf said. 'So, please take charge of the horses and oversee the other volunteers. Okay?'

'*Ja*wohl! The former stable master spoke with an eagerness Elli had not heard from him before.

'Great.' Hans took charge again. 'Now, who knows anything about rope hoists?' Four arms went up. 'Come closer please.' Hans pointed to one of the men. 'Herr Hauser, Armin Hauser am I right?'

'*Ja*wohl, *Herr Bürgermeister*.'

'Armin, if I remember correctly, you were a foreman at one of the coal mines,'

Hans said.

'*Ja*, I was with the Glückauf-Mine for forty years,' Hauser said. His voice was a deep growl, seeming muffled by his beard. His body was straight and powerful, only his weathered face showed his age and the hardship of a miner's life.

'Armin, I assume you are familiar with hoists.'

'Yes, I am. I've got some hoist sets and spare rope pullies in my wagon. I knew that we would need them one day,' he said proudly. 'A good hoist can do more than ten men.'

'We are lucky to have your skills, Armin. You'll be in charge of the hoists then.' He turned back to the others. 'Now, everyone, these are the experts who will handle the horses and the technical stuff with the hoists. Armin and Manfred will select their teams, but everyone else please follow their directions. We'll split into six groups, three groups working, and the other three resting. Are there any problems, objections? Please say so now. Anything we've missed?'

About thirty people clustered together at the back, a discussion going on.

'Well folks, what is it? You there in the back, anything you want to share with us?'

They turned to Hans and the discussion stopped. They stayed silent.

'Okay, then let's do it,' Hans turned to Jochen. 'As it was your idea, how about you organise the crossing?' He hesitated. 'Although I should ask—have you actually done anything like this before?'

'Yes.' Jochen smiled. 'I was in an engineering battalion; we built bridges.'

'Sehr gut! Hans was relieved. 'Rolf and I will organise the rest.

Let's go.'

Back at the wagons, Elli noticed a large group of people gathering. Curious, she walked over. In the centre of the group, someone was addressing them. She had to elbow her way through. The speaker was Heinrich Schulze, one of the two soldiers who came with Jochen.

When she reached the front, she stared in disbelief at the woman leaning against Heinrich. There was no doubt that she and Heinrich were in some kind of relationship, he held her tightly in his left arm as he gesticulated with the other to emphasise his speech. It was Ruth. Elli was shocked. That man had arrived here only a few days ago and they were openly showing that they were lovers. Didn't she have any shame?

Ruth had been a widow for more than two years but this man—he was so young!

She slowly calmed down and then felt guilty. Her sister was an attractive woman and nearly forty. So, she was attracted to a younger man. There were not too many available men around these days. Elli, she told herself, you are such a hypocrite! Aren't you looking at Jochen in exactly the same way?

When they were younger, Elli and Ruth had lost contact for a long time. Ruth studied painting in Breslau and her lifestyle, with ever changing lovers, did not encourage interaction with the family. Then she met Horst and to everyone's amazement they married; shortly afterwards Hubert was born and, two years later, Elfi.

Horst had encouraged Ruth to continue painting. After her first exhibition, critics said Ruth was 'the most interesting expressionist since Otto Dix'.

At first, Elli did not really like her sister's paintings but she became increasingly fascinated by Ruth's way of interpreting landscapes and people. Horst, even though he was a down-to-earth engineer, loved her work—but then Horst loved everything about Ruth. Until Horst was sent to the Eastern Front, Ruth's house was the hub of Breslau's art community.

When they drafted Horst, Ruth returned to Krummhübel but avoided contact with most people, but her family. Then Claus was drafted and Elli started work again in restaurants. For a long time, Elli and Ruth saw each other only at their children's birthdays and other family reunions.

By 1940, many artists, including Otto Dix, were declared by the government to be sick or deranged and their paintings were banned from galleries. Ruth was one of the targeted painters. She was not only prohibited from exhibiting but she had to endure weekly visits from the Gestapo.

When the telegram arrived announcing Horst's death, Ruth fell apart. She became a recluse and refused all invitations to art festivals. Even though her paintings were banned, her work was still in demand by art lovers. It was more of a black-market trade. Everyone was careful, as the Gestapo was ruthless in their pursuit of Entartede Kunst, 'Degenerate Art', and the artists.

After Elli moved back to their parents' house, Rolf persuaded Ruth to move back too.

Looking at Heinrich, Elli was astonished that her sophisticated sister could be attracted to this immature man. Deep in thought, she was for a moment totally distracted. Then what Heinrich was saying began to sink in.

'It is insane to cross the river here when a few kilometres down the road is a perfectly solid bridge. Crossing here would take days and endanger all of us. We would be sitting ducks for any passing Russian or Polish troops.'

Elli saw many nodding in agreement and making supportive noises.

'There are no troops here but they will certainly be in Ostritz.' Elli moved closer, placing herself directly in front of Heinrich and Ruth. 'I don't get your point, Heinrich. If you think we are sitting ducks here, what will we be when we are all bunched up in that bottleneck at Ostritz? Dead ducks? What is the matter? Are you just too lazy to put a bit of physical work into saving your hide? The bridge at Ostritz is a certain trap, it is the only crossing point for the *Wehrmacht* and the Red Army. They'll both keep the bridge free of slow-moving refugee traffic. We would get slaughtered. Any thinking person can see that. Maybe it's asking too much from you?'

'*Blödsinn*!' Heinrich's face flushed with anger as he screamed at the top of his voice. 'How can you know all that? I heard you were a cook. Since when is a female cook a military expert?'

Elli moved even closer, looked straight at him. She spoke slowly, emphasising each word, her voice becoming louder sentence by sentence.

'Listening to your hysterical garbage, I can't help thinking that anyone would be a better military expert than you, Herr Gefreiter, even a female cook. Maybe you really should try crossing at Ostritz, along with anyone else equally stupid.'

She felt her face glow as she held his look. Heinrich's face was white; he let go of his hold on Ruth and stumbled back, repelled by Elli's outburst. He glowered at Elli and stretched out his arms as if he wanted to grab her, but stopped.

'You have a foul mouth and a bad temper but I won't let a woman provoke me.' He turned back to the crowd. 'You know I'm right. Think about what I've said. The safest way for you and your families is to use the bridge in Ostritz, not this foolish idea of crossing over the ice here.

No one knows what the actual situation is in Ostritz, but whatever it is it will be less dangerous than crossing here—even if we have to wait several days before we can get onto the bridge.'

'You are right, Heinrich, no one knows what is going on in Ostritz...,' said Elli.

'I'm glad that you finally see...'

'...but look at it logically, and consider. For many kilometres in each direction the river flows in a deep bed between steep banks. The only crossing point for heavy equipment has to be the bridge. Right? Neither our glorious *Führer's Wehrmacht*, nor the Russians, nor the Poles, will give a shit about refugees if they get in their way. Do you understand, you *Arschloch*; do you?' She turned to the others. 'Have you already forgotten what the Russians are doing to women? And what about the dead refugees? Russians or SS, what makes you think that it would be any different in Ostritz?'

The crowd erupted. Elli felt she had finally got through to them. 'Listen people, listen, please.' Heinrich tried to take control again. 'Not only is the crossing here too dangerous but it's impossible for another reason. It would take too long. If you have doubts about that, listen to the expert. Jochen, tell us what we discussed before.'

Jochen, who had listened to the exchange, came to the front. 'The crossing is not without dangers,' he said. 'We may have to shift the crossing point several times to avoid the ice cover becoming too stressed. I think any cracks will refreeze overnight and with careful spacing of the wagons and horses, we should be all right.'

'*Ja, ja*.' Heinrich tried to dismiss Jochen's assessment. 'Even if you are right, which I doubt, it still leaves us with no food.'

'We are not that short of food.' Elli said. 'How long would it take us to cross, Jochen?'

'Well, I made a rough estimation considering that we have about two hundred rigs to dismantle.'

'How long?' Elli tried to be composed.

'Considering the width of the river,' he said, as he took a crumpled piece of paper out of his pocket, 'which is about forty metres, the strength of the ice would not support more than one wagon every ten metres. That allows only four wagons to cross at any time.'

'*Ja*, come to the point.'

'Also considering the time it will take us to get each wagon and the horses down onto the ice and up again on the other side...'

'For goodness' sake! How long?'

'... furthermore, we have at the best only six hours of daylight...' 'Jochen.'

'Two weeks,' he said.

'What? That is insane! We don't have two weeks! We have just enough food for another five or six days! Beside that, if we hang around here for two weeks, you can be sure that Russian or Polish troops will wipe us out. We have to move. There must be a faster way.'

'Maybe, but I can't see any.'

'There you are.' Heinrich's voice was loaded with sarcasm. 'We can't cross here in under two weeks, and we can't wait that long because we would starve.'

'You think that being raped or slaughtered in Ostritz would be preferable to being hungry? What is it with you? Why do you refuse to see what you'll be walking into? Ostritz is a trap.' Elli's voice rose to a scream.

'Listen to this hysterical woman.' Heinrich said without looking at her. 'But of course, as a good daughter she has to support the insane ideas of her father. In Ostritz, we at least have a chance. I'm convinced the bridge is still under Wehrmacht control. It's clearly a better choice than to cross here. We have no food and would be an easy target for the Poles and the Russians and if that is not enough, breaking through the ice and drowning would finish us off.'

Feverish discussions followed Heinrich's speech.

'Why didn't you say before that it will take two weeks to make the crossing?' Elli said to Jochen.

'I wasn't told that we only had food for a few days.' He shrugged his shoulders, looking helplessly at Elli. 'Not that it would have made any difference.'

'We can't let this happen. They'll be killed if they go to Ostritz. Look, if we get everyone to work now, surely we should be able to make the crossing faster? There is no choice. We have to do it. Please Jochen, recalculate the crossing with maximum manpower. I'll talk to the others.'

Ruth, who until now stood passively beside Heinrich, came towards Elli but seemed to change her mind and went back to Heinrich.

'It's strange, most of them are more afraid of crossing here than in Ostritz,' Jochen said. 'Despite the dead people we found, and everything else, they still believe that it won't happen to them.'

'They'll listen if we explain it more clearly,' Elli said. 'Papa must talk to them.'

'Maybe,' Jochen said. 'I'll see what he says. And I'll see if we can speed up the crossing.'

Chapter 7

Ruth wasn't at the wagon. Elfi and Hubert saw their aunt coming and tried to run to her. Elfi, waist deep in snow, made some progress but Hubert was only half his sister's height, and barely visible.

'Come here you little rascals,' Erika Schlichte's voice boomed. 'Elli, I'm so glad to see you.'

'*Guten Morgen Erika*. Are they giving you trouble?' The children were racing around Elli, until she grabbed Hubert. 'Well young man, are you giving Aunty Erika trouble?' The little boy laughed.

'Aunty! Aunty! Snowball?'

'No snowball. Where is Mama, Hubert?'

'*Da da*.' Hubert pointed to the pine forest in the distance.

'Mama is gone painting,' Elfi said. 'Mama is very sad, Aunty. Can you make Mama smile?' The little girl was close to tears.

'What's wrong, Erika?'

'When Ruth and that young man came back, they had a terrible fight and then Ruth snatched her easel and brushes and walked off.' The older woman was breathing heavily and coughed after each laboured breath.

'You don't sound too well, Erika.'

'It's my weak chest. It gets me when I'm too excited,' Erika said. 'Did you see where Ruth went?'

'Over to that ridge near the pine forest,' Erika said. 'Just follow her tracks. You can't miss her.'

Elli followed the footsteps through the snow blanket. She could see Ruth in the distance, sitting on a cleared tree-stump. She was drawing on a large sheet of paper clipped to a board with wooden laundry pegs.

Even though her movements were rapid, she seemed to have difficulty using her cold fingers. One glove did not have an index finger and thumb and occasionally Ruth put the uncovered finger and thumb into her mouth to warm them up.

Elli watched her for a while, and then walked around to have a closer look. The squeaking of the snow compacting under her feet must have alerted Ruth, but she continued drawing without looking up.

The detailed pencil drawing revealed a scene Elli remembered all too well. People stood beside frozen corpses. In the foreground of the drawing was the body of a child, its dead eyes turned to the viewer. Elli moved away, nauseous.

'Elli, *Liebling*, are you alright?'

'*Oh mein lieber Gott*! I didn't know that you saw them.'

'*Schwesterlein*, I didn't see them but I was told what you and the others found. I have tried to recreate it.'

'I didn't know you could draw like that,' Elli said. 'Like what?'

'So real.' She felt compelled to look at the drawing again and the nausea slowly subsided.

'You mean it's realistic enough?'

'Realistic? It's terrible, I feel like I'm back there.'

'*Danke*, that's what I was trying to achieve. That is the biggest compliment you have ever paid me about my work.'

Ruth continued drawing as Elli watched. Suddenly she stopped and looked at her sister.

'Elli, I have been waiting to say something for a long time. I'm very lucky to have a sister like you. Forgive me if I've ever hurt you. I envy you so much because you are so capable and can handle everything, even in this awful time. I can't. The only way I can express myself is through this,' she said, pointing to the drawing. 'And nobody wants to see it because what I do is too horrible for most people. But that's just how I see it, how it is, there is nothing beautiful about what's happening around us.'

Elli did not know what to say.

Without looking up from her drawing, Ruth said, 'I know you're afraid that I'll leave with Heinrich and the others who want to go to Ostritz, but don't worry, I won't go with him. I wouldn't go with an SS man.'

'An SS man? Who, Heinrich? Where did you get that idea?'

Ruth told her that she discovered an SS blood group tattoo on the inside of Heinrich's arm, halfway between his armpit and his elbow. Elli was familiar with the tattoo. She had seen it on SS men when they took their shirts off during drunken brawls at her restaurant. The purpose of the tattoos was quick blood group identification of a wounded SS man. The drawback for any SS man was that Germany was losing the war and they could easily be identified.

The Russians were particularly keen to check every male in the right age range, and discovery of a tattoo meant execution. If a captured soldier had an injury or scars on the inner left arm, they shot him. Rumour said that even left arm amputees were shot. The Russians hatred of the SS allowed no margin for error.

'I saw the tattoo when I slept with him.' With a sad smile she continued. 'Heinrich isn't the first SS man I have been with, but do you know what that means for you, my darling sister?' She looked Elli straight in the face and spoke slowly. 'Heinrich is with the SS and when he came to us he was with two other soldiers, Jochen Pohl and Wilfred Meyer.

Correct?'

'*Ja*, but...'Elli's voice was hardly perceptible.

'They said that they were left behind to care for two injured comrades. Elli, SS men don't serve in *Wehrmacht* units. All three of them must be SS.'

'No, stop it, you are wrong,' Elli said, her voice rising.

'I think they were left behind to cover up evidence,' Ruth said. 'If I am right, the other two will also have the tattoo on their arms. Elli, think, have you seen anything like that on Jochen? Or maybe an injury on the inside of his left arm or the other man's?'

'No, I haven't. I mean I don't know about Wilfred, and with Jochen it's impossible to tell because of his shoulder injury.'

'He has a shoulder injury?'

'*Ja*, but not what you think. It isn't just on the inside of his left arm, the abrasions cover his shoulder too, and the whole arm.'

'It covers the inside of his left arm?'

'Stop it, Ruth. He had an accident. He was dragged by a car.'

'Maybe! Let's hope he isn't checked by Russian soldiers. They will execute him on the spot. Elli, tell me the truth, is there something between you and Jochen?'

'Nothing at all, but I like him,' Elli said. 'I don't think you are right, but even if you are, so what? They are trying to survive, like us. They haven't done anything but help us, so why should we be afraid of them? The war is over.'

'*Ja*, the war is over but is it over for the SS? There are many stories around about the atrocities they have committed. The Russians will not rest until they have shot every last one. Sooner or later we will run into Russians and if they find SS men here they will kill all of us.'

'That's insane, Ruth.'

'Yes! The war is insane and we endanger ourselves if we harbour them.'

They stopped arguing when they saw Rolf and Hans walking towards them. Both men were shouting and they totally ignored the sisters.

'You have the diplomacy of a charging bull,' Hans said. 'Telling them to get lost if they don't like our idea of crossing the river here was really bright. You have annoyed most of them so much they'll probably leave. We'll be lucky if there are more then ten wagons left.'

'Come on Hans, don't be so naïve. They had already made up their minds. You saw how they were lapping up every word from those two idiots. Besides, a bit of straight talk is good for them. Anyway, whoever leaves now would be unreliable and might fall apart the moment it really gets tough.'

'What is going on?' Elli had never seen the two men talking to each other like that.

'When we started to organise the work groups Wilfred and Heinrich confronted us,' Hans said. His voice was hoarse as he tried to control his anger.

'Confronted you about what?'

'They had convinced most of the people to go to Ostritz; they accused us of trying to lead them into danger by crossing the river here. It wasn't really going our way but your father told them that they are *Arschlöcher* and to pack up and leave and that did it. Most of them will try to make the crossing in Ostritz.'

'Is Jochen going with them?' Ruth said.

'Jochen? No, he is staying and thank goodness for that, because we really need his expertise,' Hans said.

Ruth stood up abruptly, dropping the wooden box with her painting utensils and splattering them into the snow.

'Well, that's a shame because it would have solved our problem,' she said.

'What problem?' Rolf said 'Getting rid of three SS men.' 'What SS men?'

'Heinrich is an SS man; I saw his tattoo,' Ruth said quietly. '*Verfluchte Scheisse*, since when have you known that?' said Rolf. 'A few days.'

'Why didn't you tell anyone?'

'There didn't seem to be any reason to make a fuss.' 'Does he know that you found out?'

'I don't think so, Papa.'

'Ruth thinks that the others must be SS as well, because they were together when they came to us,' Elli said.

'*Ja*, you could be right,' Rolf said. 'We have to be sure. I'll talk to them.'

'You think that's wise?' Hans said. 'If they are SS, they won't hesitate to kill you if they think you will expose them.'

'We have to find out if Ruth is right and if she is right, why they are here. Then we have to deal with it. Come on, let's do it now.'

'How are we going to approach them?' Hans said anxiously, trailing behind Rolf who was striding off towards Elli's wagon. Ruth and Elli followed at some distance, trying to keep up with their father.

Jochen was preparing the wagon for the haul over the river when they arrived. Without any warning Rolf shouted at him, 'Are you three with the SS?'

Jochen dropped the hammer. His face drained of blood. He spoke slowly.

'*Ja*, we are. We are deserters from the same Waffen-SS unit.' Elli held tight to her sister. Oh, *Vater im Himmel*, he is one of these murderous bastards, she thought, and shivered with terror. This man had been sleeping in her wagon and playing with her children.

'*Schwein*, SS-*Schwein*!'

She threw herself at him and battered him with both fists on his face.

Jochen took the blows without moving, or trying to stop her. Hans and Rolf tried to pull her away. She pounded Jochen again and again, as tears ran down her face, stopping only when she was too exhausted to lift her arms.

Rolf held his shivering and sobbing daughter in his arms. 'When you came to us, it was close to where we discovered the massacre. Did you have anything to do with that?'

Jochen held a handkerchief to his bleeding nose. His voice was barely audible. 'No, that must have been an SS-Einsatzgruppe. I know that the special units were operating in the area. We are just draftees; they do not use draftees from the Waffen-SS for anything like that. The SS command sees us as too unreliable. They are quite right; we ran away the first chance we got.'

'I thought all SS men were volunteers.'

'*Ja*, in the regular SS, but in the Waffen-SS, there are many draftees like us. Most of us were public servants who thought we were safe from the draft because we had jobs essential to the war effort. Well, that changed. I was a local government engineer, repairing roads and bridges, but that didn't help me. Heinrich and Friedrich were postal clerks, essential jobs needed to keep communications going. But that didn't save them. We were drafted.'

'Do you really think we are stupid enough to believe your lies?' Elli shouted.

Without giving him the chance to reply she continued ranting at him. 'I don't care if you were drafted into the SS or not! Next time we meet some Poles or Russians, try to explain it to them! Maybe they will let you finish a sentence before they shoot you. Drafted or not, you were part of a bunch of murderers, not regular soldiers. Spare us your excuses, SS-man.' She stepped closer to him, spat in his face and walked off.

Ruth gave him a puzzled, solemn stare and followed her sister. An hour later Rolf and Hans came to Elli's wagon.

'Jochen swears that the only thing he did during his time in the Waffen-SS was to get involved in engineering jobs. He feels bad because he didn't tell you before,' Rolf said slowly. Elli was reminded of the way he looked when she had been a child, angry and outraged with him, and he had tried to calm her down. She felt patronized and her anger rose again.

'That's fine if you believe it. I don't,' she said, 'and it doesn't minimise the danger they have put us all in.'

'We need Jochen. It's safer here than in Ostritz for everyone, including him,' Hans said. 'We talked to the others as well and they want to stay.'

'That is stupid, Hans,' Ruth said. 'If they stay, they'll endanger all of us'

'Maybe, but if they were discovered in Ostritz the Russians would wipe out the whole convoy. It's better to have them here.'

'How about us, did you ever consider what would happen to us if they are discovered?'

'What do you want us to do, Ruth, kill them?' 'Why not? It's us or them.'

'Wouldn't that put us into the same category as the SS?'

Ruth's face was red and the veins at her temples stood out when she shouted at Hans. 'You are a fool for harbouring these men and endangering us all!'

'I can't see any other solution.'

Ruth did not say anything. She stared at the ground, her *jaw* working as if she were chewing something. Her chin jutted out as her eyes closed to slits. As a child Elli had seen her sister's face become distorted with rage, but never like this.

By the evening, they had finished preparations for the next day's crossing. The people who had decided to try crossing at the Ostritz Bridge would leave in the morning.

It was a cold and clear night, with no moon and only faint light from the canopy of stars. Suddenly, a shot rung out.

Elli sat up, straining her ears. She could hear people shout, and the high-pitched screams of a woman. She got up and went outside. From the distance, a light came closer. Elli was terrified; she wanted to call out to the others but only a hoarse whisper came out.

'It's okay, girl, it's just me!' Rolf said as he came closer. 'What was that? Where did that shot come from?'

'I don't know; somewhere from the back. I'm on my way to check it out.'

'I'll come with you. Wait, I'll get my lantern.'

They walked through deep snow past two camps. At the next one, they were greeted by angry voices and crying.

'Ruth and the Schlichte family are in this group; what's going on Papa?

Out of the dark, someone came over to them. Erika. 'What is it, Erika?' Rolf said.

'Ruth ...'

'Ruth? What's happened to her?' 'She's okay but...'

'But what, woman, what?' 'She shot Heinrich. He's dead.'

'What? Ruth shot him?' Elli said.

'*Ja*, with this,' Erika handed a pistol to Rolf. '*Mein lieber Gott*,' Rolf said. 'Why?'

'The only thing I got out of her was that the 'SS-Schwein deserved it'. I don't know what she meant.'

'Look at the pistol,' Erika said.

'Oh God, it's a Walther HP, an SS officer's side arm.' 'Is she in your wagon?' Elli turned to Erika.

'*Ja*, Elfriede is with her.'

Elli climbed into the Schlichtes' wagon. Ruth was with Elfriede, sitting on one of the plump, crocheted pillows Erika used to make. She was talking quietly to Elfriede, holding a steaming cup of coffee.

'Thanks Elfriede. That is...' She stopped. 'That is real...' She stopped again, unable to find the word.

'Coffee?' Elfriede said.

'*Ja*, that is real coffee.' Her shaky voice could only just be understood.

'Ruth, what happened?' Elli said.

'I shot the Schwein,' Ruth said, emphasising each word.

Elli felt helpless, unsure what to say. 'Even knowing what he was...' Her voice was a whisper. 'I don't know if anyone has the right to do what you did. Oh God, Ruth, you killed someone.'

Ruth showed no reaction. 'He was part of an Einsatzgruppe,' she said, in a faint voice. 'A special commando group. They took prisoners from a labour camp and executed them.' As she continued, she sounded clearer and more in control.

'They did what?'

'He said, that they were closing the camp as the Russians drew near. The Einsatzgruppe was told to take the prisoners out of the camp and execute them somewhere in the forest.'

Elli had heard many rumours about the SS labour camps and the brutalities taking place there. Like most others, she had believed it to be no more than enemy propaganda.

'Who did they keep in these camps, criminals?'

'Hardly, mostly Jews, gypsies, and others who do not fit into the Nazi philosophy.'

'Where was the camp?'

'I'm not sure but it was somewhere round here. Heinrich worked there before he joined the Einsatzgruppe. He lied to the others. He was in the regular SS, not a draftee in the Waffen-SS. The other two really are deserters from the Waffen-SS. He found them somewhere and convinced them that he had deserted too. He intended to hand them over in Ostritz.'

'How do you know all that?'

'He talked a lot when we were together—not because he trusted me. His arrogance didn't allow him to think that a woman sharing her bed with him, an SS-man, might not admire him.'

Despite her apparent calmness she trembled. The trembling escalated into spasms. Elli took her into her arms. They held on to each other as if they were drowning, caressing each other's face, wiping tears away, holding each other's heads as if they were in danger of breaking off. In between gasping breaths, Ruth said again and again, 'I had to do it. He boasted about slaughtering women and children. He was evil!'

Chapter 8

In the first light, the horrors of the night before seemed unreal. Elli and Ruth never heard what happened to Heinrich's body but neither really wanted to know. By now, everyone knew of the night's drama.

The families leaving for Ostritz were busily preparing their rigs for departure. No one spoke to Ruth and Elli as they walked through the camps.

Rolf had persuaded a few families to stay and went from wagon to wagon, still trying to talk people out of leaving, even after rigs had started to move out of the convoy. Most people gave him a cold stare; if that did not deter him, they swore at him.

'Stop trying, Papa. They have made up their minds.' Elli wanted to pull him away. Rolf tried to brush her arm off but she held on like a steel clamp. After allowing his daughter to drag him along for a few metres, he shook her off and strode back.

'You fools are running into a trap!' he said. 'Can't you see that you're putting your families in danger? Don't go to Ostritz; I beg you.'

'Get out of the way you *Arschloch*,' a fat, red-faced man said when Rolf tried to block his way. 'You are the fool. You'll break through the ice and drown like rats.'

Rolf stepped aside, his shoulders sagging, his face ashen. Elli had not thought her father as old at fifty-nine, but at that moment he looked eighty. She knew that he felt responsible for these people and was devastated at letting them down.

'We have to do something. All these people ...'

'Leave them Papa. You tried,' Elli said. 'I hope you are wrong.' Rolf did not respond and at last allowed his daughters to lead him away.

Most of the departing people pulled away quietly, doubt on some faces but others glowering, occasionally swearing at people staying behind. Some families were obviously leaving reluctantly, hugging, crying and kissing their friends goodbye.

The departing rigs had to pass Rolf's lead wagon. He stood there beside his horse, straight as a post, arms folded, trying to make eye contact with those who left. Nearly everyone looked away as if afraid of his disapproval.

Slowly the newly formed wagon train pulled away and disappeared into the distance.

Only twenty-six rigs remained, but Rolf did not give anyone time to grieve. He immediately started to organise preparations for the crossing.

Luckily, neither Manfred Leber, the former brewery stable master, nor Armin Hauser, the hoist expert, had left.

Manfred went straight into action, supervising the preparation of the horses.

'We'll take Margot first,' he said to Jochen. 'Nothing excites her and she follows every command without misunderstanding anything.'

'Margot? Who is Margot?' Jochen said.

'The Kruse's adopted her.'

'Manfred, what on earth are you talking about?' Jochen said. 'Manfred is talking about one of his former charges,' Elli said.

'Margot is the Kruse's horse.'

'I'm glad you stayed with us,' Jochen said.

'*Danke*', Manfred said. 'I nearly left with the others. Most of my horses are with them but the animals here need me more.'

'You stayed because the remaining horses need you more?' Jochen said.

Manfred must have seen the bewilderment on Jochen's face.

'They don't need my help in Ostritz to go over a bridge.' He stopped as if listening to an internal voice, and continued hesitantly, close to tears. 'If Ostritz is a trap like Rolf thinks, I hope that the Russians or Poles look after them—and don't slaughter them. All my...' His eyes went wet as he struggled to stay in control. He turned around and walked away mumbling as he went. 'Have to organise the ones we still have.'

'He really cares for those animals,' Jochen said.

'Ja,' they are his life. His decision to stay is more like a father deciding which of his children needs him more.'

'It's odd that the road leads directly to the river and then turns away along the bank. We're lucky the river bank isn't too steep here,' Hans said to Rolf and Elli.

They were watching the preparations for the first horses to be lowered down to the ice.

'Nothing to do with luck,' Rolf said. 'This is where the original wooden bridge to Berthelsdorf was. Look, on the other side you can see the road starts up again.'

Elli couldn't see a road on the other side of the river, only a cut through the dense pine forest. Ice covered most remnants of the former bridge, but a few stumps poked out like a widely spaced fence.

Manfred led Margot to the edge of the slope. The river was some twenty metres below; if the slope had not been solidly iced over it would have been easy for him to walk the horse down.

Armin and his crew had tied a rope hoist to a pine tree with three men holding on to the control rope. Manfred attached the horse's harness to the hoist and gently edged her down the slope. Margot's backwards movements were slow but steady as she placed her hooves onto the ice, supported by the rope harness.

Suddenly her left rear foot broke through the ice into a hole. With jerky movements, the horse desperately struggled to free the trapped foot. 'Steady Margot, steady!' Manfred called, but the horse continued to kick with her right leg against the ice, trying get a grip.

'Hold me,' Manfred directed Jochen and Hans. He looped a rope around his waist and threw the other end to them. 'I have to go down or she'll break her leg. Quick, hold on to me.' Without waiting for a reply, he slid down the slope.

'That's insane,' Hans said. 'The horse will squash him!'

Margot was shivering. Her eyes stared widely around. The kicks increased in panic. Jochen and Hans strained at the end of the rope.

Suddenly they started to slide towards the edge of the bank. Elli and Rolf jumped to their aid, grabbing the rope.

'Manfred will make it. He knows his horses,' Elli said.

They hauled on the rope with all their weight. The stomping and snorting stopped.

'Elli?' It was Manfred.

'Yes, I'm coming. Keep holding on,' she told the men as she let go of the rope.

'*Liebling*,' Rolf panted as they struggled to compensate for her depart 'Just tell him to hurry up with his rescue. He is heavier than he looks.'

Elli crawled to the edge, fearful of slipping. Manfred and the Clydesdale were still ten metres above the river. The horse's foot was out of the hole and both the horse and Manfred were pressed against the icy slope. Manfred held the horse's head and was murmuring in its ear.

'Manfred, are you all right?'

'We are both fine,' he smiled back at her. 'Tell them to lower us very slowly.'

'What is going on down there?' Hans called out. 'Be quick!' 'He is talking to Margot,' Elli said.

A long desperate groan came back from the men holding the rope. 'Talking? Well, I hope they are having a nice chat.' Rolf forced

the words out through clenched teeth. 'Tell them to hurry up, or we'll join them. *Scheisse*! Too late. We're slipping! For God's sake, hang on!'

Elli tried to hurry back up the slope to help them but she was too slow on the slippery surface.

'Well done,' Manfred's voice came from the ice. 'We are safe. You can let go of the rope.' Seconds later the three men slid, shouting, down the slope, one behind the other, hanging on to the rope, gathering speed as they bounced over outcrops, until they stopped, crashing into each other in the middle of the frozen river.

'Some help,' Elli heard Manfred say, 'more like children bobsleighing!' Both man and horse seemed to be laughing as the dazed trio struggled back, still holding on to the rope.

'Elli,' Manfred said, 'get Karla into the hoist and go down with her. Just in case Karla decides that she doesn't like it.'

'And what do you suggest I do then?' Elli said. The image of sliding down the icy slope alongside a panicky horse made her stomach clench.

'Simple: talk to her, be very calm, and talk sweetly.' She heard Manfred laugh.

'*Arschloch*,' she shouted back. She knew Karla might react badly if the horse felt abandoned by her, so she picked up the harness.

'Good girl,' Hans said and Rolf smiled approvingly. Elli gave them the dirtiest look she could muster.

'Just hold on to my rope and don't slip again, you two useless men.'

'What was that about?' she heard Hans say, as she started her careful descent with Karla.

'She's worried about her horse,' Rolf said. 'You know how women are.'

'*Ja*, you are right,' Hans said.

I'll kill them both if I make it back alive, Elli promised herself.

Karla seemed to know that she was safe with Elli beside her, and slowly, step-by-step, the horse allowed herself to be lowered onto the ice. Elli beamed with pride.

'You are beautiful, *Liebling*, the cleverest horse there is. *Grossartig*!'

Once down on the ice it was easy. Hans and Elli led the two horses to the other side and tied Karla first into the waiting lifting gear. Two men at the top of the riverbank, and Elli and Hans on the ice used both hoists to pull Karla up in one clean swoop. The upward movement was more comfortable for the horse as Karla could see where she was going.

All but four of the other animals were brought over the same way, but pulled up with the much greater strength of Karla and Margot at the top of the bank. The four horses left behind were used to lower the wagons onto the ice. Once there, the horses on the other side pulled the wagons across.

By late afternoon all the wagons and horses had been transferred and the families were moving their personal belongings over the ice.

Toboggans were loaded then, with one or two children on top, they slid down the slope, over the ice, and were pulled up on the other side. The atmosphere was like a snow festival in Krummhübel. The children loved it.

Close to nightfall, everyone was safely across and the whole group seemed confident and relaxed. Although they were exhausted, Rolf insisted on moving away from the riverbank to a forest a few hundred metres away. Too tired to protest, they did as he said.

Even though the convoy was only a fraction of what they started with, they stuck to the concept of five wagons sharing cooking facilities and the preparation of meals. Elli worked for her group. She planned something warming and quick.

'It's starting to snow again, thank God. Daughter!' Rolf pointed suspiciously at his plate. 'What's that? It's pink.'

'*Labskaus*, Papa. Don't poke around in it, eat it.' Elli smiled. 'I'll eat it, but tell me what I'm eating?'

'It's a recipe I got from a neighbour from Friesland, you know? In the north, near Hamburg?'

'Good for her, but what is it? It's pink!'

'Oh Papa, you are such a baby sometimes! It's herring, potatoes and beetroot put through a mincer. She serves it with fried eggs on top, but we are out of eggs; taste it.'

Rolf moved his spoon through the steaming, pink slosh with the fishy smell and Elli could have sworn that his face turned slightly green.

'Why did you say, 'Thank God' that it's snowing, Papa?' Elli said, trying to distract him.

'It will cover our tracks. The devil knows who'll be looking for us after the others arrive in Ostritz. It looks like the snowfall's getting stronger too.'

Beyond the ring of light created by their campfire the snow fell like a white waterfall, becoming increasingly dense in the eerie silence.

'Want some more Papa?' Elli looked at her father's empty plate. 'I'm glad you liked it.'

'Ah, no thanks,' he said. 'Have to go and see Hans. Thanks for the meal.'

'You are welcome.' Elli politely ignored the steaming hole in the snow where he was standing. Maybe it would have been better with eggs on top.

Back at the wagon, the peaceful sounds of her children and Lara breathing in their sleep and Jochen's snoring from the luggage area, welcomed her. Ignoring the mumbled protests and groans she slid herself between the children and after several attempts managed to extinguish the spitting carbide lantern. Sleep came fast.

Someone was screaming at her. She ignored the sound but the screams persisted.

'Elli wake up, come on, wake up!' It wasn't a dream; Jochen shook her awake, but still the screaming continued.

'Go away! Don't touch me!'

'Elli, wake up. Listen! Can't you hear the screams? I'll check it out; stay with Lara and the children, okay?'

Elli peeled her blankets off and climbed out of the wagon. At first, the sounds didn't make any sense but then she distinguished crying and shouting. She couldn't stand the anguish of the screams. Her heart raced and breathing hurt. Her head spun. She clasped her ears with both hands, trying to block out the sounds and her fear, but they didn't stop.

In the flickering light of the campfire, Elli saw a group of shadowy figures close to the fire. As she got closer, she recognised people from the Ostritz group. Five women. She reached Jochen and tugged his sleeve.

'What's going on?'

'Your father was right; Ostritz was a trap. The Russians took Ostritz but kept on moving into Saxony, leaving the Poles in charge. Most of the men were shot and the women were gang-raped. They don't know what happened to the children. These are the only ones who could escape.'

'*Mein Gott*, how did they manage to come back here and find us?

It must be fifteen kilometres on foot through deep snow,' Elli said.

'They came back along the frozen river; otherwise they would

never have found us. Rolf has arranged for them to stay with families. Come on, let's go back to bed or we'll freeze to death.'

'What?' Elli looked incredulously at him. 'Don't you understand what has happened? Fifteen hundred people, our people, nearly our whole town was massacred in Ostritz! Men shot, women raped and God knows what they did to the children, and you want to go back to sleep?' She looked him up and down as if she saw him for the first time.

'I didn't mean... I...' Jochen tried to say something but Elli left him and walked over to the fire.

She crouched down beside a young woman in her twenties who looked familiar. The woman shivered so violently that the blanket around her shoulders started to slip off. When Elli reached out to rearrange it, she jerked away and screamed.

'No, no, don't touch me! Don't touch me!' She jumped up and moved away from the fire. In the flickering light Elli saw the woman was covered in bruises and there were bloodstains on her clothes. Then she recognised her.

'*Mein Gott*, Hildchen! Is it you?'

Hildchen Ehrenberg was a teacher at her children's school. She warily came back and looked hard at Elli.

'Elli?'

Elli wrapped her arms around Hildchen, helped her to sit down and let her cry, not saying anything, only rocking the young woman. The crying stopped and slowly Hildchen began to talk.

When the convoy had arrived at the bridge, Polish soldiers herded them onto a field next to the river where they were separated into three groups, women, men and children. The children were dragged away by soldiers kicking and pushing them when they tried to break away to get back to their mothers. The women screamed and shouted as their children slowly disappeared down the road pushed along by their guards.

The men were separated from the women and prodded by soldiers to the steep river bank to form a line facing the river. Ten steps behind the men soldiers formed a second line, facing them. The officer walked in between the two lines and shouted in broken German that the men were regarded as enemy soldiers who had obviously deserted from their units as they were out of uniform. He ignored the feeble protests from the men and stepped back behind the line of soldiers.

A sharp command in Polish. The women cried out in horror when the soldiers lifted their rifles and aimed at the men. A second command, a volley of shots, and all but five men collapsed and slid down the riverbank. The remaining trembling men turned around. They stared at the soldiers, ashen faced. The officer shouted again and with a second volley the five men collapsed and disappeared over the edge. The women could see the bodies at the end of blood trails where they came to rest on the ice. Some were still alive, trying to crawl away.

The women's cries of terror died down when the execution squad turned around facing them. Most faced the soldiers silently expecting their turn. Some older women fainted. No one picked them up, all stared at the soldiers. An older woman in front of Hildchen lost bladder control, and looked around, mumbling apologies. A middle-aged woman in the front row stepped forward and shouted abuse at the soldiers. The women beside her grabbed her and pushed her back behind them.

The soldiers did not act at the provocation, only stared at them like a pack of wolves surrounding a flock of sheep.

Another shouted order and Hildchen was sure that now they would die, but the soldiers unhooked hand grenades from their belts, turned back to the river and tossed them after the men. The explosions broke the ice and swallowed the dead and dying men. A few pools of blood remained on the ice.

Hildchen's voice faded to a hoarse whisper.

'Don't talk anymore,' Elli said. 'You need to rest and be looked after.'

Hildchen grabbed her as another of the Ostritz women came over and took her arm, trying to lead her to a wagon. She brushed off the woman's arm.

'But I have to tell you what happened then,' she whispered and continued.

The soldiers divided the women into small groups and led them to empty houses along the river. There were five in Hildchen's group; the youngest was a girl of thirteen. The oldest was older than her grandmother.

'They told us to take our clothes off and lie on the ground. It was very cold.'

She stopped, wiped her face and continued, barely audible. 'They raped us. Ten of them, or more. One after the other.' She stopped, breathing in painful short gulps.

'Here Hildchen drink this.' Elli held a cup of hot tea to the woman's lips. 'Please drink.'

Hildchen stopped rocking back and forth, grabbed the hot cup and greedily gulped it down.

'*Danke*. I passed out and when I came round, they were still on me. I heard the old woman beg for the girl's life but they just laughed.' She paused and tried to continue but choked on her tears. Elli held her tight, crying with her.

'How did you get away?'

'They... they went outside.' Elli could barely understand.

Gasping, Hildchen went on. 'We heard them laughing and then someone shouted. I think it was an officer who ordered them off. No one came in. There was a door at the back and it wasn't locked. We just walked out. We could hear the soldiers on the other side of the building. We crawled through the snow down the river bank, onto the ice and kept crawling until we were out of sight.' A sad smile lightened Hildchen's face. 'We followed the river, not even sure if we were going in the right direction. But we were lucky.'

Every one of the refugees listened to the woman, their faces horrified. As the reality of what had happened sunk in, many were crying, holding on to each other for support. Except for this small group of twenty-six families, and the five women, the population of Krummhübel had been either wiped out or had ended up in Polish work camps. They stayed at the fire, feeding it as if its warmth and light could hold back their fears. Only when the snowfall became too dense and firewood scarce, did they move slowly to their wagons.

Sleep did not come easily. In Elli's nightmares she saw the raped and murdered people at the Ostritz Bridge.

It was still dark when Rolf came back.

'Come on, everyone, get up! We have to pack up and leave before sunrise.' He didn't wait for a response and was already off to the next wagon.

'It's still dark, what time is it?' Elli said into the darkness. 'About six!' Jochen said. 'It'll be dark for another three hours.' An hour later, all the wagons were loaded; the horses were ready.

Most people had finished a hasty breakfast and listened to Rolf explain what was to happen next.

'Let me make it short. We are in danger. By now the Poles will have an idea where our people came from. They could be looking for us. We have to get away from the Neisse River.'

The river was the border between Silesia and Saxony and Rolf was convinced that the Poles would not follow them into Saxony, as the Russians only gave them control over Silesia. Even though they were now in Saxony, they had to get away from the border, away from Polish patrols and Czech partisans. Their best option was to get to the Elbe River.

Rolf suggested they use back roads to Berthelsdorf and from there to Ebersbach, which was close to the Bohemian border. After skirting the border for a few days they would come to Suhland, from there they could travel to Neunstadt, and finally reach the Elbe River near Bad Schandauwhere they would be able to cross.

Rolf warned that the towns they would be passing through were small, and a starving refugee convoy could be seen as a threat to meagre food supplies, but he was hoping that they would be able to barter for some food.

Most people had never heard about the towns Rolf mentioned. Too weary to object, they accepted Rolf's plan.

Chapter 9

The road was only lightly covered in snow, so a clearing team in front of the horses wasn't necessary They reached Berthelsdorf in four hours. Most of the houses in the small town were arranged around a circular marketplace.

The wagons took up positions surrounding the marketplace, which gave the refugees a tight central space.

They were visible from every house adjoining the marketplace place and their noisy approach should have alerted the population, but no one appeared. The only sign of life was a dog, which emerged from the garden as Manfred and Otto walked to one of the houses.

Elli expected the dog to bark at the men but it kept its distance from them, limping towards Elli and Lara. It was a large dog, but so undernourished that its massive head seemed a misfit on its wasted body. Step-by-step, it came closer until it was only two metres from her.

'Come on boy, don't be scared; come here.' Gradually the dog crawled closer, until he was in reach of Elli. He lay down, head on his front paws, wagging its tail.

'Lara, look! What's that on his side?' The animal flinched at Lara's touch.

'He is bruised,' Lara said,' but it doesn't seem too bad. I think someone kicked him. You poor Liebling, who has done this to you?' She looked around but still nobody was there. 'I'll keep him. There is enough space in our wagon. Come on.'

The dog looked at Elli and did not move. 'I think he has decided already who his new owner is,' Lara smiled. The dog followed the women, close to Elli's heels.

The town was largely undamaged, except for a burned-out church and two ransacked shops. It was peaceful. It was also deserted.

'It doesn't look like the Russians came through here,' Elli said. 'Everyone is gone, but how did they leave? Look Lara, there are wagons still in the barns.' Open barn doors facing the market place revealed farming equipment neatly stored as well as the wagons. Closer to the house where the men had gone, the dog stopped and lay down.

'Come on boy. Don't lie down here; you'll get a cold belly, you skinny thing. Come on.' Elli patted him but the dog refused to get up. He laid his head on outstretched legs and whimpered like a child in pain.

'Manfred and Otto are coming back, Elli.'

The men stumbled out of the door, fell down and helped each other up.

'What's the matter with them?' The women rushed over. 'Manfred, Otto, what's wrong?' Elli stared at the men. Their red eyes contrasted with their white faces, as if both had been crying. Then Manfred clasped a hand over his mouth and collapsed to his knees, dry retching.

'There are bodies everywhere,' Otto said. His face was drained of blood, even his lips were white. He reached for his handkerchief, and wiped his face.

'Everyone is dead...everywhere bodies. All dead! Women, children, all dead.'

By now they had retreated to the waiting group of refugees. The people around them reacted with fear.

'We're cursed! Everyone is getting killed!' '*Ja*, we should have stayed in Krummhübel.'

'The Polish animals would kill us all. We had to leave.' Some people were hastily withdrawing to their wagons. 'Wait!' Rolf tried to take charge. 'Let's not panic. Jochen and

Armin, come with me. We'll have a look. Everyone else stay here please.'

The three men went to the house where Otto and Manfred had been. Moments later they came out again.

'Wait, please! We'll check the other houses too.' Rolf said as some made attempts to follow them.

The crowd in the market place watched in silence as the three men hurried from house to house.

Then they came back. No one said anything.

Jochen and Armin sat down beside Manfred and Otto, covering their pale faces with their hands. Rolf walked into the crowd as they made space for him, forming a circle around him.

'This place is a slaughterhouse. Everyone has been murdered. There are bodies everywhere. There is nothing we can do for them.' He hesitated. 'But we can't leave yet—we have to go in again. We have to find food. Make no mistake; if we can't find food, we'll soon be as dead as these people. Search everywhere. If you have to move a body to get into a cupboard or cellar, do it. We have to find food! Split up in groups of three—and stay together.'

The women were not excluded from the grim task. The house Elli, Lara and Elfriede entered was a dark pit, the windows barricaded with boards. The light from the opened door lit only a small rectangular space, beyond which was darkness. Elli was aware of her scalp tightening, sending shivers through her body.

Ice crunched under her feet. The house smelled acidic, almost like a stable, and of something else, which she almost recognised. Her left foot kicked something soft. She bent down, horrified at what she might find, but compelled to find out.

A mattress.

She sighed with relief, and stepped away—onto something firmer. It was harsh underfoot, irregular. The crunching sound indicated something frozen. She tried to focus on the thing at her feet but there was only darkness. She turned around and tried to move towards the bright outline of the door but her feet stepped on soft bundles, slowing her down.

She heard the rustling of countless small feet and a shrill whistling. Rats!

Thousands of rats.

The air was cold, and thick with the half-remembered smell. And then she knew; the smell was like this in the hotel's cool room where sides of beef and pork hung. No: it was more pungent, more like when the cool room had become too warm and the meat had spoilt. Her chest hurt. Breathing was painful.

There was another sound she had heard somewhere before—years ago, during a walk in the forest, when she stumbled over the carcass of a horse.

The hum of cadaver flies!

She screamed and waved her arm around as the insects crawled over her face trying to get into her nostrils and ears. She knew they were not interested in a living body but she had stirred them up, disturbed their feast. She felt her stomach push up a hot burning fluid and stumbled towards the bright light of the entrance, knowing now that what she was stepping on were corpses.

In every house there were corpses. The men had been executed SS style, a single bullet through the back of their heads. Most of the women were mutilated, their bodies slit open, breasts and limbs cut off, lying with their intestines beside them, in pools of blood.

But they found food, large stores of food.

Later sitting on the driver bench beside Jochen and her father Elli asked, 'Papa, what happened here? This wasn't an ordinary village. Everything is intact, hardly any destruction or signs of panic and the dead don't look like village people. What happened here?'

Rolf told her he had found documents in the church office, which showed that a special commando unit, an Einsatzgruppe, operated in the area and the village was their headquarters. There were reports detailing the thousands of people that the Einsatzgruppe had killed. The victims seemed to be mostly Polish Jews, POWs and Polish civilians. The bodies were Russians and Poles who had been used as servants, then murdered when the SS withdrew. What happened to the original townspeople was unclear.

'And now we have to move fast because sooner or later Russian troops will find this place. If we are still anywhere in the neighbourhood they will kill us,' Rolf said.'

'Why? We are just refugees,' Elli said

'*Ja*, German refugees found in a place littered with dead Russian and Polish people.'

Rolf drove the group relentlessly and by dusk they were settling in the forest near Ebersbach. This evening they had plenty of food but most were not hungry. The memory of where the food came from was too vivid and when Elli, who had prepared the meal, said that she felt like a grave robber, some of the few who were eating started to choke.

The ghosts of the slaughtered SS slave workers kept them awake as they huddled around the bright campfires, keeping the darkness at bay.

Chapter 10

"'Elli, wake up, your father was here. We have to get going.'

The air in the wagon was musky, heavy with the smells of people living in their clothes with little opportunity to wash. It was still dark.

Between Jochen's snores, coming from the lower compartment of the wagon, she could hear the breathing of her children. The shadowy outline of a head moved into view.

'Come on Elli. Wake up. Jochen, wake up,' Lara said. Elli tried to clear her sore throat, and rubbed her eyes.

'Tell him to go away.' She fell back on her bedding.

'Don't fall asleep again. Jochen get up!' A yelp from Jochen showed Lara's determination. Seconds later Elli's blankets were ripped away.

'Up now! Both of you!'

Elli sighed and levered herself up.

'Why? It's still dark; we can't move before daylight.'

'I don't know why, but Rolf is franticly running around telling everyone to get ready for immediate departure. He wants everyone to meet at the fire. Hurry please.'

It took longer than five minutes but eventually they crowded around the burned down campfire, as close as the heat from the glowing embers permitted. Occasionally their cold backs forced them to turn around and face the white wall of falling snow.

'Verfluchte *Scheisse*! I hope you have a good reason for this, Rolf,' Hans rubbed his cold hands together.

'We have to move on in a hurry. Only a few hundred metres from here is an SS convoy,' Rolf said. For a moment, there was shocked silence.

'SS? Oh God! How do you know?' Hans said.

'I couldn't sleep. About two hours ago, when I was standing here, it wasn't snowing. I saw something which looked like light reflecting off low clouds. I went to investigate what it could be. From the top of the hill, up there just behind us, I could see an army camp.'

In the red glow of the embers, he saw their wide-open eyes, heard their whispers. They pressed closer as if the fire could protect them, somehow reduce their fears.

'If you saw the reflection of their fire, they must have seen ours,' Hans whispered.'

'No, I don't think so. Our fire was nearly out at that time and now the falling snow filters out lights and sounds.'

'How do you know it's the SS?' Hans said.

'The armoured vehicles, only the Waffen-SS uses them. But there is something else, something strange, about this convoy. The command vehicle had the number 1'.

'So what?' Hans said. 'The commander is a typical Nazi egomaniac and sees himself as number one. Or perhaps he is number one in this region.'

Rolf didn't agree with Hans. He couldn't imagine that the SS would make a mistake like that. Too many Russian troops are in the area. What puzzled him was that normally all military vehicles, including Waffen-SS have an individual identification, usually letters, and two to three numbers, not just a single number. He was convinced that the SS convoy escorted some important military or civilian person.

'Something else—I don't think their being so close to us is a coincidence.

They are only a few hundred metres behind us and most likely they saw our tracks before fresh snow covered them. If they have chosen to stay behind us, it's deliberate. Their vehicles are ten times faster than ours.

I can think of only one reason. Should we run into Russians, they will hear it and be warned. They are trying to escape to the West by quietly following us.'

'But if the Russians discover them so close to us, they will think we are part of the SS. They'll kill us!' Jochen said from behind Elli.

'*Ja*, I agree,' Rolf said. 'And that's the reason we have to get away fast.'

'Wait a minute,' Hans cut in. 'Your idea that the SS is quietly following us is silly. Armoured vehicles make more noise than our rigs. If there are Russian patrols nearby, they would hear them before us.'

'Perhaps,' Rolf said. 'Nevertheless, the falling snow filters most noises out. In any case, I don't trust them to stay behind us for long. God knows what they are up to.'

'But how can we get away? We are leaving tracks a blind man could follow and we certainly can't outrun them,' Jochen said.

'Maybe we should go to them and ask for their help? They are German troops after all,' Ulrike Kruse said. 'They are our people, not Russians.'

Elli cringed. Despite Ulrike's family background, she had never before heard her supportive of the Nazis. After all that they had experienced, how could she suggest asking the SS for help? It wasn't just stupid; it was suicidal.

A murmur travelled through the crowd. Up to now they had passively followed the discussion, gripped by fear, but now a few people supported Ulrike's suggestion.

'It is stupid to run away from the *Waffen*-SS,' Otto Schlichte shouted.

'*Ja*, they are Germans. Better them than Poles or Russians. If they are heading westwards, we should ask them for help,' Erica Schlichte supported her husband.

'Does anyone else think so?' Rolf said sharply.

They stared at him in silence. Otto and Erica glowered at him red-faced but they kept quiet.

'What is Ulrike on about, Elli?' Ruth whispered.

'Think about what Rolf said,' Hans said. Elli saw that he was tightly holding his wife's hand. 'They could easily catch up with us but they deliberately stay behind. Whatever their reasons are, it would be safer to be as far away from them as possible.'

Ulricke looked increasingly uncomfortable during the discussion, looking down and avoiding eye contact with anyone.

'I think...' She hesitated, flicked a strand of her auburn hair out of her face, and started again. 'I think that Rolf is right. We can't rely on the SS supporting us in any way,' she said.' They are being hunted and would do anything to survive.' She stepped back and, without looking at anyone moved to the back of the crowd.

'What was all that about?' Ruth nudged her sister. 'First she comes up with an idiotic idea and then she is the greatest supporter of Papa.'

'Our father and Hans are playing politics,' Elli said. 'He wanted to identify any opposition. Look at him.'

The barely perceptible smile on Rolf's face as he seized the opportunity to regain control told Elli that she was right.

'I have studied the map and I think we can make a clean getaway.

We are only a few kilometres from the border with Bohemia. The plan is to move along the border until we reach Bad Schandau at the Elbe.

The Bohemian country in this area is like a peninsula, surrounded on three sides by German territory. I think we can get rid of the SS if we cut through instead of moving around the peninsula.'

'What stops them from following us?' Otto Schlichte said. 'It would be too difficult for them,' Rolf said. 'The road is narrow and goes through a canyon. They would be easy prey for partisans operating in that area, but they won't bother us, and it would cut out a few days travelling. We'd get to the Elbe much quicker.'

'But you said yourself that the Czechs kill refugees who cross into Bohemia. Sounds to me like hopping from the fire into the frying pan,' Otto said.

'I know the area quite well. It's mountainous and mostly unpopulated. With a little luck, we won't be seen by anyone.'

'And what if we run into partisans?' Otto said.

'I don't think we will. This was partisan country earlier, during the war, but they aren't hiding anymore. Now, they are chasing *Wehrmacht* troops and there are none in the area. We have to be more cautious of local people who might be interested in our food. But, as I said, hardly anyone lives there, and in any case, we can defend ourselves.' 'Defend ourselves! How?' Otto said.

'We have some guns,' Rolf said. 'We have guns? Where from?'

'We found them. Troops on the run get rid of them. There are guns in virtually every roadside trench,' Rolf said.

'And why do you think they get rid of them?' Otto said. 'Because they are trying to camouflage themselves as civilians. The Russians will slaughter us if they find any weapons here. Have you lost your mind? This is crazy, Rolf.'

'I don't think there is a risk of running into Russian troops around here.'

'You don't know that,' Otto said.

'No I don't, but it is unlikely. If we can't defend ourselves against people trying to rob or kill us, we might as well give up. Remember what happened in Ostritz. The risk of running into Russian troops is minimal, and we need the guns. We have to be able to defend ourselves.'

Otto stood with his arms folded over his chest. He opened his mouth, but seemed to swallow what he wanted to say as he faced Rolf.

'The short cut through Bohemia must be safer than being trailed by the SS.' Rolf gazed around, avoiding Otto's stare. 'I agree with you that we probably shouldn't have weapons with us. But we must be ready to deal with looters and any others who see us as easy prey. You're right about what would happen to us if Russians found our weapons. We'll get rid of them when we cross back into Saxony.'

'Looters will be everywhere, even in Saxony.' Otto came back at him. 'We may lose a few possessions, but if the Russians find any weapons, they'll massacre us.' Without waiting for a reply, he walked off, followed by his wife.

'There is no alternative,' Hans broke the silence. 'We have to get away from the SS so we can't continue on this road. I think we all agree on that. Keeping weapons on us is dangerous but I agree with Rolf that the danger from armed looters is greater. I think we should keep our weapons but be prepared to get rid of them at the earliest opportunity.' The meeting concluded with support for Rolf's plan.

'I just hope Rolf knows the area as well as he claims,' Jochen said later at their wagon.

'I don't know what the fuss is about,' Lara said. 'Since we left Krummhübel I have carried a pistol. No Schwein will rape me again.'

'That's crazy Lara. You have to get rid of it! We will all be killed if the Russians find it,' Elli said.

'No! No one will hurt me again,' Lara said. 'No one!' She wrapped herself in her blankets, pulled them over her head, and did not respond any more.

The Clydesdale tolerated Jochen and Elli's hurried preparations for the night march as Rolf dashed from wagon to wagon.

'Please, people, try to do everything as quietly as possible. We don't want our escorts to wake up.'

'Don't worry, Rolf. As you said, the snow will dampen any noise we make,' Jochen said.

'*Ja, ja*, but sharp noises can be heard.'

The narrow road was nearly snow free under the shelter of trees and overhanging rock. The falling snow transformed the walkers in front of the convoy into moving snowmen. Whenever Elli started to fall back, Karla, the lead horse, gently nudged her or snorted hot air on her neck.

'*Ja, ja*, I am going, you silly nag.'

Daylight was coming. The snow had stopped and ground fog had moved in, an eerie mixture of night and day filtering out the landscape.

Elli could sometimes see the tops of trees floating in the air without any visible connection to the ground. When the fog lifted, Elli saw a bridge ahead of them spanning a deep gorge. When they came closer, she could hear the sound of rushing water.

The bridge was old. The two main beams were oak trunks, still with their bark on. The planks connecting the beams were thick but the gaps between them were as wide as the planks. The railings on both sides were broken. Elli saw that the main beams were anchored to the rock walls by four struts. Two of them were broken. As the convoy slowly, carefully, picked its way across the creaking timber Elli desperately avoided looking down.

On the other side, the road opened up into a plateau. After the next bend and out of sight of the bridge, Rolf stopped the convoy. After the last wagon arrived, Rolf selected a dozen of the strongest horses, which included Elli's Karla.

'Bring the horses back to the bridge. We have a little job to do.' He did not give any explanation. Elli was too tired to argue and took Karla out of the wagon gear to follow Rolf and Jochen back to the bridge.

'Okay, Jochen, Hans, Fritz and Helmut, take the bowsaw and cut through the main beam on the left side. Hans and Fritz you two will

have to go under the bridge. The rock shoulder should make a good work platform. Be careful, it will be very slippery.'

'Why are we doing this, Papa? Did I miss something?' Elli said. 'I'm sorry *Liebling*, I thought you knew.'

'Knew what?'

'We're going to demolish the bridge. It is possible that the SS will try to follow us into Bohemia. We'll have to make sure they can't.'

'But, Papa, you said they wouldn't come after us! You said the road is no good for their vehicles!'

'I know, I know, but the road is frozen. It could be firm enough to support their vehicles. They might try it. We have to make sure they don't. Maybe I'm too cautious. In any case, it's relatively easy to collapse the bridge and will take no time.'

The four men walked over to the bridge. The chosen two carefully climbed down onto the narrow rock shelf.

'Cut from outside through the rail. There! *Ja*, there, just behind the main pylon. *Ja*, good! That's the right place.' Rolf was hanging so far over the railing, directing the men, that Elli was afraid he would lose his hold. 'Be careful, just cut it to about three-quarters through. When you hear cracking sounds, get out from there and come back to this side quickly.'

The men under the bridge pulled the blade down, then the two on top pulled it up. They quickly developed a rhythm as the saw easily cut through the old timber. Halfway through the beam, they slowed down and listened carefully for cracking sounds. Elli could see their anxiety increase with each stroke as they approached the three-quarter point.

'That's it! Get out of there and come back to me!' Rolf said.

He had two ropes with him. He tied them around the partially cut beam.

After everyone was safely back on the other side, they attached the ropes to the horses' harnesses and the animals started to pull. The horses strained and struggled until loud creaking sounds came from the bridge. The beam did not move.

'The angle is too shallow. Get the horses closer to the edge.' Rolf stared at the bridge. Despite the cold, he was sweating. Suddenly, the beam broke, but still it did not fall. 'Quick, cut the horses out of the gear or they will go down with the bridge!' Rolf said. Seconds after they cut the last rope, there was a loud crack, and the bridge slowly broke up.

First, the cut beam went down, taking with it the top boards. Then the supporting structure of the other beam collapsed and the rest of the bridge disappeared. All the time Elli held her breath.

'My God, a few seconds longer and the horses would have gone with the bridge. That was stupid, Papa.'

They stared down into the gap where the bridge had vanished. '*Ja*, that could have been disastrous.' Rolf was pale, trembling.

'But if the bastards are following us, that'll slow them down.' With a wide grin, he slapped Jochen on the shoulder. 'You are good at building a bridge but I think I'm pretty good at demolishing one, *ja*?'

Elli took Karla back to the camp and rubbed her down. Soon her father joined her.

'*Liebling*, you have the binoculars I gave you last Christmas?' '*Ja*, sure, Papa. Do you want them?'

'I want see if I was right.' 'Right about what?'

'The SS following us.'

'You mean you are going back to the bridge?'

'*Ja*. From the boulders on this side, I can have a good look at the bridge—I mean where the bridge was.'

'I'll come with you.'

'No, no, that's too dangerous.'

'Fine, forget about the binoculars then.'

'You are a very stubborn woman, Tochter. I don't know where you got that from. Your mother was such a gentle person.'

'*Ja*, I sometimes wonder too.'

After about an hour, freezing in a space between two large boulders, Elli cursed herself for insisting.

'Papa, let's go back, they aren't coming. Come on, I'm freezing to death.'

'Just a little longer.'

Her feet were almost numb. They hurt when she started to stamp up and down. She hopped from foot to foot to increase her circulation.

'Come on, Papa. They're not coming.'

A vehicle turned the corner on the other side of the departed bridge. Elli ducked behind the boulders. '*Verfluchte Scheisse*, you were right! They are here!'

Four armoured personnel carriers stopped at the gap. Six soldiers in grey uniforms got out and walked to the edge of the gorge, shouting at each other. An officer and a civilian joined them. Through her binoculars, Elli could see that the officer's greatcoat had red shoulder flashes and red edgings to its collar.

'You were right, Papa. That is an important person. A general, I think.'

'Let me see.' He grabbed the binoculars. '*Ja*, that's a general, but who is the man in the black leather coat? He looks like Gestapo.' The general said something to the officer beside him. He waved an arm and the soldiers hurried back to their vehicles, followed by the officer. The general and the civilian started to walk back to the vehicle with the numeral '1', written on it. Rolf jumped up in clear view and shouted, 'Didn't count on that you *Arschloch, ja*?'

Both men turned around, shouting. Soldiers emerged from the vehicles and started shooting. Bullets ricocheted off the rocks around the hiding place. Elli pushed her father down so forcefully that she fell on top of him.

'Are you totally mad, you old goat? Why did you do that?'

Rolf did not answer but the broad grin showed that he was satisfied with himself.

'So what?' he said later at the camp when his furious daughter explained to the others what had happened. 'There is no way they can follow us. Should they decide to cut us off by taking another road, they would have to go through the area the Russians are moving through.'

'You are proud of your little stunt, aren't you?' said Elli. '*Ja*. I haven't felt so good for a long time.'

'Calm down Elli,' Ruth said. He probably saved our lives.' '*Ja*, and he nearly got himself shot. He acted like a kid.' '*Ja*, that's what Mama always said about him.'

'Only ten kilometres more and we'll be at the border. The first town on the German side is Saupsdorf. From there, it is only forty kilometres to the Elbe. With a bit of luck, we should make it in two days,' Rolf said. 'We shouldn't hear anything from the SS anymore. Even at high speed it would take them two weeks to catch up because they have to go back to Ebersbach and then take the long way via Oppach and Neustadt.'

The people standing around him were too cold and too tired to respond. Few showed signs of relief. Everyone was glad to be out of Bohemia, away from this dangerous road hugging the mountainside. The only one who was wide-awake and active was Elli's father. He was beaming with energy and restlessly running from wagon to wagon, organising people. Elli was convinced that he was actually enjoying himself.

The convoy moved on.

Elli and Lara were sitting, wrapped in blankets, on the wagon's steering bench. Karla moved steadily along the narrow road, with her reins loosely attached to the steering bench. The horse knew where to go and Elli did not attempt to interfere. She envied her horse. The steam coming from under Karla's blanket showed that she wasn't cold.

No steam was coming from Elli and Lara. They tried to cheer each other up by talking about the hot dinner they would have at the campfire, and by telling warm stories. Eventually the cold even penetrated the dirty joke competition with which they tried to keep each other alert. When Elli felt the burning pain of frostbite in her toes, she decided to walk.

'Lara, come down here with me, your feet must be as frozen as mine. Come on, let's get some circulation going.'

She had to stop talking as her frozen toes protested with a stab of pain as she started to walk.

It was easy moving through the powdery snow and she strode ahead in front of Karla. Lara stayed on the wagon and Elli could hear her muttering something about 'madness'. Don't listen to me, girl, she thought. Just freeze your arse off.

Elli's was now the third wagon behind Elfriede Schulze. When she came alongside Elfriede's wagon, Elli heard her humming. Elfriede held a large bottle of schnapps, which immediately disappeared when she saw Elli.

'Elfriede, you rat! You hoarded some alcohol and to make it worse, you didn't share it with me! Come on, woman, get it out or I will tell everyone about your filthy crime.'

'Shut up! Don't scream like that or we will have to share it with everyone.' Elfriede looked anxiously over her shoulder.

The schnapps felt like liquid fire and after a few gulps Elli could not feel her hurting toes anymore.

'Wow, that feels good. Where did you get that stuff? I thought there was nothing left.'

'That's nothing, look at this.' With a broad grin, Elfriede stood up and lifted the lid of the steering bench.

'*Mein Gott*, French cognac! That's fantastic, where did you get it?'

'There is plenty of it, look.' It was filled to the brim with bottles.

'Got it in Ebersbach. There was plenty more of it—and only the best.'

For a moment, Elli felt a sharp stab of guilt. Then the calming effect of the alcohol drowned the feeling.

'What the heck, they won't need it anymore but we certainly do.'
'That's my girl,' Elfriede said. 'Let's have another gulp.'

Elfriede's horse ignored the erratic jerks of the reins and delivered them safely to the evening camp.

When Rolf came around both women managed a warm welcome grin before they passed out.

Chapter 11

'What's the matter with you two?' Ruth said.

Elli and Elfriede staggered to the campfire. They tried to hold each other up but slipped occasionally, landing in the fresh, soft snow.

'Want some?'

Elli tried to avoid looking at the piece of pork Ruth was holding up. Its oily surface glistened in the sunlight, and watery blood oozed out where Ruth had stabbed it. When the smell hit her, Elli stomach heaved and sparks flashed in front of her eyes. Elfriede must have had similar problems. Each desperately tried to hold on to the other.

'You look awful, both of you. Are you sick?' 'Just a bit of a cold,' Elli said.

'A bit of a cold? You look like death.' As she came closer the alcohol fumes hit her.

'Wow! Sister, I didn't think a proper Frau like you had it in her. You stink to heaven. Where did you get the booze? Come on, tell your big sister.'

'Go away, *Arschloch*.' Elli's head spun and her tongue got in the way of her words.

'If you can't hold it, don't do it. Leave the boozing to people who can, like me. Now, be a good girl and tell your big sister where you got the schnapps from and most importantly, if there is any more. Here! Have some porridge; you look like you need some food, and then tell me all about it.'

Elli looked at the unappetising, slimy substance in the bowl; then she smelled the sour steam rising from it. Within seconds, her stomach lurched and shot something hot and burning into her throat. She tried desperately to keep her mouth shut but the pressure increased. She had to let go. She knelt in the snow until the vomiting and dry retching eased into infrequent spasms.

She heard a voice out of the haze, taking a few seconds before she registered that it was Ruth.

'You poor things! Come with me. I have something that will help you.'

She grabbed both women and dragged them to her wagon where she let them drop. Elli came to rest with her face squashed in the snow, wondering if her eyeballs would freeze if she didn't get up. With great effort, she turned over. Beside her was Elfriede, also face down in the snow. Elli tried to roll her over but soon realised that there was no danger of her friend suffocating. Her vomit had dissolved the snow under her face.

From the wagon, Elli heard her sister rummaging through her belongings. Finally, Ruth emerged with a small golden box. In it was a white powdery substance.

'What is it, baking powder?' Elli said.

Ruth placed a small amount into two cups with water. After she stirred the mixture, she handed the cups to the sick women.

'Here, drink this. In a few minutes you'll feel newborn.'

Elli gulped the mixture down, absolutely convinced that Ruth was insane. Nothing would kill this hangover: certainly not baking powder.

Maybe a glass of schnapps would do it.

The mixture was almost tasteless but there was a hint, a tingling on her tastebuds, which Elli could not identify. She fought to keep the fluid down. Moments later the burning in her mouth and throat had gone. She felt an odd sensation travelling through her lower body, a warm wave slowly spreading out. The pains and spasms disappeared. When the warmth reached her head, her eyesight cleared and she became aware of a variety of smells. The rush of energy and feeling of unlimited power overshadowed everything. She felt hungry.

'That is unbelievable! A minute ago, I wanted to die; now I feel fantastic,' Elli said. 'What is that stuff? Can you spare some?'

'For a bottle of schnapps, I could spare a bit, but not much. I got it from a friend who died a few months ago and I wouldn't know where to get any more,' Ruth said.

'*Mein Gott,* I've never felt so good, can I have some too? What is it??' Elfriede said.

'Cocaine.'

'Cocaine? Isn't that something they put in cough medicine?' Elli said.

'*Ja*, I guess you could take it as a cough medicine, but like this you have to be careful,' Ruth said.

'Ah, come on, why should I be careful with cough medicine, especially if it cures more than a cough? That stuff is better than schnapps. I'll swap a few bottles for some,' Elfriede said.

'I'll give you some, but only a little bit, and that will be all. I need it myself.'

'Don't be so selfish Ruth. What do you mean you need it?' Elfriede said.

'I've been using it for a while. It gives me energy and inspiration but when I stop taking it, I want to commit suicide. I have to have it, or I fall apart.'

'Fall apart? What are you saying?' Elli said.

'My whole body hurts; I get spasms, shakes and I want to kill myself—until I take another dose.'

'And you gave that to us, are you crazy?' Elli said.

'Nothing to worry about if you only take it a few times. It'll wear off in two or three hours. That's all.'

'Where did you get it in the first place?' Elli said.

'A few months ago, a friend offered me some after a party. I had a terrible hangover, and it felt so good I got more.'

'How did you do that?' Elfriede said.

'I slept with him. For a while we had the perfect relationship—we both got what we wanted, and the sex was good.'

Elli was not sure if Ruth was trying to shock her. 'Where did he get it?' Elli asked.

'I really don't know, but for SS officers it's easy to get what they want.'

'You slept with an SS officer so that he would supply you with cocaine? That's sick.'

Elfriede looked uncomfortably from one to the other.

'*Danke*, Ruth, for the medicine. I have to lie down for a while,' she mumbled and rushed off.

'Come on, *Schwesterlein*, save me the moral outburst. I've been through hell and this stuff was the only thing that kept me from stringing myself up. No one looked after me, including you, only the white powder.'

'*Unglaublich!* Have you looked around recently? We are all going through hell. Can't see it, ha? Of course, you can't, you never had to.

All your life you were pampered and only had to snap your fingers to get whatever you wanted.' Elli's voice was rising. 'Papa spoilt you rotten and that imbecile husband of yours continued with it, even though you treated him like dirt. Now you have the audacity to say I didn't have any interest in you? My poor, big sister. No, I didn't, but good old Papa made me, forced me to look after you.'

The last few words she screamed so loudly that her voice snapped and she ended up in a coughing fit. Ruth looked at her quietly, tears slowly running down her face.

Here we go again, Elli thought. The selfish bitch deserved that and it was long overdue, so why do I feel so bad?

'Papa told me to be strong and independent, like you,' Ruth said, her voice so low Elli could barely hear her. 'But I couldn't.'

'*Ja, ja, ja,* du armes Mädchen. Stop that! Don't give me that 'poor little girl' act. You are a tough bitch if you want to be. I've seen you in action often enough.'

'*Ja*, I can give a good show but it's just that, a show. Horst looked after me and protected me. I became so dependent on him that when they drafted him, I felt like a cripple. All of a sudden, I had to do all the unpleasant things he had kept from me, and I couldn't cope. Not that I was stupid, but I had forgotten how to look after myself.

'Horst never held my moods against me. He was always there and made sure I could function, not just as an artist but as a person. When he didn't come back, I couldn't go on. I was so scared of everything, especially people. Alcohol helped, but cocaine was better.'

Elli struggled with anger and pity. Ruth was someone she looked up to. People saw Ruth as an important artist. She was proud of her but often felt inferior in the crowd her sister moved in. She did not feel strong at all.

'Why didn't you say anything? You could have talked to me or Papa.'

'I couldn't. I felt like a failure.' 'A failure, you, the famous artist?'

'*Ja*, Papa was so proud of me and showed me around like a prized possession, even after the Nazis banned me. What could I have said—I'm sorry Papa but I'm falling apart because Horst isn't here to look after me anymore? And by the way, because I'm feeling like shit, I'm sleeping with the SS to get cocaine so I can feel better—is that what I should have told him, *ja*?'

'You never said anything to me either.'

'I felt ashamed. Papa hammered into me that I had to look after you, my little sister, and when he changed his sermon to my needing to become as strong as you, I couldn't.'

'Maybe Papa was trying to tell you to look after yourself better.

You should have talked to me.'

'How could you understand? You weren't part of that insane crowd.'

'That's why. As an outsider I could've been more objective.' 'You had enough trouble with Claus missing. God, I envied how you dealt with that. Papa is right, you are the stronger one.'

'Envied me? I lost my husband! Do you know how I felt when I got the telegram that said Claus was missing?'

'That was two months before Horst died. You kept on working. I never saw you crying. You were so strong.'

'Strong? God no! I talked a lot to Papa and that helped, but mostly I was hiding in my work. Talking to you wasn't on because you were constantly at some shitty art function, and after Horst died, I didn't see you at all.'

'I tried to go back to painting. I tried anything—anything but thinking. Parties, alcohol and men helped, but cocaine really worked. I got my energy back and could see colours again. I could paint again—at a price. I had to sleep with SS men and party officials who supplied me with the stuff. *Ja*, I was their whore but I could paint again and felt no pain. Nothing else mattered.'

'I thought you weren't interested in anything or anyone. You painted, and nothing else seemed to exist.'

'I must have looked like a total selfish and uncaring bitch.' 'How are you now?' Elli said.

'I'm using less. Soon, hopefully, I won't need it at all. My painting is getting better too, no more rose-coloured happy pictures,' Ruth said. A crooked smile, a hint of mischief lit up her face. 'In fact, the Nazis' art guardians would lock me away, not just ban me, if they got a look at my recent work.'

'If your other work is as graphic as the one of the dead refugees, I wouldn't be surprised,' Elli said. 'Do you still take that stuff?'

'Only when I'm very down. I had to stop using as much anyway. Couldn't stand the nose bleeds.' 'Nose bleeds?'

'That happens when you sniff the powder. It works faster but your nose will continue to bleed. I have seen what it does if you don't stop.'

'What?'

'It eats away the wall between your nostrils.' Ruth looked at her sister with a sad smile. 'Please, *Liebling*, don't tell Papa. I can't face him. Please.'

'I won't tell him but I think you should. He'll tell you that you are stupid—and that he loves you.'

'*Ja*, you're right, but not yet, I'm not ready.'

❄

Chapter 12

'That sign said 'Saupsdorf—3 Kilometres'. Did you see that, Elli?' Lara said.

'Only three kilometres and we'll be out of Bohemia.'

'I'm glad. This place gives me the creeps,' Elli said. 'It must be the most desolate area I've ever seen. It's so eerie and dark you could think witches and gnomes are in every shadow, keeping their eyes on us.'

They wound their way along the side of a vertical mountain wall. On the other side of the narrow road was a sheer drop to the bottom of the cliff, invisible in the snow.

Around the next bend, the road opened up into a plateau, with overhanging rock walls on both sides. Beside the road was a hut; across the road was a boom gate. Lights were on in the hut.

'The border's guarded. Oh God, what do we do now?'

An older man and a young woman came out of the hut. When they came closer, Elli saw that both wore bits of uniform: badges, a cap, a gun belt. German uniform trophies. Both carried guns. Rolf jumped off the wagon and walked over to them. Elli flinched when the woman pointed her gun at Rolf. She could not hear what they were talking about but the response of the man was sharp and short. He walked over to them.

'Get off the wagons; we have to search you.' He waved his gun at them to support his demand. None of the refugees moved.

'You heard what I said. Off, off.' He fired his gun into the air and then pointed it at Rolf.

'You heard the man. All off the wagons. Stay calm and let the border guards have a look in the wagons. No one will get hurt.'

The shots had alarmed everyone. Pale and trembling, they climbed out of their wagons. Children cried but most of the adults were quiet, shuffling away from their belongings, glancing cautiously at the guards. The male guard went from wagon to wagon, stirring through the luggage of the refugees, as the female pointed her gun at them. Suddenly a woman screamed, then a man shouted.

'That's Lara! My God, I didn't realise she was still in the wagon,' Elli said.

A shot rang out.

'Stop!' The woman guard fired her weapon, stopping them from running to the wagon. Lara emerged, covered in blood, a pistol in her hand. The female guard shouted at her to stop, to drop the gun, but Lara continued to walk towards her. Almost simultaneously, two shots rung out. Both women fell. When they reached Lara, they saw a small bullet hole in her forehead. Under her head was a pool of blood. She was dead. Elli knelt down. The warm blood steamed in the snow. Lara's face was smooth; it seemed to reflect disbelief. Only her glassy eyes showed that she was dead. Gently, Elli closed them.

'The guard is alive. Over here, someone, please.' Jochen called.

When Elli got up, her trousers were soaked with blood.

The female guard was on her back. Frothy blood came in convulsions from her mouth.

'She has blood in her lungs. Turn her on the side to let it run out or she'll suffocate. She must have a chest wound. Her lungs have collapsed; we have to patch the entry wound,' Jochen said.

When they tore open the woman's blouse Elli stared at a hole as large as a fist. *'Oh mein lieber Gott!* Cover her up again; there is nothing we can do. She is dying.'

After a few minutes the gurgling sounds stopped. Elli checked her pulse. 'She is dead.'

'Where is the other guard?' Jochen said.

'He is dead too. Lara shot him; he is over there,' someone said, pointing at Elli's wagon.

'We have to get going; other guards will be here soon. They told me that they were due to be relieved,' Rolf said.

They wrapped Lara's body in a blanket. As they lifted the bundle one man slipped and exposed Lara's head. The back of the skull was missing. Blood and lumps of brain tissue dripped down in the snow.

'Stop!' Elli wrapped her scarf around her friend's mutilated head, trying to avoid getting more blood on her. They hurried with their bundle to the wagon and carefully placed her in the back. Elli fell on her knees and vomited.

'What about the other bodies?' Jochen said. 'We can't leave them here.'

'We have to. We must hurry,' Rolf said. 'If the new guards find us here with the bodies of their dead comrades, they'll execute us on the spot.'

Elli's children sat close to Jochen and Rolf on the driver's bench. Elli went into the back. Lara's hand had fallen out of the bundled blanket. It was cold and stiff already when she carefully tucked it back under the blanket.

'We'll get you back on German soil my girl. It's my fault. You told me you had a gun and that no one would rape you again and when I told Papa he agreed that you needed it to feel safe. Oh, *mein armes Mädchen*. When that man came into the wagon, you must have been terrified that it would happen again. I don't blame you. I understand.' Elli kept talking as she wept over the bloodstained blanket. Rolf climbed into the back of the wagon and took Elli into his arms.

'Oh God, I forgot the gun; I forgot,' he said. Elli hugged him. His body was trembling and he was sweating, despite the cold.

'So did I, Papa. I don't think it's anyone's fault. This poor girl had so much happen to her; raped, her father murdered. I bet having a little bit of control again felt good, at least for a moment. Papa, she died as she said she would: not allowing anyone to touch her again. It wasn't your fault or anyone else's.'

From the distance, they heard voices.

'We have to hurry up. That will be the relief guards. We're still too close to the border,' Rolf said, wiping his eyes.

No one followed them. After an hour, they reached Saupsdorf.

It was like a ghost town. The street ahead was covered in an undisturbed blanket of snow. Doors were shut and the dark windows seemed to be grimly staring at them, warning of horrors locked inside. Elli shivered at the thought of what might lie there. She didn't want another Ebersbach. A child's teddy bear dusted with snow lay on a doorstep. A pile of logs half-buried in snow had been knocked over and lay shattered on the road. Not a sound could be heard except the rattle of the wagons and the snorting of the horses.

'I think we should move on. This place is giving me the creeps. There is no one here, not even dogs,' Elli said.

The men searched several houses but there were no bodies and very few personal belongings. It looked as if the occupants had just packed up and left.

They buried Lara in the town's graveyard. Elli, Ruth and Elfriede rolled Lara's body into the grave on one of Elli's rugs.

'That poor girl, we don't even have a decent coffin for her,' Elli said.

'*Ja*, but it's a very nice rug,' Elfriede said.

'That was a family heirloom,' Ruth said. 'Why did you use

Mama's best rug?'

'She was my friend,' Elli said.

The grave was shallow, as the frozen ground did not allow easy digging. Instead of flowers, every one of the twenty-six remaining families laid a personal item on Lara's body—a hand-mirror, a lacy mat, a silver spoon. The service was short as they were anxious to leave. As soon as they had lowered the body into the grave, and covered it with rocks, people moved to their wagons. The river Elbe was close and once they crossed the river they would be in Saxony, and safer.

Armin Hauser had managed to get a basic diode-radio going, giving the refugees the opportunity to catch up on latest developments. Radio Gross-Deutschland and the BBC agreed, for once, that the *Wehrmacht*'s fierce resistance at Breslau was holding up the Russians.

'That won't last long,' Rolf said. 'And the moment they are on the move again Dresden will be their next target.'

'I don't know. Dresden is unimportant to them. I think they'll just bypass it,' Jochen said.

'If you are right, there's even more reason to get over the Elbe and away from this area as fast as possible.'

Rolf went from wagon to wagon organising the departure. Elli's wagon was supposed to be second, behind Hans and Ulricke's rig, on which her father still travelled.

'Hurry up, Hans! Get your rig in position so we can line up.' Hans ignored her shouts and then started to move his rig in the opposite direction. Frustrated, Elli looked for Jochen and her father but neither was in sight.

'Children, hold Karla's reins until I came back. I have to talk to Uncle Hans.'

As she went over to the Kruse's wagon, she saw five other wagons moving out of the line-up. Jochen and Rolf were running towards Hans's rig. Elli arrived moments after the two men.

'Hans, what are you doing? The others told us that they are leaving with you for Dresden. That can't be true.' Hans stayed on the driver's bench. His face was set, his eyes looking away.

'There are six of us,' he said. 'Six families, who have decided not to cross the river over the ice in Bad Schandau. Dresden is only twenty kilometres from there and we can cross over a bridge in Dresden.'

'What? That is insane, Hans! Dresden is not safe. Of course, there are bridges in Dresden, but you would be stuck there,' Rolf said.

'It isn't only the crossing that concerns us. All of us have relatives in Dresden,' Hans said.'

'Relatives? Does that mean that you want to stay in Dresden?' 'It's a possibility.'

'You have heard on the radio what is happening in Dresden!' Rolf's frustration increased. 'Thousands of refugees from Silesia and Prussia are converging there.'

'We all have relatives. They'll give us somewhere to stay.' Hans's voice was becoming louder. Elli could see that he wouldn't change his mind, but Rolf kept on.

'How do you know that your relatives are still in Dresden? Everyone is trying to escape to the west.'

'Well, if they're gone it will still be better. Crossing the river in Dresden is easier; there are many bridges. It's not like Ostritz.' He hesitated for a moment. 'If Ulricke's uncle and his family have left, we'll get on a train or maybe stay at their house.'

'Hans, the Russians will be in Dresden soon. You know how they treat civilians, women in particular. Who knows what they'll do to the city? It isn't safe there.'

'Come on Rolf. Safe? Where is it safe? Crossing the Elbe?

Continuing through that frozen hell? Being killed by passing troops?' Hans jumped off the wagon and stood in front of his old friend, fists clenched, face glowing. 'There were more than two thousand of us. Look around you.' He pointed at the remaining wagons. 'Look what's left. Not safe in Dresden? That is a very bad joke, Rolf.'

Rolf reeled back from the outburst. 'I did what I could...' He stopped, ashen faced, searching his pockets for a handkerchief.

'The Elbe is huge and far wider than the Neisse. Didn't we have enough trouble crossing that one? We have twenty-six heavy wagons. If one breaks through the ice, we drown like rats. Isn't it enough that we just lost one young woman? How many more will we lose if we follow your lead?'

Rolf looked like as if Hans had physically assaulted him, his face was red, the veins on his head stood out like ropes and his restrained voice was barely audible.

'Would it have been safe for you if you hadn't followed my lead and crossed the frozen Neisse, but went to Ostritz to be killed or captured? Lara is on my conscience. I wish I had stayed at Elli's wagon. Maybe I could have prevented what happened, maybe.'

'Stop this Papa.' Elli positioned herself between the two men. 'It wasn't your fault that Lara was killed. She was terrified of men. She said that it would never happen again and she made sure that it didn't. That's not your fault,' Elli said. She turned to Hans with an icy stare. 'How dare you blame Papa! If it weren't for him most of us would be dead.'

Hans trembled with anger. He tried to say something but only a distorted mumble came out. Finally, he regained control.

'Dresden has many bridges. Even if we do nothing else but use one of them, it will be safer and easier.'

'The Elbe is not as shallow as the Neisse. It flows more slowly and its ice will be thicker.' Rolf continued with grim determination. 'The ice will be strong enough for our vehicles and we'll have easy access to the river. The riverbanks are not as steep as the Neisse's.'

'But we are so close to Dresden and its bridges.' Hans said pleadingly, his anger gone. 'Some of us just don't want to go any further. Dresden has been a safe place during the war. As far as I know, it has never been bombed. Why go further?'

The five families left with Hans and Ulricke. Before they went it was agreed that the remaining convoy would wait at the Elbe for two days to give Hans and the others a chance to rejoin them, should they change their minds, or if the situation in Dresden was not what they expected.

'The two days will give us a chance to do some repairs and give the horses a rest,' Rolf pointed out. 'Hans, Ulricke, all of you, my friends, I wish you the best of luck. Dresden is a wonderful city. I would love to see the Zwinger again. It is one of the most beautiful palaces in the world. I hope you find your relatives.'

After a tearful farewell, the six rigs sheared out of the convoy and moved slowly away. Elli continued to cry as Hans's group gradually became black dots in the white snow and eventually disappeared over the horizon. The remaining twenty wagons moved slowly out towards the frozen river.

The gloomy mood at the camp gave Elli an excuse to prepare a special meal. In Ebersbach Rolf had given her three geese he found among the supplies at the SS base. The freezing temperatures had kept the birds in excellent condition. Elli had hidden them and her father must have forgotten about them, or he would have protested when she served Labskaus again. When she unwrapped her hidden treasure and started to prepare the birds, people appeared from everywhere.

She cut the geese open and removed the viscera. There was no shortage of volunteers to wash the smelly intestines Elli needed for sausage skins. The wings, necks, livers, and other offal, mixed with goose fat and flour became the sausage filling. An oven, roughly constructed of rocks and two metal plates, was slow and needed a lot of fuel, but there were helpers everywhere collecting wood, turning the sizzling birds, or waiting hopefully. The aroma was so powerful that no one was able to move away.

Finally, everything was ready.

Elli served the geese with dumplings and red cabbage, a traditional Silesian Christmas dinner, even though it was February. None of the people wolfing down the rare delicacies were concerned about the timing.

'You outdid yourself, daughter,' Rolf said licking his plate so as not to waste any gravy.

'Papa, where are your table manners? A grown man licking his plate, what a terrible example for the children!'

Slowly people went back to their wagons, smiling and sharing stories about previous Christmas dinners. For the moment, the gloom had lifted.

Chapter 13

Hans and his group crossed the Elbe at Pirna, close to Dresden. From the outer suburb of Heidenau their progress became very slow, as all the streets leading to the city centre were crowded. They decided to separate. Three families had relatives in different parts of the city and left immediately. The remaining three families aimed for the central railway station, but eventually Hans and Ulricke lost the others in the chaos.

Dresden, as Saxony's railway hub, was a magnet for refugees from the Eastern provinces. The Red Army's rapid success had sent an ever-increasing flood of desperate people into the city.

An endless procession stumbled through the streets. They could hear the dialects of Eastern Prussia, Pomerania and Silesia. Many people walked through the snow-covered streets beside horse-drawn vehicles and battered trucks, clinging to a few possessions. At every intersection, police and SA groups directed the stream of misery towards marshalling points near the central railway station. But there were also Field Gendarmes checkpoints.

The checkpoint corporal bellowed commands that stopped the wagon ahead of Hans and Ulrike.

'You there, down here!' The corporal pointed at a boy. *'Schnell, schnell,'* he hurried the frightened boy. Hans heard the fearful gasps of the boy's mother.

'How old are you?' The corporal said.

'Fifteen, Herr Gefreiter,' the boy said trying to stand to attention in front of the soldier towering over him.

'The *Führer* and the *Vaterland* need you. Be proud, you'll become a soldier.'

'No! No!' The boy's mother jumped down from her wagon, stumbled over to the corporal and fell on her knees. 'Please! Don't take him, he is only a child.' A violent kick from the soldier knocked her down, into the icy slosh on the road.

'You whore, you dare to object to your duty as a citizen of the Reich?' He turned to the other two military policemen. 'Get all of them on the truck. If this woman makes any more trouble, shoot her.' He marched off, pushing the unlucky boy ahead of him.

The woman's daughters, two small girls, tried to help their mother up. Soaked and barely conscious, she managed to get back on her legs, only to see her son among other boys being loaded on a truck.

'No! Not my Konrad! He is only a child. No!'

'*Mutti*, please don't.' The girls were desperately hanging on to their mother, trying to stop her from following her son.

Hans jumped down to support them, placing himself between the two military policemen and the woman.

'Out of the way.' The soldier made attempts to push Hans aside with his gun.

'She'll be all right, sir. We'll look after her.' Hans said calmly and turned to the woman wondering if the soldier would shoot him or smash him with his gun.

'Come on Peter, leave them! We have to go!' He heard the other soldier urging his colleague. The man who had trained his gun on the woman and Hans mumbled something, and left. Hans helped the woman back to her wagon. An older woman waiting there tried to give Hans a grateful smile, despite the tears streaming down her face.

'*Danke, Danke.* Brigitte, come here, let me help you. Our poor Konrad! These animals.' They went into the wagon. The two girls climbed back on the driver's bench and arranged the horse's reins.

'Will you be all right?' The girls solemnly looked at him, then one said something but it was lost in the noise and shouts from vehicles pushing past them.

'Get going, you *faules Schwein*. Where are the police? You're blocking the road. Out of the way.'

The girls urged their horse on and slowly moved back into the stream of refugees.

Ulricke held Hans tight when he came back, both ignoring the shouting and abuse from other vehicles.

'Oh God, I thought I'd lost you. That soldier—I thought he would shoot you.'

'So did I,' Hans said. 'That poor boy. What insanity is that, to draft children?

What chance do they have against Russian tanks?' The tormented face of the mother and the haunted expression of the two girls stayed with him, as they continued their struggle towards the centre of Dresden.

After less than a kilometre the traffic came to a halt again. 'Look ahead,' Ulricke said. 'As far as you can see, thousands of vehicles, all trying to get to the central railway station. We need to go through there. Uncle Hubert lives in Meissen at the other end of Dresden. We'll never get there.'

'Don't be so negative. We've made it this far and we'll get there.'
'There are so many people here. The streets are choked,' Ulrike said.

'We will, *Liebling*, we will. At the next intersection we'll get off this street.'

Hans tried to move their rig into a side street but police stopped them.

'Keep moving. You are blocking the street,' a policeman shouted at Hans.

'We want to try the back streets. It's too crowded here.'

'This one's a dead end. Down there is the Elbe's dyke. Go back.'

As they came closer to the city centre, the absence of *Wehrmacht* soldiers became obvious.

'The *Wehrmacht* has given up on Dresden,' Hans said. 'I haven't seen one soldier in the last few hours. Considering that the Russian army is only a few kilometres away trying to destroy 'Fortress Breslau', as Hitler calls it, that is strange.'

'Maybe Dresden has been declared an open city to save it from destruction,' Ulricke said. 'The Zwinger, Semperopera and the Meissner Porcelain factory are not exactly dangerous.'

'Yes, but I have a bad feeling about it. With all these refugees here, there'll be a bloodbath when the Russians get going again. We have to leave, as fast as possible.'

They moved with the stream of people towards the central railway station until they came through the Tiergartenstrasse, by the zoo and the Grosse Garten.

The park was changed. Leafless trees were the only indication this had been a beautiful park, now it was a huge camping ground for refugees.

'Let's find a space and stay here overnight,' Ulricke said. 'We are close to the railway station anyway.'

'I agree, *Liebling*. There'll be total chaos at the railway station.

We'll try it tomorrow.' He manoeuvred the wagon to the side of the street, ignoring protests from other refugees. 'Look, under that oak tree that would make a good spot for us.'

He moved the rig off the street and negotiated their way past other camps. The space under the oak tree was not open; it was cluttered with logs and broken park benches.

'That's why this spot is still free. The gardeners used it as a dump,' Ulricke said. 'It's a shame. It looked like a nice place for us.'

'It still is,' Hans said. 'We'll use the horse to pull the logs aside, just enough for our wagon. Easy, you'll see.'

It was not that easy and their efforts created protests from their new neighbours, but they managed.

'This is actually safer than setting up camp among all the others. Here we have our little fortress around us.' Hans tried to give his wife an assuring smile.

'I don't know. It's like being in the middle of a funeral pyre,' Ulricke said. 'I hope no one is playing with matches.'

'Ah, come on. These are logs, they don't burn that easily. Dresden is just an administration centre. When the Russians are in control it will be the same. The war won't last much longer. Nothing has happened to the city up to now. I think it's safer than most other places in the Reich.'

'But all these people here. It's too crowded.'

'Maybe the Russians are holding back to give the authorities a chance to get the refugees out—save them a lot of trouble later on,' Hans said.

The camp under the oak tree was at the edge of the huge refugee camp. There were tents, horse-drawn wagons of all kinds, horses, dogs and people, thousands of people.

Darkness was setting in and they could see campfires starting up everywhere. Despite the noise, it was a peaceful picture, except for the police moving around and telling people to extinguish their fires. Most refugees ignored them or merely reduced their fire. They had to cook and keep warm; they scoffed at the fact that the nearby city centre was blacked out to prevent identification by enemy bomber planes. There was continuous coming and going as more refugees arrived and tried to find a space to stay.

Two police officers came to Hans.

'Well, you are certainly in the right position here. No one will run over you with all those logs around,' one of them said.

'*Ja, Danke*. It looks like the whole park is becoming one large refugee camp,' Hans said.

'It is already, and more people are arriving every minute. We are running out of open spaces,' the officer said. 'Everyone wants to get to the central railway station and insists on staying close. The place is a mess, and it stinks. You'll have to dig a toilet. Health regulations.'

'Of course. Will there be trains tomorrow?'

'*Ja*, there'll be extra trains. The authorities are trying to get all the refugees out. Health and sanitary conditions are stretched to the limit. The public toilets in the park were not built for this. Even the ground is frozen. Don't forget to dig a toilet pit. Good luck. *Auf Wiedersehen*.'

'Thank you. *Auf Wiedersehen*,' Hans said.'

Hans and Ulricke watched the officers go from camp to camp, repeating their advice.

'I think we should leave,' Ulricke said. 'With all the people here, we have no hope of getting on a train if we can't stay with Uncle Hubert.

We still have time to go back to the others. This is not the Dresden I remember, Hans.'

He looked at her astonished. 'But it was your idea to find your uncle and see if he could help us to get to the west.'

'*Ja*, I know, but I don't think so now. Just look at this place. Thousands upon thousands of people all fleeing, all trying to get on a train. Getting through the city centre to Meissen is impossible.'

'Well, let's see tomorrow. We could stay in Dresden if they have space for us. I mean, what's the difference between Dresden, Hanover or Munich? Germany is finished. Wherever we go there'll be occupiers: Americans, English or Russians. We'll have to learn to live with them.'

'I feel bad about this place, Hans. Let's get back to Rolf and the others.'

'How about staying here tonight? It's too late to go anywhere else anyway, and tomorrow we'll try to get on a train. Forget about Uncle Hubert,' Hans said

'*Ja*, but if we do that what do we do with our rig? We can't line up at the railway station with a horse and a wagon; we wouldn't even get close. Then if we can't get on a train we would be without transport if we get rid of the rig.'

'I didn't think of that, you are right.' Hans said. 'If we don't stay in Dresden we can't risk being without the rig. You're right; let's go back to Bad Schandau to our friends.'

Chapter 14

One by one the campfires died down, and the park disappeared into vague, dreamlike shadows. All around Hans were the sounds of the refugee camp, horses snorting, dogs barking, children crying, a couple somewhere having a loud argument.

This was one of the rare, clear nights, without fog or snow, since they had left Krummhübel. It was peaceful, except for the occasional *Wehrmacht* truck rattling down Tiergartenstrasse.

Hans stared at the star canopy and wished he could identify constellations. That bright one there, just above the horizon? He shivered; it was getting colder. He tried to remember where the spare blankets were. Oh, how beautiful: a shooting star! I can have a wish. There, another one! Two wishes—and then he saw three, no, ten more! He gave up counting.

A red-hot pain seared his body as he remembered. Last year—Breslau—the air raid. The 'shooting stars' were bomb markers. The Breslau people had called them 'Christmas trees.'

This is an air raid. Why are there no sirens?

No! He told himself. No sirens meant no air raid. And why should there be one here? During the whole war, Dresden had only been hit by a handful of bombs. No more lights. It was a drill, an over-efficient local commander no doubt trying to scare the refugees clogging his city.

More lights floated down over the park, bathing the refugees' wagons in a ghostly, white glow. Bundles of beautiful lights. There was a hush as if the park held its breath.

Oh God help us, he thought, this is no drill.

From the distance came the dull vibrating sounds of aeroplanes, many aeroplanes.

'Ulricke, wake up *Liebling*, it's an air raid!'

Ulricke was awake. She had been looking at the light through the rear of the wagon. Hans found her sitting among the pillows and blankets, shaking violently.

'*Liebling*, come out please.'

'You said they wouldn't attack Dresden.'

'I was wrong. Come quick. *Scheisse*! It's too late to find a shelter, it's already started.'

The sky was alight now over the city. The bomb-markers, bright magnesium flares on parachutes, slowly drifted down. They looked so pretty that people who saw them for the first time laughed with delight until moments later, when they found out that the pretty lights were heralds of death.

The bombs seemed to explode above the buildings, the soundwaves thumped through their bodies even though the explosions were not close by. Ulricke clung to Hans; they stared hypnotised at the sky over the old city.

'What are they doing?' Ulricke said. 'They are not aiming for the buildings.'

Around them, people were shouting and running for shelter. Hans didn't answer. He hoped that he was wrong.

He watched until he was sure.

'Oh my God! How can they do that?' he said. 'What?'

'They did it two years ago in Hamburg. They dropped percussion bombs that explode over buildings and shatter the windows to make the firebombs more effective.'

'I don't understand,' Ulricke said.

'The *Schweine* are creating a firestorm. Look, there in the sky— the dimmer lights. They're the firebombs.'

Thousands of small glowing lights were raining down on the city. Moments later, the inner city burst into flames. They could feel the heat as a huge, red, mushroom column rose into the sky—and then came a strange wind, blowing towards the fire.

'Down here behind the logs!' Hans screamed through the howling airstream. 'I'll look after the horse.' But the horse was gone.

'The explosions must have scared it off.' He crawled back to their shelter under the logs. 'It's gone. The poor thing has run away.'

'Why are they doing this?' Ulricke said. 'There are only people and old buildings to burn in Dresden. There are no *Wehrmacht* barracks here are there?'

'I don't know *Liebling*. Maybe that is just what they want, to burn people.'

The sound of the bombers faded, replaced by the sirens of ambulances and fire engines. All raced towards the column of fire and smoke rising over the city.

'We have to stay here.' Hans said. 'Not much can burn here and we are far away from any buildings which catch fire.'

'Oh God. It must be like a furnace there. Why is the wind so strong?'

'The fire is so intense it needs oxygen, so it sucks up the air.'

They held each other tight, watching the inferno in the distance, and the chaos around them.

Horses were galloping through the camps, crashing into people and tents. From everywhere came screams. People were running about, searching for relatives.

An older woman peered in at them.

'I can't find Waldi! Have you seen my Waldi?'

'No one came to us,' Hans said. What does he look like?' The woman looked at him without answering, her eyes wild.

'Waldi, where are you, you naughty boy?' She turned and stumbled back into the darkness.

'I think she was looking for her dog,' Ulricke said.

After a while the noise lessened. People moved purposely as the panic subsided. The fires still illuminated the night with an eerie light as Hans and Ulrike gathered some of their belongings, ready to leave.

Despite flames and smoke, through the fallen trees and collapsed buildings they could see the burning old city centre. The Frauenkirche, the church of our Lady, a round building with a solid rock dome, looked like a torch. Jets of fire were blowing out of the shattered windows. The Kreuzkirche next to the Frauenkirche was also on fire, but not as fierce, more of an internal glow. The most intense fires were in an area where the old palace of the Saxon rulers was, the Zwinger. The palace buildings were burning fiercely, priceless treasures in its museums being consumed by the fire.

Hans and Ulricke were clinging to each other, crying with their tears immediately drying in the hot air hitting their faces.

Without warning, the shock waves of fresh explosions travelled through the park, followed by the thrum of vibration from aeroplanes, hundreds of aeroplanes. The explosions drew closer. Hans and Ulricke scrambled back into their makeshift shelter under the logs. Ten metres away, with a whooshing sound, followed by a thud, a firebomb came down. The shoebox size device exploded into a fountain of fire and sprayed a burning, jelly-like substance in every direction.

Close to them, a man with his face and hands on fire stumbled and fell down. The fiercely burning stuff continued to cook his head until it exploded.

A woman came along; she carried something in her arms. Hans thought it was a burned doll but realised she was holding the shrivelled body of her incinerated child.

Wherever he looked there were smouldering and steaming corpses. Abruptly there was the whistling sound of falling bombs, followed by sharp explosions that rocked the ground.

'That came from the Central Railway Station!' Hans screamed over the noise. 'We are too close. Open your mouth or your eardrums will burst.' More shock waves, like physical punches, resonated through every fibre of their bodies. The shallow hole under the logs protected them from direct radiating heat, but not from the wind. Breathing became painful as nostrils stuck together and their throats dried.

'I'm a fool. We shouldn't have come here,' Hans said between desperate breaths.

'I love you my darling. Hold me close.' Ulrike's breathing became shallower and she was wheezing.

The oak tree towering above them started to disintegrate, its burning branches sending showers of sparks flying through the air. The wind now was a burning stream of heat. Tents flew into the sky wrapped around their unlucky occupants, and loose objects became deadly projectiles.

A woman, speared through the chest by a branch, crashed down in front of them and was catapulted away by the wind, howling and clawing at the branch. An elderly man with a young child in his arms staggered past. Whenever he lost balance and fell down he made sure not to drop the child. He was so careful, but the child was cut in half with its intestines dragging behind.

Hans wanted to close his burning eyes to shut out the horrible images but he couldn't.

More hissing sounds and thuds of firebombs followed by screams.

Objects picked up by the wind bombarded their shelter, and burning people stumbled past. Only metres away, a woman fell down on her knees and crawled towards their shelter. Hans reached for her hand when a piece of corrugated iron sliced off her arm. Her face showed no pain, but disbelief as the air stream picked her up. She disappeared into the maelstrom of debris, leaving Hans still clutching the amputated arm.

The heat increased. They were forced to blink frequently as the hot wind dried out their eyes. Breathing became torture. Hans wet his handkerchief in the muddy ground under their bodies tore it in half and handed a piece to Ulricke.

'Breath through this and keep your face close to the ground. Don't lift your head.'

But the moisture in the handkerchief evaporated fast. Each breath was like sucking in fire. He tried quick, shallow breaths. No better.

Strange, I'm floating. It occurred to him that he was losing consciousness, possibly dying, but it was not important, even breathing was unimportant. No more pain.

An explosion nearby showered their shelter with debris and brought him back into the heat and pain. For a moment he wanted to sink away and let go but a new, sharper pain forced him to open his eyes. The logs they were sheltering under had started to burn and were singeing his leg.

'We have to get out.' Ulricke did not move. 'Ulli, we have to get out.'

He lifted her limp body and shook her. Her eyes were open but her head rolled from side to side like a broken doll.

'Wake up!' He cried out in terror. 'Please don't leave me! Oh God, please, not her, please!'

He searched for her pulse but there was none. He gasped for air as he pressed his ear against her mouth, begging to hear her breathe. But the roaring of the firestorm suppressed all sound. He dragged her out of the hole, away from the burning logs. The heat was unbearable. Afraid of being picked up by the wind, he crawled away from the hole, dragging Ulricke along by the arms. He stayed close to the ground after a flying piece of bark grazed his arm like a bullet, cutting away clothes and skin.

The park lawn had changed from a snowfield to a mud flat. And still the heat increased.

Hans's hands and legs were numb and his vision blurred. He blinked, tried to focus again, but everything was fading. An explosion pressed him to the ground, then all of a sudden breathing was easier and the wind eased. He picked up Ulricke's body and stumbled out onto the street.

Tiergartenstrasse was lower than the surrounding park and zoo, making it a natural shelter. He had barely climbed down from the park's wall when the wind came back. But it was blowing over them now: on the footpath, they were in the lee of the wind. He tried to tie both of them to a lamppost but had to give up; the post was too hot. The wind strengthened, swirling into their space. He tried the lamppost again, but it was even hotter. But there, half buried in dirt between the wall and the cobblestone of the footpath was a metal rail where a garden bench had been attached. The dirt was soft enough for him to dig under the rail and tie both of them down with his belt and Ulricke's scarf.

The frightening howls of the firestorm increased. People were picked up and rolled along the street. On the other side of the street the warped-iron fence of the zoo became a net catching debris, branches, roofing timber and bodies of people and animals. It looked like someone's nightmarish sculpture, which constantly changed as the wind added features and blew others away. Anything loose was picked up by the airstream. The trees, which had lined Tiergartenstrasse for centuries, were reduced to their trunks and larger branches. The storm raged, blowing everything to the centre.

'We'll be safe here. The wall will shelter us.' He looked at his wife's lifeless face and gently pressed her head against his shoulder. 'We'll have to get back to Bad Schandau. Rolf said they'd wait for two days.'

He looked around, more aware of their surroundings. Along the park side of the street there were semicircular bays where the wall formed stone benches, like large steps. The bench they were tied onto had names crudely scratched into the bricks, reminders of happier days. 'Peter and Hannelore from Hamburg 1943' said one inscription. They missed both firestorms. God! Why did I come here? Hans thought.

Two metres away on the opposite side of the bay, exposed to the wind, were a dead man and woman. Their skin was shrivelled, they had bulging eyes, and swollen tongues hanging out of their mouths. They had died holding each other tightly.

The explosions gradually decreased but the storm continued for hours, even though the fire did not come closer.

'Only a little longer and we can walk out of here.'

He tenderly straightened Ulricke's body. The storm lost its intensity. People appeared again, walking and stumbling down

Tiergartenstrasse, away from the furnace that was Dresden. Some walked silently, too dazed to be afraid. Others moaned or cried as they dragged their injured bodies. Most were covered in burns, their faces blackened, lined with red cracks of open wounds. Their clothes were smoking and falling off, disintegrating as they walked along.

'Come on *Liebling*, we have to go now or we'll miss Rolf.'

He untied them, lifted Ulricke's body in his arms and walked down the middle of the avenue towards the outer suburbs.

The bombardment had stopped and there were no more bombers in the sky. Behind them the column of fire and smoke rose and mushroomed out over the city.

Hans stumbled under the weight of Ulrike's body, avoiding slippery ice patches.

Then he heard the dreadful sounds yet again.

The bombers had returned. They came in high, aiming for the burning city centre. Soon came the deep growl of powerful explosions. The people fleeing down Tiergartenstrasse too numb to care, ignored the air raid and continued their escape.

Suddenly, low flying planes appeared ahead skimming over the treetops.

Fighters! Lights flashed from their wings. Oh God! People exploded. Limbs flew through the air. There was no cover as the fighters' bloody harvest continued unchallenged.

Hans walked straight into the gun flashes, until the punch of the slugs hitting Ulricke's body knocked him down. He rolled her aside and crawled over her, covering her entire body, pressing himself against her face.

Two fighters came back for the final destruction of the few moving, upright, bodies. Soon there was no one left to kill, and they were gone. No more agonised screams, or moans. Only the rush of the wind feeding the fires.

The pain in his hands caused by immersion in the refreezing sludge of the street, made Hans aware that he was still alive. Ulricke's body had protected him, or he would have frozen to death in the icy muck.

'Ulli, you always protected me. If not for you I'd have ended up in the cellars of the Gestapo, but you protected me. Forgive me!'

He lifted her body. Around him other survivors, most of them injured, staggered among corpses and body parts. Hans, oblivious to the misery around him, carried his dead wife away.

From everywhere survivors flooded the streets, desperate to escape.

Among the people were injured and frightened animals from the zoo. A group of zebras passed Hans. The animals stayed close together but ignored the people on the street, only to hurry away when an injured lion came to close. An elephant with a large burn wound on his back, trumpeting and trampling on people in its pain and fear, made Hans stop and seek cover for a moment.

Ulricke's body was heavy now, forcing him to rest frequently.

Even though it was cooler in the outer suburbs, denser smoke made breathing difficult.

He reached the frozen river and remembered how the Ostritz survivors had travelled back to the convoy. Getting Ulricke's body down the riverbank exhausted him, but he persisted.

'Don't worry I won't leave you here. We'll get back to the others.' And then he started the long way back to the convoy, dragging his wife's body behind him.

Chapter 15

Two days earlier.

It was a day when the brilliance of fresh snow, blue sky and a blazing sun dispelled any gloomy thoughts. The landscape was bathed in light: light so intense that closing her eyes made no difference. The air was bitingly cold, despite the sun, but fresh.

Elli pushed away the pain of Ostritz, and her distress of losing the families that had departed for Dresden.

'Come out, you lazy bums, it's beautiful.' Elli pounded the wagon's tarpaulin cover to dislodge the snow. 'Come on, get up.'

'What is wrong with you? Why do you have to be so damn cheerful? God, it's cold!' Swearing followed clanging and crashing. Elli hoped he had only damaged his head and not something in the wagon. Jochen emerged head first out of his compartment under the children. He squeezed his eyes shut, missed a handhold, and dropped to the ground like a sack of potatoes.

'Too much glare,' he said.

'Congratulations. You're alive after all. Well, sort of.' Elli laughed at him.

'Hey, stop that,' she said, as he wrote his initials in a stream of urine. 'Do that somewhere else, you Schwein.'

At her outcry, Jochen lost his aim and pissed on his feet. Cursing her, he moved further away and without warning disappeared in a snowdrift.

'Much better! Stay there until you've finished!' Jochen looked sheepish when he struggled free.

'Had a good time?' Elli said with an infuriating grin on her face. Jochen gave her a blank look and started to climb back into the wagon. He was barefoot, wearing only his long underpants.

'Aren't you cold?' Elli said. 'Cold?'

'*Ja*, cold. I would be cold, standing in my underwear, barefoot in the snow.'

He looked at his feet and his sleepy expression became a pained one. Yelping, he hopped from foot to foot and scrambled back into the wagon.

'My goodness, that took a while.' Satisfied, Elli walked off to the communal kitchen.

'Clean yourself up and hurry if you want some breakfast, and bring the children along,' she shouted back over her shoulder.

Close to the wagon Ruth had set up her easel and was painting. 'I'm glad you're preserving this glorious day in a painting.' Ruth ignored her and Elli came closer. 'Oh my God. Not that again.'

It was the same graphic scene of the massacred refugee convoy, but now, instead of the black and white pencil sketch, there was the vividness of oil paint. The centre was still filled with the face of the dead child, but the painting had more depth and the eyes of the dead child followed Elli. She shivered. The child's expression confronted her. She forced herself to look away and break the mesmerising spell.

'Ruth, come along and get something to eat.' No reaction. 'Come on, you have to eat something. Get away from that depressing painting.'

'Depressing painting? Are you saying that you don't like it?' 'The drawing was bad enough, this is terrifying.'

'*Danke*,' Ruth said. 'After I finished the drawing, I wasn't sure if it would be possible to convoy it in an oil painting. Looks like I've managed.' A broad smile lightened her face. 'An art critic would possibly have given a lengthy, meaningless analysis, with my mental condition as the centre part, but you, sister, manage to give me valuable feedback in a few words.'

Elli gave her a bewildered look. 'Ruth, there is enough misery around us. You are a fantastic painter, but you don't see anything positive.'

'I agree. I don't see anything positive. This fresh snow only temporarily covers all the horrors beneath.' She hesitated and gave Elli a sad smile. 'That's the difference between us. You can still see positives. I wish I could.'

'Come on now. You need something to eat and a warm drink.' Ruth looked up. 'My practical sister. But what food is there?

Porridge without milk, no eggs, no bacon? You really think it's worth making the effort?'

'*Ja*, I can't stand the slimy porridge either, but there is fresh bread. Smell!'

Ruth sniffed the cold air like a hunting dog and her face lit up. 'My God. You are right. Wait for me.'

Freshly baked loaves were cooling on a sheet of metal. Aromatic steam, carrying traces of walnuts and yeast, rose in the cold air.

Someone handed Elli a warm chunk of bread, smothered in melting butter. The sisters were on their second piece when a large *ja*r of *ja*m appeared and for the next few minutes, there was nothing more important than stuffing as much as possible, as quickly as possible, into their mouths.

'Where is it all coming from?' Elli said. 'I thought we were out of butter and jam. I haven't seen any for ages. I didn't even know that such delicious obscenities still existed.'

'We found a stash of food in a cellar, mostly *ja*m and pickles but also some butter and flour. Someone hoarded the food and must have forgotten it,' Rolf said. 'I hope that all that fresh bread won't make you sick, *Schweinchen*.' He skillfully avoided the empty cup thrown at him as he walked off.

Later, Rolf and Jochen allocated repair tasks, enough to occupy the group for the two days they had promised to wait.

'Friends, I think it would be better to cross the river further upstream, closer to Dresden,' Rolf said. 'The ramps at Bad Schandau's ferry port and the river banks are too steep for us. Further upstream, close to Naundorf, the banks are lower, and the edges will be frozen. If that doesn't work, in Naundorf itself there's a shallow concrete ramp for the ferry, which would let us drive straight out onto the ice. If we pace the rigs carefully, we should be able to do the crossing in a couple of hours.'

'The banks of the Elbe may not be as steep as the Neisse's but they are still dangerous because they'll be slippery. Our wagons could become toboggans,' Jochen said.

'*Ja*, we will have to be very careful,' Rolf said. 'But it will still be easier to get on the ice here than it was at the Neisse.'

'Two days of preparation for the crossing is not enough. We'll have to do a hell of a lot of work,' Jochen said.

'Like what? Except for a few minor repairs, aren't we ready?' Elli felt her father's irritation. He wanted to get away from the Elbe as fast as possible. But Jochen was in his element.

'Each wagon needs special brakes that can dig into the ground to prevent sliding, and all the horses need some kind of shoes to stop them from slipping. Moreover, that's just to get onto the ice. On the other side, we'll have to get the horses and wagons up again. Even if the banks are not as steep as at the Neisse, we'll have to use hoists and that will be slow.'

'How slow?'

'I don't know. It depends on too many factors, but 'a couple of hours,' is a very optimistic assumption.'

Elli saw the faint smile on her father's face. Even though the interaction with Jochen was heated, he was obviously glad that Jochen had taken control of the technical details.

'All right. Jochen, you and Manfred organise the preparations and the horses. There are not that many of us left. Everyone will have to help.'

He looked around. No one objected. 'In the meantime, I'll go towards Naundorf with a few people, and look for a good spot to get onto the ice. There should be a few openings in the riverbank where the locals get their stock to the water and launch boats.' Elli and Ruth looked at each other and Elli raised her hand.

'We'll come with you, Papa.'

'Don't you have to do some repairs?' 'Jochen has fixed everything,' Elli said. 'What about the children?'

'Oh, they'll be all right; they can help Jochen. If we take two horses, the trip should take only a few hours, right?'

Rolf hesitated but Elli and Ruth were the only volunteers. Most people were already walking off to prepare their rigs.

Elli and Ruth were sitting astride Karla, high above their father, who could only muster one of the few normal horses, and it was small, more like a pony.

'Will you watch where your monster is going? She nearly stomped me into the ground.' Rolf said, his voice a low grumble.

'What was that, Ruth?' Elli said. 'I thought I heard a voice, but no one is there.'

'*Ja*, I heard it too but I can't see anyone.'

'Very funny, you two clowns. Slow down and let me pass. I am fully aware that you instructed your beast to shit on me,' Rolf said.

'Did Karla do that?' 'She missed.'

'Then it was an accident. Karla never misses.'

When their grim-faced father passed the two sisters, they were choking with laughter, only just managing to stay on their horse.

After about two hours they arrived. The Elbe River Valley, carved out of the surrounding sandstone, was deep below them. The frozen river, covered with snow, looked like a wide road meandering through the countryside.

'That's so beautiful,' Ruth said. 'Elli told me to concentrate on something positive, and look at this. I would love to paint it.'

'No time for that. We have to find a place to cross,' Rolf said. 'The road here must be pretty steep. It's at least two hundred metres down to the river. And look, even from the road that runs beside the river there is another steep drop to the ice,' Elli said.

'See the houses down there? That's Naundorf. It's only a few kilometres. Let's have a look at their ferry ramp,' Rolf said.

They were lucky. The ferry ramp was accessible and had a gentle slope onto the ice. The town of Naundorf was actually on the other side of the river. It looked deserted, no people were in sight, and no smoke came from the chimneys.

When they got back to the others, Rolf immediately organised the departure for the river. It was getting dark when they arrived in the hills above the river valley.

'We'll stay here in the shelter of the trees for the next two days,' Rolf said. The warm glow of campfires and the smell of hot food soon wafted over the hillside.

Repairs, and the sewing of hessian socks to give the horses better traction on the ice, continued late into the night.

Slowly fires died down and people retired to their wagons. Elli and Ruth were poking their fire's glowing embers, trying to revitalise it.

'Can you hear that? What is that noise? Elli said. They stood up, trying to recognise the sounds.

Second by second the noise increased. Against the star-studded sky, the silhouettes of large planes flying in formation became visible, low above them. A sound rose from the valley below; at first looking like shadows of the planes above, more aircraft appeared. They were stacked at two levels.

'Bombers!' Ruth said. 'Are they going to…?' 'Dresden!'

'God help the poor people! All those refugees: it'll be a massacre.' The sisters held each other. The sky was filled with huge black shapes, like flocks of giant migrating birds, passing above and below them.

'Hans and Ulricke, and the other five families, will be there by now. Oh God, Hans thought he would be safer there.'

People who had already retired stumbled out of their wagons, staring into the sky, their shouts and cries drowned out in the noise.

Wave after wave of enemy aircraft passed them, flying along the valley from Czechoslovakia, using the river to navigate. Small fighter planes suddenly came into view, buzzing protectively around the bombers like nervous cattle dogs. Several fighters dived down with high-pitched screams, passing at treetop level above them.

The refugees stood there, unable to move, glued to the ground by the physical force of the noise, and their fears.

The sisters were holding each other so close that Elli felt the warm flow as Ruth lost control of her bladder, and realised the same had happened to her.

They continued to stare into the sky, unable to move or look away as the shadowy planes passed over them. Soon they heard other sounds, despite the noise from the passing aircraft, this time the deep rumbling of distant explosions.

On the horizon, the outlines of Dresden's tallest buildings were unexpectedly visible in the flash of explosions. Glowing fireballs rained down on the city, like stretched strings of pearls, illuminating targets for the bombers.

After the planes offloaded their cargo, they climbed back to safer heights above the reach of the anti-aircraft guns. An unnecessary precaution: Dresden was unprepared. Still more planes came along the river valley.

In the centre of the city a column of light appeared, rising higher and higher.

Even though it was dark, they could see a black column under the centre of the light. The outline of a huge mushroom cloud, thousands of metres high, was visible against the clear sky.

As they watched, they felt a strange wind, blowing hard towards Dresden.

'They've created a firestorm! A funeral pyre for Dresden. The fire is sucking air in from around it. That's what causes the wind. God help them,' Rolf said. He turned to his daughters, his face distorted. 'I should have stopped Hans. Why didn't I stop them? They were heading for the central railway station. They'll all be dead.'

Elli tried to say something comforting but her few words were lost in the unrelenting thunder of the planes as her father stood up and staggered away.

The column of fire against the darkness of smoke was an eerie sight, paralysing the refugees huddling on the ground as they prayed and cried into the night. Elli felt numb, as she tried to comprehend what was going on. Why did this happen? The war was almost over and yet they burned thousands and thousands of civilians in an undefended city.

Wasn't there something on the radio, the BBC, stating that the Allies were liberating Germany? Ruth still clung to her, sobbing and shaking.

'Why, why? God in heaven, why do you let this happen? Why?'

The last wave passed and except for the fading sound of planes returning to their bases there was silence. It was broken by Rolf.

'Take cover! Don't stand around like targets. Over to the trees! *Schnell, schnell.*'

People rose and staggered to the nearby trees. Elli and Ruth went to their wagons to change their clothes. As they came closer, Elli heard the screams of her terrified children.

'Mama, I am scared! What was that? Where were you?'

Just when the children were calming down, the sound of aeroplane engines rose up again and an unending line of bombers passed over them. The children clung to their mothers. Elli felt them tremble as the planes drowned out their cries.

Then there was a break and again it became quiet. By now the glow from the burning city bathed the countryside in reddish light. This must be what hell looks like, Elli thought, or maybe we are already there.

In the light of the early morning a group of grey-faced people gathered around the fire, trying to calm each other down. They avoided looking at the burning city in the background.

It wasn't over yet, another wave of bombers was coming in. They sounded different and further away. The new wave flew higher and came from a different direction, not along the river valley.

'The planes are bigger,' Rolf said. 'They are not the same as the night bombers.'

'My God, they're still bombing Dresden! Why?' Elli said. 'They want to make sure that nothing is left. The day shift has arrived,' Ruth said. 'Looks like they intend to go on through the day.'

'Why? Surely there's nothing left to destroy.'

'The railway station is not in the city centre. Maybe they didn't get it last night and so they are coming back for it. That must be their main target. There is nothing else worth bombing, except the civilians,' Ruth said.

'So they not only burn civilians and refugees but they also want to prevent them from getting out?'

'*Ja*, that's what I think they are doing,' Ruth said grimly. 'Oh God, all those people, and Hans and the others!'

The bombing continued well into the evening. When at last it stopped, the refugees were exhausted and numb. No one could cry anymore. The terror they had witnessed was too vast to talk about, it forced them into silence.

The moon came up and washed the whole countryside in pale light, overlaying the unnatural, red glow from the burning city. The only sounds coming out of the darkness were the far-away rumble of explosions.

They were waiting.

At the same time as the night before the bombers returned. Again, they came along the river valley but this time without fighter planes. There was no need to protect the bombers from the burning city.

They saw the strings of light falling from the planes again, and with each passing bomber the firestorm on the ground increased in intensity.

'Look Elli,' Ruth said abruptly. 'Look, they are coming back!'

The planes were close to them, occasionally visible when they crossed the face of the moon.

'*Ja*, they are returning; they have dropped their bombs,' Rolf said. All of a sudden, they heard a high-pitched noise directly above them.

'Bombs! Take cover!'

Seconds later, there was a loud explosion. Debris flew through the air. Large chunks of rock hit the ground around them.

In the panic there was a mad scramble for shelter among the rocks and trees. Horses galloped into the forest. Mothers screamed for their children. Some, immobilised by shock, remained where they were. More planes passed high over them.

The whistling sound of a bomb again, followed by a loud explosion. Elli felt the ground shake. The explosion was not as close as the previous one.

'Please, friends!' Elli could hear her father shouting. 'They are not bombing us! They are offloading unused bombs on their way home. Looks like they're going back along the river valley, the way they came in. They are not after us. That first bomb was just coincidence.'

There were more distant explosions. Their panic subsided. The bombardment of Dresden continued through the night.

Morning came with yellow light and a strong smell of burning. Elli had slept only a couple of hours, like most others.

'Ruth, look, look! It's so smoky, the sun is hardly visible, look.' Ruth coughed and tried to clear her burning eyes.

'The fires must be still burning but the smoke is so thick I can't see anything far away,' she said. 'At least there are no more bombers.'

'The poor people, there can't be much left of the city.'

The deep vibrating noise of the bombers started again. Second by second the noise increased.

The day shift was back.

The bombers continued to come through the day and into the night. After forty-eight hours the bombing finally ceased.

The refugees crawled into their wagons, too tired even to comfort each other.

Elli insisted that Ruth and the children stay in her wagon.

Chapter 16

'Elli, help me. Please Elli.' The pleading penetrated her dreams. Someone was coughing. Go away; let me sleep, she thought.

'Elli, I can't breathe. Elli.' That irritating voice again. Her throat burned. She took a deep breath. Fire rushed into her lungs. Coughing did not relieve the pain.

She opened her eyes. It was almost dark, only a little light entered through cracks in the tarpaulin, and in it moved bluish shadows. What was that stink?

'Elli, please.' Ruth's voice was down to a scratchy whisper. Elli wanted to answer but managed only a croak, resulting in violent coughing. She realised that everyone around her was coughing. Smoke! The wagon must be on fire. We have to get out. Sparks in front of her eyes blotted her vision. Vomit filled her mouth. She reached to the side and felt the frozen tarp. She pushed against it and felt fresh air coming in. She could breathe again but she continued to cough.

The outside air was smoky too and the light was wrong.

Everything looked yellow. Nothing seemed real. All the colours seemed false. In the sky Elli saw a yellow disc and it took her a while to realise that she was looking at the sun. The other wagons were just shadowy outlines but their occupants were audible. Coughing was coming from all sides.

'Out, out everyone, get out!' Elli ran from wagon to wagon, opened the tarps and shouted. 'Get out!' There was smoke in the air but it was much easier to breathe outside than in the wagons where there was no air movement and the smoke had concentrated.

The children stumbled out, coughing and vomiting. Anna and Elfi were crying between coughs and dry retching.

'Come on all of you, breathe deeply and hold this in front of your mouth and nose.' Elli handed the children rags with snow rubbed into them. Ruth had already recovered and stopped coughing. She tried to help Jochen, whose face was white and his eyes so bloodshot that pupils and irises were invisible. He stood up and staggered off. A few metres away he fell on his knees and convulsed in dry retching. When he came back, he looked puzzled; Ruth was not affected by the smoke.

'How come you are so well?' he said.

'She is a chain smoker who ran out of tobacco ages ago. A bit of smoke in the air just makes her feel like having a cigarette,' Elli said.

'Thanks sister.'

Jochen's breathing became easier and his stomach settled back where it belonged.

'*Oh mein lieber Gott*, what is that terrible stink?' he said.

More people were coming out of the wagons, all affected by the smell and the smoke.

'It must be from Dresden,' Elli said, breathing through a scarf filled with snow. The hazy figure of her father appeared in the distance. Her burning eyes had trouble focussing on him but his voice sounded amplified as he barked commands.

'Keep moving, people. Get yourself some wet cloth to breathe through and stay out of the wagons. Open the tarpaulins to ventilate them and get ready to leave.'

'Where is the smoke coming from?' Elli said.

'Dresden. The smoke is drifting along the river valley, and we are directly in its way. We have to get down to the river. It should be better there. We have to—my God what was that?'

From one of the wagons came a bloodcurdling scream.

'Oh God, she won't wake up! Hildchen, my baby, wake up! Hildchen, wake up! Oh God, help me, my baby won't wake up!'

Elli, Ruth and some of the others ran over to the wagon where the screams came from. Hanna, a widow who had lived in their neighbourhood, was holding in her arms the limp body of her daughter. The child's head hung back and the lifeless eyes were open.

The small face was as white as a china doll. Even before Elli checked for a pulse, she knew the girl was dead. She carefully let the cold arm go and held her ear against the girl's mouth. There was no breathing. Hanna watched her anxiously.

'What is the matter with her?' Hanna whispered. 'Why doesn't she wake up?'

'Hanna, she is gone. I'm so sorry,' Elli said. Hanna did not react for a moment.

'I should have checked her during the night,' she said. 'It's my fault, I should have checked.'

Elli tried to say something comforting but the body of the dead child made anything she wanted to say useless. An older woman gently took the dead child out of Hanna's arms. She did not resist. She stared into nowhere as she sank to her knees.

'*Danke*, both of you,' a woman said. 'We'll take care of her. Thank you again.'

Two of Hanna's cousins lifted her gently up and led her away. Elli and Ruth went back to Elli's wagon.

'Papa,' Ruth said, 'why did you leave?'

'I felt useless. You two handled the situation well.'

'Handled the situation? I didn't know what to say to the poor woman. Thank God, her cousins took care of her or I would have become a sobbing mess.'

'That little dead body will haunt me forever,' Elli said. 'What makes it even worse was that I felt somehow relieved that it was not my child. I don't know how I would have reacted.' She grabbed a large handkerchief and noisily blew her nose.

'Papa, what is that smell? The smoke is bad enough but that smell makes me want to throw up all the time.'

Her father gave her a sad look, turned around and walked off. Elli looked perplexed at her sister.

'What's the matter with him? I just wanted to know what the smell is.'

'Elli, what do you think was burned in Dresden, besides the buildings?' Ruth said.

'Well, I don't know. How should I know? Stop playing games; I don't...'

Her eyes opened wide. 'Oh no, you don't mean...' '*Ja*, that's what I mean.'

'People, the smell of burning people,' she said. 'Oh, I can't breathe anymore. I feel sick.' She tried to swallow her vomit, but failed. She felt as if her body was trying to turn itself inside out.

If Ruth had not held her tightly, Elli would have collapsed. Slowly, her stomach calmed down.

'Sit here for a while, but not too long or you'll freeze your bum off. I'll look after the kids,' Ruth said.

Elli felt the coldness of the snow. It was thick, but as grey as the sky. The spasms in her guts subsided. She grabbed a handful of snow to clean her face but the snow tasted bitter. Disgusted, she spat it out. The snow was covered with a brittle layer of ice. She bent down. It wasn't frost, it was something different. Then she realised what it was.

'Oh, *mein lieber Gott*.'

'What?' Ruth came back. 'Oh, you poor thing, still sick.' 'That is not snow,' Elli whispered. 'That is ash, what's left of the burnt people and I put it in my mouth.'

'Elli, pull yourself together. Of course, there is ash everywhere. They burned a whole city.' Ruth scooped up a handful of snow. 'It isn't only ash. Here, look!'

Small scraps of paper, singed at the edges were mixed into the icy crust.

Elli picked up a larger piece. Something was printed on it. It was difficult to decipher but Elli recognised the words. It said: 'Dresden Zoologischer Garten'. The singed piece of paper was part of a ticket to the zoo in Dresden, carried by the firestorm for more than twenty kilometres. Elli felt sick again.

They had to delay their departure to search for the horses that had run off, scared by the explosions. Luckily they were close by. The horses were in better condition than most of the people.

The preparations continued into the middle of the day, when it started to become darker.

Then came the rain.

The ash of the burned city mixed with moisture came down as a thick liquid, burning their eyes and sticking to their faces, hands, clothes, everything.

'Close the wagon down and get under cover, *schnell*. I have to warn the others.' As Rolf rushed off, Elli closed the tarps and tried to calm the children.

'Mama, it's too dark. Can I come out?' Anna begged. 'No, stay where you are. It's raining.'

'Raining? I love raining. The rain will melt the stupid snow. I want to come out.'

'Stay inside, all of you, or you'll get...'

The large drops which came down first, changed into a steady downpour. Each raindrop was abnormally large and hit the wagon's canvas cover like a drumstick. The noise drowned out the shouts of the children. Elli rushed outside to cover Karla with blankets. She was soaked to the bone and shivering when she climbed back inside.

'Yuck, Mama, you have slime all over you.' Heinrich tried to avoid touching his mother.

'Don't be so stupid,' Anna said. 'Help me.'

The children ripped the wet and slimy clothes from their mother. Elli felt totally paralysed by the cold and did not resist. The children bundled her into blankets and then all three rubbed her. Their enthusiasm increased as Elli yelped in pain but eventually she felt warm again. She managed to give her torturers a crooked smile when they released her.

'*Danke*, all of you monsters.'

'More, Mama?' Anna said. Her eyes sparkled as she attempted to start again.

'Go away from me, you witch,' Elli said, laughing.

By now the rain had changed colour. It was darker, almost black.

It looked as if it was raining mud. A few minutes later the rain slowed, stopped, and the sun came out.

Elli heard her father in the distance, shouting instructions as he passed the wagons.

'Are you all right?' Rolf gave Elli and the children a reassuring smile. He wore an oilskin and looked reasonably dry.

'That was the strangest rain I ever saw.'

'That is the result of the firestorm. All the heat and moisture combined with smoke and ash. I'm afraid it's not over. We can expect more like it. You'd better change Karla's blankets. They are covered in the stuff.'

Finally, they resumed their journey. They reached the river just before nightfall.

'Let's camp over there, at the edge of the forest.' Rolf pointed to a field between the river and a pine forest. 'At first light, we'll make the crossing, so try to get some sleep. It will be a big day tomorrow.'

They were all tired: exhausted. The lingering smell was on their clothes, on their skin, in their minds. It had destroyed the need for food. Everyone at the campfire coughed, even though the smoke from Dresden had gone.

'Papa, do you think Hans and the others are dead?' Ruth said. 'When they left us, they were only half a day's travelling from

Dresden. Ulricke wanted to find her relatives,' Rolf said. 'Did they live in the old city?' Elli said.

'I don't know. Hans said that they would try to get on a train to Munich. I think the railway station was a main target. God help them if they were near the station. I hope they made it.'

'But you don't think so,' Ruth said.

'I hope that they are alive,' Rolf said quietly. 'I just hope.' 'Why would they bomb the city centre? There is only the Frauenkirche, the Zwinger, and all the other old buildings.'

'I don't know *Liebling*. Maybe because Dresden had so many government buildings, or just because it is a large city. I don't think Stalin, Roosevelt and Churchill were too concerned about how many people would die.'

'But that is madness,' Elli said.

'*Ja*, it is. Our *Führer* and his generals don't have a monopoly on madness; it seems pretty common these days.'

In the warm glow of the fire, Elli saw wet streaks on her father's face.

'Poor Hans and Ulricke,' she said. 'They thought they would finally be safe.'

'*Ja*, poor them,' her father said, 'and poor us.' He stood up and left.

'It's late and we have to get up with the first light,' Ruth said. 'I put Elfi and Hubert in Elfriede's wagon. They are coughing so much I thought it would keep everyone up. I'd better join them.'

'Where has your father gone?' Jochen said after Ruth left.

'He is staying with the Schlichte's. They have plenty of room, he told me, and he won't have to fight for space or get kicked in the face by the kids.'

They looked across the river. The fire that had been Dresden had died down. It was quiet, no sounds at all.

Jochen must have noticed her shivering, and took her in his arms.

For a moment, she stiffened, then relaxed.

The sparks and smoke of the fire still blocked the gentle light of the star canopy but now the air was clear. For a few moments, only a few moments, Elli focussed on the peaceful picture around her. Then the cold entering her bones bought her back to reality.

She bent his head down and kissed Jochen. 'Let's go inside. I'm freezing.'

The children were huddled together in search of warmth, asleep. Elli and Jochen slipped under Elli's blankets. Getting out of their layers of clothes in the narrow confinement was a challenge, but their enthusiasm overcame it. They explored each other's bodies in the darkness. Elli felt Jochen's excitement and hesitated for a moment; it had been a long time.

Her fears were overcome by her body's reaction when Jochen entered her. They stopped for a moment when Heinrich's sleepy voice called out.

'Mama, is it raining again? The wagon is rocking.'

'Sleep my *Liebling*. Everything is fine, it's only the wind.' 'What wind?' Jochen whispered into her ear.

'Keep going. Don't worry about the wind.'

Chapter 17

'*Vater im Himmel*, take this child to you, Amen.' Rolf concluded the service and walked over to the mother of the dead child. Elli and Jochen followed him.

'Hanna, you have no idea how much we feel for you. Please accept our condolences.' Elli was surprised by her father's formality but struggled for words herself. How could she say anything supportive to the woman when she felt relieved that it was not her own child who was dead? She took Hanna into her arms.

'Hanna, what can I do? Please tell me.'

Hanna gently took Elli's face between her hands.

'Thank you. I need some time alone with my daughter.' She smiled at Elli, but not with her eyes. Elli gave her a tight hug and left. Halfway back to the wagons she looked back. Hanna stood at the grave, not moving, as though in a trance. Fresh snow had covered the ash and brown rain of the night before and made the fresh soil from the grave stand out like an ugly blotch.

Elli saw Hanna's cousins go over to her. Elli could not hear what they were saying but when they tried to lead her away, Hanna shook them off, stumbled back to the grave mound and lay down on it. Her wailing cries sounded like a wounded animal.

Elli started to walk back, but stopped. What could she say to Hanna that wasn't a cliché? Hanna's cousins would be more helpful, Elli reasoned. But the high-pitched wailing continued, penetrating like a knife. She ran off as fast as she could to catch up with her father, who was shouting orders, getting the wagons moving again.

'*Vater, ich hasse dich*! I hate you! How could you? Why can't we wait to give Hanna more time; how can we just go?' Rolf looked at his daughter, his voice trembling.

'We have to get moving, fast.'

'Why? What difference does it make if we cross today or tomorrow?'

'We are too close to Dresden and too exposed. If the bombers return, we will become the target.'

'Come on Papa, why would the enemy waste a single bomb on a group of refugees?'

'They've just bombed the shit out of Dresden, haven't they?' '*Ja*, but...'

'Dresden, the city with no factories, no army barracks, and hardly any air defense, *ja*?'

'*Ja, ja*. Still, shooing everyone back to the wagons and running around in hysterics is a terrible way to treat a grieving mother! We hardly had time to close the grave.'

'I don't mean to hurt Hanna but we have to get going. It is too dangerous to stay here any longer. Elli, please talk to Hanna, I would like her to travel with the Schlichte's. She is the only occupant of her wagon now and most of the others are crowded. Ruth and the kids can take it over for a while. They are too cramped where they are now.'

'Terrific. First, you rush her away from the graveside and now from her possessions. Why don't you tell her yourself, Vater?'

'All right, I will. Later. You may be right; now wouldn't be a good time. Later, not now, right?'

'Coward,' she said and left.

Hanna didn't object to joining the Schlichte's. 'It will be better. The wagon would be unbearable without Hildchen.'

Elli rushed back in time to see her father and Jochen stepping out onto the ice.

'Stop you two! I'm coming with you.' The men looked at each other. Rolf opened his mouth but Jochen stopped him.

'You're welcome. You can get cold feet too.'

The ferry ramp seemed to be a perfect way to get onto the ice but the opposite shore was steep, and there was no sign of a ramp to get them off.

'I don't get it. Where is it?' Elli said. 'I thought ferries went straight from one side to the other. Don't they pull themselves along a steel rope?'

'*Ja*, you are right, they normally do. This one must end somewhere else. Let's check it out,' Rolf said.

They walked over to the other side of the river but there was no ferry ramp in sight. When they climbed up the slippery bank, there was no road.

'The ramp must be further upstream or downstream. Maybe it has something to do with the current,' Jochen said.

'Listen, can you hear that?' Elli said 'Hear what?'

'Rushing water. There must be open water close by.'

'You're right,' Rolf said. 'I remember, there are rapids in this area.

The water wouldn't freeze there.'

'Terrific; that settles it.' Jochen said. 'We have to get up right here. It shouldn't be too difficult, the river bank is nowhere near as steep as the Neisse's.'

'It will be difficult; we don't have as many people to help as we had at the Neisse,' Rolf said.

'Elli, you'll go first.' Jochen said.

Elli could see that he was looking forward to the crossing, a new challenge for his engineering mind. He continued, 'At the Neisse, it was wonderful how Karla performed and she is by far the strongest horse.

After we get her up on the river bank, she will make it much easier to get the others up.'

'*Ja*, *ja*, *ja*, let's get back, my feet are freezing off.'

'The first two wagons will have to be got up separately,' said Rolf.

'When we have two horses on top we can pull the other wagons up with their horses. That would speed the whole thing up.'

'No, I don't like that.' Jochen said. 'If a horse stumbled it would be a disaster. Too risky. We are not in a hurry. Let's do it properly.'

'We must get away from here as fast as possible,' Rolf said.

'Why? There is no danger here,' said Jochen. 'No people, no troops, no more planes. Besides, who would be interested in a bunch of refugees with horse-drawn wagons?'

'*Scheisse*!' Rolf glared at Jochen. 'In the last few days, they have bombed the life out of a city only a few kilometres away and you delude yourself that there is no danger? Are you too stupid to see how exposed we'll be when we actually get on the ice? There is nothing underneath-just cold, black water.'

'Come on, Rolf, I'm on your side, but if we rush it and have an accident with the horses it will take longer.'

Rolf heard Jochen out before speaking. When he did his voice was harsh and barely controlled.

'Do it your way. I hope to God I'm wrong,' he said and walked off.

Elli rushed after him, glad to get off the ice. Close to the shore she saw something on the ice. She stopped. It looked like two bundles of rags. 'Papa, Jochen, come over here.' Closer up, she saw it was a man and a woman. The woman's body and face were iced over. She was dead.

The man was face down and was not ice covered like the woman. His clothes smelled of smoke and there were brown patches, which looked like dried blood on his overcoat. The hair on the back of his head appeared to be glued together and shrivelled.

'Armer Hund!' Jochen arrived and checked the man's pulse. 'Slow, but he is alive. He must have come from Dresden. He's burned.' Gently he turned the unconsciousness man over. His face was blistered and swollen and all his hair was burned off eve his eyebrows but he didn't seem to have any open wounds. Rolf reached them out of breath. He knelt down and opened the man's overcoat.

'Oh, no!' He went over to the woman's body and wiped her face, looking at it closely.

'What?' Elli pulled his sleeve. 'Who are they?' She leaned over the woman—and recognised her. 'Ulricke! That is Ulricke. Oh God and this must be Hans.'

Rolf stood beside his friend, unable to move.

'We'd better get him to the camp,' Jochen said. 'He is barely alive. We can leave the woman here and get some others to pick her body up. She died a while ago. He must have dragged her all the way.'

They carried Hans to the camp and put him in Ruth's wagon. As they worked on him, taking off his torn clothes and rubbing him down to get his blood circulating, Elli became aware that he was looking at her.

'Hans! You're safe. You've made it. Ruth and I will get you warm, especially your feet. It'll hurt but we have to get your circulation going.' He did not respond. His eyes followed her, but he stayed silent. 'Hans, did you hear me?' A barely visible nod was his only response. They continued to work on him. Elli knew that the massage of his frozen feet must have hurt him but he didn't flinch.

Finally, when his feet turned pink, Elli stopped. In the meantime, Ruth spoon-fed him hot tea. Hans swallowed the hot liquid but remained silent.

'Rest now, *Liebling*,' Ruth said. Do you need anything else for the moment?' After a second, he shook his head.

'See, he is recovering already,' Ruth said.

'Let the man sleep.' Elli smiled at her sister's enthusiasm.

In the meantime, Ulricke's body was retrieved. Rolf tried to insist on an immediate burial, but failed to convince the others.

'A day longer won't make any difference, Rolf,' Elfriede said. 'We are exposed here. We have to get moving.'

'We have to give Ulricke a decent funeral. Hans dragged her body all the way. She deserves it and he needs it too.'

'Hans is unconscious and will take a while to recover. We can't wait for that.'

'He is awake and reacting to questions,' Ruth said. 'He is recovering.'

'That settles it. If Hans is up to it, we'll have Ulricke's funeral today and do the crossing tomorrow,' Elfriede said. Rolf tried to protest but they all walked off.

They dug a grave beside the little girl's. During the short service Hans was silent as tears streamed down his blistered face.

Late into the evening Rolf and Jochen were busily preparing each family's rig for an early morning departure.

In the morning they found that the hessian socks on the horses had come off and had to be replaced. The crossing was delayed until midday, despite Rolf's feverish efforts to hurry it along. Rolf decided that three wagons would cross first. Elli, Elfriede, and the Schlichte had the strongest Clydesdales. When they had safely arrived, Jochen would go back and organise the rest of them.

Karla went onto the ice without hesitation. The canvas socks gave the horse such a good grip that Elli had to slow her down when the wagon skidded sideways. Rolf travelled on Elfriede's wagon, immediately behind her, followed by the Schlichtes with Hanna. Ruth insisted on being at the back of the convoy to give Hans more time to recover.

After they had been on the ice for a few minutes and were used to the crunching sound of snow compacting under the wagon wheels, Elli became conscious of another sound, a creaking, groaning sound coming from the ice. She had heard the same sound and seen cracks developing under her feet when as a child she ventured out on a frozen pond.

'The ice is breaking!'

'Don't worry,' Jochen said cheerfully, 'we are fine.' 'Can't you hear the ice? It's creaking!'

'*Ja*, I hear it, but it is not a problem, it's at least half a metre thick; it won't break.'

Jochen was sitting beside her on the driver's bench, looking for possible obstacles on the ice. To Elli the creaking was nerve-wracking; she expected that at any moment they would break through and be swallowed by the river.

'Oh my God, look!' Elli pointed at the ice. 'What? Look at what?' Jochen said.

'Look there, where the snow has been blown off! Those are cracks and they are running alongside the wagon. The ice is breaking up!' Jochen leaned out of the wagon to have a look.

'Relax, *Liebling*, that is normal, only shifts in the surface tension. You told me that when you were a child skating on the village pond, the ice cracked then too?'

'Yes and it scared me to death.' 'But it didn't break, *ja*?'

Elli was unconvinced. She looked at his face. He was serious about what he said but still-surface tension shifts'. What a patronising *Arschloch*.

They progressed steadily as there were no obstacles on the icefield, but the constant creaking sound kept Elli's tension at breaking point.

A mist descended over the ice. From the driver's bench Elli could no longer see Karla's legs. It looked as if the upper part of the horse was floating on a grey cloud. The sound of Karla's bandaged hooves on the ice was muffled and seemed to come from all sides.

Elli shivered; the fear of danger was consuming. Slowly the riverbank came in sight. Even though they were still on the ice, once they reached the shore Elli breathed easier.

Rolf and Jochen immediately went to set up the rope hoist and anchored it to a tree on top of the riverbank. Elli attached Karla to the hoist. The other Clydesdale pulled Karla up, slowly, by walking away from the riverbank.

'That was fantastic, Jochen: great job.' Rolf said.

'What do you mean by fantastic job, Jochen? Elli said. 'How about saying thanks to Karla? Without her it wouldn't have worked.'

'Okay, okay, daughter. Thanks Karla.'

After Karla pulled the Schlichtes's Clydesdale up, both horses hoisted the wagons to the top of the riverbank.

'Okay Jochen, go back and tell the others to get onto the ice. Keep them apart by about two wagon lengths, so the ice won't be too stressed.'

Elli watched Jochen slowly disappear into the mist. She knew the other wagons would not reach them for an hour, and it was already getting late. The sun was getting weaker and the cold was coming back. Although the crossing had been uneventful, Elli still trembled with fear.

The landscape behind the riverbank was quiet and peaceful. No houses, no fences, no signs of people.

The fog was closing in. In the failing light, the scene became surreal.

After an age she heard the wagons approaching. The fog carried the clanking sounds of the horses' gear before she could see them. There they were, at last. Jochen kept them well apart but she could clearly see several wagons.

'At last,' Rolf said. 'What took them so long?'

'I can see Jochen running up and down beside them, keeping them together.'

Elfriede, Hanna and the Schlichtes came from their wagons to watch the approaching convoy, which became visible as the fog over the ice dispersed. Something disturbed Elli. A sound. What was it?

'Can you hear that, Papa? What is that?'

'What? I can't hear a thing.' They stood together, silently, tense. 'Oh my God, planes!' Rolf said.

He jumped up and screamed at the approaching convoy. *'Schnell, schnell,* planes! Get off the ice!

The people in the first two wagons must have heard him and tried to hurry their horses.

'Leave the horses. Get off the ice! Take cover!'

Four twin-engine planes came in low, a single large bomb strapped under each wing.

Elli's mind was racing, evaluating, questioning. Why were the planes here? This couldn't have anything to do with Dresden. Had they been too long at the river, too visible? But the planes were smaller than the bombers of Dresden. They couldn't be American or English; too small to fly the large distance.

She could see the individual rotations of the propellers—everything around her slowed down—she made a slow, deep growling noise.

The planes came from the east—from Breslau—they were Russians! Father was right; we stayed too long. Maybe they think we are *Wehrmacht* troops. No! They are low enough to see that we are refugees. They want to murder us!

The planes lined up over the wagons, one behind the other, two on each side of the convoy.

The bombs disengaged.

Why didn't the people on the ice run faster?

The bombs hit the ice, efficiently, one behind the other, on both sides of the convoy. There were no explosions—the bombs had failed! Then the ice rose, and tilted up in a majestic fountain of snow and water. People, horses and wagons tumbled into the openings, and then the ice smashed down and came to rest.

The planes pulled sharply up to avoid the trees on the riverbank. The displaced air pushed the observers into the snow. Elli felt each passing plane like a violent punch against her body. Then there was silence, except for the sound of her heartbeat. She sat up, dazed, disoriented and tried to brush off the powdery, harsh snow sticking to her.

Her hands did not make any sound, then, with a high-pitched whistle, her hearing came back.

She turned to the river. No one was on the ice.

No people, horses or wagons. The icefield was bare.

The ice did not even seem to be disturbed, only shiny and wet. 'Oh God. Jochen, Ruth, Herman, Fritz, Anna, where are you?'

She stumbled down the riverbank onto the slippery ice, followed by the others. She fell several times, cutting her legs on shards of ice, standing like knife blades.

There was nothing left of the convoy, only debris.

The river had swallowed the people and the ice was back in place. Only the cracks and the water on the surface showed what had happened.

Elli knelt on the ice. There was something, some movement, someone alive.

'Over here! I can see someone! Get a pick! We have to break the ice. Jochen, Ruth, I am here. I'll get you out.' She hammered with her bare fists on the ice, trying to break through it.

'Elli, *Liebling*, stop.' Rolf held her bleeding hands. He was shaking, his face as grey as the ice. 'The ice is too thick and even if we could get through, the icy water will have killed them. Please, *Liebling*, get up.'

'How can you say that? We have to try! Your daughter and grandchildren are down there!' Faces appeared under the ice. The wet ice acted like a lens, enlarging and distorting what drifted underneath.

'There! Look. Someone is there.' The face of a woman became clearly visible. Elli could see the terror in her eyes as the mouth formed a silent scream.

'Oh God, you are right,' Rolf said.

The scene under the ice changed. Elli saw a child and a horse float into view only to disappear into the darkness.

'They are drifting away.' She grabbed her father's sleeve, dragging him away. 'Downstream! The rapids! There is open water. The current will bring them into the open there, hurry!'

Rolf, Elli, and the Schlichtes ran the short distance downstream. They heard the sound of rushing water.

'There!' Rolf pointed. 'There, the rapids.'

In the middle of the river small clusters of rocks emerged, on their downstream side a barricade of ice had developed. The large pool of swirling water in front of the rocks was filled with floating bodies and debris, spinning in a whirlpool before disappearing under the ice again.

They watched helplessly as bodies emerged and sank again. 'Papa, we have to do something. We have to get them out.' 'How? We can't jump in and swim over there, the water is freezing and the current would drag us under the ice.'

'We have to get them out.' 'They are all dead, Elli.' 'Maybe someone is still alive.'

'No! If the explosions didn't kill them the icy water has.'

'We can't just stand here and let them disappear under the ice. We must do something.'

The debris in the whirlpool was in constant change; wagon parts, wooden boxes, clothes, bodies and body parts. The head of a woman, floating like an egg in the nest of long hair; a hand with several rings, neatly separated at the wrist; the torso of a man cut apart at shoulder level, with no arms and head; and then a small bundle drifting towards them, a baby. Elli dropped on her stomach and slid towards the edge.

'Elfriede, Papa, hold my legs, I can reach it.' The ice at the edge was breaking piece by piece, floating away.

'Pull her back,' she heard Elfriede say. 'She is slipping.'

'No! Wait! I can reach it.' She touched the bundle, forcing her frozen fingers to close. No feeling of contact, then pain in her hand told her that her fingers had closed.

'Pull, pull! I've got it.'

She felt the grip on both her legs increase but then the ice tilted downwards and she submerged. The cold stopped her breathing. She couldn't feel her body, only an icy pressure. A sudden jerk bought her and the bundle back onto the ice.

Elfriede and Erica Schlichte wrapped her and the baby into their coats and bundled her off to her wagon. Rolf and Otto went back to where the bombs hit the convoy.

'We have to go back to the other bank,' Rolf said. 'Maybe someone is still alive.'

Elfriede undressed Elli and covered her with every blanket she could find, and Hanna slipped the cold body of the child under her clothes and held it against her skin.

'Oh God, the poor little thing is so cold. I'll keep him against my body until we have hot water.'

'Is he alive?' Elli said.

'I'm not sure, but I think so,' Hanna said.

'I have to go back. Ruth, Elfi, Hubert and Jochen, I have to find them. Elfriede, help me get dressed.'

'We can't get on the ice. It's dark and foggy. We wouldn't see where the ice is broken. We would drown,' Elfriede said.

❄

Chapter 18

'The fog is getting too dense; we'll get lost, Rolf. We might be going in circles.'

'We must be close to the other shore, Otto. The ice has a snow cover again.'

'We have to go back, there is no one left.' Otto clung to a teddy bear he had found. 'This is all there is—a child's toy. We shouldn't have crossed here.'

'What was the alternative, Otto? Murdered in Ostritz, incinerated in Dresden? Tell me!' Otto's face flushed and he looked away without saying anything. 'How do you think I feel, Otto? My daughter and grandchildren are gone. I'll tell you how I feel. Guilty! And I don't know why, because there was no alternative. My own flesh and blood died because there was no alternative!' He grabbed the big man by the collar and shook him. 'Yes, we shouldn't have crossed the river but what else could we have done? Tell me, Otto!'

'I...' Otto tried to move away but Rolf was holding on. 'I don't know Rolf.'

'Then never, ever again tell me we shouldn't have done this.' Rolf let him go and dropped down, sobbing uncontrollably. 'Ruth, Elfi, Hubert, I've failed you.'

Otto made some clumsy attempts to calm him. He had been better at that when Helene died, Rolf thought, but then I was drunk and he was behind the bar. He had known Otto and his wife all of his life, they had all gone to school together. Otto inherited the town's largest *Gasthaus* when his father died.

Rolf became involved in politics after he survived The Great War and the killing fields of Verdun. During the turbulent years of the

Weimar Republic, he joined the Socialist Party of Germany, helped set up a branch in Hirschberg and finally was elected mayor of Krummhübel. They had remained friends despite Otto becoming a member of the NSDAP, the Nazi party. Otto was a pragmatist, and covered himself in every way. Stormtroopers, communists and socialists were all welcome in his *Gasthaus* as long they didn't try to vent their political differences in his place. Even the loudmouth Stormtroopers had great respect for the huge publican who kept a wooden club handy on his bar. The rumour that Otto had a loaded double-barrel shot gun under the bar also helped.

Despite their long-standing friendship, Rolf felt Otto had become increasingly hostile towards him since they had left Krummhübel. But for Erica's calming influence, Rolf would have moved out of their wagon a long time ago.

Rolf dragged himself up. 'You are right; we have to go back. The light is fading, and the fog and open water holes will make it too difficult.'

Rolf saw tracks in the snow, just visible in the fog, but they were definitely tracks of the convoy. Something was odd about them.

'They went back!'

'What? Who went back?' Otto said.

'The wagons at the back of the convoy—they turned back after the attack! Ruth was at the back. They are alive! Hurry, we have to find them.'

'I don't know Rolf. There are tracks, yes, but many wagons came along here and all of them produced their own tracks. I mean, it wasn't a railway on a single track.'

'I know that! But these tracks show that they turned around. They went back. We have to find them.'

'If we don't go back now it will be pitch dark, impossible to get back. We'll freeze if we have to stay on this side without shelter.'

Rolf didn't seem to hear him. 'Come on, we're nearly at the ferry ramp. Come on Otto!' He stopped abruptly. 'Listen! Voices! Can't you hear them?' Rolf shouted at the top of his voice. 'Hello! Anyone there?

Hello!'

'Rolf, the fog does strange things. It makes you hear things— things you want to hear.'

'No! I can hear them. Hello! Hello!' Without waiting for Otto, he ran to where the sounds came from. There—the ferry ramp—a light—a fire. 'Ruth, Elfi, Hubert!'

People came towards him and then he heard his daughter. He dropped to his knees. They were alive!

'Papa! Papa, I thought you were dead.' Ruth bent down and lifted him up, wiping and kissing his tears away. 'Elli and the children, are they...?'

'*Ja*, they made it. Where are Elfi and Hubert?'

The children ran up to their mother and grandfather.

'*Opa*, you came back! *Opa*? Why are you crying?' Elfi said. 'Because I'm so happy to see you.'

'I'm happy too, *Opa*, but you must smile.'

'Is there anyone else with you, Papa?' Ruth said.

'Three wagons. Hanna, Elfriede, Erica, Otto, Elli and the kids, and myself, that's all. How many are here?'

'Only five wagons.'

'How is Hans? I can't see him,' Rolf said. 'Not good. He doesn't speak, just sits there.' 'And Jochen?'

'Jochen? No, wasn't he with you?'

'Yes, but he was on the ice during the attack, directing the convoy.'

'We never saw him, Papa.' They looked at each other in silence for a moment.

'We must go back to the others. I have to tell Elli.'

'We'll have to wait until first light,' Otto said. 'It's too dark now. You would drown in one of the open holes or get lost. Wait until morning.'

Rolf didn't need any further convincing. Ruth was determined not to let him go anyway.

On shore the other survivors gathered around the two men, horrified to hear that only three wagons had made it to the other side.

'How did you manage to get the five rigs back on shore?' Rolf said.

'Four of the wagons were still there, only Peter Holstein was on the ice. Peter?' she called. An older man, in his sixties, came over.

'We were lucky. The ice broke up close to my horse. If she hadn't shied and turned sideways, we would have disappeared in the river.'

'Those bastards cracked the river from one side to the other,' Rolf said.

'It was terrible. We didn't know what to do. Every wagon in sight except Peter's disappeared. And the screams. I'll never forget hearing a child calling her mother. 'Mama, Mama, Mama,' and then nothing. We searched on the ice but found no one and we were too scared to go any further. We thought you were all dead.'

At first light, Rolf and Otto went back on the ice. Ruth and the others stayed where they were. The fog lifted rapidly as the sun came out. It was a clear day, so clear they could see the other shore and people moving around there. The bomb holes had frozen over during the night but looked fragile. Both men carefully avoided them. The outline where the convoy had been was marked by upright shards of ice, like a cemetery fence. Between two large shards Rolf saw something on the ice. It looked like half a person.

'It's Jochen, Rolf, or what's left of him,' Otto said.

Jochen's body was cut in half. He was on his back, his face frozen in a surprised scream. The river had swallowed the lower part of his body.

'Elli and Elfriede are coming from the other side,' Otto said. Rolf jumped up and rushed to his daughter.

'Papa, you are alive. We thought you were gone too!'

'It was too late to come back. We stayed with Ruth and the others who survived.'

Elli stared at him open mouthed and then screamed, grabbed him by the ears, kissed his nose and jumped into his arms, like she had as a young girl when her father surprised her with a present. Rolf nearly collapsed from the pain of his injured shoulder.

'Steady girl, my shoulder, you are killing your old father.'

'Oh God, sorry Papa.' She tried to soothe his shoulder by rubbing her hands up and down his arm until Rolf stepped way from her.

'Ruth and the children are alive? Oh, *Danke lieber Gott*. And there are other survivors—how many?'

'With Ruth and the children, another four families,' Rolf said, still rubbing his shoulder.

'Is Jochen with them?' Rolf looked down. Into the silence Elli whispered, eyes open wide and face drained of blood. 'Papa? Where is he?'

Rolf looked up into her pained face and pulled her against his chest. 'He is dead, darling,' he said slowly. Elli pushed out of his embrace and stared into her father's face, mouth opening, no sound coming out.

Then she slumped into his arms.

'Papa, is that him, there on the ice?' she whispered.

'Yes, that's Jochen's body.' He held her tightly as she tried to pull away.

'Let me go, Papa. I want to see him.'

'Don't look, please. He is terribly injured. He must have died instantly. Remember him as he was.'

'Let go!' Her voice became steely. He let go of her arm but after a few metres she stopped. Rolf enclosed her in his arms again and tried to lead her away. Abruptly she shrugged him off and walked over to the dark bundle on the ice. Rolf followed her.

Below Jochen's chest was a gaping hole. The large pool of blood around him was frozen and the fresh, red crystals crunched under their feet. Elli knelt down beside him, positioning herself so that she could look at his face and avoid the mangled torso. Rolf stepped back to give her some privacy.

Jochen's dead eyes stared into space, his mouth half-open. Death must have come quickly. Elli tried to close his eyes. The frozen eyelids resisted, but the warmth of her fingers forced them shut. She let her hand glide over his face and kissed him. Rolf gently touched her shoulder.

'*Liebling*, we have to get off the ice. I'll take you back to Ruth.' Slowly Elli rose, stretched out both arms to him, moved two steps, gasped for air and collapsed.

'Elli! Elfriede, help me! I'm an idiot. I shouldn't have let her see Jochen's body.'

Elfriede felt Elli's pulse and checked her head.

'She has a bump on the back of her head. Must have got it last night when she fell on the ice. The concussion and the shock have been too much for her. Her pulse is low but regular. I think she'll be fine.'

'We'll take her to Ruth. Otto, go back to your wife and Hanna, tell them we are all right—and get the horses ready.'

'What for?' Otto said.

'To pull the rigs up when they come across,' Rolf said.

'What? Are you insane? You want the rest of the convoy to get on the ice and go through that again?

'You have a better idea? We'll space the wagons so that only one is on the ice at a time. Otto, we have to get going, there is no other way.' Otto walked off without comment. Rolf and Elfriede carried Elli ashore.

'Rolf is back.' He heard the call when they got to the ferry ramp. Minutes later everyone from the five wagons surrounded them. Ruth, after the initial shock of seeing her sister unconscious, organised four women to take Elli to her wagon.

'What happened to her, Papa? You said Elli was all right,' Ruth said.

'We just found Jochen's body. It was terrible, the ice had sliced him in half, and when Elli saw his mutilated body, she passed out.' 'Oh my God! But she is strong, she'll recover,' Ruth said.

'*Ja*, but I'll make sure that your wagon is the last. That will give her some peace,' Rolf said. The astonished look on her face stopped him. 'We'll have to do the crossing today; we have to get away from here.'

'But Papa...'

'I know, I know! But we have no alternative, Ruth. This is the only way to cross the river. We'll only let one rig on the ice at a time, and everyone but the driver will walk. There is no other way.'

Rolf walked first, alone, across the river. The most direct path, which the convoy took the night before, was unusable. The refrozen ice was too thin for the heavy wagons. Rolf walked close to shore before crossing at a safe distance from the breaks. Erica and Hanna ran on to the ice to greet him.

'How is Elli?' Erica said.

'Still out, but she'll come around.' Hanna gave him a friendly hug.

'You poor man. I'll make a warm drink and then come with you. You need help.' Rolf wanted to protest but was too tired and let Hanna pamper him. Despite his tiredness, he was anxious about wasting time.

'Otto, are the horses ready?'

'*Ja*, the horses and the lifting gear are ready but we can't bring the rigs up here.'

'Why not?'

'The ice is fractured right up to the shore. We have to find another place.'

'It's the same on the other side. So, we'll do the hoisting a hundred metres up the river. The ice will be solid enough there.'

Arm in arm Rolf and Hanna walked across the ice. For a few moments, with this attractive woman at his side on the quiet and sun-drenched frozen river, he could push away the nightmare. He could almost forget that they were walking over the place where so many people died last night. He had the impression Hanna felt the same. Then the horrors came back.

'Look, what is that?' Hanna pointed to something. It looked to Rolf like a short timber post. He bent down and recoiled.

'Oh, God, it's a leg.'

They walked the rest of the way in silence.

Peter Schleswig's rig was the first to move out. Rolf walked ahead of the horse, as Hanna accompanied Peter's family on foot at a distance from the rig. The crossing and hoisting the horse and wagon up on the other side was uneventful. Rolf went immediately back to get the next rig. By late afternoon, only Ruth's rig was left.

'How is Elli?'

'Still the same. Maybe it's best. I hope she doesn't wake up in the middle of the crossing,' Ruth said.

'Stay with Hans and the children. Elfriede will drive the rig. We have to hurry; the fog will settle in again soon.'

The crossing progressed without problems and Ruth, with the others, reached the shore safely. Rolf saw Otto waiting with the lifting horses—and then he heard the sound of a plane. He froze in fear. Regardless of the apparent ease of these last crossings, there had been an increasing sense of foreboding from the beginning. And now it became reality. The scene was so similar to the night before, fading light, fog and the threat from above. He exploded into action.

'Go Elfriede, go! The *Schweine* are back!'

The single-engine plane dived down, with a bone-penetrating, screeching sound until it levelled out, coming low towards him. There were no bombs hanging under the fuselage. Rolf sighed with relief, until he saw the flashing of the plane's guns and bullets hit the ice around him. Then the plane was gone and the sound of its engine faded in the distance. The people ashore came out of hiding.

'*Schnell*! Rolf, get yourself and the others up here before the Hund decides to have another go. We'll get the rig,' Otto said. 'Elfriede, help me with Elli.' Rolf walked to the front of the wagon but couldn't see her. 'Where are you?' He felt his heart stop when he saw the bullet holes and blood on the driver's bench. 'Elfriede! Elli!'

Elfriede lay in the back of the wagon across Elli. Several bullets had ripped through her chest. She was dead. When he rolled her body over and saw blood on Elli he screamed in agony.

'No! No! Not her!' He hugged Elli close to his chest. 'Let go, Papa,' he heard Ruth say. 'She is alive.'

Elli was unconscious but unhurt. There were bullet holes throughout the wagon but Elfriede's body had protected Elli. The blood she was covered in was Elfriede's.

❄

Chapter 19

She heard a voice, but it made no sense. She thought the speaker must be very drunk. Every word was slurred and stretched. Jochen and Papa must have had a drinking session. They must have found the hoarded Schnapps from Ebersbach. She made a mental note to give both of them a lecture about the lousy example they were setting for the others, in particular the younger people who looked up to them.

Community leaders, pah! Why don't they shut up; can't they see that she wanted to sleep?

They were speaking clearly now. Why didn't they leave her in peace? She was cold and tried to adjust her blanket but her fingers did not obey. What was going on? She tried to open her eyes. First nothing, her eyelids did not open, they were stuck, but then light, bright light, and shadows moved over her. She screamed.

'Elli! *Liebling* wake up! Please wake up!' Ruth's voice. Slowly her vision became clearer. It was Ruth. Tears were running down her face. 'Oh Elli, my poor *Liebling*, I thought you would never come out of this.'

'Ruthy, I thought I would never see you again. There was no one left on the ice—so many bodies at the rapids—and the baby. How is the baby?'

Before Ruth could answer, Elli went on. 'Papa and Otto didn't come back.' Her voice became increasingly slurred. 'I was so scared but Elfriede stopped me going to look for them. But next morning, Papa and Otto were there—alive—and then—I found Jochen.' She stared silently at Ruth, convulsions racking her body.

'Why? Why him too?' Ruth lay down beside her, holding her shaking body. Elli shot upright.

'Where are Elfi and Hubert?'

'Outside, waiting to come in,' Ruth said.

Elfi and Hubert must have heard Elli. They rushed in, pushed their mother aside, and threw themselves over their aunt. For a few moments their enthusiam suppressed every other thought.

Ruth had to support Elli when she climbed out of the wagon where Rolf waited for her with a steaming cup of coffee.

'Here drink this. It's coffee, strong coffee. 'I'm so glad to see you up again.'

'Coffee? Real coffee?'

'Real coffee, not Ersatzkaffe, real coffee,' Rolf said. The smell was wonderful.

Elli had forgotten what coffee smelt like. When Rolf handed her the cup she felt his hand tremble, and then she noticed new, deep lines around his mouth and eyes.

The image of Jochen's smashed body came back, like a red-hot poker. She gasped for air and tried to bring back the memory of the few intimate moments they had together, but the pain in her chest was a clamp, forcing her into short, shallow breaths. Ruth, still holding her arm, tightened her grip. Elli forced her lungs to expand. Burning pain, but she persisted. Breathe in. It's burning. Ignore it, breathe! It became easier; the pain subsided. She looked around. The cup of coffee was spilled in the snow as she hung between her father and sister.

'*Scheisse*, that was the first real coffee for ages,' Elli said. Ruth and Rolf's faces lit up.

'My God! You scared me!' Rolf said. 'Don't do that again, there is only one cup left.'

'You are such a clown Papa.' Elli quickly downed the second coffee and handed the empty cup to Ruth. 'I want to see Jochen's body.'

Rolf's smile vanished but he did not say anything. 'Please. I just want to see him one last time. I have to see him, Elli pleaded.'

'My poor *Liebling*, that is impossible,' Ruth said. Her sad smile made Elli even more determined.

'I remember what his body looked like. Don't worry I won't pass out again.' She tried modulating her voice and sounding in control.

'Elli, you didn't just pass out, you were unconscious for two days.

We were worried that you wouldn't come out of it,' Ruth said. Elli felt shocked but still determined.

'Two days? So what! I still want to see him.'

'We buried him with Elfriede and the others,' Ruth said. 'Elfriede!' Elli looked at her sister in disbelief. 'Elfriede is dead?

But she was with me on the ice the following day. She was fine.'

'A plane attacked us on the second crossing. Elfriede was shot,' Ruth said. Elli needed a few moments to comprehend what Ruth said. Perspiration was running down her back and face.

'I want to see his grave, please.' The nausea came back, forcing her to swallow rapidly.

'We moved on. It was too dangerous to stay at the Elbe.'

Elli felt something break in her. The nausea rushed through her, followed by the fire of red-hot pain spreading from her chest into every limb. Then the redness of pain faded, it became darker. Ruth sounded muffled.

'Papa, Papa, *schnell*! She is passing out again.'

Pain and nausea subsided as the blackness increased. Peace at last.

She woke up, abruptly.

'Keep her mouth open, Anna. Come on, don't be so clumsy,' she heard Herman say. A large spoon was put in her mouth, pushing on her tongue and making her gag as a hot liquid went down her throat and windpipe. She gasped for air and exploded into violent coughing.

'*Opa, Opa*, come here, Mama is awake but she is choking!' Seconds later someone was thumping her back.

'Stop that. What are you trying to do, kill me?' Elli said, her voice rasping and snorting.

'Mama, you are awake, oh Mama!' Between sobbing and crying, Anna tried again to force-feed her mother.

'Anna, stop that. Take that spoon away. You are killing me.' 'Mama, you have to eat. You are so skinny now. We couldn't get much food into you. It was so difficult,' Herman said. Elli tried to sit up, but dizziness forced her down again.

'How long was I out?'

Her son looked at his sister. He was biting his lower lip. 'I...I have to...I better get *Opa*. Where is *Opa? Opa!* Even though he shouted at the top of his voice his grandfather didn't come. He looked helplessly at his mother. '*Opa* said that Aunty Ruth was too rough with you and told us to call him as soon as you woke up.'

'Nonsense! Answer me.' But Herman was already gone to fetch his grandfather. Elli closed her eyes. I have to tell my patronising father to mind his own business, she thought.

'Elli? Elli, are you awake?' she heard Rolf say.

Her father was leaning over her. His face had aged even more since the last time she saw him.

'Elli, *Liebling*, I'm so glad that you are awake again.' 'Papa, how long was I out this time?

'Some time, *Liebling*.' 'How long, father?'

'A while. It doesn't matter how long. You have to eat, get your strength back and then we'll talk. Herman has some soup for you and I'll be back in a few moments,' he said and walked off.

'Father, come back here, you patronizing bastard! Answer me.

Come back.'

'Please Mama, eat this.' Herman had the big spoon, balancing it in front of her nose and spilling the hot soup on her neck.

'Ouch! Be careful, you clumsy ox.'

'Open your mouth Mama, please.' Elli resigned and let her son feed her. She felt the warmth of the soup spreading through her body. Slowly strength came back and thinking became clearer.

'Thanks, Herman, that was very good, the best soup I ever had.' 'It's the same stuff we have been feeding you for the whole week.

I'm glad you are awake because that was the last. There isn't anything else.'

'You did a good job keeping your mother alive for a whole week,' she said with a smile.

'It was actually nine days and all of us helped and we...' His face turned red when he realised what he had said. 'I have to call *Opa*. *Opaaa!*' Minutes later Rolf came in, panting.

'What happened? Are you alright?' 'Papa, tell me how long I was out.'

'*Liebling*, it is much more important that you recover slowly, because you were really unconscious for a while.'

'What happened? How come I passed out twice, and this time for nine days?'

Her father's eyebrows rose as he gave his grandson an annoyed look.

'Couldn't keep your trap shut, ha?' 'But she tricked me, I didn't...'

'Herman, who is 'she'? Are you talking about your mother?' Elli cut in. 'Please, both of you, cut out the games and tell me what happened. I won't pass out again, I promise.'

'Elli, I told the kids not to bombard you with too much information when you came out of it. It was a precaution in case the stress was too much for you,' Rolf said.

'I'm okay now, so please answer me.'

'I hope you are, but we will stop talking if you get a headache or feel dizzy.'

'Headache, me? I haven't had one for years. Come on, Papa.' Rolf gave her a worried look but then gave in.

'You got a bump on the head. Possibly a piece of ice hit you, even though you were not on the river when they bombed us. Anyway, you passed out when we found Jochen and again later, several times, when we told you all the terrible news,' Rolf said.

'I don't remember what happened. It's all a blur. I vaguely remember slipping on the ice. Maybe that's when I hit my head,' Elli said.

'Ruth and the kids looked after you each time you were out.'

'So, altogether I lost about two weeks. Is that right?' Elli said.

'That's right.'

'What happened on the ice, and what happened to Elfriede? Please Papa, tell me.'

For a moment, her father was silent and Elli could see his eyes filling with tears. He tried to compose himself but the tears ran down his face, flowing in the deep wrinkles. He sat down, grasped her hands and then enclosed her in his arms. Elli felt him shaking.

'It is... it is... I was wrong... all my fault.' She heard him stumbling for words.

'What do you mean? How were you wrong?'

'If I hadn't insisted on crossing the Elbe just then, many people, Jochen and Elfriede, would still be alive.'

The mention of Jochen hit Elli. For a few moments, she was unable to say anything. Her eyes were burning and the thought of Jochen's mutilated body took her breath away.

'Maybe Papa, maybe. Maybe if we weren't in this dreadful situation and maybe if there was no war and maybe if there was no one bombing us, maybe, Papa. I don't think that it was your fault or anyone else's. If you hadn't led us, we would all be dead. Stop blaming yourself, Papa. I need you now more than ever. We all need you.'

Rolf lifted his head and looked at her.

'There are only forty-one of us left. One hundred and sixty died in the bombardment. We have stayed under cover since the second attack, where Elfriede died. I searched the ice the following morning. Nothing, only some body parts, and at the rapids we found a few bodies. Of all the others were sucked under the ice, we didn't find a trace. The river swallowed them. We buried Jochen and Elfriede with the others at the riverbank and then moved on. We had to get away from the river. The bombers kept coming back.'

Elli swallowed hard to keep her tears back and then remembered. 'What about the baby?'

'He didn't make it.'

'Oh God, that poor little thing, after all that he went through.' 'He was too long in the water. His little body just gave up.'

Chapter 20

Forty-one people and eight wagons. They were wedged into an endless stream of refugees heading west. Occasionally, military units overtook the slow-moving refugees and forced them off the road. When one convoy of *Wehrmacht* trucks caught up with them, Elli saw that every one of the trucks was crammed with wounded soldiers. Grey faces, covered with blood-soaked bandages, stared at her from the open backs of the trucks. Only pain and horror were reflected in them.

Close to Rolf's leading wagon, a truck slowed down and stopped. Protesting shouts from the truck behind it urged the driver to move on.

'*Scheiss Kerl,* keep going or we'll all die. Schnell, schnell!'

The rear gate of the front truck dropped down and two men pushed a body over the edge. The body hit the ground, rolled over to the side of the road, and came to rest in front of Rolf's wagon. Immediately a man from a motorcycle-sidecar climbed onto the truck. The whole exchange stopped the *Wehrmacht* convoy for only a minute. As the convoy moved on, the driver of the motorcycle came over to Rolf.

'You, over there, come here.' He pointed to the dead body. 'He is gone. Dig him a grave.' The body was a young man, with a thin cover of hair on his chin. Can't be older than sixteen, Elli thought. He had a head injury, both of his legs ended in bloodied stumps but, oddly, his face looked peaceful.

'Would you mind if my friends help me?' Rolf said. 'The ground is frozen and it will take a while.'

'*Ja, ja.* Whatever, get going.' The soldier looked surprised as if he expected resistance to his request. 'Take your time; you'll be stuck here for a while anyway.'

Manfred, Otto and Elli jumped off their wagons to help. 'We'll bury him under the trees over there,' Rolf said to the soldier. 'The ground shouldn't be too hard there.'

'Just keep going,' the soldier said. They started to dig but managed only a shallow hole.

'We can't get any deeper. Too many roots,' Otto said to the soldier who restlessly paced around them. 'Gefreiter! Is that enough?'

'*Ja*, that's enough. Put him in, schnell.'

'Why is he so agitated?' Otto said. 'Didn't he say that we wouldn't be moving for a while?'

'We'll finish this job. Elli, talk to him,' Rolf said. 'Otto is right.

Something is wrong.' He handed Elli a pack of cigarettes. 'Here, give him that.'

'We'll be done in a few minutes, Herr Gefreiter. Would you like a cigarette?' Elli smiled at the young soldier who was clearly embarrassed by her attention.

'*Danke*, Fräulein. I have to get back to my unit but there is always enough time for a smoke.' He carefully took a cigarette out of the packet, handling it as if Elli offered him a fragile and expensive piece of porcelain. 'Haven't had one for ages.' Elli offered him a light and he took a few deep breaths, slowly exhaling the smoke through his nostrils. 'God, that is good.'

'Take the whole packet,' Elli said. 'You need it more than me.'

A grateful smile lit up his face. '*Danke*, again.' he said. 'That kid...' He nodded in the direction of Rolf and the burial. 'He was my cousin. Couldn't keep him alive, but it's better this way.' He looked again towards the trees, nodding slowly. He continued in a low voice, even though no one else could hear. 'Get off this road at the next intersection. A Field Gendarme checkpoint is at the second junction from here. They take every male, regardless of age, as long as they can carry a rifle. They would certainly be pulled out,' he said, gesturing at the three men completing the burial. 'The boys as well.' Elli felt her heart pounding.

'None of our boys is older than fourteen. They wouldn't draft children.'

'They do. Any male who is strong enough to carry a rifle or Panzerfaust will be drafted into the *Volkssturm* and ordered to defend towns. My cousin was fifteen.'

'But children and old men against Russian tanks, that is insane.' 'It is! Get off this road.' He didn't wait for any further response, jumped on his motorbike and drove off.

'What did he say?' Otto said when Elli came back to them. 'We have to get off this road at the next junction,' Elli said and repeated what the soldier told her.

Eventually the traffic started to move again. At the next junction a small sign said: Nickolsdorf—20 Kilometres. The road was under deep snow without any sign of recent use. Rolf directed his eight wagons onto the road, despite protests and insults from other refugees.

'What an *Armleuchter!*'

'There is nothing that way, you idiot.'

Otto came over to the lead wagon. Elli saw his red face and bulging eyes as he puffed angrily past her wagon. Poor Papa, she thought, Otto is in a bad mood.

'The man lied.' Otto spoke to Rolf loud enough to be heard in the following wagons. 'No one else is using this goat track and we haven't enough people to flatten the snow. The horses will soon be exhausted.'

'Otto you are sixty-two, correct?' Rolf said quietly. '*Ja*, so what?'

'You heard what Elli was told. So, if we stay on the main road, you'd become the oldest soldier in the *Wehrmacht*. You really want to risk that?' Without a word, Otto went back to his wagon.

Luckily, after a few kilometres the road was snow free, except for an occasional drift. From the top of a sunbathed ridge, houses became visible in the fading light. There were no lights or smoke from chimneys. The town looked deserted. Hans stopped the convoy at the edge of the town and they gathered around a bullet-ridden welcome sign.

'Willkommen in Nickolsdorf—Einwohner 256'

'I don't think there are 256 people in this village,' Rolf said. 'In fact, I don't think there is even one.'

'My God! It is like Berthelsdorf,' Hanna said.

From their vantage point they had an overview of Nickolsdorf.

The town had the same layout as Berthelsdorf, around a central market place, but it was severely damaged. Many houses were totally, or partly, burnt out. Steam was rising from the burned timber, smelling smoky and acidic. The ruins were still warm.

The wagons moved into the market place.

'There must have been heavy fighting here,' Rolf said.

'But how is that possible? Back at the main road, *Wehrmacht* units were fleeing from the Russians, yet here, twenty kilometres further west, a village is already overrun by them?' Elli said.

'This didn't have to be the Russians, maybe it was Czech partisans. Whatever happened, this town is dead,' Rolf said.

'Not again!' Hanna gripped Rolf's arm. 'We can't stay here. There'll be bodies everywhere.'

'It's too late. We have to stay.'

But there were no bodies. All the houses were empty, except for broken furniture. The search party concluded that the town had been abandoned before it was destroyed. Rolf allocated the eight wagons to the three houses without broken doors. Rolf and Hanna, Ruth and her children, Elli and her children and Hans stayed together in one house.

'Rolf, behind the blacksmith's shop is a large stable, and it's intact. There is enough space for all our horses,' Manfred said. 'I'll stay with them.'

'Karla is not used to that,' Elli said. 'Behind our house is a small stable, just big enough for her.'

Rolf couldn't help smiling. 'And I guess you'll stay with her through the night?' Elli gave him an annoyed look and led Karla away.

There was an abundance of coal and wood beside the undamaged houses. As the families settled in, heat from the ovens and stoves spread through the houses. For the first time since they left Krummhübel Elli felt really warm and dry. No icy air coming through cracks in the wagon, no suffocating stink of mouldy canvas and body odours. She felt comfortable and safe, even though she knew it was an illusion. Still, they were lucky; their house had some intact furniture.

In the attic, they found four bunks with clean, dry mattresses. The children refused to sleep in the cold rooms, so they dragged the mattresses downstairs. In the comforting safety of the family, they soon fell asleep.

Hanna and Rolf disappeared when they found a large double bed, and Hans cuddled up between Elli's boys and immediately fell asleep.

Elli and Ruth stayed in the kitchen. The large *Kacheloven* covered an entire wall and had a sleeping bench wide enough for two people. At the sides of the heater were water inlets with ceramic pipes leading to other parts of the house. The tiles were little pieces of art, covered with tiny, glazed pictures. Elli and Ruth had fired the *Kacheloven* up when they moved into the house, and the water in the ceramic pipes and hollow tiles was now warm. The sleeping bench was just the right temperature to ensure a warm sleep.

'The people who lived here must have been well off. This *Kacheloven* would have cost an absolute fortune.' Elli stretched out on the bench enjoying its warmth. She closed her eyes, slowly dozing off, when a strange sound interrupted her. She looked up. Ruth was down on her knees, rubbing her hands over the floorboards, and banging with her fists.

'What are you doing?' Elli said. 'No I don't want to know. I want to sleep. Stop it.' Ruth stood up, a satisfied smile on her face.

'A trapdoor. That is a trapdoor.'

'What? I can't see a trapdoor. Come to bed, we have to get up early.'

'I tell you that is a trapdoor. Look here, these two cracks are not part of the floorboards,' Ruth said. 'And it's hollow, listen.' She banged on the floor.

'I can't hear anything different.'

'Wait a second, I'll get a knife.' After a few moments, she came back with one of her painting spatulas.

'That should do it.' She carefully followed the outlines of the cracks, which were at a right angle to the cracks between the floorboards.

'Got it!' she said triumphantly.

'Got what?' Ruth pushed the spatula into a crack and forced the board up. With a squeaking sound from its hinges, the trapdoor opened. 'I don't believe it. You are right.' It was a narrow opening, with a steep staircase leading into the dark room underneath.

'Get a light,' Ruth said. 'We have to see what's down there.'

The kerosene lantern Elli found illuminated the way. Carefully both climbed down.

'Unbelievable! Look at that, a wine cellar,' Elli said.

'Not just wine, have a look at that,' Ruth said. The large cellar had dozens of wine racks organised like bookshelves in a public library, and between the wine racks sides of pork and beef were hanging from the ceiling.

'My poor eyes can't believe what they are seeing,' Elli said. 'How is this possible?'

'Who cares? Let's get a couple of bottles. Tomorrow we'll share it with the others. No reason to wake them up now.'

Elli climbed down and took two dusty bottles from a rack. 'Are these any good?' She showed Ruth the bottles. 'Dürkheimer Nacktarsch, Auslese, 1921,' Ruth read.

'A naked arse from where?' Elli said.

'Dürkheim is a little wine town in Rhein-Hessen. The owner of this cellar must be rich. These two bottles alone cost a fortune and there are hundreds more here.'

'Let's hope it tastes all right. Naked arses from Dürkheim, strange name.'

The wine was sweet and heavy. After drinking a bottle each, they had difficulty getting up onto the oven's warm sleeping bench. Sleep came immediately.

In Elli's sleep there was the nagging feeling that someone was watching her. She bolted upright at the sound of a suppressed cough. In the semi-darkness of the room stood a figure. Elli screamed.

'What is it Elli?' Ruth said. Then she saw what Elli was scared about. 'Hans, you have to stop doing that! Go back to your bed.'

'That was Hans?' Elli said. I nearly wet myself. Does he do that often?'

'*Ja*, every night. At least he doesn't scream and cry anymore. God, when he did that for the first time in the middle of the night, I hit him with a frying pan. I didn't recognise him.'

'That poor man. I've never heard him speak since he came back. Does he talk to you?'

'No, but the children say he sometimes talks to them. Mind you, I've never heard it,' Ruth said.

'What is the matter with him?'

'I don't know. I only know what we all know. He came back from Dresden walking on the ice, dragging his dead wife along. He never talked about what happened to them in Dresden; he cries a lot.'

'Do you think he is gone?' Elli said.

'Meschugge? No, I don't think he is crazy, just grieving for Ulricke, and possibly blaming himself for her death. He'll come around, just needs some time.'

'Who needs some time?' Rolf came into the kitchen. 'I thought I heard a scream.' Then he saw Hans standing motionless in front of the boys. 'Hans, my friend. Was it you?'

'No, only me. I was startled by him,' Elli said.

'How are you, Hans?' Rolf said. Hans didn't react. Rolf gave Ruth a helpless look.

'He wants to go back to bed, but is too polite to roll the boys aside.'

Ruth rolled the boys over and gestured to Hans to lie down between them.

Elli was amazed when Hans climbed between the boys and lay down, like an obedient dog.

'My God, he is worse than I thought, Rolf said.

'He is just in shock. He'll come out of it,' Ruth said.

'That would be a miracle,' Rolf said. He turned around to go back upstairs.

'Wait Papa,' Elli said. 'We have some good news.' She told Rolf what they had found in the cellar. 'Want to have a look?'

'That is fantastic! We'd better do it in the morning or we'll wake everyone up.'

'How about that?' Elli said, after her father left. 'He couldn't wait to go back to bed. Must be really getting old.'

'On the contrary, dear sister.' Ruth was grinning from ear to ear. 'A few sides of beef and some wine can't compete with the warm body waiting for him upstairs.'

Chapter 21

'Let's have a look around before the others wake up,' Ruth said. 'Knowing Papa, he'll want us to leave immediately.'

They snuck out of the house. It was still dark, but glowing fingers of light broke through the clouds, announcing the sunrise.

'There must have been some fighting here,' Ruth said picking up a handful of empty cartridges.

'*Ja*, but I think that was after the people left. The houses are burnt out, but it's tidy and there are no bodies. I don't think the Russians would have bothered to bury anyone,' Elli said.

'Maybe. Let's have a look at the other houses.'

They found another house with an expensive *Kacheloven* and a well-stocked cellar, much like the house they had slept in. They knew where to look now, and they found similar hoards in two more cellars.

'This is not a normal village,' Elli said. 'After seven years of war, food shortages and starvation, it's impossible that an entire town could have such well stocked reserves.'

'I can't understand why they left it all behind.' 'Maybe they had more than they could transport.'

'Food is the only thing left of value. I can't imagine any reason for leaving it behind,' Ruth said.

'Maybe they didn't leave.' 'I don't get you.'

'Papa told me that Nickolsdorf is an old mining town.' 'So?'

'The silver mine closed years ago but the tunnels might be still usable.'

'They are hiding in the mines?'

'Why not? We did the same in Krummhübel. That hill over there looks like mine tailings. Let's have a look.'

Close to the rubble they found a destroyed engine house, and a narrow railway track leading into a tunnel. The entrance was open; its heavy iron gate had fallen down into the tunnel.

'That gate was forced open. Look, the hinges have been blasted off,' Elli said. They walked a few metres into the tunnel but stopped when they smelled a familiar stench and heard the buzzing. Ruth stumbled and had to support herself on Elli.

'Come, we have to get out of here.' Elli held her sister, as Ruth was violently sick.

'Oh God, you were right,' Ruth whispered. 'They didn't leave, the

Russians found them.' She stared at the dark shapes in front of them. 'Let's go. They're all dead.' They hurried out of the tunnel and moved away from the entrance. Elli rubbed handfuls of snow into her face, trying to prevent herself from vomiting.

'Those poor people thought they were safe. The Russians must have known about the mine,' Ruth said.

'Maybe the Russians thought the mine was still operating and they were looking for silver ingots. When they found people there, they killed them. But I think only a few people were in the mine.'

'What do you mean?' Ruth said. 'There were only a few bodies.'

'It's a mine. The others could be further down the tunnel.'

'*Ja*, maybe. If they are alive surely they would have come out by now. Let's go, I can't stand it anymore. We have to tell Papa, maybe he'll check it out.'

From the distance, they could see that the rest of the convoy was gathered around Rolf.

'We have to decide where we go from here,' Rolf was saying. 'We are in Saxony now and could settle here if we choose; however, the Russian troops will occupy this place soon. If we keep going on this road, we'll come to Brausenstein and from there it will be easier to continue to the West.'

No one said anything. Grey faces reflected apathy and fear back at Rolf. A few were talking to each other in low, hissing voices. Elli could pick up what they said and she felt a cold shiver. The crowd was uneasy, whispering mostly, a few loud words but nothing definite. Why didn't Rolf see that he was losing them? They were resenting his ideas and his solutions. She knew that she should tell them what they had found, the food and the town's population, but she stayed silent.

'Why should we go on Rolf? Germany is kaput. It's the same everywhere,' Otto shouted.

'The war will be over in a few months,' Rolf said. 'And you are right; the Russians will be everywhere. From Prussia to Berlin, Germany will be under Russian occupation.'

'So why go on?' Otto said again.

Rolf explained what he had heard on the BBC; the Allies intended to divide Germany between them.

'The Americans are in control of Bavaria and the English are intending to occupy Lower Saxony, Bremen, Hamburg, and Schleswig Holstein. It looks like Germany as a country won't exist after the war is over. The Russians already occupy Prussia, Pomerania, most of Silesia, and Saxony, and they're racing to Berlin. Any part of Germany occupied by the Russians will most likely stay in their control.

'Personally, I would prefer to live in the north, somewhere near Hamburg—under the English,' Rolf added.

'Hamburg? That is a thousand kilometres away,' Otto said. 'And why? The city is in ashes. There is nothing left. It's insane to go there.'

As the others listened to the interaction between Rolf and Otto, their restlessness increased.

'What is the matter with you, Rolf?' Erica Schlichte said. 'There is nothing left of us. We started with two hundred families and now there are eight. Do you want to kill the rest of us too?'

'His family is still alive, he hasn't lost anyone!' Elli recognised Manfred Johansen, Otto's friend. Apathy was gone; everyone was shouting and closing in on Rolf.

'It's all your fault.' Otto came closer, his bulky body towering over Rolf as if to physically push him down with his accusations. 'Without you we would be still safe in Krummhübel. We could have arranged something with the Polacks. We didn't have to leave.'

'You are a fool, Otto,' Rolf said, only slightly raising his voice as he stared back at Otto's red face. 'There was nothing to arrange with the Polish settlers. They were coming in and we had to leave. There was no space for two different populations. Can't you understand that? Go back and make arrangements with them; I'm sure you'll be welcomed with open arms. And if anyone else agrees with him, they can leave also.'

As he turned around to walk away, Otto grabbed a piece of split firewood.

He swung it up and smashed it down on Rolf.

The sharp edge of the wood sliced into Rolf's exposed neck and impacted with a sickening thud on his shoulder.

Blood sprayed in every direction, covering the assailant and bystanders. Rolf's face showed surprise, no pain. His mouth opened but no sound came out. He fell on his knees and then collapsed forward on his face. The snow turned red.

Silently the crowd stared at Otto and Rolf.

Suddenly, Hans appeared behind Otto, seized the bloodied wood Otto was still holding, raised it and smashed it forcefully down on Otto's head. Otto collapsed beside Rolf, convulsed a few times and was still.

'No!' Erica threw herself over her husband's body. 'Otto! Otto! Oh no, he is dead! You killed my Otto, you murderer.' She threw herself at Hans, hitting and scratching. Hans didn't even lift an arm to defend himself.

Hanna and Elli rushed over to Rolf's crumpled body. Ruth pushed Erica away from Hans. Erica stumbled and fell on her back.

'Take Otto and leave us.' Ruth turned to the others. 'Anyone who agrees with him can leave too.' Erica sobbed, holding her husband's body. Manfred Johansen's wife helped Erica up and led her away.

'He is dead, Hans,' Hubert said. 'You killed him.' Hans didn't reply. Grim faced, Hubert turned to the others. 'Otto was right. We'll be going back with Erica to the main road.'

Elli stood helplessly beside her father's fallen body as Hanna attended to his injuries. She heard Hanna say something about setting his broken bones, but mostly was just a blur. Hubert and Peter Schleswig carried away Otto's body and put it into Otto's wagon. Everyone looked on in disbelief as Hubert and his wife made Erica's, and their own, horses ready.

'We need help, everyone!' The remaining people turned to Hanna. 'He is badly hurt. We'll have to get him back inside the house. I need six people to lift him and carry him in.'

Hanna directed the volunteers to carry Rolf inside carefully. There was a hush, the crowd shamefaced as they stared at Rolf being carried through the door.

The shrill squeaking sound from snow compacting under wheels startled them. All heads turned towards the sound as Otto and Hubert's wagons pulled out of the market place and disappeared down the road.

Elli went inside. Her father looked dreadful. His breathing was barely noticeable. He is dying, my father is dying, she thought. Fear shook her. Her father, the most stable person in her life, was dying. She was choking on her tears and felt unable to breathe.

'Hanna is looking after him. I'll try to help her without getting in the way. She knows what she is doing,' Ruth said. 'Manfred has a fire going at the stable. He has hoarded the best coffee. Go and get some. And talk to Karla. I'll join you soon.'

Outside people were still standing around, quietly talking to each other.

'How is your father, Elli?' a woman said.

'He is dying,' she said, and walked off to the stable.

Ruth was right. She felt useless inside. Others had the same idea, or perhaps they had heard that Manfred had coffee, real coffee. She joined the group gathered around the fire and gratefully accepted the cup Manfred pressed into her hands. No one said anything, concentrating on their hot drinks. Occasionally someone would go into the stable to be with the horses.

When Elli went to her, Karla greeted her with a friendly snort. The horse seemed to feel Elli's sadness as she constantly nudged her, keeping her attention. Elli felt more in control when she returned to the fire. Ruth came out of the house and joined her.

'How is he?'

'Alive. Hanna is still busy and I'm not needed. Where is the coffee Manfred? I hope you saved some for me.'

Hours passed before Hanna came out, pale, shaking, and unsuccessfully trying to close her torn cardigan.

'Is he...?' Elli could hardly bear to look in Hanna's eyes. 'No, it looked worse than it is. He is tough and has a good

chance.' She held her cold hands close to the fire. It was a few moments before Elli realised the spots on Hanna's hands were blood.

'Oh God, Hanna, your hands. Wait a minute, the water should be warm now.'

'He has a broken collarbone and he's lost a lot of blood. He passed out when I reset his collarbone, just as well. I had to change his clothes. They were soaked with blood. I think he'll make it.'

Hanna watched passively as Elli submerged her hands in a bowl of hot water.

'Too hot?'

'I don't feel anything. Could be hotter,' Hanna said, then yelped. 'Let me go! It's burning like fire.' Elli did not let go. 'Elli, please let go!' '*Liebling*, the water is not that hot. You have to keep your hands in it. The blood has to flow again.' Hanna whimpered but kept her hands in the bowl. The water had turned red from Rolf's blood.

'Hanna you are like a doctor,' Ruth tried to get her attention away from the pain. 'How do you know all that?'

'My father was a very busy country doctor and my mother was his nurse. I learned from them.'

'Why didn't they draft you? Nurses are needed everywhere.' 'My father trained me. I didn't have official training, so they didn't know.'

'Thank you. We're lucky to have you. Papa is especially lucky to have you, not only because of your powers of healing,' Elli said.

Hanna blushed. 'Thanks Elli. He is a very dear man. I'm lucky to have met him. Your boys are looking after him now. He is asleep but they refused to leave their *Opa*.'

Back at the house, the children were waiting anxiously for Elli. 'What happened to *Opa*?' Anna said, her eyes wide and red from crying. 'Aunty Ruth and Hanna wouldn't tell us anything. They dragged *Opa* to his bed. He was bleeding and they closed the door.'

'*Opa* had an argument with someone who got very angry with him. He was hurt but Hanna looked after him. He'll be fine, just grumpy for a while.'

'That's okay. He's always grumpy anyway. Will he really be all right?'

'Yes, he will.' Elli smiled at her daughter. 'You have to go to bed now. Tomorrow we have to get up early.' Ruth came out of Rolf's room. 'Any change?'

'He is asleep. Hanna is fussing around but the morphine she gave him is working.'

'Morphine, where did she get that from?'

'I don't know, but she certainly is well supplied. After she set his shoulder, she immobilised it with something like plaster. That woman is amazing. Papa's comfortable and it looks like he'll be fine, just a bit handicapped for a while.'

'Poor Papa.'

'*Ja*, poor Papa, but also lucky Papa. If not for Hanna he really would be dead,' Ruth said.' My God, I totally forgot Hans. Where is he?'

'Uncle Hans is sleeping. He came back a while ago, went into the bedroom, lay down, and fell asleep,' Anna said. 'He didn't say anything, but he looked strange Mama.'

'And he's been asleep the whole time?' Ruth said. 'Yes Aunty.'

'That's probably for the best,' Elli said. 'We'll see how he is tomorrow.'

After the children were asleep, Elli and Ruth settled down on the *Kacheloven* bench.

It was pitch dark when Elli woke up. She needed a few moments before she realised what had aroused her. The house vibrated; there were loud clanking noises and shrill squeaks. Every muscle in her body tightened. She knew those sounds—tanks. The Russians had come back.

She felt paralysed with fear. Finally, she dragged herself to the window.

A column of tanks and armoured vehicles was passing the house. The building shook each time a tank came close. She dared to peek for only a few seconds each time before she crouched back on the floor. The leading vehicle drove into the marketplace and stopped. The following tanks and armoured personnel carriers lined up alongside the command vehicle.

Someone shouted.

A magnesium torch unexpectedly bathed the market place in bright, flickering light. Elli saw the markings on the command vehicle.

It was a single digit, '1', followed by the SS runes. Fear squeezed her stomach into a tight ball. She had seen that vehicle before, with her father. They were not Russians; they were the SS group that was stranded when Rolf had organised the destruction of the bridge in Bohemia.

'Ruth, wake up,' she whispered. 'They've followed us.' It was silent for a moment before her sister whispered back.

'What? Who followed us?'

'The SS convoy we thought we got rid of at the bridge in Bohemia. They're here.'

'They're here? Where?' 'Outside, in front of the house.'

Chapter 22

'What are they doing here? We're behind the front lines. The Russians came through here ages ago,' Elli said.

'You're right. What are they doing here?'

'It must have something to do with the SS General,' Elli said. 'What SS General?'

'Remember, from the bridge?' 'Remember what?'

'Papa saw an SS General standing beside a civilian.'

'*Ja*, I remember. He was with someone who looked like a Nazi official.'

'An SS General is about as high as they come. They don't travel in little convoys and play host to Nazi officials. They must be here for another reason.'

'What has it to do with us?' Ruth said.

'*Schwester*, you are the one who had such a wonderful relationship with the SS. Don't you think that it is rather unusual to have an SS General here, in the middle of nothing, travelling in a small convoy? A whole tank division would have been more appropriate.'

'Sometimes you can be very nasty.' Ruth gave her sister an angry look.

'You don't have to rub it in.'

'Sorry, I just tried to make a point. It really is strange.'

'Come on, Germany is falling apart and everyone, including SS Generals are ducking for cover. What's strange about it? I'm surprised that we haven't stumbled over the *Führer* himself.' Ruth grinned and gave Elli a kiss. 'Don't worry about your strange General. Besides, I don't think there are any tank divisions left. They are just running away.'

'Maybe, but why are they rounding us up? With the loaded wagons in the market place, they know that we are not from here.'

'*Ja*, something is wrong.'

'Wrong? I think it's more sinister. Somehow, they were overrun or they passed by the front without being detected. If they want to get back into the *Wehrmacht* controlled area, they are doing it in a strange way,' Elli said.

'Strange how?'

'The Russians are hunting SS and this group is prancing around as if they haven't heard what the Russians would do to them.'

The SS troops were forming into small groups. An officer climbed on top of the command vehicle. Someone handed him a megaphone.

'*Achtung, Achtung!* All people in the village are ordered to assemble in the market place. You have nothing to fear. This is only a registration of civilians in the area. However, anyone found hiding will be severely punished. You have ten minutes to follow this order. I repeat, you have ten minutes to assemble in the market place.' At the end of the announcement, he shouted a sharp command at the search groups. The SS soldiers spread out in front of the houses—and waited.

'We're not going out!' Elli said.

'Didn't you hear? If they find us, they'll shoot us on the spot,' Ruth said.

'If they find us.'

'Of course they'll find us. There is nowhere to hide.' 'The cellar. We'll hide in the cellar.'

'But what if they find us there? They'll shoot us.'

'Why would you believe in an SS commando registering civilians? I've never heard such rubbish,' Elli said. Ruth didn't reply.

Crouching down Elli peeked over the window sill. From her vantage point, she could see the entire market place. Military vehicles formed a ring around the people slowly assembling in the centre. The SS officer still stood on top of the command vehicle. The eerie light of the flickering torches distorted his uniform and face and made it impossible to identify his rank but he sounded like he was in charge.

'Men to the left and women and children to the right. Scharführer, you and your men make sure no one is hiding in the houses. If you find anyone, shoot them.'

The SS herded people into groups and when two men tried to break way, they were brutally clubbed with gun butts. Suddenly, from one of the houses, Elli heard shots.

'They shot someone,' Elli said. 'Quick, into the cellar.'

Ruth did not move. Her face, covered with sweat, reflected the flickering light from the market place. Her voice trembled. 'They'll kill us. I'm scared.'

Elli took a handkerchief and wiped Ruth's face.

'So am I, *Liebling*. We'll be safe in the cellar. It's deep and well hidden. They won't find us there. Get the others.'

'We are here.' Hanna supported Rolf down the staircase. 'We were listening.'

Hans came in and opened the trapdoor to the cellar. Only the children slept on. Even when Elli and Ruth hastily bundled them into the cellar they didn't really wake up. Only Anna could raise a complaint.

'I don't want to go into that hole.'

'I found some toys down there. You can sleep there tonight and play with the toys tomorrow.'

'Girls' toys?'

'Girls' toys.'

Without further protest, Anna climbed down the staircase and settled between the wine racks with her brothers. The hatch was too narrow for the mattresses, so they snuggled into their bed coverings. Hans, silent as always, climbed down without hesitation.

'Now you, Papa.' Elli guided her father to the staircase. Rolf gave a look and turned away. 'I can't get down there.' 'No choice, Papa. You have to,' Elli insisted.

The staircase was too steep for him to use without holding on to the railing and that was impossible with his injured shoulder. Eventually, they lowered him down like a sack of potatoes. Elli and

Ruth held his good arm, as Hanna guided him from below. It was painful and slow.

'Why don't you just push me down the staircase, can't hurt any more than this.'

'Good idea,' Elli said, 'but too noisy.'

'Schnell, schnell they are coming,' Ruth urged, and she let go of her father.

Luckily, he was nearly at the bottom. Elli slid down the staircase and suppressed his cries by pressing his face against her as they pulled him away from the staircase. Hanna climbed back up and pulled the cover over the staircase, gently, quietly.

'Sorry Papa.' Ruth caressed his face. 'I didn't mean to hurt you but they're in the house.'

'Would have been much more fun to ride the whole staircase instead of just two steps,' Rolf said with the pain in his face betraying him.

'Next time Papa.'

Elli went to the staircase and climbed up, cautiously.

'Are you crazy?' Ruth's voice sounded like the sharp breath of a steam engine.

'What are you doing? They'll hear you.'

'I don't think so. The boards are very solid. Watch,' Elli said quietly and began systematically slapping her flat hand against the hatch. It made hardly any sound, but dirt rained down from the cracks between the boards.

'Why are you doing that?'

'To rattle dirt back into the cracks,' Elli said. 'Why?'

'The house is pretty dark. If dirt is back in the cracks the hatch will be harder to see.'

Moments later they heard a door opening and movement above them.

Each footstep flexed a floorboard causing dirt to sprinkle down. Then they heard footsteps from the opposite direction.

The footsteps stopped, right above them. Elli didn't breathe. She wanted to scream.

Muffled voices, footsteps again and finally, the slamming of a door.

'It worked. They've gone,' Ruth said, her voice just audible. 'Quiet! He's coming back.'

Creaking sounds from the front door, footsteps, floorboards bending under the pressure.

Slowly, someone moved through the house.

Each time the footsteps stopped, there was silence for a second, followed by sharp stamping sounds.

'The Schwein is checking for trapdoors.' Elli rushed to the stairs, climbed up and gently pushed her back against the trapdoor.

'*Verrücktes Weib*! Crazy woman! What are you doing?' Elli saw her sister staring at her in disbelief.

'A trapdoor sounds hollow.' 'What?'

'Quiet! You'll see.'

The footsteps stopped above her, followed by a sharp stomp. The vibration from the board travelled through her body. She lost her balance and fell down the staircase into Ruth's arms.

'Got you, little sister. That was brilliant. He is going.'

In the feeble light of the kerosene lantern Elli saw the wide-open eyes of the others.

There was the sound of a door being slammed. Silence!

'Well done, Elli.' Rolf said through clenched teeth as large globules of perspiration ran down his pained face. 'That trick would never have occurred to me. Where did you get the idea from?'

'It's your doing, dear father.' 'What do you mean?'

'Remember the manhole in the kitchen where Mama stored her conserves?'

'Yes, but...'

'Well, you never fixed the handle. With no handle and dirt in the cracks it was sometimes hard to find. You had to stomp around and find it by ear.' Rolf shook his head in astonishment.

'*Wunderbahr*!' He winced in pain. 'I saved our arses by not having done a maintenance job.'

They huddled under their blankets and waited. Elli felt the trembling of the children decreasing as they became drowsy. She envied them as she listened. The slightest creaks, the rustling of mice, seemed amplified and her body reacted like a tight string, vibrating to the slightest sound.

The kerosene lantern flickered one last time and died. It was pitch dark. With the light gone other sensations and irritations became overbearing: pungent body odour and itches. She tried to ignore the itching but finally gave in. Ah! Relief! But only for a few seconds and then it was back with a vengeance. She scratched again. An annoyed grump from her daughter forced her to stop.

We all need a good bath, she thought. Her last hot bath was a lifetime ago. Hot water up to her chin and steam, so thick she couldn't see the other end of the bathtub, melting everything away as she floated in perfumed bliss. Perfume? She jerked back to full alertness. There was a strange smell in the cellar.

'Do we have another light?' Elli said.

Hanna answered. 'I think I saw a couple of lanterns on the ceiling where the hams are hanging.'

Elli unwrapped herself, despite the protests from her children, and stumbled through the darkness. Guided by the salty smell of the curing hams, she found a lantern. She fumbled for her matches, found them, and lit it. The light was so strong it hurt her eyes. When they adjusted, she thought the strange smell had disappeared, until she realised the stink of the kerosene lantern had replaced it.

The room was huge and all eyes were watching her.

'This cellar must be as big as the whole house. I'll have a look around.'

'I'll come too,' Ruth said.

They walked through the storage racks towards the other side of the cellar.

'Look! There, at the other end. Doors!' Elli said.

They found a coalbunker, a potato store and in a third room, furniture. There were wardrobes, chairs, a large table, and bunk beds. Elli had a closer look and pulled back in shock.

'People! They are all dead.' She reeled back. 'Close the door. Don't let the children see them.'

In one of the beds a man and a woman held each other in death. In each of the other three beds were the bodies of two children, the youngest one not older than two, the oldest about sixteen.

'They must have died a while ago.' Elli found the strength to have a closer look. 'Look, there is dust everywhere, even on their faces. The cold has slowed the decay. Still, they smell. We have to bury them.' The look on Ruth's face was total astonishment.

'Elli, there are eight corpses here. Doesn't that horrify you?'

'It does but we have no time to deal with that now, unless we want to join them.'

'Look at them, they look so peaceful, as if they all died in their sleep,' Ruth said. Elli bent over a child's body. There was something there, a smell of bitter almonds.

'They were poisoned. Cyanide!'

The bodies of the parents were not so peaceful. The woman's face was distorted and her eyes wide open. The man had shot himself through the mouth. The top of his head was blown off, spilling his brains over the pillow. On his chest was a golden Nazi party brooch indicating a high- ranking party official. It was obvious that the couple had committed suicide after they killed their children. The pained face of the dead woman showed that death hadn't come easily for her.

'Why would they kill their children and then themselves?' Ruth said.

'I guess they thought the Russians would kill them in a much more horrible way,' Elli said. 'We have to move them. I'll tell the others.'

Without disturbing the children or Rolf she told Hanna and Hans what they had found.

'I'll stay with Rolf and the children,' Hanna said calmly. 'Hans can help you.'

They rolled the bodies into blankets, dragged them one by one to the coalbunker, and covered them with coal. Elli wasn't upset burying the adults. She reasoned that the Nazi official was a coward who had probably committed many atrocities in the name of the *Führer*, so he deserved this end. But when she wrapped the bodies of the children, her hands were shaking so much that she nearly dropped the sad bundle of the smallest one. Hans gently moved her aside and buried the children himself, rejecting any help from Ruth.

The climate in the cellar had helped preserve the bodies. They had just begun to putrefy and were easy to move. The thick clothes had absorbed most of the moisture as the bodies deteriorated, leaving the mattresses only slightly stained. Elli and Hans turned the mattresses over and quietly, without waking them up, transported the sleeping children into the bunks. They made no attempt to move Rolf. Despite lying on the hard ground the morphine haze, and Hanna, kept him comfortable. Hans went back to his blanket and immediately fell asleep again. Ruth took two bottles of wine from the racks.

'Hanna, have a look in Papa's coat pocket. His pocket knife has a corkscrew attachment.'

'Found it.'

They drank quietly.

'The parents must have found out what happened to the others in the village,' Elli said. 'I don't want to think about what the Russians did to those people in the mine.'

'I doubt if this man was the only high ranking Nazi in the village. They were too well off here. It was probably a Nazi party town, some kind of hideaway, a rural retreat,' Ruth said.

'Rubbish,' Hanna said. 'Why would the SS round up their own people? I mean they would know if this was a Nazi place.'

'*Ja*, but they saw our wagons. They knew there were refugees here,' Elli said.

Their speech became increasingly blurred, as the wine smothered everything in a comfortable haze. They fell asleep.

It was dark when Elli woke up. The kerosene lanterns were out. She found some matches and managed to start one of the lanterns again. Her watch told her that only one hour had passed, but then she realised it had stopped. She would have to remember to wind it up from time to time.

She walked into the room where the children slept and climbed into Anna's bunk. The warmth and regular breathing of her daughter helped her to relax. Sleep came immediately.

'Elli, wake up. Wake up,' she heard Ruth say.

'Why? It's still dark.' She tried to roll over but Ruth stopped her. 'It's not dark anymore, only in this hole. Look, light is coming through the cracks. It's daytime. Come on, we have to see what's going on.'

Hanna was awake, but Rolf, Hans, and the children were still sound asleep. Elli moved carefully up the staircase, trying not to make any creaks. The trapdoor lifted without any problems. Ruth was right; it was daytime. Bright sunshine was coming through the windows. Quietly the three women moved into the house.

'Oh, shit,' Elli said. 'What is it?'

'They are still here. Have a look.'

The military vehicles were abandoned in the market place, but there was no one around. No SS soldiers and no refugees. Only a few horses and dogs were in sight. A sudden movement stopped Elli's breathing. She needed a few moments to realise that her horse was peering at her through the window.

'*Scheiss Gaul*! Stupid horse, you nearly gave me a heart attack.' Fresh snow covered the market place. There were no vehicle tracks or footprints. The snow cover was untouched except for a few hoof prints. Suddenly, the peal of a bell broke the silence. The sisters jumped into each other's arms.

'What was that?' Seven more strokes answered Ruth.

'It's only the church bell. It's eight o'clock.' Elli felt relieved. A little bit of normality had returned and she felt safer.

'They must have left during the night. There are no footprints or vehicle tracks in the fresh snow.'

Carefully, they moved outside. It was quiet. The air was cold and smelt of snow. A sloshing, scraping sound froze them in their tracks, until they realized it was dislodged snow slipping down the steeple roofs. The village was totally deserted, the military vehicles abandoned.

'Look, the wagons are gone,' Ruth cried out.

The arrangement of the houses around the circular marketplace allowed them to see each house. Only Elli's wagon was still there.

'They have left their vehicles and taken our people and the wagons.' Elli said. 'Maybe they couldn't catch Karla.'

'They didn't take them away. They killed them.' Ruth said, pointing to a small pool of blood.

'*SS Tiere*! Animals! They murdered them!' Elli pushed the snow away from around the blood and uncovered a thin line of blood leading to a small mound in the snow. She hesitated but then dug into the snow.

'The dog we found in Berthelsdorf. Someone shot the poor thing.' Elli said. 'So where are our people?'

'Let's look in the houses where the SS stayed.'

'Why? To find the same as in Berthelsdorf? They've murdered them. I don't want to find any more dead bodies.' Elli dropped on her knees beside the dog, her body shaking violently as she stroked its frozen body.

'*Schwesterlein*, maybe they are alive. Maybe they have taken them away to question them.'

'Can't you see what happened here? They've have taken our people away to murder them. Can't you see that?' Elli's anger at her sister increased and she had difficulty formulating the words between her sobbing.

'But why would they take them away? In Berthelsdorf, they killed the people in the houses and left them there. Why the effort to take them away?' Ruth said.

'I don't know why. I don't know how the bloody SS works. That's your area.' Ruth looked at her. 'Please stop that, Elli.'

'I don't want to go into these houses.'

'Then I'll go on my own.' Ruth said and walked off. Elli watched her go into the nearest house. After a few minutes, Ruth reappeared, shook her head at Elli and walked to the next house.

'Wait, I'll come too.'

They entered the house together. It was dark, with only diffused light through the heavy brocade curtains. A few tossed-over chairs were on the ground but otherwise the place looked tidy. On the dining room table, everything was laid out for a large family meal. The chunky goulash, the potatoes and the red cabbage in the Meissen porcelain bowls were frozen. Molten wax covered the silver candlesticks. After the people left, the candles had continued to shine their light on the deserted table, until they were spent. In the kitchen, a Jena glass bowl with cream-covered fruits was ready to be served with a bottle of champagne. Only the people were missing.

'It looks like the people who lived here left without any panic.' Ruth said.

'*Ja*, but they left in a hurry. Maybe you are right and they didn't murder them, but where are they?'

Chapter 23

Rolf's face was pale, nearly as white as the bandages around his neck and shoulder. He leant heavily on Hanna but looked alert.

'How are you Papa?' Elli said.

'Stiff, hurting, can't move my arm, can't turn my head, but otherwise I'm fine.' His voice creaked like rusty hinges but it came out strong. Elli was surprised that he could speak at all considering the extensive bruising, which seemed to cover everywhere not hidden by bandages. The slightest head movement caused visible spasms from his shoulder to his arm and head.

'Papa has the constitution of an ox,' Ruth said. 'A bashing with a piece of timber won't stop you. Right, Papa?' Rolf's smile ended in a painful grimace.

'What happened? I remember Otto coming at me with a wooden club and then—nothing. I also vaguely recall being pushed down a staircase, but that's it.'

Elli told him everything that had happened since Otto Schlichte attacked him. Rolf listened, shaking his head from time to time. Pain distracted him until he heard the other refugees were gone.

'Where is Otto now?'

'He is...' Elli stopped. Hans sat down beside Rolf. 'I killed him,' Hans said.

Rolf looked at him in disbelief. He pushed himself up so that he was eye level with Hans.

'You killed him? Did he attack you too?' 'No. It was over before he had a chance.'

'My old friend, I never thought that you would be able to do something like that,' Rolf said.

'Neither did I. Something snapped when he stood there with the bloodied club and said that you deserved it.'

'I don't know what to say. Otto was basically a good man. I saw trouble coming, but I thought that we would clash verbally, not something like that.' His voice became fainter. 'Where is Erica?'

'She left with the Schleswigs and the Johansens.'

'My God, why didn't anyone stop them?' No one said anything as Rolf looked from one to the other. 'Now we are the only ones left.' He cleared his voice and continued through clenched teeth. 'And had it not been for your fast thinking, they would have taken us too. But why have the SS taken our people?'

'Maybe as a cover,' Elli said. 'As a cover from what?' 'Russians.'

'I can't imagine a worse disguise. They wouldn't be able to control so many people, especially with children, all the time.'

'The SS have ways to control people,' Ruth said.

'Yes, but SS men are young. Any Russian patrol would find it suspicious that there are young men of fighting age in a group of refugees.'

'Of course! You are right,' Ruth said. 'They would never pass as refugees. Even in civilian clothes they wouldn't look like refugees.'

'And the Russians will check any man aged between twenty and fifty for the SS tattoo,' Elli said.

'I can't imagine that they are so stupid as to forget that.' 'So why did they take them?' Elli said.

'It must have something to do with that civilian,' Rolf said. 'Maybe someone important enough to take such a risk. In any case we have to get out of here.'

'Why? This place is deserted and has everything we need,' Elli said. going.'

'This place is evil. It has twice lost its population. We have to get Elli wanted to argue her point but gave in when she saw the perspiration running down his face, steaming in the cold morning air as he desperately held on to Hanna.

'Papa, do you want something for the pain?' Elli said.

'Later. *Danke*.' A slight smile lit his face. 'Hanna will give me some of her wonder juice later.' His voice trailed off in a rasping cough but came back a moment later. 'There is only one direction we can take and that is along the Czech border. The other direction leads straight back to the Elbe, and Dresden. If we travel along the border for about twenty kilometres, we'll come to Giesing. From there we can make it to Leipzig.'

'The Czech border again?' Ruth said. 'Is there no other way?' 'We can't get too close to Dresden. All the roads will be crowded with refugees and military convoys. It's too dangerous.'

Elli's and Hanna's wagons, which had been sheltered in the barn with the horses, were the only ones left.

'Why didn't they take ours too?' Ruth said. They walked deeper into the barn. All the stables were open and the horses gone.

'Because Manfred had taken the wheels off, look.' Elli pointed to her wagon; it was supported on logs with the left front wheel removed.

'He told me that both wagons had cracked wheel spokes and he was going to repair them. The SS was obviously in too much of a hurry to let him complete the repairs.'

'They have three wagons then. There are at least ten SS men, and all our people if they are still alive. That will make the wagons awfully crowded,' Ruth said.

'Let me get the figures straight,' Rolf said. 'There were forty-one of us left. Otto dead, and the Schleswig, Johansson and Erica Schlichte gone, that makes thirty-seven; minus the ten of us leaves twenty-seven people abducted; twelve adults and fifteen children. You are right, if there are ten or more SS, the three wagons are very crowded.'

Hans, Elli and Ruth managed to get the wheels back on the wagons.

'Manfred hadn't finished fixing the spoke on my wheel. I hope it'll last,' Elli said.

Beside Karla, one other horse had been left behind. By midday they had finished their preparations and Rolf insisted on immediate departure. Hanna objected.

'The wagons have no suspension. They're not coaches, they're hay wagons. Every bump in the road will hurt you. You are already in pain and travelling in one of these wagons will be hell. We have to wait until you are better.'

'We can't wait. We'll be killed here. I'm fine. A bit of rattling is nothing. Let's get on with it.'

'We'll put him on one of the mattresses, that should make it more comfortable,' Elli said.

'I don't need a mattress. Will you two stop fussing about me? I'm fine,' he growled. Elli gave him a sharp look.

'Sure you are. It's the mattress or staying, Papa.'

Hanna's smile broadened but she didn't speak. Rolf looked surprised. He opened his mouth to say something but swallowed it down and smiled.

'You win. Tie me to the mattress.'

Before they left, Elli and Ruth inspected the deserted SS vehicles. All of them were hybrid tanks and trucks, with tyres at the front and chain-drives at the rear. There were no personal belongings, papers, or anything else left by the previous occupants.

Except in the last one. Elli lowered herself through the top hatch. This vehicle was different. No benches, just two swivel seats mounted opposite destroyed radio equipment. She climbed to the front, into the driver's compartment. There was no steering wheel, just two pedals and two big handles on each side of the driver's seat. Above was a small hatch, barely big enough for a lookout. Curious, Elli climbed on the driver's seat and poked her head through the opening. On each side of the hatch were narrow metal shields. Perhaps, to give the driver some protection from the weather and whatever else might hit his face. On one shield someone had stuck a small paper square. It was a road map.

'Ruth, Ruth! I found something. It looks like a map.' Someone touched her from behind. Elli pulled her head back and banged her neck against the edge of the hatch.

'*Scheisse*! That hurts. You didn't have to sneak up on me. I nearly had a heart attack.'

'What did you find?'

'A map, in there,' she said, pointing up at the hatch.

Ruth found the map and carefully opened it. It was very detailed, but didn't make any sense to them. Rolf was irritable when they woke him, but he became almost cheerful when he saw the map.

'That's a logistics map. Most of the symbols don't make any sense to me, unfortunately. But look here, that must be this town. It's the last one ticked off.' All three were staring at the small map. Finally, Elli could see what her father was getting at.

'That large marker, I assume, is Dresden, *ja*?'

'*Ja*, that's right, and this one must be Nickolsdorf, where we are now and if you follow that line, which is this road, I think they had the same idea as us.'

'As us? What idea?' Elli said.

'They'll move along the Czech border and then cross over to Leipzig.'

'Oh God! That would mean they are moving ahead of us,' Ruth said.

'Travelling with our people will slow them down. We could catch up,' Rolf said.

'Catch up? Why? You want us to free them? Are you totally mad?' Elli said. 'I think that we should travel in any other direction but where they are going.'

'We could stay behind at a safe distance. They wouldn't expect anyone to be following them, especially not a few refugees.'

'But why?' Elli's voice was getting shrill. 'Maybe they'll cover their rear and see that we are following them.'

'*Ja*, that is possible, but we are just another bunch of refugees travelling in the same direction. I think we could get away with it.'

'But why, Papa?' Elli said. 'Even if our people are with them, what could we do? It's suicidal. They would kill us.'

'I don't think we have much choice. We have to find out what happened to our people.'

'This is nonsense! Three women, children, and two old men against a group of SS soldiers? They'll kill us.'

'Elli, *Liebling*, come on,' Ruth pleaded. 'Papa is right, we have to find out what happened.'

'You are both mad. Think of our children. Do you really want to expose them to such a stupid act? And my dear Papa—have you already forgotten that none of the cowards you want to rescue lifted so much as a little finger when Schlichte tried to kill you?'

'I know, I know, but we can't just walk away from them,' Rolf said.

Hanna listened and did not say anything until there was a break. 'Elli, maybe there is nothing we can do, and yes, we will endanger ourselves. But we have to find out, or for the rest of our lives we will live with the guilt of not having tried. I would have great difficulty with that.'

Elli wanted to scream at her, telling Hanna that she had no more children to lose and that it was easy for her to make such a decision, but Hanna was right. They had to find out.

'Elli, I feel scared too,' Ruth said. 'But if we walk away from this, how would we justify it later to the children?'

'*Ja*, if we survive it, and if not, we won't have to justify anything, anyway.'

Elli knew she had lost the argument, not against the others but herself.

They finally agreed to follow the SS, at a safe distance.

'What will happen if we have to do something? Elli said to Rolf.

'Look at us. Do you really think that we would be able to intervene? You are fantasising.'

'I guess that depends on the situation,' Rolf said with a thin smile. 'I trust that one of us will come up with an idea.'

They followed the narrow road. The tracks of the three wagons were still visible ahead of them.

'Look what I found, Mama.' Herman called out. Proudly he presented his discovery, a squashed can with some smelly pieces of fish still sticking to it.

'Where did you find that?' Elli said. 'There, at the side of the road.'

Elli showed the crumbled can to Ruth. 'Have a look at that. They aren't far ahead.'

'You conclude that from smelling an empty sardine can?' Ruth said.

'It's not an empty sardine can, it's an empty anchovy can.'

'Oh, apologies for my underdeveloped sense of smell,' Ruth said, her voice dripping with sarcasm. 'Sardines or anchovies, so what?' 'French anchovies. They are impossible to get unless you have access to imported food like the SS, or what we found in Berthelsdorf, which was SS loot. This tin is most likely from our wagons.'

The weather started to worsen. Dark snow clouds were moving in and the wind was picking up.

'We have to find shelter, a hell of a snowstorm is coming up,' Elli said. 'Look, we should be close to the next place marked on this map. I hope it's a town and not something else.'

The darkness intensified very quickly. Ten minutes later, Elli sat up, alert. 'I can see something. Look, it must be the village Papa talked about. What did he call it?'

'Brausenstein.' Ruth said. 'Look, there, on the other side of the road.' She was right, there was a signpost. 'Brausenstein *170 Einwohner*'—170 inhabitants. A few houses came into view, on both sides of the road. All seemed deserted. There were no lights, no fires, and no people. They stopped at a house with a large barn beside it. Both wagons fitted comfortably into the cavernous building. They rubbed the horses down and let them start on the hay stored there.

'The house has been cleaned out. They took everything. Everything, but for some broken furniture and several mattresses,' Hans said when he came back. 'There is a large cellar but it's empty except for wood and coal.'

'Let's stay in the barn. There is plenty of hay to keep us warm. At least we are out of the weather,' Elli said.

The wind grew stronger. Whenever a gust hit the barn the timber creaked and groaned. Suddenly there was a flapping sound in the darkness. As Elli held the lantern high a shadow sailed past her. She nearly dropped the lantern.

'What was that?' She was scared. Her voice was a hoarse whisper. 'Look, ghosts.' She pointed to the shadows gliding through the darkness. Then she remembered where she had heard the sound before. 'No, it's pigeons! We must have scared them.'

'We scared them?' Ruth said. 'The filthy things scared me to death. Hans, why don't you have a look? Hans!'

Hans was asleep, or pretended to be, and Ruth gave up.

It was getting colder and snow was coming in the cracks between the floorboards. Elli shivered; the white powdery stuff seemed to be alive. It entered through the narrowest holes in the boards. Nothing seemed to stop it.

They moved the horses into a tight space between two large hay bales and covered them with blankets.

'It's getting too cold here. Let's go into the house,' Elli said.

'I'll stay here with Rolf,' Hanna said. 'He is still asleep and if we stay in our wagon, we'll be fine. We have enough blankets. I think the horses will also be happier if someone stays. *Ja*?'

Getting everyone to the house, which was only a few metres away, was more difficult than Elli anticipated.

'Come on, move, children. Hans hold on to them, *schnell, schnell*.'

The children started to cry when the icy wind hit them. Sharp ice particles, not snow, hit their faces. Elli could barely open her eyes and desperately tried to see something through the scarf she had wrapped around her head. When she took it off the cold froze the moisture in her nostrils and stuck them closed. She exploded into a coughing fit when she tried to breathe the icy air through her mouth. Finally, they made it.

'That was a marvellous idea, sister,' Ruth said, in between spitting and coughing.

'Whoa! Think how close the barn is to the house, yet we nearly didn't make it! That's unbelievable! The Russians must have brought their Siberian weather with them. It must be colder than minus twenty,' Elli said.

'Thank God we found shelter. The horses would have frozen to death if that had hit us in the open.'

'Not only the horses,' Elli said.

The house was solid and windproof. There were enough mattresses for all of them and soon the children and Hans were asleep. There was a fireplace in the room where they bedded down, and Elli and Ruth used broken furniture and coal from the cellar to start a roaring fire.

'It's a shame there isn't a supply of food and wine like in the last cellar,' Elli said. 'A nice glass or two of that wine would do me well.'

'I have something better,' Ruth said, opening her coat and proudly presenting a bottle of cognac to her sister.

'You are an angel, an alcoholic angel but so what! Where did you get that?'

'A fiercely guarded leftover from the place of the flies,' Ruth said.
'Flies? You mean, you kept this since Berthelsdorf?'

'*Ja*. Still interested?'

'I'm too cold to care. The only thing I'm thinking about is that at least it was warm then. Terrible, isn't it?'

'Here, have a sip,' Ruth said.

Chapter 24

The howling of the wind went on through the night. Curled under their blankets they waited for daylight. The house creaked and moaned like an animal in pain as the wind continued its onslaught, a frustrated monster trying to shake them out of their hideout. Sometimes its fury increased and Elli's heart stopped, fearing the roof would be ripped off and the monster would suck them out; however, the old house was used to these assaults.

It rattled and swayed but kept them safe. Through the whole night, as the wind battered their shelter, Elli drifted in and out of a dreamless sleep. She woke up abruptly. Something was different.

There was silence.

The wind had stopped. No sounds came from the outside. She heard only the gentle breathing of the children, and something else. It took a minute to recognise the strange gurgling noises as her sister's snoring.

Carefully, without waking anyone, Elli peeled the blankets off. The daylight coming through the windows was dull and barely illuminated the room. Her breath was a thick fog in front of her. It was very cold.

She tried to open the front door but couldn't push the door handle down. Her hand stuck to the icy metal and hurt when she rattled it in frustration. All of a sudden, the handle turned and the door opened into the room with such force that she was slammed against the wall by an avalanche of powdery snow.

Her shouts woke Ruth and Hans, who rushed in to find Elli buried to her neck in snow. She tried to push herself out of it but the snow was like loose sand and held her in a tight grip.

'How did you manage that, sister?' Ruth said. 'Wouldn't it be more appropriate to shovel the snow out of the house rather than invite it in?'

'If you don't give me a hand, I'll murder you when I get out.' 'Temper, temper. Didn't anyone tell you to check first before you

open a door after a stormy night? Never heard about snowdrifts? The wind blew against this side of the house, so we'll have no trouble getting out through a door on the other side. But didn't you notice that all these windows were covered with snow?'

The back door opened easily into a snow-free clearing, surrounded by steep walls of snow at the edge of the wind shadow. The front of the house and the barn were gentle white slopes, the buildings invisible under the snow. Snow covered the barn windows and kept the inside semi-dark. Rolf and Hanna were just waking up.

'*Guten Morgen*, my lovely daughters. Did you all have a good night?' Rolf's glowing face smiled at them.

'Papa, you are obviously much better!' Elli said. '*Ja*, Hanna is magical. Fantastic.'

'I bet she is,' Ruth said. 'But did you get any sleep?' Even in the bad light, they could see Hanna blushing. Rolf roared with laughter.

'We didn't get much sleep because we were scared the wind would blow the roof off,' Elli said.

'It was windy? Really? We didn't hear a thing,' Rolf said. Elli looked at her sister who was grinning from ear to ear.

'*Ja*, Papa, it was windy.'

The children came in, pleased to see their *Opa* alive and well.

'*Opa, Opa*, wasn't it windy last night?' Anna said and gave her grandfather a bear hug, which made him wince. '*Ja*, your mother said something like that.'

'Mama, there are other people here!' Herman and Fritz came running back. 'Come on, Mama, have a look.'

Puzzled, the adults followed the boys. The barn was dark but there was something in the back, something partially covered with hay.

It was one of their missing wagons.

'*Vater im Himmel,* they were here.' Elli would not go any closer, she was afraid of what they would find in the wagon. They waited as Ruth climbed into the wagon. Moments later she re-emerged.

'It's empty. Come, see for yourself.'

In the faint light, Elli saw that the wagon was indeed bare.

'I found something.' Ruth said. Elli felt her hair rising at the back of her neck when Ruth continued. 'It's a child. No, wait, it's only a doll.'

The doll was large, the size of a baby. It had long, blonde hair, a lively face and its blue eyes opened and closed when Ruth moved it.

'It must be the Schuster's wagon. I remember that doll. They bought it in Berlin. Angelica came around every morning to show it to us. Every morning, rain or snow, every morning. She wouldn't leave her doll behind.' She turned the doll over and dropped it. 'Blood! Something has happened to that child.'

'If that blood is hers, she must have had an accident. Surely the SS wouldn't be so stupid as to harm a little girl when they need her mother's support.'

'They can force anyone to obey,' Ruth said.

'But now they are crammed into two wagons and...' Her eyes widened. 'That's something like thirty people to a wagon. That's impossible! They would have to get rid of at least half of them.'

Elli sat down abruptly. The barn floor was freezing but she didn't feel it.

'You must be right; they've killed the girl—and others. There isn't enough space for more than fifteen people on each wagon, even with minimal luggage.'

'Maybe the SS killed them because they refused to play along,' Ruth said. 'But why cram together in two wagons? Why leave this one behind?'

Elli walked around the wagon. 'Because this wagon has a broken wheel too.'

'Something must have happened to Manfred and Armin or they would have repaired it,' Ruth said.

'We are insane to follow the SS. They are probably not far ahead now.

The blizzard will have stopped them too.' Elli was becoming anxious. 'What do you want to do when we run into them? Use harsh language? Because that's about all we have as a weapon.'

'I don't know what we'll do or what we can do, but we can't just abandon our people,' Rolf said. 'I think the SS will let them go when they don't need them anymore. But I doubt they will give them supplies. If we can't pick them up at that point they'll freeze or starve to death. Hans, what do you think?'

'We have to follow them,' Hans said.

'Easy for you to say, Hans, you have nothing to lose. Ruth and I, we risk our children.' Hans's face drained of blood. He looked so hurt Elli immediately regretted what she had said.

'*Ja*, I have nothing to lose but my life, and that I want to keep, but if I lived knowing I could have helped them but chose not to because I was afraid, then life wouldn't be worth living.'

Elli felt deflated. He was right, how could she turn her back on the others, even if there was only a slim chance of helping them? Still, her maternal instinct rebelled.

'Elli, I feel the same,' Ruth said. 'I would like to run as fast as possible in the opposite direction, but I can't.'

'It doesn't have to be a suicide mission. Their tracks are easy to follow from a safe distance. We won't run into them. Believe me, *Liebling*, the last thing I want is to endanger us,' Rolf said. 'Following them at a safe distance won't be more dangerous than travelling in any other direction.'

The road meandered through a white countryside with snowdrifts like sand dunes. The extreme cold made the snow so powdery that the Clydesdales moved through it like boats on the sea.

They came to a small cluster of houses wedged around an intersection. A building facing both roads was partly demolished.

'Look at that.' Elli pointed at tracks going across the front gardens of several houses. 'Our convoy ran into someone else. Hanna, is Papa awake? Ask him to have a look.'

'Daughter, I'm stiff as a board, this had better be good.' Rolf emerged from the wagon.

'My God, that was a tank!' he said, staring at the tracks. area.'

'Tanks? Russians?' Elli said.

'Who else? I don't think there are any German troops left in this

'What happened to our people?' Elli said. 'This looks more like a raid than just checking out a refugee convoy. Look at the damage they did to that house.'

'No, I don't think they clashed with a Russian patrol. There would be signs of it, debris. I can't see anything. Can you?'

'No, only the tank tracks. We'll have a look around. Back in the wagon with you.' Hanna, Elli and Ruth lifted Rolf up before he was able to object. 'Look after *Opa*, children.'

The muffled response from under the blankets mingled with Rolf's protests.

'Hans, stay with Rolf, we'll call you if we need help.' Ruth stopped Hans as he started to climb out of the wagon.

They searched the houses but found nothing. On their way back Elli saw something in the snow. Small brass tubes; empty gun cartridges.

'I'll show them to Papa,' Elli said and rushed back to the wagon. 'They look unusual,' Rolf said. 'Not like German or Russian ammunition.' He hesitated. 'I can hear something. Listen, isn't that Ruth calling?'

Elli saw her sister and Hanna in the distance, shouting and waving their arms.

Both were standing between shallow dirt mounds, only lightly covered with snow.

'I think we have found our people,' Ruth said. The dirt mound looked fresh.

'I'll get a shovel; we have to check who is buried here.'

'Wait,' Elli said. 'I don't think it's them. Look.' She pointed to a sign uprooted and lying on the ground. It said: *Dorf Friedhof*. 'This is the village graveyard.' Elli pointed at the many small mounds around them. Some of them had tombstones, partially visible under the snow.

'But these two are new,' Ruth said.

Elli cleared the snow from the two graves. Flat on the ground next to one was an engraved head stone. The inscription read, 'Heinz Waldman, *Geb*. 14 June 1892, *Gest*. 14 February 1941.'

'The man in this grave died four years ago,' Elli said. 'Let's go.' Hanna and Ruth followed her quietly.

'I could have told you that,' Rolf said, when they told him about their find. 'If the SS or Russians killed anybody, they wouldn't bury them. We would have found bodies and their belongings. I think they are alive; but those tank tracks just don't make sense. If tanks run into wooden wagons, we should see something.'

'*Ja, ja*, wise man. Maybe the tanks came later,' Ruth said. 'Came later?' Elli said.

'Maybe the tanks did not confront the convoy but found their tracks and decided to follow them.'

'If so, there shouldn't be any wagon tracks for us to see, only the tracks of the tanks following them,' Rolf said.

'Let's find out,' Ruth said.

Elli walked slowly along the icy road, following Ruth who was already way ahead. Eventually she caught up when Ruth stopped to check the road.

'I can't see any tracks, from the convoy or from anything following them.' Ruth pointed at the cobblestones of the narrow road. 'I don't think we'll find anything. This powder snow doesn't stay on the road. Besides, tanks are wider than this road, so there should be tracks at the sides but there are none.'

'You are right. Let's go back,' Elli said.

Once they were back with the wagons, it started to snow again. The wind had died down and it was warmer. The snowflakes were large and stayed put, unlike the powder snow.

They covered the horses with more blankets. Elli took one of her father's hats, cut ear-holes into the brim, and fitted it onto Karla. The Clydesdale snorted loudly, expressing her concern about the unusual cover, but settled down, flicking her right ear occasionally.

'Like it, *ja*?' Elli was pleased and continued to fuss over her horse. 'Now I have to find something for your ears. I know! Papa's gloves!'

At their next brief rest, she snuck into the wagon. Later, she heard her father talking to Hanna.

'*Liebling*, what is that on Elli's horse?' 'On Elli's horse?'

'There! On the animal's ears. It looks like... Oh my God, my gloves! Elli!' Elli poked her head in the wagon.

'What is the matter? Why are you shouting?'

'What are my good gloves doing on your horse's ears?'

'Well, I thought you could spare them and Karla certainly needs them. So what is the fuss about?'

'My good gloves! I have worn those only once, to the opera! She put them on her dirty horse's ears.' Most of what followed Elli could not understand, until Hanna's loud voice cut in.

'For goodness sake! will you stop it? When do you think you will have an opportunity to use your fancy opera gloves again? The horse has more need of them.'

Silence, then only a barely audible muttering from Rolf.

Poor Papa, she thought. Not only does he have to share his opera gloves with a horse, but his woman agrees to it. I'll get him new ones when we make it to Hamburg, she promised.

The snowfall was dense. The road and the countryside became one. Only the snow markers, long black poles on both sides of the road, showed that they were still on the road.

'We have to find shelter, Papa. How much farther to the next town?'

'I don't know Elli, but we should be in Bömchen soon.' 'We need shelter now. Anything sooner?'

'There is a small village before Bömchen but I can't remember its name.'

'You are right Papa,' Ruth said. 'Look, over there. It looks like a couple of buildings.'

It was not the village, but a deserted farm. The main house was badly damaged by shellfire but the large barn was intact.

Elli and Ruth tried to open the huge double doors. The metal handles were frozen and when Elli accidentally touched them with her bare hand, she was stuck.

'*Scheisse*! Please help me, I'm stuck to the metal! Oh, it hurts, hurry please.'

'Wait! Don't move or you'll rip your skin off. Why didn't you wear your gloves, *Dummkcpf*?'

'Had to scratch myself,' Elli moaned. '*Scheiss Läuse*,' shit lice. 'Hurry up.' 'Patience.' Ruth bent down close to Elli's stuck hand anc blew warm air on her fingers.

'What are you doing,' Elli groaned through clenched teeth as Ruth lifted her hand off the door handle. 'Oh that hurts.'

'A bit of skin decided to stay behind,' Ruth said. 'Put my scarf around it and wait.'

She came back with a Schnapps bottle. 'What a waste, here, pour that on.'

'Will it hurt?'

'*Ja*, of course, it'll hurt me. It's my last little bit and I saved it for a special occasion, not for my stupid sister.'

The barn was in semi-darkness but they could see that part of it was filled to the roof with hay. The free spaces between the haystacks were crammed with farm machinery. When Elli came closer, she saw someone laying on the ground. Three bodies were stacked of top on each other.

'*Vater im Himmel*! Ruth, come here.' The bodies were loosely wrapped in blankets. 'Who are they?' Elli felt her voice trembling. Ruth pulled the blankets off.

'One man and two women, but not our people,' she said.

'They must be SS,' Elli said. Ruth pulled a blanket further down, away from one of the bodies. The man had a large chest wound and his blood-soaked uniform looked like frozen strawberry *ja*m. All three were dressed in olive green clothes, without any identifying badges or insignia.

'No, they aren't SS.' 'How do you know?'

'The SS would be in civilian clothing. Our people's clothing. This is some kind of uniform, but it's not Russian.'

They checked the other two bodies. Both had been killed with shots through the back of the head. The bullets had lifted the top of their skulls, exposing their brains.

'We have to turn them over to look at their faces,' Elli said.

Despite the injuries, their faces were intact. Death must have been fast, Elli thought.

'They are not our people. I don't know who they are.'

'Someone ripped something off their uniforms, look here,' Ruth said. All the buttons were missing. Elli went through the uniform pockets. Nothing, all were empty. Finally, she found something. She pulled out a flat, brown object.

'What is that?'

Ruth turned it over.

'A piece of chocolate. To be precise, a piece of a Hershey bar.' 'Hershey bar?'

'*Ja*, Hershey bar, American chocolate. Look, it's written on it.

Hershey.'

'They are Americans?' Elli said.

'I don't think so. The Americans wouldn't leave their people behind and they wouldn't be here in the East. Papa said the Americans have started the invasion in Italy and Normandy. Only the Russians are coming through the Eastern provinces.'

'So, who are these people? Locals?'

'No, they are too well fed. Locals haven't much food. Maybe they're Czech partisans who got hold of some American chocolate?' They heard their father calling from the entrance of the barn.

'What are you doing in there?' 'We found some bodies.' '*Schweine*! Who is it?'

'None of our people.' A sigh of relief came from Rolf. 'Thank you, God.'

'I think they are partisans,' Ruth said. 'Where are they? I want to have a look.'

He knelt down beside the bodies, checking their outer clothes and undergarments.

'They are not partisans. They are soldiers. Someone has ripped off their dog tags. Look here, see the red marks around their necks? They've also removed rank insignia from the shoulders of their coats and sleeves. He may have been an officer and the women were...' He picked up a small metal piece shaped like an arrow. 'That is a radio battalion badge.

The women were radio operators.' 'American?'

'American? What makes you ask that?'

'We found a Hershey bar in the man's coat,' Elli said. 'Don't know. Maybe.'

'What do you think was going on here?' Elli said.

'No idea. These men probably had nothing to do with our people or the SS. I think we had better leave here as fast as possible.'

'We can't leave before morning. The snowfall is getting worse and it's getting dark,' Elli said. 'We have to stay.'

They covered the bodies with hay bales and went back to the others.

Chapter 25

The road became steeper in the foothills of the Sudeten Mountains and with the easing of the snow the temperature dropped rapidly. Hans travelled with Rolf and Hanna, so the children could stay together in one wagon. They kept each other warm, not daring to come out. The air was bitingly cold, forcing Elli and Ruth to breathe through scarves wrapped around their faces.

'I'll have a nap for a couple of hours,' Elli said and climbed into the back of the wagon. It was warmer in there, but it stank. The smell of wet mouldy canvas, mixed with body odours and urine, was overpowering. We all badly need a hot bath or at least a wash, she thought. Elli was determined to clean everyone up at the next stop, if necessary, with a snow rub.

'Come on, you little stinkers, let your mother under the blankets.' Protests came from everywhere but finally she snuggled between the warm bodies. Small arms wrapped around her. She warmed up, became drowsy, and drifted off.

'Oh! How can you sleep in here? What is the matter with all of you? You stink to high heaven.' Ruth's loud voice boomed through the wagon and penetrated Elli's dreams like a knife. I'll kill her, she thought and felt around for something to throw. A shoe would do.

'Ha, ha, missed!' Elli heard, followed by a shriek when the other shoe hit its target. With waking came itching and soreness. Just as well she couldn't smell herself. The icy air viciously attacked the skin on her face and bare arms. Shivering forced her to hold on to the frozen side of the wagon. When she pulled her hand away, some of her skin stayed there. The pain made her breathe in sharply, which started her coughing.

'*Scheisse*!'

'Hallo, dearest sister.' Ruth gave her a bright grin. 'It's nice to see you up but please, don't come too close. The brown haze around you is getting to me.'

'Do you think you look or smell any better? Ouch, that hurts.'

Ruth looked at Elli's bleeding hand. 'I'll get some bandages.

You seem to make a habit of getting your hands stuck on frozen surfaces. Papa's thermometre says it's minus ten degrees. Don't touch anything with your bare hands again, Dummkopf.'

'*Danke schön*, my dear, caring sister,' Elli said through her teeth. 'Getting back to stinking, we all need a good wash. It's a miracle no one has developed skin problems or got fleas. Let's boil some water.'

'For washing? You are joking!' Ruth said. 'The little bit of wood we found is barely enough for cooking. We won't stink to death, but we'll certainly starve to death if we can't cook. Besides, you can't wash the children in the open. It's too cold. The water would turn to ice on their bodies.'

'We could rub them down with snow.'

'Oh yes! Don't be stupid, their screams would bring any nearby Russians running.'

'But it's unhealthy. At least we could wash their faces and hands. That won't kill them.'

'We can try but have a look at yourself before you suggest it to them.'

Ruth handed her a small mirror. Elli had difficulty recognizing the reflection in the mirror as hers. Her blonde hair hung around her face like a dirty mop. There were harsh, deep lines she had never seen before. She had aged ten years in the last few months. Even her bright blue eyes didn't help, looking out as they were from deep hollows, surrounded by dark shadows.

'Don't show me a mirror again until we are in Hamburg.'

'You'll be fine after a good clean up and some fattening food,' Ruth said with a warm smile.

❄

The sun was still high in the sky when they arrived in Bömchen. There was no wind and from some of the houses smoke columns rose. They entered the main street. Loud banging came from one of the houses. As they drew near, they saw its massive chimney belching flames and black smoke. Rusting farm machinery cluttered the front yard.

Through an open double door, two men were working at an anvil. One of them held a red-hot horseshoe with a pair of tongs; the other hit it rhythmically with a sledgehammer.

In the back of the workshop, the outline of a third man was visible against a cloud of flames, pulling the bellow's chain, blowing air into the open fire pit. The flickering light gave the sweaty bodies of the three men the appearance of dancing devils, or so Elli thought. She climbed off the wagon and walked towards the blacksmiths.

'*Guten Tag*. Could I talk to you?'

The men did not react but continued to work.

Elli walked further into the workshop and touched the man with the hammer on the shoulder. As the hammer was on the upswing, he turned towards her and the hammer came down—directly at her. Elli jumped. The hammer hit the ground, barely missing her.

'Are you mad? You could have killed me!'

'Just a warning. No one sneaks up on me. Who are you and what do you want?' His voice was a deep growl.

The three men were clad in leather aprons over their pants. Rivulets of sweat poured down their faces and bare chests. The heat of the furnace burned Elli's face as the cold air coming in from the outside chilled her back.

'I'm sorry. I didn't want to startle you. I called out but you didn't hear me.'

'Who are you?'

'My name is Elli Hirsch and this is my family. We are refugees from Silesia. We need some help.'

'We can't help you. We have nothing left. Most of our food was stolen by refugees a few days ago,' he said, his face twisting in anger.

Elli stepped backwards. She thought that at any moment he would bring his hammer down on her again.

'We don't have much food either but we'll be happy to share it with you. What we really need is a bath. We haven't had a clean up for weeks and smell a bit. What are your names?'

The three blacksmiths looked at each other and slowly their faces lightened.

'My name is Wolfgang Müller and these are Emil Krause and Heino Schnabel, my apprentices.'

'We won't stay long, Herr Mueller,' Elli said, 'just long enough for a good clean up and some washing.'

'Please call me Wolfgang, Frau Hirsch. You can have a hot shower. The furnace heats a large boiler. There will be enough hot water for all of you.'

A hot shower! Elli thought she was dreaming. This must be the only place in Saxony which had hot water, and they had found it.

'Thank you, thank you. You can't imagine what that means to us—and please call me Elli.'

She rushed back to the others, who welcomed the news with screams of delight. Soon the five children and four adults were milling around the blacksmiths. Hans took the horses out of their gear and led them to the stable.

'Emil and Heino will show you where the shower is and how to operate it. It's a bit tricky.'

Elli noticed that all three men kept some distance from them. At first she thought they were shy until she saw Wolfgang discreetly holding his nose. My God, we must be stinking to heaven if even these sweaty men can smell us.'

'Is Hans not coming?' Elli said.

'He'll rub the horses down first, and have a shower later,' Hanna said.

The shower was a drum with holes at the bottom, hanging from the ceiling. Pipes from a boiler and a coldwater tank fed into the drum. Getting the right temperature was frustrating but they managed. The mist in the shower shed was thick and Elli didn't notice the woman before she called out.

'Ach du meine Güte! So many naked people! No wonder the boys were so keen to bring in the towels. I'm Sophy, Wolfgang's sister.'

Elli felt instantly drawn to the plump woman with the neat white apron and the warm smile. Sophy started to rub the children in thick fluffy towels when she saw Rolf.

'My God. You poor man, let me have a look at that.' She carefully inspected Rolf's shoulder.

'Papa, you've done it again.' Elli saw her father's embarrassment. 'Can't keep the women away from your body*, ja*?'

Being naked and subjected to close inspection by a strange woman was too much for Rolf. He grabbed a towel.

'Thank you for your concern but I'm fine.' Even through the mist, Elli could see him blush.

'Fine, ha! That wound needs cleaning and dressing. It's amazing that you didn't get an infection.'

Hanna came to his rescue. 'That's because I boiled the dressing every day. I've been looking after him.'

Sophy was not convinced and continued to fuss over Rolf, with Hanna watching her closely.

Later, in the living room, the children squeaked with delight when Sophy brought in a large pot of steaming hot chocolate, something they had not seen for a long while.

'You said that refugees stole your food, Wolfgang. Is that right?' '*Ja*, four days ago. There were fifty or more people in three wagons. Just like yours,' Wolfgang said. 'They were very strange.' 'Because there were so many in three wagons?' Elli said excitedly.

'No, strange because only the men came down from the wagons. We offered them showers but the women and children were not allowed off.'

'Not allowed?'

'*Ja*, I heard the men shouting at them to stay where they were.' They came through here, Elli thought. They were alive.

'The men, were they young?'

'*Ja*, that's right. They were all young, except two of them. What was so strange about them was that they looked like soldiers. They had weapons, so when they took our food we didn't argue.'

'You are lucky you didn't. They might have shot you. They were SS.'

Everyone stared at Elli.

'How do you know that?' Wolfgang said. 'Have you anything to do with the SS?'

'No, but the women and children were our people.' Elli explained the situation.

'If they are your people, what happened to the men who were with them?

'I don't know. Are you sure that there were only young men?' 'Yes, except for two of them. These two were the only ones who spoke to us. They wanted some repairs done to the harnesses and the wagons.'

'Is it possible that there were more men, older men, in the wagons?' Elli said. She was scared of what was coming.

'No, the women opened the wagons up to air them. It was a sunny day. There were definitely no more men.'

'The bastards murdered them,' Rolf said, 'and I bet it happened in that last village, where we found the bodies.'

'Why would the SS kill your men?' Wolfgang said. 'To take their place,' Rolf said.

'To take their place? That doesn't make any sense.'

Elli saw that her father was trembling and sweat was running down his face. She came to his side to support him.

'He is not well. Bring him inside,' Sophy said to her brother. The blacksmith lifted Rolf up like a child and carried him into the house.

'We have to go back to Brausenstein,' Elli said.

'Go back? Are you mad? We nearly got killed making it to this place, What for?' Ruth said.

'Maybe they are still alive. We can't just leave them there. We have to go back.'

'Elli, Ruth is right,' Hanna said. 'We don't know if the SS got rid of them in Brausenstein. They could have killed them anywhere between here and there. With the thick snow cover and more snow coming down all the time, we have no chance of finding anyone, dead or alive.'

Sophy prepared a meal that they contributed to with their reserves. The kitchen was large and warm. The central *Kacheloven* and the stove were producing enough heat to allow the refugees to peel off several layers of clothes.

On the large table was a massive bowl filled to the brim with thick, steaming broth. From wooden baskets the scent of warm bread, fresh from the oven, spread through the room.

'You are lucky. We just finished baking. They didn't touch our flour. Possibly didn't know what to do with it.' Wolfgang cut the warm bread and then used the still warm knife to smear butter on the thick slices. Real butter. Elli couldn't take her eyes of it. The smell, the maddening mixture of sourdough and fresh butter put her saliva glands into overdrive. Her sister's loud voice interrupted her.

'Pull yourself together. A grown woman drooling! What a pathetic picture.'

'Eat, *Liebling*, there is plenty,' Sophy said.

Only after two large slices did Elli remember her father. 'How is Papa, Sophy?'

'Weak, but he is resting. I think the news about your people threw him.'

'He needs a few days rest. I want to go back to Brausenstein. Could the others stay with you for two or three days? We have our own food and they will do some work around your place.'

'*Ja*, of course, all of you can stay. Right, Wolfgang?'

'*Jawohl*, Sophy.'

'Why do you want to go back to Brausenstein?' Sophy said.

'We have to make sure that nobody has been left behind.' Elli smiled at her sister's words.

'*Danke.*'

'How will we do it?' Ruth said.

'Tomorrow morning we'll take Karla and ride back. Without a wagon, it will take only half a day. We'll leave at first light and be there by early afternoon, if the weather holds.'

When Rolf woke up, they told him their plan.

'*Verrückt*! You are crazy. The devil knows what happened in that town. You'll get yourself killed. Haven't we lost enough people already? I forbid you to go.'

'Papa, it would haunt us for the rest of our lives,' Elli said. 'We have to make sure that we didn't leave anyone behind. You would do it yourself if you were in better health. I mean, why did you insist we follow the convoy in the first place?'

'*Ja, ja, ja*, but we know now that only women and children are in the convoy. They got rid of the men,' Rolf said. 'Besides, I'm much better now. If anyone goes back, it will be me. A little ride in the fresh air will do me good. Much better than the stink in the wagon.' Elli saw that he meant it. His face was red and his eyes sparkled with anticipation.

'Fine, Papa.'

'I'll get the horse ready,' he said and turned around to walk off. Elli followed him and tapped him on his shoulder. He stumbled and screamed out in pain.

'Why did you do that?'

'Sorry Papa, just to make a point. You are in no condition to ride. We'll go.'

'That was cruel,' Ruth said.

'Papa wouldn't listen to arguments. I had to show him that he is not able to ride.'

'*Ja*, but that was a bit brutal. You didn't have to hit him.' 'I didn't hit him. I just gave him a tap on the shoulder.' 'On his injured shoulder,' Ruth said.

'I had to convince him. He would have taken a clap on his healthy shoulder as encouragement.'

Ruth did not say anything, just gave her sister a look. Rolf limped over to them, as they prepared the horses.

'I'm afraid for you two, but you are right Elli. I wouldn't make it. Be careful.' When Elli gave him a gentle hug, he gasped.

'They might have left the men behind, instead of killing them, to ensure cooperation from the women,' he said.

'It's a long shot, but we'll look, Papa.'

'The church would be a good place to start. There would be enough space there to imprison a group of people.' Rolf said. 'I hope you find them. Be careful'

The icy wind was at their back, blowing them along. If it continues to blow from that direction, we'll freeze our faces off on the way back, Elli thought. After a few hours, Elli's hips were aching. The Clydesdale's back was too wide for comfort. The only parts of Elli not chilled were the contact points with the horse.

'Papa is not so well, *ja*?' Ruth said.

'Considering the damage, he is making good progress. He's tough, but Hans worries me,' Elli said.

'*Ja*, I thought he was coming out of it when he defended Papa, but that lasted only for a short while.'

'Is that why you and the kids came back to me?'

'I couldn't stand it anymore. The children love him. He is like a big silent bear—they can do anything with him, but he doesn't talk much.'

'Still, I was surprised when you came back. I thought something was developing between the two of you,' Elli said.

'*Ja*, I thought so too. When he looked at me with those big, sad, puppy eyes, I was convinced that he felt the same, but it never developed any further—and believe me, I tried.'

'*Ja*, I can imagine,' Elli said dryly. 'That reminds me; I didn't see him last night at all. Did he stay overnight with the horses?'

'Papa said he came in later. He thought Hans felt too embarrassed to shower with all of us—or maybe just with me,' Ruth said. They continued to ride in silence.

The sun came out. In the distance Brausenstein's church steeple came into view.

'We've made it, Elli. Another hour and we'll be there.' 'Ruth, look. What is that on the road?'

'What do you mean? I can't see anything. Where?' 'There, close to the horizon.'

'*Ja*, I can see it now. Don't know. Some cows?'

'No, it's smaller. Oh my God! People. A group of people coming towards us.'

Chapter 26

Eight men dressed in rags, their faces hidden under ice-encrusted scarves, stumbled towards Elli and Ruth.

'It's Elli and Ruth. They came back for us!' The two men in front took their scarves off.

'Manfred, Armin, you're alive! The other men took off their head covers. Two stood back as the others surged forward.

'Hugo, Alfred, Udo, Jürgen. Oh my God!'

They hugged and kissed the sisters, as tears of relief ran down their faces. Soon the excited babble gave in to exhaustion as they held each other up, leaned on crutches, or dropped to the ground. Most had bruises and open wounds. Their torn clothes had given them little protection from the cold.

'You can't know how glad we are to see you,' Armin said. 'Did the SS let you go? Is my family safe?'

'We really don't how your family and the others are, Armin. It was only yesterday we learned that you men were not with the SS. That's why we came looking for you.'

When Elli explained what had happened to the women and children Armin unexpectedly swayed and dropped down. His scarf came off, exposing extensive swelling on his face.

'Armin, my God, what happened to you?'

'The SS beat us up,' Armin said. He continued but his words were slurred. 'They rounded us up and threatened to shoot us if we wouldn't tell them where these two men were,' Armin said, pointing at the two men still waiting quietly aside from the others. Elli had never seen them before. They were not from their refugee group.

'Who are they?' Elli said.

'They escaped from the SS. I think they are Tommies. When the SS couldn't find them, they rounded us up, worked us over with their rifle butts, and told us they would execute us one by one, starting with the youngest. They took my son, Peter, Hans Schneider and Willi Meister and dragged them behind the church.' Armin's voice was breaking. 'I tried to stop them but they hit me with their rifle butts until I stayed down.' His voice was barely audible. 'They went on questioning and beating us, but we had nothing to say. Then—they shot our boys.'

'Oh God, what happened then?'

'They separated the six of us from our families. We were sure they were going to shoot us too but they locked us in the church crypt. That's where we found these two men they were looking for.' Armin stumbled, another man supported him. 'Because these bastards didn't come out, they shot my sons.' His voice became shrill. 'Our boys would still be alive if these two hadn't run away! It's all their fault!'

'Come on Armin,' Manfred said. 'That's not true and you know it. The SS murdered your sons, not these men. You can't blame them for hiding from the murderous *Schweine*. They were just lucky they got away.'

Armin, a bear of a man, sat in the snow at Elli's feet and wept.

Elli felt helpless as she sat down beside him. She didn't know what to say. No one could blame the two strangers, but how could she say that to the father of a murdered boy? Finally, Armin pulled out a large handkerchief, wiped his face, and gave Elli a pained smile.

'It hurts so much. My son is dead and my wife and daughter have been taken by the SS.' He turned to his friends 'I'm all right now.' He cleared his throat and continued. 'When we finally got out of the crypt, everyone was gone; the SS, our families and our wagons.'

'They took all the women and children with them?' Elli said. 'We don't know. After they left we only found the bodies of our boys.'

'Why did they take the families?' Elli said.

'Maybe as a cover to get out of this area. Their trucks were out of petrol,' Armin said. 'That's why they left them behind.'

The men stood around them, nodding. There seemed to be nothing else to say. One by one, the exhausted men began to collapse. Three of them sat down heavily in the snow.

'Please get up,' Elli said. 'You'll freeze to the ground. Ruth, help me.' They hauled the men up again. 'Support each other and don't sit on the ground. You have to get moving or you'll die. Ruth, keep them moving, especially those two.' The two strangers wore thin shirts and trousers barely warm enough for a mild spring day.

'What is your story?' Elli said, turning to them. They looked at each other and finally one spoke.

'Believe me, you have no idea how sorry we are about what happened to these people,' the man said in fluent German. If I had known that SS were going to shoot hostages because they couldn't find us, we would have given ourselves up. We only learned what happened when the others found us in the crypt.'

Both the trembling men were on the point of collapse.

'It wasn't your fault. Why did the SS want you so badly?'

'They were taking us to Berlin. They followed your convoy for a long time.'

'Why?'

'They used you as scouts, I think, hoping you would run into any danger before them. They recognised you as the refugees who got away by destroying the bridge in Bohemia.'

'How did they recognise us? Refugee convoys all look the same.' '*Ja*, but only your convoy had such big horses. When they found you again they decided the only way they would get out of this area alive would be to disguise themselves as a group of refugees.'

'But that's insane!' Elli said. 'They would never pass a Russian inspection. The Russians are not so stupid as to believe that young men are refugees. They must be soldiers or SS.'

'I know, I know,' the man said, 'but they were desperate.'

'Let's talk about it later. We have more urgent problems now,' Elli said. 'Ruth, stay with them, but keep them walking. I'll see if I can find a wagon, or something else Karla can pull. I don't think they are able to walk to Bömchen.'

The houses were only a few hundred metres away. In the central market place were the vehicles the SS left behind, but Elli could not see any wagons or sleds. She was about to go back to the group when she noticed that one of the deserted trucks had a trailer attached to it.

Tying Karla to it was difficult because the trailer had no brakes and the connection bar was too short for such a large horse, but Elli had no choice. She slung a long rope between the horse and the trailer and let Karla slowly pull the trailer as Elli walked alongside.

Karla seemed to know that she should walk slowly without jerking the trailer. Luckily, the road was straight and the horse had no problems negotiating it.

In the distance, Elli saw Ruth with the group. They were stumbling along, as Ruth persuaded them to keep moving, sometimes by swearing and kicking when they slumped down. They swore back at her but continued to walk.

A scramble broke out when Elli reached them with the trailer.

'Wait! There is only enough space for three or four people. Only those really too sick to walk can ride in it,' Elli shouted.

Before they could sort this out, one of the two strangers spoke. 'Please lady, do you have any spare clothes?'

'I saw some blankets in the trailer. Wait a moment. Ruth, give me a hand.'

In the trailer were piles of blankets. To their surprise, under the blankets were neatly stacked uniforms and boots.

'Why did they leave these behind?' Ruth said. 'There are enough clothes for a whole battalion.'

'If they want to be taken for refugees, these would be a total giveaway,' Elli said. 'I guess that's why they left the stuff in the trailer.'

'Well, whatever the reason, there are enough warm clothes here for all of them.'

None of the men hesitated before accepting the army boots, but some were worried about wearing the uniforms. Only the two strangers happily accepted the clothes Elli handed them. As they tried them on, they talked to each other. Elli realised they were not English.

'Are you American?' She said in English.

'Yes,' the younger one said, clearly surprised that Elli understood him. 'I'm Alf Smidt and my friend here is Henry Welsh, US Air Force.'

'What are you doing here?'

'We were shot down.' He made a sound like a failing engine and made his hand fall, much as a child would show a shot-down plane.

'Shot down over Saxony?' 'Yes.'

'How did you end up with the SS?'

'We escaped from a concentration camp.'

'You were in a concentration camp?' Elli said. 'I thought all enemy soldiers and airmen were sent to POW camps.'

'They decided we were spies and handed us over to the Gestapo,' Smidt said.

'Why were you seen as spies? Weren't you in uniform?' Elli said. 'We flew a reconnaissance plane.'

'A spy plane,' Elli said. She sounded disapproving. 'Reconnaissance is not spying. Our plane was unmistakably marked as a US Air Force plane.'

'So, what happened after you were found?'

'They interrogated us for days. Beating us, no sleep, no food, no water. We never got out of the cell—until something strange happened,' Smidt said.

'What?'

Smidt stomped around, testing his new boots and buttoning up the long coat Elli handed him. He visibly relished the warm clothes. 'One

day we heard gunfire, people yelling. It went on for hours but eventually it died down.'

'It didn't sound like the SS were executing people, we'd heard plenty of that, it was more like a riot,' Welsh said.

'A riot, in a concentration camp?' Ruth said. 'That would have been a bloodbath. The camps are guarded by the regular SS, they wouldn't hesitate to kill rioters.'

'We didn't know what had happened. For two days, we didn't see anyone. No guards, no food, no water, nothing. Then out of the blue the door opened and regular army soldiers took us out. There were no SS in sight but a lot of damage had been done to the buildings,' Schmidt said.

'There were bodies everywhere,' Welsh said. 'Where was that camp?' Elli said.

'I'm not sure,' Smidt said, scratching his head. 'Somewhere close to the Czech border. They called it a labour camp—Treblinka, I think, something like that.'

'I've heard about Treblinka,' Elli said. 'Ruth, isn't that one of the big ones?'

'Couldn't be Treblinka, it's further east, but there are some labour camps in this area too,' Ruth answered in English. 'How did you get out?'

'Everything was in chaos so we just walked out. We were recaptured by an SS group,' Smidt said. 'Listen lady, I…'

'Elli, Elli Hirsch and this is my sister Ruth Bredien.' 'Elli, I don't want to sound pushy, but is it possible to get something warm to eat?'

'We'll soon be in Bömchen,' Elli said. 'Here, have this.' Elli handed him the bread and wurst she carried in a bag. 'The sausages are cold, frozen actually, but it will occupy your stomachs until we get back.'

The Americans took the food gratefully and started to eat. Ruth spoke quietly to Elli.

'Are you sure about the *Wehrmacht* stuff we gave them to wear?' Ruth said. 'The SS left those uniforms behind for a reason. If these men dress in *Wehrmacht* and SS uniforms, and the Russians find us, they'll shoot us all.'

'They are freezing and we all have to walk back to Bōmchen. There's no choice.'

The cold wind and the drifting snow made it easy to convince all the men that they must wear the uniforms. She insisted that they pile them on, several coats on top of each other. The need for warmth overcame their fear that passing Russians would mistake them for soldiers.

'In Bömchen, a long hot shower and hot food are waiting for you,' Ruth said. Now let's go.'

'Hot showers. Food. Right!' The enthusiasm died down when Elli explained how they would use the trailer.

'We have only one horse to pull the trailer, so only a few can ride in it. The others must walk. Every half hour we'll change and let others have a rest. Everyone will get some time on the trailer. Like this, we'll all make it. Hopefully in six hours we'll be back.'

The group dragged themselves to the trailer. Every half hour they stopped and the men in the trailer reluctantly came out to give others a turn. Elli and Ruth never rested but constantly coaxed the men to keep moving. Elli could see that some of them came close to attacking her and Ruth. Better angry than dead, she thought.

'We can't continue to drive the men like this,' Ruth said. 'They need rest and hot food.'

'If we don't push them, they'll freeze to death. We have no food and nothing to make a fire and hot drinks. Nothing. We have to keep going.'

'Look at them. I don't think they'll make it back,' Ruth said. 'They have come this far with an occasional rest in the trailer.

They'll make it.' Elli looked closer at her sister. Ruth looked exhausted; she was holding herself up by leaning on the trailer. 'How are you? You don't look too great.' A dusting of powdery snow, covered Ruth's head and shoulders. Around her eyes and mouth, the snow had melted and re- frozen. Elli gently rubbed the ice off her face. Ruth smiled and fussed in the same way about Elli.

'*Liebling*, you look pretty much like a frozen corpse as well. I think both of us should get one of the army blankets. We have a few spare.'

'They'll get heavy after a while.'

'Then you'll put it back in the trailer and get a dry one. We have more than enough.'

Elli and Ruth walked beside Karla, who pulled the wagon easily.

They made steady progress. The Americans walked directly behind them, followed by the rest of the men, spread out in a long line.

'Where is Armin?' Manfred said at the next changeover.

'He was behind me,' Hugo said. 'I didn't look back. I thought others were behind him.'

'Do you remember when you saw him last?' Ruth said.

'I don't know. Not that long ago,' Hugo said. 'God, I'm tired.' 'He can't be too far,' Ruth said. 'I'll go and look for him.'

The wagon and the struggling people waited until Ruth was out of sight. It was getting colder. Without moving, the cold was unbearable.

'Listen to me, all of you,' Elli said. 'We have to wait for Ruth and Armin, but we have to keep moving. Don't sit or you'll freeze to death. Come on, we'll walk around the trailer.'

Everyone was too tired to protest. They stumbled slowly around the trailer.

At last, two figures emerged out of the drifting snow. Ruth was dragging Armin by the arm.

'Oh God, am I glad to see you!' Elli said. 'Where did you find him?'

'Not far from here, but I had trouble getting him up.' Armin did not say anything, just groaned.

'Help me get him into the trailer,' Elli said. 'We have to get going.

They are all at the end of their tether. Surely, it can't be far now.'

Elli and Ruth kept the men close together. The Americans were leading Karla as Elli and Ruth drove the men. They harried them like guard dogs, making sure none dropped out. It was getting dark, and the snowfall was increasing.

'Oh, *Vater im Himmel*, look, we are back!' Elli pointed to the lights of Bömchen, just visible in the distance.

When they arrived at the blacksmith's house, the big Clydesdale smelled a warm stable and gave a loud, triumphant snort.

'My poor horse. Without you, we never would have made it. You'll be first to get something to eat and some dry blankets.'

The door opened. Hanna and Sophy rushed out. They led the half frozen men into the shower room and helped them to undress.

'Wow, you people have interesting customs,' Smidt said to Elli, who undressed beside him. 'I guess I could get used to it.' His broad grin of appreciation at the sight of the two naked women among the men, earned him a friendly thump from Elli.

'Ruth, these men are recovering fast. This one here is already getting cheeky.'

Hours later, fed and showered, Elli, Ruth and the two Americans were sitting beside the warm *Kacheloven*. Most of the others were asleep, having dropped close to the *Kacheloven*, wherever they found empty floor space.

'Elli. May I call you Elli?' Smidt said. Without waiting for an answer, he went on. 'If it wasn't for you two, we would be dead. That was incredible what you did.'

Ruth grinned.

'Not bad for two women, *ja*?'

'Yeah, not bad for anyone. How come you speak English so well?'

'We all speak English. Papa studied in England and insisted that his family learn it too. All of us are interested in foreign languages. My husband is of ethnic Russian origin, so I learned Russian too. I speak it quite well.'

'You are an amazing woman, Elli.'

'*Ja, ja*. Now it's your turn, American.' Elli smiled at him. 'Tell us your story. That was pretty incredible stuff you told us earlier.'

Chapter 27

Smidt took a handkerchief out of his trouser pocket. He blew his nose, one nostril at the time, and carefully folded the handkerchief up and put it back into his trouser pocket. Elli followed this laborious procedure with increasing impatience until finally she cleared her throat, noisily. Smidt looked up and blushed.

'Sorry, got a bit lost in my thoughts.' He gave his itchy nose a final squeeze. 'We were on a reconnaissance mission when the weather turned foul. Our flight path was low, within range of German air defense, so they shot us down. We managed to bring the plane down in a rocky field near the Czech border. The landing was rough, very rough. The plane was ripped apart, but all five of us got out with only a few scratches, before the tanks blew up. The fire must have alerted everyone in the area, so they captured us within an hour. I've told you the rest. That's the whole story.'

'Wait a minute,' Elli said. 'Five? You said the five of us. Where are the other three?'

'I don't know,' Smidt said. 'The bastards always interrogated us separately. When the others were taken out of the cellar in the last village, they locked us in. Welsh and I managed to escape but not the others.

The catacombs under the church were perfect for hiding. We heard the SS searching but they didn't find us. Mind you, we nearly didn't make it out either. The place was pitch dark and a maze of tunnels. We oriented ourselves by the voices of your men locked in the crypt.'

'I have no idea what happened to your men,' Elli said. Ruth pulled her sleeve and whispered in her ear. 'What is it?' Smidt said.

Elli looked at his clothes. He was wearing dark uniform trousers and a light blue shirt.

'Are your clothes part of a uniform?'

Smidt gave her a puzzled look. 'Yes, what's left of it.' 'It's okay then. They wouldn't be your men.'

'Who wouldn't? What are you talking about?' Smidt's voice grew louder.

'Not far from here, we found three dead people in a barn. But they weren't your men. They had dark green uniforms on.'

Smidt stepped back. His face was white. He attempted to say something but only choking sounds came out. His shoulders sagged as he turned to his companion. Welsh's face was moving as if he was trying to chew something tough.

'Our three men were regular army. They were in green uniforms,' Welsh said. He slumped down against the warm *Kacheloven*.

'Maybe they were not your men,' Elli said. 'Why should the SS murder them if they wanted information?'

'Maybe they already had the information and our men were in the way. The SS couldn't guard your people and prisoners and pretend to be refugees. So, they killed them,' Smidt said.

The room seemed to get colder. Everyone shuffled closer to the warm tiles of the central *Kacheloven*.

'I have just the right thing for a cold night like this,' Sophy's cheerful voice interrupted the silence. 'I'll make some Friesian tea, that'll warm you up.'

The tea was as dark as Russian samovar tea, looking more like weak coffee. Sophy served it in delicate Prussian Blue, Meissen cups. First, she placed a large piece of rock sugar in each cup and then poured the hot tea over it. She filled the cups only halfway so the sugar poked out of the tea like an island. The drink was completed with a glob of cream on top.

'Beautiful! It looks like a mountain with a white ring of clouds,' Elli said.

'The trick is to slowly sip the tea without dislodging the sugar, or it will end up in your lap,' Sophy said. 'It's an old Friesian custom. My husband's family came from Husum on the North Sea.'

When they were greedily munching Sophy's *Pfefferkuchen*, Ruth picked up the thread of Smidt's story.

'I didn't think an American spy plane would be interested in this area.'

'Reconnaissance plane, not a spy plane,' Smidt said.

'Okay, reconnaissance plane,' Ruth said. 'But Silesia and Saxony are overrun by the Russians. The Americans are in the South. So, what were you doing here?'

'As I said, we flew a reconnaissance mission.' 'For the Russians?'

Welsh, who up to now had let his comrade do the talking, became abruptly alert. 'Wait a minute, ladies. Why, are you interrogating us?' he interrupted, sharply.

'I'm just puzzled as to why Americans were flying into Saxony,' Ruth said.

'The Russians are our allies,' Welsh said. 'Is it so surprising for us to support them?'

Elli had quietly followed the interaction. 'Where were you shot down?' she asked.

'Near the Czech border. Why?'

Rolf jumped up, his face reflecting surprise and anger. 'Elli, what do you think an American spy plane was looking for in this area?'

'How should I know Papa?'

'Come on daughter, it's not that difficult. What could an American spy plane find so interesting around here?'

'I don't know Papa. Stop playing games, what is on your... Oh my God. You mean...'

'Yes, I do.'

'Dresden!' You were doing reconnaissance over Dresden, gathering information for the bombardment!'

The two men did not respond.

'You were involved in killing thousands and thousands of innocent civilians.' Elli stood up with her fists clenched. 'How can you live with yourselves, you murderers?'

Welsh slowly moved his large frame off the chair. He was considerably taller than Elli and towered over her, his face an angry grimace.

'We followed our orders. We were told to take photos of a large German city. Our main target was the central railway station. They are hubs for troop movements and legitimate targets for aerial bombardment. We are at war with your country, lady.'

'Bombardment? That railway yard around the *Hauptbahnhof* was the only place where refugees from Silesia and the other eastern provinces had a chance to board a train to the west, the only place for escape. Except for a few soldiers trying to get on a train to the west there were never troops garrisoned in Dresden. You burned a city and its entire population. Why?' The ferocity of Elli's attack made Welsh take a step back.

Elli's voice dropped. 'There was nothing but old buildings there, beautiful old buildings, and people. Why?'

'That's how it is in war, lady,' Welsh said meekly. 'Nothing makes sense. We followed orders.'

'Followed orders by setting fire to thousands of civilians? What is the difference between you and the SS? They say they just follow orders too.'

'We are US Air Force officers lady.' Welsh shouted back at her. 'Comparing us to your degenerate SS is an insult.'

'I hope the civilians you burned in Dresden appreciate that. What do you think?'

He did not respond; he looked away.

'Answer me, *Herr Amerikaner.* Are you a nicer murderer than the murderers you fight?'

'I am a soldier. I didn't want to be a soldier but I'm here to do my job as a soldier. And, lady, you seem to forget that it was your bloody *Führer* who started the war.'

'And that's how you justify murdering all those people in Dresden, *ja*?'

Welsh opened his mouth to respond but turned around and left.

Smidt and Rolf had followed the argument without comment.

Both men's faces showed surprise at how Elli stood up to Welsh. Rolf's expression slowly changed into a broad grin.

'Elli, you are right,' Smidt said quietly. 'It's the same. Murder is murder, only the justifications differ.'

'I need to know something,' Rolf said abruptly. His smile was gone. 'Did you take photos of a convoy heading towards the Elbe?'

'A convoy? What kind of convoy?'

'Refugees.' Rolf's voice was rising. 'Horses pulling wagons. There were women, children, and old men walking beside them. Our people. Did you see them?' He was shouting at the American.

Even though Rolf screamed directly in his face, Smidt did not flinch or look away. The sad expression on his face became more intense. He spoke slowly and enunciated each word carefully.

'After we finished the reconnaissance mission we tried to make it back to our base, got lost, came under heavy fire, and crashed.'

'But did you see a convoy moving towards the Elbe?'

'There were several convoys in the area. I wouldn't know if they were troops or refugees,' Smidt said.

'Ah, so you did see us. You radioed back that we were moving towards the Elbe, *ja*? Another brilliant bit of spying. Only this time you drowned your victims. Does that make you proud, hero?'

'Papa, please, calm down.' Elli put her arms around her father. 'Calm down? Why? Have you forgotten what happened to our people? Remember what Jochen looked like when we found him?' 'Please Papa. I haven't forgotten. How could I?'

Smidt said something, but neither Elli nor Rolf heard him. 'You were right, daughter. They're nothing but murderers. You should have left them where you found them.' Smidt tried to say something.

'What? Speak up man,' Rolf said.

'When were your people attacked?' Smidt said.

'We crossed the river the day after the bombing finished,' Elli said.

'Then it wasn't us! We flew over Dresden six weeks ago. Long before the bombardment of Dresden and your convoy.'

'So what,' Rolf said. That wasn't your only mission, was it?' 'You are right, that wasn't our only mission, but it was our last one. As I said before, they shot us down when we returned from a reconnaissance flight, six weeks ago.'

Rolf spat in the snow with a snarling, dismissive sound.

'Papa, did you hear what he said? They were shot down, captured and in a concentration camp long before Dresden and our convoy were bombed. They can't have had anything to do with it.'

'They are lying.'

'You heard that they were in the SS group that followed us. They can't have anything to do with it. They were prisoners then.'

Rolf looked at them, turned around and walked off. 'I'm sorry,' Smidt said.

'Papa blames himself for the death of our people.'

'Sounded more like he was blaming Welsh and me.'

'*Ja*, I guess for a moment he thought he could offload some of his guilt onto you.'

Elli was not sure why she bothered to explain her father's reaction to the American. Her own helpless anger still boiled in her. It also bought back her pain. She saw Jochen's mutilated body again, his sightless eyes, the coldness of his face when she closed his eyelids. She stumbled as she heard herself shouting.

'No, not him. My God, don't take him away!' The frozen ground rushed towards her and blackness closed in.

'Elli, Elli,' someone called. Hanna? No, it was Ruth.

'*Liebling*, wake up.' She heard her sister again. Jochen's clouded eyes still stared at her but slowly the image lost its intensity. She tried to open her eyes.

'I'm so sorry,' she heard Smidt say. 'Was it what I said?'

'I don't think so,' Ruth said. 'Elli lost someone close to her when our convoy was strafed.'

'Someone very close?'

'*Ja*, Jochen was very close to her. He died on the ice. He was literally ripped apart and Elli found him.'

'No wonder she reacted so strongly when your father brought it up.'

'That was stupid of Papa, but Elli is tough. I don't think that fainting spell had anything to do with reliving a horrible memory, but with her injury.'

'She was injured?'

Elli heard them talking about her. Anger began to rise, anger with her sister for telling this stranger about her loss. She opened her eyes.

'Yes, I was hurt. I bumped my head and was out for two weeks.' She glared at Ruth. What else did Ruth tell that man, when she was unconscious? The pain of her memories slowly ebbed away. The sadness stayed in the background.

'*Liebling*, I'm so glad. How do you feel?'

'Groggy, and I have a headache. That bump is still there.' 'Did you see a doctor?' Smidt said.

'A doctor? Where do you think we would get a doctor? In Dresden?'

Elli felt like slapping him but Smidt's expression showed her that she had overreacted again.

'I'm sorry. I meant that a doctor should have a look at your skull. You may have a fracture. Passing out under stress is not exactly normal.'

'It'll have to wait,' Elli said. 'I don't think there will be any doctors around for a while. Whatever doctors are left will be stitching up wounded soldiers or crushed and burned civilians. I'll have to tell Papa not to get me too excited.'

Then she remembered that her father had walked off. 'Papa, oh my God. Where is he?' She pulled herself up and wobbled out. Her head was throbbing and walking was difficult on the icy ground. Hanna was standing beside the wagon. When she came closer, Elli saw she was crying.

'What happened? Where is Papa?'

'Over there, at the shed. He wouldn't talk. He just looked at me. I have never seen him like that. I'm scared, Elli.'

It was getting dark. The landscape was a featureless mass of white and grey. She could not see her father but she heard his rasping breath. He sat hunched over on a pile of firewood. She took him into her arms. He was trembling; she could feel every bone in his emaciated body.

'Oh Elli.' He whimpered like a wounded dog. Elli fought back her tears. He said something, lost in his moaning.

'Papa, talk to me. Papa.' His breathing lost the rasping sound. 'It's my fault Elli.'

'What are you talking about?'

'If I hadn't insisted that we cross the Elbe on the day after the bombardment, they would still be alive. If we had waited they wouldn't have bombed us.' He spoke slowly, each word forced out.

'That's wrong! A day after, a week after, what does it matter? How could you have known? That had nothing to do with you. We all decided to cross the river. The planes just came then, no one could have foreseen it.'

'We should have waited. I should have known more planes would come after the bombing.' Rolf's voice was rising.

'We couldn't stay at the river. We were visible from every direction. It would have been only a matter of time before Russian patrols found us. We all agreed that we had to leave.'

She felt small convulsions travel through his body.

'Elli.' She could hardly hear him. 'It was my fault,' he repeated. 'If I hadn't insisted on crossing the Elbe that day, they would be alive.'

'We were in the wrong place at the wrong time, Papa.' 'Oh yes we were and how I wish we weren't.'

'You can't do this Papa. We have to continue. We need you. We have to decide what to do now.'

'Need me? Look at me, I'm a wreck, just a burden to you.' 'Papa, you are not well, of course, but you are not a wreck. Okay, maybe we should leave you behind, but Hanna insists on dragging you along. We wouldn't be able to cope without your whining. So, you'd better come back to the others and see if you can make yourself useful in some way.' She couldn't see his face but felt him straighten up and breathe in sharply.

'You made your point, daughter. You didn't have to slap me in the face.'

'What would you like me to say? Something mushy, so you can indulge yourself more in your misery? How do you think I feel? I should have stopped Jochen when he went back on the ice.'

'*Ja*, maybe, but...'

'*Ja*, but what? Hindsight is a wonderful thing isn't it, Papa?' Rolf opened his mouth, closed it.

'I should have stopped him but I didn't.' She dissolved into tears, clinging to him. They wiped each other's cheeks.

'Let's go back to Hanna and the others,' Elli said. 'They will be worried about us.'

'Like this? I'm a mess.' Rolf fumbled for his handkerchief and blew his nose with a loud trumpeting sound.

'Great, anyone could hear that, kilometres away,' Elli said. 'Let's go.'

As they walked back, Rolf all of a sudden stopped. 'Elli.'

'*Ja.*'

'*Danke.*'

In the darkness, Elli didn't respond. She could see someone walking towards them.

'Elli, Rolf?' It was Hanna. Despite the dim light, she must have seen Elli's smile. She rushed over to Rolf and covered his face with kisses. Elli left them alone and went back to the others.

'Where is Papa?'

'With Hanna. They will be fine. Papa and I had a long cry together.'

'Should I talk to him too?'

'Tomorrow—now he needs Hanna more than anyone else. He still blames himself. It's really eating into him.'

'I know,' Ruth said, 'but he must know the attack on our convoy wasn't his fault.'

'That's how he feels. He tried to do the best for all of us and then that happened. I think he's reached his limit, you know. His injuries are healing, but his mind isn't. When that maniac tried to kill him, he damaged more than Papa's shoulder. It's lucky for all of us he has Hanna.'

'I'll talk to him tomorrow. We have to find a place to sleep; I forgot to ask Sophy. Everyone else is asleep, but what about us? There are no beds left,' Ruth said.

'Over there.' Elli pointed to the *Kacheloven*.

'The *Kacheloven*, of course! No one is using the benches.'

'First warm night for ages,' Elli said. 'As good as sleeping with a man.'

'You're losing it, sister. Nothing is that good.'

Elli looked with admiration at the *Kacheloven*. It looked like a tiled wall reaching to the ceiling. The built-in bench was long enough for both of them to sleep on, and it was as wide as a single bed. Despite the hardness of the bench Elli felt her body relax on contact with the warm tiles.

'This is beautiful, a bed with a built-in heater,' Ruth said. 'Amazing what they make these days.'

'Actually, they're been around for a long time,' Elli said. 'I think the Russians built them first. It's a clever way of preventing people freezing to death in their beds.'

'How come we see these ovens so rarely?'

'They are very expensive to build,' Elli said. 'Wolfgang told me he built this one himself. He made a few improvements on the original design. This one has pipes filled with water. When the oven heats the water, it circulates through the pipes, cools down and flows back, gets reheated and so on. In a very cold winter, Wolfgang can let the water pass over the furnace in the workshop. He says it's a masterpiece of engineering.'

'Sounds like it,' Ruth said, already half asleep. 'Jochen would have been impressed.'

'*Ja*, he would have liked it.' She thought so, but not as much as she would have liked him here beside her on the warm bench, alive.

It was still dark when Elli woke. She tried to ignore the painful pressure in her bladder and drifted back into her dreams, but they were all about going to the toilet. She woke up again with the realisation that her body was about to give up the fight against the pressure. She jumped off the bench and stumbled through the darkness to the toilet. She tripped and fell onto someone.

'What the hell is going on?' Welsh said. 'I have to go to the toilet.'

'And that's why you walk on me?'

'You're blocking the door. Look, I can't hold on much longer. If you don't move and let me out, I'll pee on you. Would you prefer that?'

'There's a toilet down the hallway. You don't have to use the outside one. Let me get back to sleep.'

Elli was tempted to give him a sharp answer but then what he said sunk in.

She rushed down the hallway. Welsh was right! The Müllers really did have an inside toilet, unheard of in rural areas. There was a ceramic toilet basin and cistern. Wonderful! Wolfgang Müller had built more modern conveniences into his house than she had ever seen before. She lit the kerosene lamp on the wall beside her and held her breath in wonder at what was revealed by its light.

Toilet paper, real toilet paper! It was soft, delicate, and white. Elli hadn't seen toilet paper for ages. Her bottom really appreciated its smoothness. Since they left Krummhübel, they had used old newspapers, and when that supply dwindled, usually leaves.

Toilet paper was in short supply before they left Krummhübel, and no one had thought of bringing something so mundane on the journey.

How many times had she cursed the frost burn she had developed on her behind, when she crouched down in the snow somewhere? Getting your bladder or rectum to release when you were exposed in minus ten degrees was difficult. Muscles refused to cooperate. The ultimate in discomfort was a bum-wipe with a handful of snow or a scratchy fallen leaf.

Elli never realised that a heated toilet and soft toilet paper were the true symbols of civilisation until she had to shit in the snow.

The Müller's must be rich people. Anyone who still had a supply of toilet paper in these days must be very rich.

She made it back to the warm oven bench without stepping on anyone.

'That took you a long time,' Ruth said. 'I thought you must have got lost somewhere.'

'*Ja*, I can see how worried you were,' Elli said. 'How is your bladder? Don't you have to go?' For a moment, there was silence.

'You bitch. You had to say that, *ja*? Now I do have to go.'

'If it makes it any easier, the Müller's have an inside WC and— get this—toilet paper.'

Ruth jumped off the bench, stepped on swearing bodies, swore back, and disappeared. Elli woke up when Ruth crawled back under the blankets.

'That was fantastic!' she said. 'I never thought that it could be such a pleasure to wipe my bottom. Real, soft, toilet paper and an inside toilet. Heaven.'

'Did you use it all?' Elli said. 'What?'

'The toilet paper.' 'No. Of course not.'

'Thank goodness. I have to go again.'

Chapter 28

'That is total insanity. You can't be serious.' Smidt was shaking his head. 'You're going to follow the SS convoy?'

'It isn't an SS convoy. They are our mothers, wives and children. What choice do we have?' Rolf glared at the American.

'The SS is travelling westwards,' Elli interrupted. The argument between her father and the Americans was becoming aggressive. The other men looked on in bewilderment; they didn't understand a word of English. 'The next state is Lower Saxony,' she said, 'and that's where the English are. I guess they want to get the convoy there as fast as possible because it's safer there. It would also be safer for us.'

'Yes, it would,' Welsh said, 'but following the SS, particularly as closely as you intend to, is anything but safe. Before they reach Lower Saxony, the convoy will almost certainly run into Russian troops.'

'*Ja*, we are aware of that, but you are not listening. The SS is travelling with our families. We can't just walk away from them. Isn't it also in your interest to get out of this area and back to your people, or maybe you would prefer the Russians?'

'That's not the point, Elli. Following the SS is crazy enough, but as I understand it, you want to follow them without letting them out of sight.'

'No one said anything about following them that closely, just close enough to help if they harm our families.'

'And how would you help against a group of armed SS men?'

'I don't know, but what I do know is that we have to stay close to them. Maybe we can help and maybe not. We can try at least.' Her eyes filled with tears and her voice started to choke. 'We have lost so many, we have to stay close.'

'I still think that what you are intending to do is crazy,' Welsh said, 'but I understand why. And you are right, we would also like to get back to our people.'

After Rolf translated the American's concern, the discussion continued unabated. When everyone finally agreed to follow the SS group, some were anxious to start immediately.

'Impossible!' Rolf said, shouting to get his voice heard. 'We have to make space for everyone on the two wagons, do repairs, give the horses a rest, and find food. It will take at least one, or maybe two, days.'

'We can't stay here for that long,' Elli said. 'Or we'll never catch up.'

'We will. Don't forget the SS will also have problems—and they'll be travelling slower than us, with women and children.'

The group dispersed after some argument about the various jobs to be done. Ruth, who had been quiet up to now, approached Rolf and Elli.

'Papa, why should our family, follow the SS? They're not our relatives. Why risk our lives?'

'Don't be ridiculous,' Rolf said. 'These are our people, and we are part of them. If anyone in our family was in that group, how would you feel if someone used your argument? We can't just walk away from them.'

'I don't agree,' Ruth said. 'Why should I risk the lives of my children, your grandchildren, to follow this insane idea?'

Elli followed the argument between her father and sister. Neither she nor Hanna said anything. Rolf slowly levered himself out of the chair. Supporting his shaking body by leaning heavily on the table, he faced his daughter.

'Insane idea? Is there anyone you care for other than yourself?' Ruth looked straight at him. Her face was ashen but calm, although her voice trembled with anger.

'Papa, don't do this,' she said slowly, carefully enunciating each word. 'I'm responsible for the safety of my children and I'm not prepared to endanger them by being in this pursuit. I have decided we will stay.'

'Stay? Stay where? Here, with these people?' Rolf grabbed her hands. 'Ruth, you can't stay here. This place will become little Russia. Of course, I am concerned about you and my grandchildren. It's not safe here.

We have to go west.'

'No, we are staying. I think it is less dangerous here than following that convoy.'

'But you were for it, you even convinced me,' Elli said. 'I've changed my mind!'

Elli wanted to say something but the steely determination in her sister's voice stopped her.

'When the Russians come through again, they will do the same to you as they've done to other women; they'll rape you,' Rolf said. 'Even your four-year-old daughter will be in danger. Are you prepared for that?'

'We managed to avoid trouble in Krummhübel, and we'll do it again. Besides, that sort of thing could happen in any occupied area.'

'But why stay in this godforsaken place? What would that solve?' 'I asked her to stay,' Wolfgang Müller said quietly as he joined them.

'What? Why would you? Why?'

'Papa, leave it. It's pretty obvious why,' Elli said. She turned to her sister and took both her hands. 'Ruth, are you sure? I don't know what you and Wolfgang have between you, but whatever it is, you've only known each other for a few days.'

'We'll stay,' Ruth said. She pulled her hand away and walked out. 'Look, it's not what you think,' Wolfgang said. He sounded embarrassed. 'I asked Ruth to stay because there is room for her and the children and we need her. There is plenty of work. We hid our women before, when the Russians came through, and we'll do it again if we need to. I didn't ask her to stay because...for any other reason.'

Elli looked at his flushed face. The big man had a sheepish smile on his face. He opened his mouth to say something but the words didn't come.

'You mean, you're not trying to take advantage of the situation. Your invitation is not based on sexual motivation?'

Wolfgang's face changed from red to purple. Elli thought he would burst. His mouth opened like an oxygen-starved goldfish and his eyes bulged. He turned and left the room.

Elli and Rolf broke out into laughter. Rolf had tears running down his face and had to support himself on his daughter.

'Oh, that was cruel,' he said at last. 'I didn't know that you could be so cruel.'

'I couldn't help it,' Elli said. 'For the last two days he has been following Ruth like a lovesick puppy, and then he comes out with this sanctimonious nonsense.'

'You don't like him,' Rolf said.

'I don't know. Maybe it's not his fault Ruth decided to stay, but his invitation certainly contributed to her decision.'

'*Ja*, maybe. As much as I hate it, it's Ruth's decision. There's nothing we can do about it,' Rolf said.

It took them two days to get ready for departure.

Wolfgang fixed up an old wagon he found standing in the machinery yard. He fitted long benches into the wagon, enough to seat all the men. Constructing a wind shelter for the wagon was complicated as they were short of canvas. Luckily, they had the spare blankets from the SS trailer to fill the gaps.

Food was their greatest problem as their supply from Nickolsdorf was running out. Elli and Hanna decided to go on a bartering trip through the village. They had no idea if the village population would be willing to trade with them, or if there was any spare food to trade. The pile of blankets Elli had, compliments of the SS, came in handy.

People were reluctant at first but eventually they managed to get some food in exchange for the blankets.

The wagon started to fill up, mostly with potatoes. The villagers were happy to have bits of warm uniforms, but they would only swap them for a few potatoes. The army boots, however, were worth their weight in salami. Jewellery, which Elli and Hanna collected from the other refugees, was not so popular. Elli nearly cried when she gave a gold necklace to a farmer in exchange for a side of pork and some salami.

'Elli, we can't eat the jewellery,' Hanna said. 'I'd much rather be alive and poor than rich and starved to death.'

'*Ja*, fine, me too. But that Schwein knew that he was getting an incredible bargain; he gave us only a miserly side of pork and a handful of sausages. What a bastard.'

'Stop ranting. We are lucky to have this much food.'

'We've only got a couple of drawings and a landscape painting from Ruth left to trade,' Elli said. 'I wonder if we'll get more than a handful of potatoes for them? I bet no one in this place has heard of her.'

'Is she a well-known artist?' Hanna said.

'She was until the Nazi party labelled her deranged. Idiots. After that, her paintings were burned, or they just disappeared.'

'I saw one of her paintings in Wolfgang's house. Dead people, half buried in snow. It was very moving.'

'I didn't know that she had given that one away. Remember the dead people we found before we cut through Bohemia?'

'I heard about that but I didn't see them,' Hanna said. 'They were refugees like us. It was terrible.'

'How did they die?'

'Shot. Papa found empty cartridges from an SS pistol.' 'The SS shot them? Anything to do with the *Schweine* who abducted our families?

'I don't think so. They must have been killed shortly before we went through. That's why we left the main road there, to avoid running into the SS responsible,' Elli said.

'Perhaps they came back and started to follow us. It's too much of a coincidence that a few days later we see an SS group behind us.'

Elli rubbed her head. What Hanna said made sense. Why hadn't she thought of that?

'Maybe those poor people resisted them. I don't know. You could be right. That could be the explanation.'

'And Ruth painted the scene?'

'*Ja*. She was actually sick at that time and didn't see the bodies. The painting was based on what she heard from others.' 'Amazing. We should keep it and the drawings.'

'It's obvious we are wasting our time. We won't get anything for a painting in this place,' Elli said.

'Maybe. Anyway, we have only the one house left, that big one over there. We might as well try.'

An elderly woman opened the door and went to get her husband.

When he looked at the painting his face lit up. He introduced himself formally.

'My name is Erich Schnabel. This painting is beautiful and I certainly would like to have it. I can only offer you some potatoes and a few pieces of smoked pork for it. Would that be acceptable?'

Elli and Hanna nodded, too surprised to say anything.

Later, after they had loaded the last of the food onto their wagon, Schnabel and his wife came over.

'Would you like to see where we will hang the painting?'

Politely, Elli and Hanna followed them back to the house, into the living room.

'You have a beautiful place—so many paintings,' Elli said. There were pictures on every available wall space. When Erich

Schnabel pointed out where Ruth's painting would go, Elli saw something that astonished her. The paintings on the wall looked familiar. She had a closer look at the signatures. Yes they were Ruth's paintings!

'I don't believe it! All of these paintings are by Ruth.'

'You know the artist?' Schnabel was surprised. '*Ja*. She is my sister.'

Schnabel's face flushed with excitement as he grabbed Elli's hands.

'Ruth Harder's sister! Such an honour. *Mutti*, make some coffee, real coffee and chocolate cake. Ruth Harder's sister is our guest.' Schnabel's wife, a big smile on her face, hurried into the kitchen. 'Please, Fräulein Harder, take a seat, please.'

'Actually, my name is Hirsch.' Elli smiled at the babbling man. 'Harder was my maiden name.'

He waved a hand brushing her comment aside. 'How is your sister? Is she still in Silesia?'

'No, she's here.'

'Here? What do you mean?'

'Here, in this village, and she intends to remain here.' '*Mutti*, did you hear that?' His wife nodded. She piled pieces of rich chocolate cake onto delicate china plates. 'Ruth Harder is in our village! The honour, the honour! Where is she staying?'

Elli hesitated, but surely Ruth could only benefit from an adoring admirer.

'At the Müller's.'

'The Müller's? Ruth Harder can't stay at the blacksmith's. I'll have to fix that,' Schnabel said and hurried off.

'I hope Ruth enjoys that,' Hanna smiled.

'*Ja*, so do I,' Elli said.

The wagons were loaded. After tearful farewells, the passengers climbed on.

Wolfgang and his sister gave Rolf last minute advice about difficult sections of the road, as Ruth gave Elli a final hug.

'If he doesn't treat you right, I'll come back for you,' Elli said.

'When we arrive in Hamburg, we'll let you know where we are and you'll always be welcome.'

'*Liebling*, I'll be fine. He's a good man,' Ruth said. 'I'm more worried about all of you. I still think you are all insane, especially Papa.'

'Don't worry. I'll keep an eye on him,' Elli said with a sad smile. She climbed up beside her father. 'Come on, get Karla moving.' The huge Clydesdale obeyed and threw herself into gear sending shudders through the overloaded wagon but failed to move. In the other wagon, where most of the men were, the same thing happened. Both wagons were too heavy.

They had to offload all the non-essentials, including some of Elli's personal belongings.

'I'll look after your stuff,' Ruth said. 'Look, maybe you could stay too? I'll talk to Wolfgang.' Elli did not respond, just shook her head.

Even though the wagons were lighter now, they were still too heavy for the horses. Wolfgang came up with a suggestion.

'I have two large sleds in my yard. If I join them together there would be enough seating for everyone.'

'That's fantastic, Wolfgang,' Elli said, 'but wouldn't it still be too much for one horse?'

'No, actually it would be less weight than your wagon. With good solid snow, a sled is much easier to pull than a wheeled vehicle. Just

slides!' He made a wide sweep with an arm to show how easy it would be. 'That's a fantastic idea,' Elli said. 'Can we make another sled out of my wagon?'

'No, that wouldn't work; besides a big sled has some drawbacks.'

'Like what?'

'Well, it's hard to start. The men will have to get off, shove hard, and jump back on when it's moving.'

'So,' Elli said. 'I can't see any problems with that.'

'It could be a big problem for the older men to run after a moving sled and hop on again,' Wolfgang said.

'No problem. They'll move or they'll walk.'

Wolfgang's eyebrows rose. 'You will have to avoid roads that don't have a good snow cover.'

'That shouldn't be a problem either,' Elli said. 'There is a solid snow cover everywhere.'

'*Ja*, except on roads used by tank columns. They will have churned the roads there to mud.'

'I don't think that the SS convoy will follow roads that have carried troop movements.'

So it was agreed.

The sled was huge but the Clydesdale moved it without difficulty. Elli did several test runs through the village. From every doorway, people watched as Elli trained the men to jump on and off the moving sled.

'Come on, a bit faster, or you'll have to walk. Good, now off again. Next lot jump on. *Ach du meine Güte*! Are you stupid or what? You have to let the others off first, *Dummkopf*.'

After several trial runs up and down the main road, Elli was finally satisfied. The applause from the houses told her that the locals had enjoyed the performance.

They were ready to leave, but Rolf objected.

'We can't let them wear the uniforms. When they sit on the sled they look like a bunch of soldiers. We have to get civilian clothes for everyone.'

'Rolf is right,' Wolfgang said. I'll organise that.' He gathered the men together and sent them into the furnace room. 'Now, take off the uniforms. It is warm enough in here, so you won't freeze. I'll be back as soon as possible. I need someone to come with me.'

'I'll come,' Elli said.

They collected the discarded uniforms. Elli couldn't help smiling.

The men stood huddled together in their underwear and although the furnace produced a lot of heat, the icy draught coursing through the workshop made them very uncomfortable.

'We'll be back soon, so keep turning round, to get warm on all sides.'

She ignored their replies.

They went from house to house.

'Come on, Emil,' Wolfgang said to a man standing firm in the doorway of his house. 'These people have lost everything. They need civilian clothes. You can choose from these uniforms. They can't travel in them, much too dangerous. A few spare rags are all they need. Stuff you don't wear any more, anything. If it doesn't fit anyone they can trade it for food.'

'Wolfgang, these are bad times. Anything good enough to trade for food, I can't give away. My own family needs it. I already traded some food for uniforms. I just don't need any more.'

'You are a hard man, Emil, but you are right; these are bad times. By the way, aren't your horses due for new shoes?'

'*Ja*, but...'

'A new set for each in exchange for some warm clothes—deal?' Elli was fascinated. The huge blacksmith manipulated, begged, pleaded, even intimidated, until he had enough warm clothes for all the men. Only a few of the villagers dared refuse his demands. Finally, they were ready to leave.

'Papa, you have to say goodbye to Ruth.' Rolf gave her a sharp look but did not answer. 'Wolfgang is a good man. Ruth and the children will be safe here. Come on.'

'He is a blacksmith and she is an artist. It'll never work.'

'He is a good man Papa, and patient. Ruth needs that.'

'Ruth is a city person, an artist. He is an uneducated clot.'

'He is intelligent and strong,' Elli said. 'Look at this village. Wolfgang is holding it together and he keeps it going. He is a natural leader.'

'But will he look after Ruth and the children?'

'Papa, let's go. Ruth and the children are safer here than with us.'

'Why don't you stay too if you think it's safer here?'

'He didn't ask me, and besides I don't want to stay,' Elli said.

Everyone was eager to leave. The whole village watched as the men on the sled performed their mounting act perfectly.

The farewell between Ruth and her father was terse. Rolf avoided looking at her and concentrated on his grandchildren.

'Look after your brother, Elfi.'

'I will, *Opa*.' Her voice stumbled as tears rolled down her cheeks. 'Shall I look after Mama too?'

'Especially after your Mama, my *Liebling*.'

'Oh Papa, you silly man,' Ruth said. She grabbed his face and kissed him. 'We'll be fine. I am more concerned about you. Lucky you have Hanna to look after you.'

Elli looked back at the small crowd waving their arms, until they were a tiny blur on the white landscape.

Rolf, Hanna, and Elli sat beside each other on the steering bench of the wagon, with the three children safely in the back, wedged in between luggage.

'We started from Krummhübel with more then two thousand people and now there are only fifteen of us: you two, our three children and myself, and on the sled there's Hans, Manfred, Armin, Hugo, Alfred, Udo, Jürgen, and the two Americans. That's all.'

'Don't forget there are six women and thirteen children with the SS,' Elli said.

'I didn't forget them, and I haven't forgotten what happened to the three boys. I hope the women and children are still alive.'

They made good progress and reached the next town before dark. The people they met were cautious, and became hostile and uncommunicative when asked about the SS convoy.

'I think we had better keep going,' Rolf said. 'The SS took what they wanted from here and beat anyone who objected. I can understand why they are suspicious of us.'

'*Ja*, we'll leave,' Elli said. 'At least we found out that the SS are moving very slowly. The women and children are probably slowing them up.'

'We need a plan for when we catch up with them,' Hanna said. 'We have to get closer first,' Rolf said. 'I don't think they suspect anyone is following them. We would have seen them checking up on us if they knew we were here.'

Fresh snow covered the road and no vehicle tracks were visible. Darkness closed in. Hanna steered the sled. The men complained of cold and hunger. Suddenly one of them pointed at the road.

'Hanna, look, wagon tracks, fresh ones.'

Moments later Hanna pointed to a small clump of trees in the distance.

'Look there—a fire.'

It was getting darker. The faint light of the fire was clearly visible. The night camp of the SS was just ahead of them.

Chapter 29

The two vehicles stopped. Everyone spoke in whispers.

'We can't just go over there and ask them to hand back our people and our belongings,' Elli said. 'They would shoot us on the spot.'

'We'll get off the road and camp here for the night. They're not going anywhere,' Rolf said.

'But we are too close. They'll see our campfire. We can't eat cold food; we need the heat, Papa.'

'It will be safe if we get a small fire going behind those rocks.' 'With a small fire it will take ages to prepare a meal. So we'll have it cold, *ja*?'

'God, no. We need warm food and a hot drink more than anything else. You've made your point,' Rolf said. 'We'll move back a bit further. The hill we came around a short while ago should give sufficient cover.'

Turning around on the narrow road was not easy. Karla managed without much direction, but the wagon was creaking dangerously as it was forced into a tight turning cycle. Fortunately, nothing broke or fell off. The large sledge presented more of a problem. Even when the horse was disconnected it was too long and it hung dangerously over the road embankment. Elli told all of the men to hold on to the back of the sledge as the horse was reconnected to the front by a long rope.

When the horse started to pull the sledge, the men held on to the back and tried to guide it in the right direction, but they were too cold and exhausted. Only after Karla was connected to the rear of the sledge did they manage to save it from going over the edge.

The whole manoeuvre was conducted in near silence. They were more afraid of the SS group hearing them than of losing the sledge over the embankment. Finally, when they reached the cover of the hill, they collapsed into the snow crying and laughing.

'I swear I'll never to ask you to turn around again,' Rolf gasped. 'You won't. If you ever mention it again, I'll push you over the edge,' Elli said.

There was enough cover to have a large fire. The terrain was flat and they were in a clearing bordered by a dense pine forest.

'We'll stay here. We are only a few kilometres from the next town. Once there we should be able get close enough to see what condition our people are in, and possibly make contact with them,' Rolf said.

'Why wait until then?' Hanna said. 'Why not get closer tomorrow at daylight?'

'Too risky,' Rolf said. 'Imagine what will happen when someone recognises us.'

Hanna and Elli nodded. They could imagine the cheers, the joy, and the loud excitement their arrival would cause. 'I don't think the SS would accept that we are just here by coincidence. They'll probably stop in the town and try to mingle with the population. It shouldn't be too difficult to get closer then.'

'Fine, and then what?' Elli said.

'I really don't know. We'll have to improvise when we know what the situation is. We'll have to find out if our families are able to move away from the wagons or if the SS is keeping them inside. Now, I think we must move our transport into the forest. We are too exposed here at the roadside.'

'Oh no! It's getting dark and the undergrowth here is too thick, too dense,' Elli said.

'*Ja, ja*, I can see that, but we're still too exposed. We must not be seen by anyone passing by.'

The men were already setting up camp. Rolf insisted despite the loud protests and they reluctantly agreed to move.

It took more than an hour to move the wagon and the large sled into the trees. After a lot of swearing and sweating, they finally completed the task. When they had a fire going, Elli and Hanna employed everyone in the preparation of the meal.

'You want to eat, *ja*? There are the potatoes, start peeling—and we need more firewood.'

Everyone was tired and cold but the promise of hot food and a warm fire got them moving. When Hanna and Elli were ladling out the steaming stew, Rolf called for everyone's attention.

'We'll need guards tonight—two people at a time, okay?' He did not wait for any response, as he must have seen their expressions. 'Stay together and keep each other alert. It will be very cold, so we'll change the guards every two hours. Any problems?' Most people were too occupied with their bowls of stew to respond. Rolf ignored the few grumbles, and set about organising the guards' roster.

Elli, Hanna and the children crowded into the small tent and the men stayed in Elli's wagon, packed in like sardines. It was warm but the tent walls dripped with condensation. The women had to choose between wet backs or pressing their faces into a wet surface. They were just getting fairly comfortable in their smelly confinement when Rolf came around again.

'I think you should pack snow around the tent. Cover it completely, make a kind of igloo but be careful not to collapse it. It will get very cold tonight and the snow will help keep you warm.'

Elli and Hanna peeled themselves out of the tent, slipped into their near-frozen boots, threatened to kill Rolf, and carefully began shovelling loose snow against the tent walls. The children helped by pressing from the inside against the tent walls, helping the women to compact the snow. Both were half frozen when they settled down in the tent again.

'I hope Karla doesn't mind us sleeping on her straw,' Elli said, her teeth rattling.

'We aren't eating it, just sleeping on it,' Hanna said. 'She should be grateful to get warm straw in the morning.'

'Mama,' Anna said, from between her brothers. 'Fritz is kicking me.'

'Not true, she pushed her feet into my face,' Fritz said. 'She kicked me in the face too. Tell her to lie still, Mama,'

Herman said.

'Be glad that you can sleep together and keep each other warm,' Elli said.

The children were indeed warm, squeezed between Elli and Hanna. One by one they fell asleep again.

Elli tried to ignore the maddening itches from by the straw's fauna. She drifted into scenes of sunshine and a green landscape without snow. There was a feeling of gentle rocking. The rocking increased. Now she heard a voice. She tried to ignore the voice but the rocking went on.

'Elli, wake up,' she heard her father's voice. 'Come on, it's your turn.'

'Go away. Why is it always you? Go away.'

'Come on. It's your turn now. I'm going back into the wagon. I'm frozen.'

Elli struggled out of the tent into the icy night air. She shivered violently.

'Oh my God, Papa, this is crazy! I'll freeze to death, if I have be out here for two hours.' She struggled to get into her frozen boots.

'Just keep walking around the camp. We left nice tracks for you. It's not that bad,' Rolf said and walked off.

'Papa, come back. Shit! What am I suppose to do?'

'Guard the place. Stay awake or you'll freeze to the ground,' she heard his muffled reply.

It was quiet, no sound at all, only the blood rushing in her ears.

The sky was clear and the stars were sharp, like minute searchlights. In the distance, a dog started to howl, then more joined in.

'I didn't know you had wolves in your country,' a dark figure said in English as he walked towards her.

'Smidt, you idiot. Did you have to scare me like that? What are you doing here?'

'I'm your guard buddy. Didn't your father tell you?'

'No, he wasted no time getting back into his warm wagon.' 'Well, we'd better start walking. I can feel the cold through my boots already,' Smidt said.

The previous guards had left a track of compacted snow, easy and safe to follow. The moon came out and a pale-blue landscape developed in front of them.

'What do you mean by wolves? There are no wolves in Saxony.' Puffs of mist came from his mouth. He was laughing at her.

'I was born and raised in Colorado. Wolves are part of our wildlife. Believe me, I know what wolves sound like.'

'Ridiculous, this is Europe not... what was its name? 'Colorado.'

'And there are wolves?' 'Yes.'

'Sounds like a wild place.' 'Yes, it's wild—and beautiful.'

'So, what do you do in your wild country when you're not flying spy planes over Germany.'

Only the profile of his face was visible, a black silhouette against the starry sky. She was convinced that he smiled. He hesitated when he spoke, putting careful emphasis on each word.

'I'm a teacher. I was drafted, and trained to fly planes.' 'You are a teacher? What do you teach?'

'German and Latin,' Smidt said.

'You teach German! My God where did you learn that?'

'In Heidelberg. That was the most beautiful time in my life, but when the war started my parents pulled me out.'

'Why? Germany wasn't at war with the USA in 1939,' Elli said. 'I'm Jewish,' Smidt said.

'Oh.'

They continued to walk around the camp. It was bitterly cold and they had to breathe through their scarves. They lost themselves in conversation, fascinated with each other's background. Smidt was about the same age as Elli and he was intelligent. He had never married, even though he was easygoing and able to talk about anything. He looked at his watch.

'Elli our two hours are over. We have to wake the next two up.' Only now did Elli realise how cold she was.

'Thanks, Smidt, I enjoyed your company. You never told us your first name.'

'Joshua,' he said.

'Ok Joshua, let's wake them up.'

'Elli, can you hear that? What is that sound?' A faint rattling came from far down the road.

'Is it tanks? Oh my God, whatever it is it's coming our way. Listen.'

The noise grew louder, moment by moment.

'We're in trouble,' Smidt said. 'It is tanks, dammit! Look, there, down the road, coming around the bend. We have to get out of the clearing.' They rushed back to the tree line.

'Maybe they are your people,' Elli said. She hesitated for a moment. 'No, more likely Russians.'

'Right. There are no American troops in this area. The Germans are long gone. Elli, stay here behind the trees. Keep an eye on the tanks and don't show yourself. I'll go back to the camp and check the fire is out. I can't see anything from here but maybe the Russians could.'

He disappeared into the darkness. Elli hid behind a fallen tree.

Three tanks came slowly down the road. They came directly towards her. The noise increased. The first two passed by. Elli started to breathe easier but the last tank slowed down and stopped. The heavy diesel engine ran for a moment, then coughed a few times and died. In the moonlight, Elli could see the red star on the side of the tank. She felt her heart beating so loud she was afraid the Russians would hear it.

Two soldiers climbed out of the tank, guns hanging over their shoulders, swearing loudly to each other. They detached two Jerry cans and a large funnel from the side of the tank and poured fuel into the tank. After they completed the refuelling and fastened the empty jerry cans back, they started walking towards Elli. She pressed herself deeper into the snow, expecting to be discovered any second, but they stopped, and stood there, facing her hiding place. She needed a few seconds to realise that both were peeing. They finished and started to walk back to the tank. Relieved, Elli turned to hurry back to the camp. The sharp crack of the twig she stepped on sounded like a gun shot. The Russians stopped and turned back.

They pointed at her and shouted. Her profile stood out clearly against the skyline.

She saw flashes and heard bullets whistle around her, followed by the sharp crackling of sub-machine guns. She ducked close to the ground to get away but a powerful blow on her left leg knocked her down and then came the pain.

They had shot her.

Her left leg was like fire. She screamed. Moments later they reached her. A kick in the side of her chest rolled her over.

Through the red haze of pain, she saw the two men. They were laughing. The shorter one dropped his gun and started to fumble with his belt. They were going to rape her. She tried to get up. When she put weight on her left leg, a fierce pain shot through her body. She stumbled, fell down. There was a short exchange in Russian between the two men. The taller one stepped behind her head and pinned her arms to the icy ground. The other man bent over and ripped Elli's shirt off. He forced her legs apart and tried to kneel between them. She screamed and tried to close her legs. The Russian grunted and she felt a stinging slap on her face.

He tore her knickers down and then hit her on the wound. The pain was a red-hot poker. It overrode every other sensation. There was only pain, burning through her body, devouring her. He dropped her leg, pulled her up by the hair and hit her again. Her head hit the ground and the pain in her leg lessened. She stopped struggling. She saw only a red haze. Nausea. A different feeling between her legs, as he penetrated her.

Her throat and mouth filled. She opened her mouth and a fountain of steaming vomit splashed into the Russian's face. He shouted, pulled out, and jumped back. The man who pinned her down let her arms go, stepped away and laughed.

The rapist shouted at his comrade and bent over Elli again to continue where he had left off, but the smell of the steaming vomit covering Elli's body seemed to stop him.

Suddenly, there were two sharp cracks. Shots. The Russians crumpled to the ground.

Elli flinched when a hand touched her.

'Elli, oh God, Elli.' It was Smidt. 'I shouldn't have left you.'

There were another two shots. Moments later, Rolf's face bent over her.

'*Mein Liebling*. Don't worry, you'll be all right.' Elli lifted her head. 'The Russians?'

'The animals are dead,' Rolf said. 'I shot them.' The pain disappeared and blackness closed in.

She ran through the woods chased by a black monster. It came closer and closer. She felt its hot, stinking breath. Its paws clawed her body. She stumbled over a root and its hairy body came down on her. It forced her legs apart and pushed itself into her. She felt cold. Pain rushed through her body, into her leg. She moaned in agony.

'Oh, my poor girl.' Elli heard Hanna's voice. 'I have to change the dressing on your leg.'

Elli opened her eyes. It was daytime. Bright sunlight came through the tarps covering the wagon. She felt movement. The wagon was moving again.

'Here, take these.' Hanna held out her hand. 'What is it?'

'Painkillers, my last ones. I kept them as a reserve for your father but you need them more.'

'What happened?'

'Take the pills. Good. That will help you sleep for a while. Your leg needs a lot of rest.'

Despite Hanna being careful, changing the dressing was agonising. Elli moaned and sweat ran down her face, but then the pain eased.

'You'll get it right with practice,' Elli said. 'It was uncomfortable when you started. Now it doesn't hurt at all.'

'Thanks, but no thanks. That is the drug, not me,' Hanna smiled. 'Whoa. That's good stuff,' Elli said drowsily, her tongue wayward. 'How is my leg?'

'Just a flesh wound. You were lucky.' 'Some luck.'

'Sleep now.'

Elli felt herself sinking down into a warm safe place, no pain, no fear.

When she woke up, the pain in her leg was still there but bearable, just pulsating. It was dark.

'Hanna, Hanna?' There was no answer. 'Hanna?'

Panic gripped her. The pain in her leg increased. She heard movement. Someone came to the wagon.

'I'm here, *Liebling*,' Hanna said. 'I'm sorry, I just went out for a bit of fresh air.'

'Where are we?'

'We're still following the SS.'

'We are moving again? What happened back there with the Russians?'

'When we heard the noise of the tanks and then the shots, Smidt and Rolf ran back.'

'What happened then?'

'Your father saw the Russians raping you'

'One of them was already...he stopped because I threw up on him. I don't remember what the other one did.'

'Your father and Smidt shot them.' 'They shot them?'

'Actually, Smidt shot them first but they were only wounded.' 'So they are still alive?'

'No, they aren't,' Hanna said. 'I don't understand.'

'Your father finished them. He killed them.' '*Vater im Himmel*. The Russians will kill us!'

'We got rid of the bodies. There was no one else in the tank.' 'But their tank was in a convoy. There were three tanks; I saw them. They stopped because they'd run out of fuel. When the Russians realise one of their tanks is missing, they'll came back looking for it.'

'Smidt drove the tank into the forest and by now the snowfall will have covered our tracks. They won't find anything. This morning, we reached the town but the SS and our people had been and gone. They may have heard the gunshots or been scared off by the Russian tanks. Our people were okay. The townspeople said they were like any other refugee group, bartering for food and fodder for their horses. They must have been spooked by the shots and left in a hurry.'

'What now?'

'We're still following them. The next town is not far away. We'll catch up with them there, because they'll need food. They didn't have time to get any in the last town.'

'My leg hurts, Hanna.'

'Here, take these,' Hanna said, handing her two more tablets. 'The same as before? They were terrific.'

'*Ja*, the same, they'll make you sleep again. It's only a flesh wound but it'll take a while to heal.'

'Only a flesh wound,' Elli said through clenched teeth. '*Scheisse*.

Give me the tablets.'

Chapter 30

Awareness grew—voices, the smell of bacon, a dull rumbling in her stomach. The rumbling got louder. The smell of wet canvas confirmed that she was in the wagon and her rumbling stomach told her she was hungry. She pushed the tarp aside, and immediately closed her eyes to keep out the light. Even with her eyelids tightly closed it hurt. Slowly she tried again, but there was only glaring white. Despite the feeling of burning, and tears running down her cheeks, she kept her eyes open and slowly they adjusted. Shadows turned into people standing around a campfire.

She climbed out of the wagon and tried to walk towards them. Too late, she realised she couldn't feel her injured leg. There was no leg and no pain. Fear struck; she fell flat on her face.

'That was a silly thing to do,' Elli heard her father say. 'You're not healed. You should have called someone.'

'Oh, thank God it's still there! For a moment, I thought someone had amputated my leg. I couldn't feel it.' She looked up. 'Now that you have had your fun, will someone help me up please, or is that too much to ask?'

'Well,' Rolf said, 'at least your mouth is still functional. Hanna, give her a hand, I can hardly stand myself.'

'Here *Liebling*, lean on me.' Hanna helped her up in one swift hoist.

'My God, you are strong,' Elli said, balancing precariously on one leg.

'Straight back and bend the knees—an old nurse's trick,' Hanna said.

'That was terrifying. My leg wasn't there,' Elli said. 'I still can't feel a thing.'

'Quite normal! You feel pain but don't know where it is. The nerves have to reconnect and that takes a while, I'm afraid,' Hanna said. 'I've made some crutches for you.'

'Crutches, great!'

'Elli, you are lucky to be alive and relatively unharmed. If it weren't for Smidt those two Russians would probably have killed you.'

'Smidt? I thought Papa shot them.'

'No, they were still alive after Smidt downed them. We had to decide something fast. Leaving them injured was not an option. So, Rolf killed them?'

'Papa killed them?'

'Yes! Smidt drove the tank deeper into the forest and we arranged the two bodies to make it look as if the *Wehrmacht* shot them. Let's hope that when the Russians find the tank, they don't look too closely at the bodies.'

'What do you mean?'

'Well, it's rather difficult to get yourself shot in a tank. Blown up, yes; burned, yes; but shot?'

'I don't think they'd be too concerned about details, Hanna. I only hope they aren't found for a while.'

'Well, we've travelled quite a distance in the last two days so our tracks should be mixed with those of other refugees, and covered by snow.'

'I was out for two days?' Elli said. '*Ja*, with the help of a little morphine.'

'Elli, you are up again!' Smidt's voice boomed at them. 'I was afraid your nurse would have you sleeping all the way to Hamburg.' Hanna gave him a playful slap on the head. 'See, she wastes her drugs on you, and tries to beat others unconscious.'

'Thank you,' Elli said. 'You saved my life.' Smidt raised a dismissive hand, fumbled with the buttons of his jacket, and blushed.

'That assault wouldn't have happened if I had got back earlier. I shouldn't have left you alone,' Smidt said. He sounded so serious and remorseful that Elli wanted to hug him.

'If I hadn't panicked it wouldn't have happened. I owe you one,' she said.

Smidt gave her a boyish grin. 'Great! Next time I panic, I'll count on you to get me out of trouble.'

'Deal,' Elli said. 'Next time some Russian women try to rape you I'll shoot them.' Smidt's face changed to the colour of an overripe tomato. He is really a nice man, Elli thought, just a touch on the shy side.

'When will we catch up with the SS?' Elli said. Her father was standing nearby at the fire, watching her and Smidt.

'We have already.' Rolf said.

'Was he listening in?' Elli said to Hanna, ignoring Rolf limping over to them.

'Of course, he always needs to know what's going on.'

'The SS are in Dippoldiswalde, only three kilometres away,' Rolf said. 'We'll stay here overnight, and when daylight breaks, we'll go into the town.'

'What, just walk in? Is that your carefully developed plan, dear father?'

'Sarcasm doesn't become you, dear daughter, and yes,

Dippoldiswalde is large enough for us to blend in. The SS won't know we're outsiders, not immediately anyway.'

'So why wait until tomorrow?'

'Tomorrow is Sunday. There'll be a market in the town square. Lots of people from everywhere.' 'A market?'

'*Ja*. The Dippoldiswalde art market is famous.'

'An art market? In the middle of a war people buy art?' 'Well, right now it isn't so much an art market.'

'So what is it?'

'A black market of course,' Rolf said.

'What, an open black market? You are joking. The Gestapo would arrest everyone.'

'I don't think they'll bother now. They're all hiding or fleeing westwards.'

'But what is there to sell? Most people are starving,' Elli said. 'You would be surprised. Many people still have things to barter, food, anything.'

'We need food but there's hardly anything left to barter with.

We'll have to find something,' Elli said. 'That's my girl.'

'*Ja*, terrific. Any ideas?'

'No, but I'm convinced you will find something.' Rolf was bewildered by his daughter's irate look. 'What, what did I say?'

As Elli set off back to the wagon, Hanna called after her. 'Elli, wait. I have to talk to you.'

'I have to lie down; my leg is killing me.'

'I'll give you something for it.' She helped Elli back into the wagon and rummaged through her doctor's bag. Finally, she came up with a menacing looking syringe and two small bottles.

'No, wait!' Elli panicked at the size of the syringe. 'That thing is big enough for a horse. I thought you'd give me a couple of tablets.'

Hanna held up the two bottles. In the dim light of the carbide lantern, the fluids in the bottles looked sinister.

'This one is for the pain and it'll help you to sleep. And this one,' Hanna looked straight at her, 'is for what the Russian possibly left you with.' Elli's stomach cramped.

'*Scheisse*! That *Schwein* made me pregnant?

'No, I checked you when you were unconscious and I don't think he e*ja*culated...'

'He didn't...how do you know that?' Hanna's clinical language alarmed her.

'...but he possibly had syphilis. Smidt said the Russian had a rash which looked like severe sunburn and he had patchy hair loss. Both are symptoms of advanced syphilis. I've already given you two penicillin injections. This will be the last one.'

'Oh no! I was afraid that he could have made me pregnant, which would be bad enough, but not this. I feel sick.'

'You'll be fine. You were lucky that I still had some of the penicillin; I used nearly all of my small supply on your father. Okay, now turn around, skirt up, and knickers down.'

The injections were painful and Elli did not attempt to suppress her cries. 'My goodness, what a fuss,' Hanna said, and in the same breath, as Rolf poked his head into the wagon, 'Get out, or I'll give you one too.'

'You could you have given me the painkiller first,' Elli said, as the morphine kicked in. 'But that would have spoilt your fun, *ja*?'

It was dark when her bladder woke her up. She could identify the breathing of her children and her father's snoring but there were others sleeping in the wagon, as she realised when she stepped on them.

'What on earth is going on? Where are you going in the middle of the night, young lady?' Elli was sure she had never heard that voice before and didn't answer. Finally, outside the wagon she located her crutches and stumbled through the snow. At a comfortable distance from the wagon, she relieved herself. Her urine left a steaming hole in the snow.

'What are you doing here?' The man's voice made her jump. She looked up to see Smidt's smiling face.

'*Arschloch*! Why did you sneak up on me like that, Smidt?' 'I'm on guard duty. Guards sneak up. Makes it easier to find out who wants to sneak in.'

'Very funny.' She threw a handful of snow at him.

'No! Not snow in my shirt.' He stumbled back from her onslaught. 'Calm down. I didn't mean to scare you. I didn't see anything.'

'I didn't know we still had guard duty,' Elli said. 'After what happened to you? Of course, we do.'

As Elli relaxed, she started to shiver. Smidt must have heard her teeth rattling.

'Here, put this on,' he said and pulled a jumper out of his rucksack.

'But don't you need it?' 'It's a spare one.'

Elli pulled the jumper over her clothes. It was a man's jumper, very thick, with several holes in it.

'It's beautiful. How come you have a spare jumper?'

'I took it from the Russians.'

'From the Russians? Do you mean the Russians who raped me?'

'Yep. Had some problems getting the jumpers off them,' he said, calmly, as if he was talking about the weather.

Elli felt like ripping the jumper off, but it was warm. Certainly, the Russian didn't need it anymore.

'What are the holes?'

'Bullet holes. I had to make them bigger. Couldn't get the blood off.'

'Pretty mercenary behaviour for a teacher.'

'I guess you're right,' Smidt said. 'This bloody war is changing all of us and not for the better.'

'Bravo, teacher. I hope the Russians realise that when they see that we are both wearing Russian army jumpers,' Elli said.

Smidt shook his head, opened his coat, and pulled his jumper from the back of his neck.

'Have a look at this.'

'It's a garment label. So what?'

'It's an American garment label,' Smidt said.

Elli had a look at the label. He was right, it said: 'Made in USA'. 'Oh shit, they were Americans!'

'No, they were definitely Russians, but wearing jumpers we supplied to them. They are our allies, after all.'

'Great allies you Americans have.'

'As I said, the war is brutalising all of us,' Smidt said.

'What an absolute pile of shit. Those men were common rapists. Only a man could come up with such a stupid rationale. I wonder how you would feel if they raped you.'

'I'm sorry Elli. I didn't mean it that way.' He stretched his arms out to hold her.

'Don't touch me. You're no better than them.'

'Elli, I said I'm sorry. I didn't mean to be derogative. I actually meant that the war has changed me. Twelve months ago, I couldn't imagine that I could have shot someone and then worn his clothes, for Christ's sake.'

'I do not know what it is with men,' Elli said furiously. 'A gun in your hands and the excuse of war is all you need to act like animals. All these killings and rapes in the name of a better country. Americans, Russians, Germans, you're all the same. You make wars and women have to bear the consequences.'

Smidt opened his mouth to respond but the rage on her face stopped him.

'When we left our town,' Elli said, 'Polish soldiers raped one of our women. Later we found out that we were actually lucky. We heard that in some towns the Russians systematically raped every woman. It didn't matter what age the women were. They raped babies, children, and old women. I didn't think it could happen to me.'

Something was breaking in her and a tidal wave of anger and humiliation washed away her protective barrier. Again, she was there— the pressure on her arms holding her down, the tearing of her clothes, the forcing apart of her legs, the brutal penetration, a man's face close to her.

She lashed out, felt the contact of her fist and heard a scream.

Then everything became grey, the sharp stench of vomit. That will be hard to clean, she thought and passed out.

Her back felt cold. She opened her eyes, and saw Smidt's face over her. The moonlight gave him a sickly colour, which matched the worried expression on his face.

'Did I hit you?' she said. 'Yes you did.'

'What am I doing here on the ground?'

'After you broke my nose you decided to pass out.' 'I broke your nose?'

'You did.' 'Does it hurt?' 'Yes it does.'

'Good! I would have been embarrassed if it didn't. You deserved it.'

'What? I may have made a few clumsy remarks, and for that I deserve that you rearrange my face?'

'I'm sorry. I don't know what came over me. For a moment, I was back there and felt them holding me down. I can still feel him.'

'Well, I'm glad that the punch wasn't really meant for me. By the way, you didn't break my nose.'

'I didn't? Well, let me fix that,' she said and swung her fist at his face. He stopped her by enclosing her in his arms.

'Let go, you bastard.'

Smidt let her arms go, grabbed her face with both hands and, after looking for and getting permission, kissed her. His stubbly face and cracked lips hurt her, but she stopped struggling. It felt good. Only when his tongue started to explore, did she give him a gentle kick.

'That hurt.' He winced and rubbed his shin.

'It was supposed to.' Elli smiled. 'But I'm glad I didn't break your nose.'

The smelly vomit stains on her jumper were proof that she hadn't imagined being sick. 'Eeh! How could you have kissed me, smelling like that?'

'Didn't smell a thing,' he said, lying.

Back in the wagon, she snuggled in between her complaining children.

'Don't push me, Mama. You're cold. Where were you?' 'Shhh! Sleep now!' she whispered, still smiling when she fell asleep.

Voices raised in argument, among them her father's, woke her. He shouted something, and there were muttered responses. She climbed out of the wagon without disturbing the children. All the adults were standing around the fire.

'We can't walk into town as a group,' Rolf said. 'The SS will be expecting trouble, they'll be nervous. Remember how fast they took off last time.'

'Rolf, there are ten, maybe fifteen of them,' Hauser said. 'I think it would be safer if we stay together.'

'Safe? They have guns. How do you think they'll react to a large group of men recognised, maybe even greeted, by the women and children they kidnapped? It would be totally insane to stay together. If we want to find out how our people are, we have to be as inconspicuous as possible. The SS have nothing to lose. They would kill us and the women and children if they felt threatened. You must realise that, Hauser?'

'No, but I mean...maybe you are right.' Hauser looked down and stepped back without completing his sentence. Rolf glared at each man, inviting further objections, but none came. Elli wanted to protest at her father's intimidating behaviour, but he was right.

'The SS are armed,' Smidt said calmly. ' I agree with Rolf, approaching them as a group would be dangerous. Even in pairs it would be dangerous. They might recognise some of us again.'

'How? We were bashed and covered in bruises and black eyes,' Hauser said. 'I wouldn't recognise myself.'

'There is still a chance they'll know you,' Rolf said. 'So what do we do?' Hauser said.

'They have seen me, but only from a distance at the bridge and they definitely haven't seen Hanna, Hans or Elli,' Rolf said. 'So we'll check the situation before any of you go into town.'

'Wait a minute.' Elli was alarmed. 'That's crazy! You can hardly walk straight with your injured shoulder, and I'm on crutches. Hanna would have to hold both of us up, which leaves only Hans.' She turned to Hans, who was sitting quietly on a log. 'And Hans isn't exactly well. I'm sorry Hans.' Hans didn't say anything, only acknowledged her with a sad smile. 'So, where would that leave us if anyone tries to get tough with us? I'll clobber them with my crutches and you'll finish them off with harsh words, while Hanna and Hans hold us up, *ja*?'

'Can you imagine a more harmless looking group?' said Rolf, grinning infuriatingly.

'No I can't; but we're not only harmless, we're helpless. Two cripples with their helpers, that's really the best idea you can come up with?'

'The plan is actually not that bad,' Smidt said. 'Even if the SS see you, you won't be a threat.'

'Hanna, say something. What do you think about this insanity?' Elli said.

'I think it's risky, but I can't come up with anything better. Rolf's right. They might recognise some of the men and they'd almost certainly know the Americans.'

'*Liebling*, believe me, I would prefer to do it on my own, especially after what you've been through. Maybe it would be better if only Hanna and I go,' Rolf said.

'Over my dead body. It would be better if you stayed here, Papa. Two women, one on crutches and the other helping, would be even less suspicious.'

'No,' Rolf said. 'I might be limping, but you need me for the details.'

'You think two women are too stupid for that?'

Rolf looked at his daughter with a determined expression.

'No but I'm more experienced. Could we stop arguing now and discuss a practical plan?'

'I could go by myself,' Hans said unexpectedly. Everyone looked at him. Since the incident with Otto, Hans had been a little more animated, but he was still withdrawn and rarely contributed to discussions.

'No, too dangerous,' Rolf said. 'We have to do it as a group. Also, my friend, after Dresden, I don't think you are in any condition to do it alone.' Rolf's voice was determined and the subject was closed.

The sun was at its highest point. No clouds diminished the glaring reflection from the snow, which covered the road into town in a fresh, fluffy layer. The four of them were dressed to look like local peasants, they hoped.

'Look after each other,' Rolf said to his grandchildren. 'We'll be back soon.' Herman, Fritz, and Anna, looked at them, wide-eyed and tearful.

'Mama, will you come back?' Anna said.

'Of course, my *Liebling! Opa* is with us,' Elli said, with a smile for her father.

'Mama and Hanna are with *Opa*,' Herman said, reassuring himself. 'And Uncle Hans will look after them.'

Hans smiled. '*Ja*, I'll look after them.'

'Here Mama, my sled, you wanted to have it,' Fritz said. 'Thank you, my *Liebling*.'

'What's the sled for?' Rolf said.

'For me to sit on, while you pull me along. You didn't think that I would stumble along through the snow on crutches?'

'Oh, Father in Heaven! Why did I sire this child?'

'I could tell you,' Elli said grinning from ear to ear, 'but not in front of the children.'

Elli sat on her children's sled, crutches across her knees. The sled was thirty centimetres above the ground, with large runners and a seat big enough for two children to sit one behind the other. When the children used the sled, they stretched out flat, their heads and legs hanging over front and back.

Elli sat upright on the sled and Hans and Hanna pulled her along. Rolf walked beside her. Periodically, Elli encouraged Hanna and Hans to let her father pull.

'Come on you two; don't let him get away with that. His shoulder isn't that bad.' Rolf glared at his daughter.

At the next bend, the pine forest opened up, with a spectacular view over Dippoldiswalde.

'It's larger than I remembered,' Rolf said. 'Shouldn't take us more than half an hour to get there.'

'It's all downhill from here. I'll see you there,' Elli said.

'Too steep for sledding; you won't be able to steer it with your injured leg,' Rolf said.

'Envy doesn't become you, dear father. I know how to handle a sled. Have a good walk.'

'I hope you break your other leg.'

The light snow cover gave her a slow start but the speed increased. She leaned back, holding on to the steering rope. The pine trees on the roadside became a blur. Her teeth rattled each time the sled hit a bump. At larger bumps, the sled became airborne and Elli desperately clawed the sides to stay on. Too fast! How could she slow it down? The next bump came. She lost hold of the sled and was airborne. The snow cushioned the landing, but the pain from her leg was excruciating. She continued to slide down the road, twisted around, and disappeared head first into a snowdrift.

Snow was all around her upper body, but she could still move her legs. She was stuck head down with her legs straight in the air. The pain from her injury prevented any attempt to get out. Suddenly she felt hands around her ankles. Hanna and Rolf heaved her out.

'Aaaah! Not my sore leg. You idiots are hurting me!'

'Leave her there, I can't stand the complaining anymore,' Rolf said. 'Please, tell us again how well you can handle a sled?'

'*Ja, ja, ja*. Very funny. Let's get going. Where is it?'

'All over the road, a bit here and a bit there. You completely smashed it. I'm so sorry, but you'll have to walk,' Rolf said. 'You're lucky that I found your crutches.'

Elli was convinced that if his grin were any wider, his face would split.

'Leave her be. He is only pretending,' Hanna said 'You should have seen his panic when you disappeared down the road.' 'Panic, me? That's a vicious lie.' Rolf said.

Hanna interrupted him. 'Are you all right, *Liebling*?'

'My leg hurts.'

'At least you made good progress. You won't have to walk so far.

We're nearly there, look.'

Through the trees, stone houses hugged a narrow, cobbled street. All the houses were in neat rows. In front of a larger building was a flagpole with a crumpled, red flag hanging limply on it.

'Looks like the Nazis are still in charge here,' Rolf said.

Oak trees formed a snow-covered canopy over the street. Beams of sunlight came through the gaps, giving the impression of a tunnel.

There was no wind and fluffy columns of smoke from chimneys stood over the houses. No people were in sight, but they could hear dogs barking.

Close to the houses was a windbreak of large pine trees. Elli saw something that seemed familiar.

'Look, over there, in the gap between the trees. What is it?' 'It seems to have a canvas top,' Rolf said.

'Give me your binoculars. Come on, quick.' Rolf rummaged around in his bag.

'Here, what is it? What?'

Elli looked through the binoculars. He was right, there was canvas on a box container. When she followed the tree line, she could see something else through the gap.

'That's a wagon—and it's one of ours! They are here, we've found them!'

'What? Let me look.' Rolf peered through the binoculars. 'I can't see anything. I lost it. Where?'

'Look at the gap in the tree line on the left of the boxy thing,' Elli said.

'*Ja,* I got it. Is it a wagon wheel?'

'That's the wheel we put back on the wagon when it came off

in Bohemia. Remember there were two spokes missing where it hit the rock?'

Rolf put the binoculars down. He smiled.

'You are right, Elli. I think we have found them, but there seems to be only one wagon there. I can't imagine that the SS would leave it behind and go on with all the people in just two wagons. Something else has happened. We must have a look at that wagon.'

'You wait here; I'll have a look. Look after them, Hans,' Hanna said, as she climbed up the steep roadside bank.

Elli tried to follow her but her injured leg cramped and she slipped down onto her father. Both ended up on the road.

'Up, daughter, not down.'

'How about you leading the way, father?'

Rolf had difficulty climbing with his injured shoulder and he slipped back again after a few metres.

'Neither of us is good at this.' Rolf looked at Hans. 'Go after her, we are all right here. Hanna may need help.' Hans hesitated for a moment.

'But Hanna said...'

'Go, she needs help,' Rolf said. Hans shrugged his shoulders, climbed up and disappeared.

They waited. Elli felt something cold and wet on her face. It was snowing. At first large flakes drifted down, then more and more joined them until the tree-lined street was invisible.

'They have been gone for ages. We have to do something,' Elli said trying to suppress the tension in her voice.

'We have to wait here,' Rolf said. 'We can't do anything. They'll be back.'

Chapter 31

All of a sudden, Hanna slid down the embankment. 'What happened? Where is Hans?' Rolf said. 'Hans? I haven't seen Hans.'

'He went after you.'

'I didn't see him.' Hanna looked helplessly around, panting with exhaustion. 'My God, something must have happened to him!'

'Did you see the wagons?' Elli said.

'I'm not sure, the snow made it very hard to see anything, but it looked like there were three wagons in the meadow behind the pine trees.'

'We have to wait for Hans,' Rolf said.

'You think it's possible that he walked into the town? Elli said. 'Why would he? No! He went after Hanna to help her and he

would have come back here if he couldn't find her. Something must have happened to him. Maybe he had an accident, fell into a hole or something, and dragged himself to the nearest house for help.'

'Some scenario,' Elli said. 'More likely the SS caught him. We have to see if we can get help in the town!'

'Help? Who in his right mind would help us against SS?' Rolf said. 'The three of us have a chance of finding him if he's had an accident.'

'The weather is clearing. If we're going to look for him, we'd better get moving before it starts snowing again.'

It was late afternoon and getting dark. Most houses were in darkness. They couldn't see any people in the few buildings with lights.

'Strange,' Rolf said. 'No people.' 'Listen,' Elli said.

'What?'

'Music. I can hear music. It's faint, but it's definitely music.' 'Can't be,' Rolf said.

The snowfall reduced visibility to a few metres. The music grew louder as they advanced into the town.

Unexpectedly the street opened up into a market place. They stood at the edge of a fair. There were lights everywhere; coloured glass lanterns hung around sausage stands, produce tables, and craft stalls.

Lights were dancing through the sky—a carousel! The drifting snow distorted lights and sounds.

Scents of hot bratwurst, fresh honey cakes, and roasted nuts drifted by, making Elli's mouth water and her stomach growl.

Like a magic theatre, the falling snow formed a curtain that opened up new scenes and closed others. People appeared from nowhere and then faded out. Rolf, Hanna and Elli stood transfixed, unable to believe what they were seeing.

'What is this? Where are all these people from?' Elli said. 'From all the towns around here,' Rolf said. 'I knew this market was famous but I didn't expect this. There are people everywhere! How do we find our people in all this?'

'Simple,' Hanna said. 'We look around and we ask.'

No one in the crowd looked twice at them. People seemed used to strangers. There were no shortages here; the food stalls close to them had an abundance of offerings.

'I don't get this,' Rolf said. 'Everywhere else food is rationed, but here they have plenty. Look at these stalls, I haven't seen some of these goodies for years.'

Elli stared at the stalls; the smells drifting over nearly drove her mad.

'My God, I'm so hungry. I have to have one of these knackwursts. I didn't know they still existed.'

'We have no money,' Rolf said, 'but maybe they'll give you one because you are drooling so nicely.'

'Wait here,' Hanna said and walked over to the nearest sausage stand.

'What is she doing?' Rolf said. 'Begging for a sausage?' Hanna said something to the man behind the sausage stand, huge man with

'Emil's' printed on his apron. The trader smiled at Hanna, nodded, and handed her three sausages.

'I don't believe it! He gave her some,' Elli said, as she and Rolf hurried over.

The knackwursts, thick sausages with tight skins, came wrapped in hefty slices of bread. Elli's gave a loud crack as she bit into it, and a fountain of juice flowed over her hand.

'Hanna, where did you get the money?' Rolf said.

'Not money, I gave him a ring. Money would have been useless anyway. It's worth nothing, no one accepts it anymore. Seems like most people pay with other things. I saw his stash of traded goods behind the counter.'

Elli could see his open cashbox. It held very little money but all kinds of jewellery; even a cuckoo clock sat next to it.

Elli concentrated on her knackwurst again. The taste and smell were heaven. The sauerkraut had been prepared with goose fat, a taste she had forgotten. Rolf and Hanna likewise wolfed down their sausages, noisily enjoying every morsel.

This was bliss. Heaven was a hot knackwurst with fresh bread and sauerkraut.

When at last she looked up, Elli felt an icy shock through her body. Three Russian soldiers, Kalashnikovs over their shoulders, walked towards them. Elli breathed in sharply, and the last piece of sausage lodged in her windpipe. Desperately she tried to warn the others but could only cough until Rolf whacked her between the shoulder blades.

'Too greedy. Eat slowly,' he said with a fatherly smile.

Elli tried to talk but managed only a gurgle. 'Slow down,' Rolf said. 'I can't understand you. What did you want to...?' He stopped when he saw the Russians. The soldiers ignored them, talking to each other as they stopped at the sausage stand.

'Oh God, what do we do now?' Elli said. Her voice was quiet as she tried to make herself inconspicuous, fighting the urge to turn and run.

'Smile,' Rolf said. 'What?'

'Smile, laugh, talk to me. Act as if you are enjoying yourself.' Elli looked at the strained grin on his face and tried to comply even though his smiles and laughter were so false that surely the Russians would not be fooled. But the soldiers only glanced at them.

'There's something very strange going on here,' Rolf said. 'Did you see?' Hanna said. 'They act as if they are part of the town population. There must be more of them here or they wouldn't be so relaxed.'

'*Ja*, possibly a garrison of some kind. They act more like policemen, not like an army patrol,' Rolf said. 'Look.'

The trader handed each of them a sausage and the soldiers left. 'They didn't pay,' Hanna said.

'But they didn't just take the sausages either. The man gave them willingly,' Rolf said.

'So what?' Elli said.

'They could have taken them with threats. It looks like there's no looting here,' Rolf said. 'Wait a moment.'

He walked back to the sausage stand and talked to the dealer.

Both were laughing. The dealer handed Rolf three sausages and Rolf came back.

'Come on, come on,' Elli said. 'What did he say?'

'That he owed us a second lot of knackwurst. Hanna's ring is more valuable than he first thought. Here,' he said, handing each a sausage.

'What did he say about the Russians?' Elli said.

'We were right. There is a garrison in town. The Russians took over the town hall and some of the houses. He also said that the war is over.'

'The war is over? Since when?' Elli said.

'What he actually said was that the war is over for them. The Russians run the town now.'

'Is that what they are celebrating here?' Hanna said.

'No, this is the annual winter fair. The Russians gave them permission to hold it. He thinks this is a clever ploy by the Russians, to get hoarded goods brought out. It saves them having to supply food to a starving population.'

'I don't believe that,' Elli said. 'Why would people openly display their reserves when the Russians could just take everything?'

'I agree, it sounds strange,' Rolf said.

'Did you ask him where they got all the food?' Hanna said.

'He is a butcher and he used a couple of pigs he had hidden. Most of the other traders are selling or swapping goods they've hoarded. This is really a black market dressed up as their annual fair.'

'*Wunderbahr*,' Elli said. 'What about our people?' 'Oh *Gott*, I didn't ask!'

'Typical, thinking with your stomach again,' Elli said. 'Wait here.' 'Hallo *süsses Fräulein*,' the man at the sausage stand greeted her.

His high-pitched voice sounded excited. 'You three must be very hungry. I can understand that. Emil's sausages are the best. You get hungrier the more you eat.'

He towered over her, his big arms strong enough to strangle an ox.

'Emil? *Ja*, your sausages are fantastic.'

'*Danke schön*.' As he smiled, he looked like an oversized cherub. 'We're from Silesia, Emil, and we're going north to Hamburg.' 'From Silesia? I have relatives in Hirschberg. Where are you from?'

'Near there, from Krummhübel.'

'My goodness and you want to go to Hamburg! That's a long way.'

'*Ja*, it is. Have others from Silesia come through here recently?' The butcher looked at her, and then took a long knife and sharpening steel from a sheath on his hip. For a few moments, there was silence, but for the sound of the knife sliding over the steel. At last, he spoke.

'I heard that a group of Silesian refugees arrived two days ago. Apparently, they are staying in the Müller's horse field.' 'Where is that?

'What direction did you come from?' 'Bömchen,' Elli said.

'Well, then, you passed them. The field is close to the main road, behind a row of large pine trees.'

Elli laughed loud and long. '*Danke schön*, Emil, you are very helpful.'

'*Bitte schön*,' Emil said, beaming with delight. 'And if you need any help—with anything—my shop is down the main road.'

'How do we get to your shop from here?'

'Just follow the road back to the east end, but be careful to avoid the Russian Commissariat.'

'The Russian what?'

'The Russians set up their headquarters in the old police station.' 'A building with a swastika flag in front?'

'Swastika? That is the Bolsheviks' red flag.'

'*Mist!* We should have had a closer look,' Elli said. 'Do you know what happened to our people?'

Elli wasn't sure how Emil would react if she told him too much. The people here had come to an arrangement with the Russian occupiers, and might pass information along about the presence of SS. This could be lethal to the abducted families.

Emil's baby face tightened and he shrugged his shoulders. 'No, but be careful.'

'You had a long talk with him,' Rolf said when Elli came back. 'Does he know anything?'

'You were right, Hanna. The wagons you saw in the pine trees do belong to our people.'

'Are they still there? What happened to the SS?' Rolf said. 'I didn't ask.'

'Why not?' Hanna said.

'For these people, the war is over. The Russians are in their town.

Heaven knows what would happen if they learned about the presence of SS men,' Elli said.

'We have to go back to where we saw the wagons. We have to find out what is going on,' Rolf said.

'What about Hans?' Hanna said.

'It would be insane to just walk into the SS camp. Emil didn't know anything about them; the SS seem to keep to themselves. I think we should go back to the others and discuss it with them,' Elli said.

'We can't go back. We have to find Hans,' Hanna said.

'We'll never find him without help,' Rolf said. 'Elli is right. We have to go back.'

'If Hans has had an accident, he'll freeze to death before we find him.' Hanna was becoming desperate.

'*Liebling*, neither Elli nor I are able to search for him, which would mean you would have to do it alone. What chance would you have of finding him in the dark?'

'I'll ask Emil if he has heard anything about Hans,' Elli said.

Elli turned around but Emil was gone and the sausage stand had faded away in the drift of falling snow. For a moment the fire under the pot was visible, but then it disappeared too.

Lights, rides, and people appeared magically, only to be swallowed by a moving white curtain. Like in a dream, everything happened in slow motion, with little sound. Finding the street on which they had come into town, proved difficult.

'There, that must be the street,' Rolf said. 'Though they all look the same.'

As the light of the fair disappeared, the white wall swallowed them. They held on to each other, afraid that one wrong step could mean that they would be separated and lost.

For an eternity they stumbled along, holding onto picket fences. Finally, there was a gap, an opening in the row of houses, and they could make out the flagpole. They had reached the police station.

No lights: the station seemed deserted. The snow had slowed now and vision was a little better.

'Maybe we should ask the Russians,' Hanna said. 'Too dangerous, we have to go back,' Rolf said.

Their progress was slow, walking up the steep road, and Hanna had to support Rolf and Elli.

'We won't make it before midnight,' Elli said. 'We might freeze to death first.'

'If you hadn't smashed the sled, it would be easier,' Rolf said. 'And who would have pulled the sled uphill? Just keep walking or I'll let you slide down again,' Hanna said. 'Move, don't slow down, move.'

Elli wanted to protest, yell at Hanna to leave her alone. She needed a little rest. Just a little rest.

'Get up, Elli! Move!' That witch doesn't let up, Elli thought. She promised herself to tell her father that Hanna was no good for him, too pushy and demanding. 'Move Elli!'

Suddenly, like a beacon of hope, promising warmth and rest, the light of the campfire appeared.

'They're back. Quick, get them to the fire.'

Elli and Rolf stumbled to the fire. Hanna took charge, despite her exhaustion.

'Boil water and get every hot water bottle we have.'

Everyone but the two Americans scrambled. Smidt and Welsh, with their few words of German, couldn't understand what Hanna had said.

'Elli, what happened? Did you find them and where is Hans?' 'Out of the way.' Hanna was outraged by the American's insensitivity.

'What did she say Elli?'

'She wants you to get lost.' Elli couldn't help but smile when she saw the hurt expression on Smidt's face. 'Hanna knows what she is doing, and to answer your questions: I don't know what happened to Hans and yes, we found them but couldn't make contact.'

Hanna pushed him aside and started to stuff hot water bottles into Elli and Rolf's clothes.

'Elli, tell him we have to wait until morning before we can do anything, and press the point that if he doesn't lay off now, I'll shove a hot water bottle down his throat.' Elli felt her frozen face hurting from the grin as she translated Hanna's message.

The pain in her leg woke her up. It was still dark but she heard the crackling of the fire and voices. Someone had taken her clothes off and dressed her in py*ja*mas and several jumpers. Getting dressed was painful but she persisted without seeking help. Everyone was at the fire.

Rolf was explaining what had happened to them without bothering to translate to the Americans.

'What is going on, Elli?' Schmidt said.

'All right,' Rolf was saying, 'we will spread out at the point where Hans and Hanna separated from us. Stay in sight of each other.'

'What are you doing, Papa?' Rolf looked at her and the Americans and switched to English.

'We'll search for Hans by combing the meadow where he disappeared.'

'It's very close to the SS. They could see us coming,' said Elli. 'We have no choice. Hans could be in that field, injured, maybe frozen to death—or he could have been captured.'

'If they caught him, they'll be waiting for us,' Elli said.

'Maybe not. They have never seen Hans before, and not too many of our people knew Hans *Bürgermeister* personally either.'

'Didn't know their *Bürgermeister*?'

'Even, if they had seen him before, I don't think they would recognise him now,' Rolf said.

'It's very risky, Papa.'

'*Ja*, I know, but we can't just leave him there.' 'What happens if the SS see us?'

'They will see us only from a distance. We won't get too close to their camp.'

'Yea, but they could still shoot you even if you're not too close,' Smidt said.

'Not with the Russians around.'

'Oh Papa, this sounds like one of your crazier plans.'

They took the sled and the wagon to the spot where Hanna and Hans had climbed up the embankment. Two men stayed with the horses as the others lined up five metres apart across the meadow. Despite the clear weather and sunshine, their progress was slow. The ground was covered in deep snow that hid any holes and depressions. Occasionally one of the men disappeared into the snow and had to be pulled out.

There was no sign of Hans. Slowly they drew closer to the row of pine trees where they had seen the wagons. For the last hundred metres the meadow sloped down, into a long ditch running parallel to the trees on the ridge above them.

There was no sign of the wagons.

'Where are they Hanna? Shouldn't we be able to see them by now?' Elli said.

'I was closer,' Hanna said.

'*Ja*, but it was snowing then. I think we should stop here, where we can't be seen so easily.'

Rolf had already reached that conclusion, and gestured to the searchers to come over to him.

'We are close to the first houses. Look down the depression, you can see roofs,' Rolf said. 'We have to find out if the wagons are behind the trees. Hanna, Elli and I are not known to the SS, so we'll take a look.'

'What if they see us? They'll have guards,' Hanna said. 'Pretend you are from the town. Bluff your way into the camp,' Rolf said.

'Splendid plan, Papa,' Elli said.

Rolf gave her an irritated look. 'You have any better ideas? Anyone else? Now is the time to say so.'

No one spoke. Elli didn't want to go, but she felt unable to refuse.

Every one of the men, including the Americans, was well known to the SS. This left her father, Hanna, and her.

'If it's okay with Hanna we'll go, but without you, Papa,' Elli said.

'Out of the question,' Rolf said.

'Two women, one injured and leaning on the other, look harmless, but if an older man also injured, struggles along with them, it would surely look unusual. Would you agree with that, Papa?'

'Yes, but...'

'It'll be difficult for me to get up the slope, even with Hanna's help, but at least I can crawl on all fours. You can't use your arm and you wouldn't make it.' Elli saw that her father was resigned to her argument. His irritation was gone, replaced by fear for her and Hanna.

'There must be another way.'

'Maybe Papa,' Elli said gently. 'But I don't know it and there is no time. We'll be careful.'

Slowly, they progressed up the hill. Close to the ridge it became steeper, forcing them into a crawl. The snow was deep and powdery, easy to push through, but their passage formed a trench and the sides collapsed onto them. Breathing became difficult as moisture froze on the outside of their scarves, choking them. Elli tried to breathe through her nose without the scarf, but the icy air instantly froze her nostrils shut.

After a while, Elli could see the tops of the trees appearing above the horizon. They were close to the ridge. Without warning Hanna dropped flat down.

'They are right in front of us.'

'What?' Elli crawled beside her and carefully lifted her head. The SS camp was only twenty metres away, the wagons partially hidden by the trees. At the campfire, women and children were preparing food, peeling potatoes, and stacking firewood. On an improvised table, made from boards laid over large boulders, four women were preparing chickens. Elli felt herself salivating.

Two grey-haired men were sitting on a bench close to the fire, ignoring the activity around them. Close to the wagons, three younger men were feeding the horses.

The peaceful scene clashed painfully with what she expected, no prisoners, no guards, just collaboration.

'What is going on here, Elli? Are these our people? '*Ja*, they are ours,' Elli said.

'But how could they work like this with these bastards, after they shot three of their boys and locked the rest in a cellar to die. How could they?'

'I don't know.' Elli hesitated. 'Something else is wrong. I can see only five men. Where are the others?'

Her question was answered seconds later by the sharp click of a gun being cocked behind her.

'Well, well, and what do we have here? Two *Fräuleinchen*!'

Chapter 32

Hans followed Hanna's tracks, thinking he would easily catch up, but he was wrong. It was getting darker and the gale-force wind picked up the powdery snow, dissolving Hanna's tracks before his eyes. To make it worse, even though it was only midday, the light was dull and grey.

He had to find Hanna, but which way to go?

He remembered Hanna had seen the wagons hidden behind trees on top of a ridge. He could see the meadow rising ahead of him so, as he had no other directional indicator, he shook off the snow and started climbing.

When he reached the top there were trees but no sign of Hanna.

He had climbed the wrong ridge.

Nearly crying with frustration, he turned to go back. His tracks were gone and there were no clues to what direction he should take.

The cold was creeping up from his feet and the ice crystals in the wind stung his face. He needed shelter urgently. After a few attempts to dig a hole in the powdery snow, he gave up. It was like trying to make a sandcastle with dry sand.

He knew that the leaden tiredness he felt was really the sign that he was slowly freezing to death. His only chance of survival was to reach the town. It was close, he knew, but where?

He stumbled down the ridge, not knowing if he was retracing his steps.

Visibility was down to a few metres. The gritty snow blowing in his eyes felt like sand. He closed his eyes and continued.

The need to sleep grew stronger and stronger. Sleep—just for a moment. He jerked upright. Don't give in you fool, you'll die! He continued dragging himself along, stumbling into holes that were invisible under the snow, and crawling out again.

He lost track of time, but kept going, knowing that the town's first houses were close by.

He kept crawling.

Only a little sleep, only for a moment. No, he must go on. Go now.

Something kept poking into his side; he ignored it and crawled on.

The poking continued. Annoyed, he stopped, pushed himself up, opened his eyes.

A tree was looming over him. Must have run into a branch, he thought. Then the tree moved. Someone grabbed him under the arms and lifted him up. Not trees, two people standing beside him. Then he realised they were talking to him. But he couldn't understand Russian.

Elli and Hanna turned. Two men pointed pistols at them. 'Why are you spying on us?' The older one said. Elli thought feverishly for an explanation.

'We came to look after our pigs.'

'Your pigs? What kind of a stupid lie is that?'

'But it's the truth,' Elli said trying to sound scared and desperate—which was not difficult at all. 'My father is a butcher and he's hidden a couple of pigs at the far end of this field.'

'You are lying. There are no pigs here.'

'Papa built an underground shelter into the hillside,' Elli pointed to the far end of the open plain. 'You can't see it from here.'

'What's your father's name?' 'Emil Strausser.'

'Is he a small man?'

'Oh no, Papa is big. Some say fat, but to me, he is cuddly.' The tension on the man's face relaxed, he must have heard of or seen the butcher and his *Würstchenbude* —Emil's sausage stand.

'Walk ahead of us, to the fire. We'll look for your pigs later.' Elli stumbled when she stood up. Hanna rushed to help.

'Why are you limping?' the SS man said. Elli decided that the truth would be best and might get her sympathy.

'I was raped and shot by the Russians when they came through our town.'

The SS man looked at her in surprise, but didn't say anything.

Elli's fear of being exposed by people in the camp increased as she came closer to the fire. All activity had stopped as everyone stared at the new arrivals. Elli tried to avoid looking at the faces watching her and Hanna, hoping no one would call out. She saw Heicke, Armin Hauser's wife, their two daughters and grandchildren, all staring at her but none of them, not even the children, gave any indication they knew her.

The two men on the bench were watching them closely. 'We found these two women on top of the ridge. They were observing our camp, *Gruppenführer*.' The SS man finished his announcement by clicking his heels, despite standing in soft snow. Papa was right, Elli thought, it is an SS General. And although the Russians are almost within shouting distance, and they are in civilian clothes, they behave like an SS unit. The General was an archetypical SS officer; lean and wiry, his face scarred by traditional swordplay. He had a short military haircut and a monocle squeezed in his left eye. Even camouflaged as a refugee, his clothes were spotless and without creases; he still looked like a soldier, and an aristocrat.

'No titles, you idiot! His voice was without emotion, making it sound even more menacing. The SS man responded hastily.

'*Jawohl*, Gr... sir.'

The other older man was dressed like the others, but his casual appearance showed that he was used to civilian clothes. His bloated face, and his watery eyes with deep bags underneath, gave him the appearance of an old cocker spaniel. However, the harmless image dissolved when he spoke in an out of breath, high-pitched voice.

'Two pretty *Fräuleins*! I wonder why you are spying on us?' He was trying to sound friendly, but the words came out as sharp as rapiers.

Elli repeated her story, surprised that the General let the other man take charge.

'If you are not lying, why didn't we see you yesterday, or do you only feed your pigs occasionally?'

'We feed them whenever we have leftovers, but we check them every day.' Elli said. 'They are very intelligent and find lots of edible roots under the snow.'

'So where are the leftovers for the pigs?' the man said stretching each word as he spoke.

'There aren't any. Yesterday was Sunday, when we go to church, and in the afternoon it snowed. That's why we had to check them today.' Elli prayed that he didn't ask more questions.

'They are obviously harmless,' the General cut in. 'We'll let them go when we move on.' The reaction from the civilian surprised Elli.

'*Gruppenführer,* use your head. We can't let them go. They know that we are not a normal refugee group. Execute them!'

For a moment both men stared silently at each other, then the General spoke. 'Don't be stupid, Vogel, we can't shoot them without being heard. The Russians are too close.'

'We can,' Vogel said. He reached into his long overcoat and pulled out a pistol fitted with a silencer.

Oh God, I don't want to die, Elli prayed. I hope the others got away. My poor children will need their grandfather.

'Still too risky. I say no,' the General said.

'*Gruppenführe*r, must I remind you that the Gestapo is in charge of this operation? Get rid of them.'

Reluctantly, the General took the Gestapo man's gun, and handed it to one of his men.

'Take them away from the camp.'

Two men guided Elli and Hanna through the camp as everyone looked on silently. Almost at the end of the camp, Elli heard a child's voice calling her.

'Aunty Elli, Aunty Elli.' Elli's heart stopped for a moment. A little girl, not older than six, with her arm in a sling, tore herself from her mother and ran towards Elli. It was Angelica Schuster, the girl whose blood-covered doll they had found.

'*Halt,*' she heard the General. 'Bring them back here, and the girl.'

We are finished, Elli thought. Now they will find out who we really are. They'll capture the others—and we'll all be shot.

'I found your doll, Angelica. Did you get hurt?' Elli said. There was no reason to pretend any more.

'I fell off the wagon. Oh goody, where is my dolly?' 'In my wagon. Anna took good care of it.'

A satisfied smile creased the General's face. 'So you know each other. Which means no pigs at the end of the meadow? I knew that we didn't get all of your godforsaken group. You've given us nothing but trouble. Where are the rest of you?'

'We are the only ones. We hid in a cellar. Yesterday we reached this town and saw the wagons.' Elli hoped that he would believe her. They would too easily find the men if they searched.

'She is lying,' Vogel said. 'They must have found the men you refused to execute. Maybe they even found the Americans.'

A murmur travelled through the women and children, who up to this moment had been quiet.

'Quiet!' Vogel screamed at the top of his voice, coughing, his face flushing. 'Any more disobedience and we'll execute your brats!'

The crowd fell instantly silent with only occasional whimpers to be heard. 'Much better,' he said in his oily voice. 'Search for them. They'll be hiding close by.'

After Elli and Hanna had been gone for more than an hour, the others became restless.

Huddled in the snow, Rolf was well protected in the centre of the cluster they had formed to keep each other warm. Because of his injured shoulder he did not have to rotate with the others and he stayed warm on all sides.

'We can't wait here until our arses turn to ice,' Rolf said, pushing against his companions. 'It's probably too late anyway; I can't feel anything below my waist.'

'Sit still, Rolf,' Smidt said. 'I was just getting a bit warmer and you, you idiot, have to wave your arms around.'

'*Arschloch*!' Rolf stood up, disregarding the protesting howls of his companions. 'We can't wait any longer. We have to go after them.'

'Shhhh! Shut up, and get down.' Smidt pulled Rolf down. 'You hurt my shoulder. *Miststück, verfluchtes*!'

'Stop whining, and listen!' Smidt said. Rolf gave the American an irritated look, searching for an insult in response. Then he heard voices— male voices shouting commands.

'*Oh, mein lieber Gott!* they got them.' They strained to hear more but it was quiet. Rolf could see that all of his group, including the Americans, were on the edge of running away. Rolf felt like running too, but not away. He wanted to run in pursuit of his two women, defending them, killing anyone who would harm them. He trembled, wanting to scream, and stood up. The fear in the other faces stopped him.

'What is going on, Rolf? What did the American say?' Manfred said.

'We have to get away from here. You heard it—they caught

Elli and Hanna but there were no shots. They must have captured them. Knowing what the SS can do, they'll soon find out that Elli and Hanna were not alone. We have to get into the town and get help.'

'Even if we make it, who would help us against the SS?' Manfred said.

'The Russians would be interested,' Rolf said, and translated for the Americans.

'The Russians? Are you insane?' Smidt said.

'Who else? The town's people certainly won't help, and we can't do anything alone, against a bunch of armed SS. They would shoot us on the spot. The Russians, though, they would love to get their hands on them. Enough palaver!' He rapidly explained in German, and in

English to the Americans. 'We have to get away from here. They'll be looking for us.'

'Okay, anything's better than freezing our arses off in this snow hole,' Smidt said.

'Yea, instead we'll freeze everything else off crawling on our bellies to the town,' Rolf said.

'Rolf you've been there. Do you remember the way?' Smidt said.

'*Ja*, I'll lead. Follow me.' Rolf hesitated when he saw their grins.

'What now?'

'Come on Rolf,' Smidt said. 'You are moving like a drunken sailor with your damaged shoulder. I'll lead. You follow behind with Welsh.'

'You are not quite in control here, *Amerikaner*.' He felt stupid as soon as he had barked at the American. Smidt was only trying to help him, but no way would he let himself be ordered around by this arrogant ...

Smidt took Rolf's outburst in his stride. But when he smiled, Rolf was ready to throttle him. The other men looked on confused, as Rolf didn't bother to translate.

'I'm not trying to control anything,' Smidt said. 'But it would be easier for you if I walk ahead, to be your snowplough.'

Rolf looked at him suspiciously, but saw only Smidt's pacifying smile. 'Well, go ahead then,' he said and added hastily when he saw Welsh's barely suppressed grin, 'but I'll give you the directions. And tell your ape to get his hands off me. I can walk without being pawed by him.'

Welsh let Rolf go.

After two hours of crawling and stumbling along the ravine, without hearing or seeing anyone pursuing them, they saw the rooftops of the first houses.

Rolf felt a sapping, paralysing tiredness and not only in his body. His mind could focus only on sleep and warmth.

'Come on buddy, keep moving.' Welsh prodded him like a cattle dog. God how he hated the brutish American, but Rolf was too weak to swear.

'Look buddy. We made it! Houses! We made it!'

'Call me 'Buddy' once more and I'll kill you.' Welsh's words sunk in. 'What? Where?'

Even without translation the others understood. 'Dippoldiswalde, we made it! Not a moment too soon, I'm nearly dead.' They stood up, hopping excitedly around.

'Get down, you idiots.' Rolf felt relieved, even though he was stiff and could hardly understand his own voice. 'There are Russians everywhere, so shut up.' He turned to Smidt who was still crawling along. 'Smidt, stop! We have to discuss what we do from here.'

There was warmth all around him—beautiful warmth soaking into his body, loosening his frozen limbs and joints. Even the biting pain in his legs from long exposure to cold was bearable, as the heat dissolved it. He couldn't remember ever feeling so relaxed. Gently he slid back into sleep—until his nose was below the bathwater and he exploded into violent coughing. He opened his eyes. The bathtub he was submerged in was filled to the brim. The steam rising from it hid any details in the semi-dark bathroom. Hans's thoughts were racing. The last thing he remembered was voices, Russian voices! How did he end up in here?

He saw his lean body in the soapy water. His eyes were burning. He touched his head and felt soap in his hair. Someone had undressed him and washed his hair.

A noise came from beyond the door. He dived deeper into the water as if the soapy water could protect him from whoever entered the bathroom.

The door was stuck and the invader pushed hard. It flew open with a bang and a large woman in Russian army uniform stumbled over the doorstep, followed by a small man in civilian clothes. He was the size of a starved twelve-year old and had the owlish face of a middle-aged bureaucrat.

Hans instinctively covered his crotch when he saw the woman's leering glance. He realised that she must have undressed and washed him. She turned to the grey man and asked something. Hans only understand only '*Nyet*'. No: her request was denied. She shrugged her shoulders, patted Hans on the head and left.

'You are lucky, Svetlana likes you,' the stone-faced man said in German. 'And even luckier that your friend watched her when they undressed and bathed you. Svetlana can be very rough when she likes a man.'

'My friend watched her! What friend?' Hans said.

'Later.' The man dismissed his question. 'How do you feel? We thought you would have severe frostbite but it seems you were lucky.'

'Where am I?' Hans said.

'In the bathroom of the Russian Commissariat.' 'Who are you and why are you taking care of me?'

'My name is Jürgen Schmalke. I'm the appointed Political Officer of this town.'

'But you are German.'

'*Ja*, and a dedicated communist trained at the NKWD in Moscow.' He paused. 'Here are some dry clothes your friend has laid out for you. If you feel better, get dressed, then come into the next room. We'll be waiting for you.'

Hans was confused. After drying himself with a towel—so soft, he had forgotten such a thing existed—he slipped into the clothes lying on a chair. They fitted perfectly. Strange he thought. Then he saw the label on the shirt collar—Schulze, Finest Tailor of Krummhübel. It was from his own tailor—and it was his own shirt. What was going on here?

He opened the door into a large office. Close to the window at the back stood three people. Schmalke and the Russian woman were facing him. The third person was a woman with her back to him. The light was behind her and her face was in the dark. Then he heard her.

'Hello Hans, I'm so glad you are all right.' 'Ruth?' Hans whispered. 'Is that really you?'

❄

'We can't just walk into the town,' Smidt said.

'Why not?' Rolf said. 'The town is occupied, by the Russians, your allies; you'll be greeted with flowers.'

'More likely shot,' Smidt said.

'What silly talk is that? Why should the Russians shoot two of their American allies?'

'Because we know things that the Russians wouldn't like to get back to the States.'

'You'll have to explain that,' Rolf said.

'When the Russians started their winter offensive it became clear that they intended to be the first in Berlin. That is their ultimate prize.'

'*Ja*, so what?'

'Well, the US decided not to participate in that race, and to concentrate on securing the south of Germany. But the English are more competitive; they are as keen as the Russians to be the first in Berlin.'

'Okay, I get it, but what does that have to do with you?' Rolf said. 'We were sent to check the advance of the Russians. Stalin is paranoid about the Allies depriving him of his prize.'

'Understandable,' Rolf said. 'So?'

'So, American planes flying over areas the Russians occupied, or are intending to occupy, were shot down.'

'Let me see if I've got it right. The Russians, your allies, are shooting down your planes because they don't want you to know how close to Berlin they are?' Rolf grinned and continued. 'I must say that's rather funny. Aren't your people objecting to it?'

'Sure, we are,' Smidt said. 'But whenever one of our planes is lost over their area, the Russians say that it was either accidentally shot down or the Germans did it.'

'And as you survived being shot down by them, they are keen to keep you silent,' Rolf said. 'I can see why you are reluctant to fall into their hands.' Rolf hesitated then his face lit up. 'Oh, I get it. That's why the Nazis were after you and wanted to take you to Berlin. If the Nazis could demonstrate to the allies that the Russians are pushing through to Berlin and shooting down allied planes, it would be rather embarrassing for the Russians. Correct?'

'Yes.' Smidt said.

'Hilarious! The Russians, your allies, want to silence you—and the Nazis, your enemies, want you alive.'

'Yes, Smidt said, grimfaced. 'Except that it's not funny.

'I don't know what you two are babbling about,' Manfred said. 'But you can forget about any plans you had. The Russians are here.'

Russian soldiers suddenly emerged from everywhere, pointing their guns at them. A small, grey-looking civilian came towards them.

'Colonel Smidt, and Captain Welsh, how are you?' the civilian said in English.

No one said anything, but some of the men identified Smidt and Welsh by looking at them when they recognised the Americans' names. The civilian smiled, stretching his right arm out to shake their hands.

'Jürgen Schmalke, Political Commissar and translator. It's a pleasure meeting you gentlemen.'

'What, to shoot us?' Smidt said.

Schmalke looked astonished. 'Sir? Shoot you? Why should we shoot our allies?' Schmalke laughed. 'I know what you mean. Well, the war situation has somewhat changed. I assure you that you are absolutely safe.' His grin became even broader. 'Berlin has fallen to the Red Army; Hitler is dead and the only fighting still going on is in the north. The war is almost over, and the information you have has become irrelevant.'

Smidt and Welsh were too overwhelmed to say anything.

While Rolf was translating for the others, tears were running down the Americans' faces.

'Would you please follow me?' Schmalke said. 'We learned that you had survived the crash and were taken by the SS, and we were hunting them. In Bömchen we found out that the SS had kidnapped a refugee group, but our source could not tell us where you were—with the SS or left behind with the other men. So, we carefully followed the SS only to find you here. Astonishing!'

'Who was your source?' Rolf said.

'Your daughter, Ruth,' Schmalke said. 'She and her two children came with us from Bömchen. They are waiting for you. Also, some American officers are waiting for Colonel Smidt and Captain Walsh.'

The news that Ruth and the children were there sank in slowly. Rolf's immediate concern was for Elli and Hanna.

'Did you find two women, Elli and Hanna? They were trying to find the SS group.'

'No, we only found a man, nearly frozen to death, who told us about this group being somewhere close. His name is Hans Kruse.'

'Oh God, Elli and Hanna must have been caught by the SS,' Rolf said.

'We'll find out soon when we take them out.'

'Take them out? Our women and children are their hostages!'

'We'll make sure they don't get harmed,' Schmalke said.

Elli saw the search team returning, without prisoners. Her relief lasted only moments. Two SS men roughly pushed Elli and Hanna to the fire where the General and Vogel were talking to the searchers.

Vogel fondled his pistol, taking the silencer off and slowly screwing it on again.

'Well, my *Fräuleins*, it looks like they got away. So, I'll ask you really nicely, if you know where they are.'

As he was talking, he loaded and unloaded the pistol, played with the bullets like worry beads. He pointed the loaded gun at Elli.

More than the gun, his voice dripping with barely suppressed violence paralysed Elli. She knew that he would shoot her. Her mind raced. Think woman! Think!

'The two Americans said something about getting information back to their people.' Elli had no idea why the Nazis were so keen to get hold of the Americans, but the reaction on the men's faces told her that she had stayed their execution—at least for the moment.

'Ah, so you know them after all. But maybe you are just lying, as you did before.' Vogel tried to smile, but only a few muscles obeyed. His lifeless eyes held hers, a predator ready to devour its prey.

'They were flying a spy plane and were shot down.' Elli tried to avoid his stare. 'I think they had some photographic film.' She hoped that he wouldn't press for details, as it would immediately become clear that she was lying.

'She is lying,' the General said. 'If they had a film we would have found it.'

Vogel looked at her. 'You are lying. Aerial photography films are big. We would have found them.'

Think Elli! Think! Vogel aimed his gun at her again. 'When we found them, they had a metal cylinder,' she said. It worked. He lowered the gun.

'You are wasting time,' the General said to Vogel. 'We had the Americans in our custody for a long time. They didn't have anything like that. She is lying.'

Vogel looked at Elli and Hanna, stood up, and handed his gun to an SS man.

'Take them away from the others and finish them off,' he said without any further hesitation.

The SS man marched Elli and Hanna through the camp. All the women and children stood beside the wagons, crying and hugging each other for comfort, avoiding looking at Elli and Hanna.

Elli felt sad for them, having to watch as they were led away to be executed. She knew that any objection would result in the same fate for them or their children; if she were in their position, she would do the same.

About a hundred metres into the meadow, out of sight of the camp, the SS man stopped.

Elli looked at him. He was in his early twenties, blond, blue-eyed, a perfect Arian specimen.

'Sit down. I'll fire a couple of shots in the air and go back to the camp. You stay here for a while after I've gone.'

Elli and Hanna stared at him in surprise, unable to say anything.

The SS man smiled, pointed the pistol in the air and fired. The shots from the silencer sounded like a pea-gun. He turned around and walked off.

He hadn't gone more than five metres when a volley of shots hit his body, ripping him apart. Then shots came from the camp, followed by an eerie silence.

Too afraid to get up, they stayed in the snow, still surprised at being alive. Shadows fell on them. Elli looked up—into the grinning faces of Russian soldiers.

'Gute Fräuleinchen. Schnell! Schnell!'

A dozen or more heavily armed Russian soldiers marched them back to the wagons. As they passed the body of the SS man who had let them get away, Elli saw a Russian soldier cutting off the man's ears. She had to stop and vomit. A painful kick, accompanied by some grunts from a Russian guard, urged her to get going again.

The first thing she saw was that the women and children seemed to be unharmed, and that the Russians did not seem to be interfering with the women or girls.

A few SS men had been shot but most of them were alive, including the General and Vogel. All were stripped down to their underpants, their arms in the air. The Russians pointed their guns at them and occasionally gave them a prod. But in general, they were unharmed.

A Russian officer shouted at the women and children. He wanted them to load up their wagons ready to be escorted to the town.

Silently, too shocked to resist, they followed the directions.

Two hours later they arrived at the Commissariat. Rolf, Hans and the other men were waiting for them.

A familiar-looking woman stood beside her father. Elli needed some time before she recognised Ruth.

'Ruthy, I thought I would never see you again!'

The reunion of the refugee families was quiet and tearful. Elli and Hanna listened in disbelief to the story of the SS and

Russians chasing the Americans.

'Where are Smidt and Welsh? I haven't seen them,' Elli said. 'They are with that little German communist,' Rolf said. 'With who?'

'A German communist who is apparently in charge here, or atleast thinks he is. Ah, here they come.'

A group of American officers, led by a civilian and a Russian officer, walked toward them. Elli almost failed to recognize Smidt and Welsh in their smart uniforms. Smidt hesitated at first but then took Elli in his arms, kissed her and stepped back.

'What? No slapping today?' he said.

'Not today.' She smiled. 'Be careful. I see that the two of you are back in uniform. The prodigal sons return, *ja*?

'Something like that.'

The civilian interjected in English. 'I am Commissar Schmalke,' he said. 'Your American friends told us that you want to go to Hamburg. They have arranged transport for you.'

'But isn't the fighting still going on?' Elli said.

'The war is over. Hitler is dead and his successor, Admiral Doenitz, signed an unconditional surrender. You can go to Hamburg.'

Hanna and Elli were still trying to comprehend what they just heard, when the Russian officer said something to Schmalke.

'The Commander asks you to come with him. He wants to show you something.'

The group followed the Russian and the German, who eagerly guided them to the back of the Commissariat building.

In the grey light and falling snow she saw Russian soldiers, standing shoulder to shoulder with their backs to them, covering what was behind. The Russian commander shouted something and the men stepped aside, revealing a gaunt timber construction of a single beam between two posts: gallows.

Eight men, short ropes around their necks, were suspended from large hooks. Elli recoiled, covered her face, and turned away.

The Russian commander turned back to them and spoke with a broad smile.

'The commander is proud that he could execute the SS. His family was murdered by them,' Schmalke translated.

Elli forced herself to look back at the executed men. Their bodies hung from the overhead beam, their feet nearly touching the ground.

Oh God, she thought, they're strung up like carcasses in a butcher's shop. On the left she saw the General and Vogel.

The General's face was distorted by pain and his lifeless, bulging eyes, stared at them. Then Vogel's body moved and she heard him gasping for air.

'Oh God, he's still alive!' Elli clung to Ruth as the dying man fought for his last breaths.

'The commander insisted they die like his wife and children, slowly suffocating,' Schmalke said. 'The knots of the nooses are at the side of their necks to ensure they die as they deserve to.'

Elli looked at the satisfied face of the Russian commander. 'It never ends.' Her voice was heard only by Ruth, as they walked away.

Epilogue

The small placard read 'Have you seen or heard anything about Peter Hoff? Missing at the Eastern Front since 1944.' The photo showed a skinny teenage boy. The icy February wind did its best to rip the placard away from the old woman's hand.

'Is he coming back today?' Elli said.

The woman's voice trembled, barely audible. 'He should be on this train. I have waited here so many times.'

As she turned to Elli, her face became still and the tremble in her voice vanished, even though tears were running down her cheeks. 'I come here every time a transport arrives,' the woman said.

She paused a moment, took a deep breath and continued. 'I had three sons and only Arnold came back. Hans died near Stalingrad and Peter is still missing. He was only sixteen when he was drafted and sent to the Eastern front. He was only a baby.'

She frowned. 'They gave me the Mutter Kreutz medal, for giving two sons to *Vaterland and Führer*. If Arnold had died too, it would have been the golden Mother's Cross. A medal for their lives! When Peter comes back, I'll have to give the medal back. One dead son does not count.' Her face softened again. 'My poor baby, he has been missing for so long. Maybe someone saw him or heard of him.' She smiled at Elli. 'Who are you waiting for, young lady?'

'My husband is coming back.'

'I'm so glad for you. You came a long way?' 'From Hamburg.'

'Oh, you poor dear, that is a long way.' 'Where are you from?'

'I lived in Wiesbaden but I moved to Friedland because I couldn't afford to travel each time a transport arrived. I don't know why the POW transports only come to this border town. Excuse me, I have to go to the main exit, so they can see his picture. *Auf Wiedersehen*.'

She rushed over to join the crowd of women displaying photos and placards.

Elli asked a Red Cross official why there were so many First Aid stations here.

'Are you waiting for someone on this transport?' 'Yes, my husband is coming back from Russia.'

'Lady, you have no idea. We were taken by surprise with the first group. Everyone thought that the Russians dealt with the POWs according to the Geneva Convention. Well, that was a mistake. Most of the men could hardly walk. They had severe frostbite and awful injuries, and they all looked like walking skeletons. I guess they are the lucky ones. They are alive, although some of them only just. Still, it's better than having died in Siberia.'

A loudspeaker bellowed. *Achtung! Achtung!* Please stay back from the platform, the special train will arrive in five minutes.'

The crowd became restless. Women lifted children up and jostled for positions closer to the platform fence.

By now, it was dark and snowing again, dulling the bubble of light over the platform. The loud whistle of a locomotive came out of the darkness. Elli strained to look down the railway track but could see nothing.

Then three faint lights became visible, the headlights of a train. As the lights became brighter, the crowd erupted into screaming and shouting. Without warning, the platform was bathed in bright light. The camera teams from the news services went into action. Elli could hear the puffing and hissing of the engine.

Slowly the train emerged out of the darkness and pulled into the station. A short distance from the end of the platform, with a screech, the engine's wheels spun in the opposite direction. The train came to a shuddering halt. For a few moments it was invisible, behind a curtain of steam.

Slowly the cloud dispersed to reveal the engine, its black paint dominated by a red star at the front. The carriages were thick with ice and snow, covering most of the Cyrillic letters on the sides.

Siberia still had its grip on the POWs. This train had come directly from Russia.

Creaking noises came from the carriages, and loud banging as impatient men tried to open the frozen doors.

The waiting crowd exploded into frenzied shouting and jostling for better positions for their placards and pictures.

'Has anyone seen Ulli Haberbaum? Please look at the photo, please!'

'Please let me through, my son must be on this train.'

The first POWs appeared. At each carriage door, Red Cross officials helped them descend onto the platform. They moved slowly and often stopped. A few smiled, but most faces showed disbelief as they stared at the crowd.

The train continued to spill out its cargo and soon hundreds of bewildered, tired men crowded the platform. Their faces looked out of the remnants of woollen scarves and uniform caps pulled over their heads.

Eyes—sunken by pain and hunger into tissue-covered skulls—looked around, weary, frightened and hopeless. Most just stood where the Red Cross men let go of them. They tried to cover their eyes, blinded by the lights of the news cameras.

Gently, the officials moved them down the platform towards the exit and their waiting relatives.

As the men came closer the mood of the crowd changed. It became quiet.

Horrified, the relatives looked at the faces, trying to identify a familiar one.

Elli looked at each man as he passed by.

Many supported each other, or hung between helpers.

Occasionally, someone slumped to the ground and had to be lifted onto a stretcher and carried away.

Then she saw him.

He wore an army coat, far too large for his wasted body.

He stumbled along, unattended, dragging his feet.

Elli jumped over the barricade, ignoring the protest from the Red Cross men as she rushed over to her husband.

'Claus! Claus! Here, it's me, Elli!'

His blank face gave no indication that he recognised her. Elli held his face with both hands, pulled him down to her and gently kissed his cracked lips. A small spark of recognition lightened his face. His eyes were smiling.

'Elli? Elli, is that you?' His voice was no more than a whisper. 'What are you doing here?' He stopped, his head down, shaking.

'Claus, look at me.'

Slowly, he lifted his head. 'Is that really you?' Both his hands came up, touching Elli's face. His hands felt like pieces of leather. She had to fight the impulse to withdraw as he caressed her face.

'Oh God, it's really you. I am back,' and he crumbled into her arms. His body was as fragile as a child's. Elli had no problem holding him up. Two Red Cross helpers rushed over and lifted him onto a stretcher.

At the exit, Elli saw the old woman again, still holding up her photo, smiling at every face passing her, still hopeful. Elli knew she would be back when the next transport arrived.

Claus, like many of the returned soldiers, stayed in the small Friedland hospital for several days. Most of the time he was unconsciousness or under sedation. After a week, Elli managed to get him transferred to a hospital in Hamburg.

The doctors found that Claus had stomach ulcers, as well as other problems related to malnutrition and frostbite. One of the ulcers was serious and he needed an urgent operation.

The operation was successful but they kept him heavily sedated for days. Elli visited him every day.

On the fifth day, the head nurse greeted her with a big smile. 'He is conscious, and constantly asking when you will be here.'

Elli rushed to his room. He was awake and beamed at her when she entered. For the next hour, Elli kissed and hugged him and said how much she had missed him.

'I heard nothing from you for years. 'Missing in action' they said. I thought you were dead. It was terrible.'

Claus talked about the POW camp in Siberia. 'Most of the others died. Every day and night some died. No food, only hard work, and the relentless cold. It was always dark, sometimes for months. I survived because I could speak Russian, even though they thought I was a spy at first and tortured me. I became a kind of clerk. I worked inside. All the others died, one by one. The Russians didn't give us enough food and clothing, but everyone had to work outside. Often the work was pointless, good only for slowly killing us. That was their main purpose: killing us after they had marched us through half of Siberia to show off to their population. Payback, they told us.' He stopped and touched her hands. 'Your turn. You haven't said anything. How come you and the family ended up in Hamburg?'

Elli told him what had happened after they left Krummhübel.

Claus looked at her, his eyes wide open, his face drained of blood. 'Is that why I haven't seen the children? Are they hurt?'

'No, no, the children are fine! They are itching to see their father.'
'So where are they?'

'Outside. I asked them to wait. I have to tell you something.'

'Are they really alright?'

'Yes, they are, all four of them.'

'Let them in.' Then it registered. 'Wait, what do you mean, all four of them? We have three children.'

'There is one more. His name is Jochen, named after his dead father,' Elli said.

'Who was this Jochen?' He sounded scared.

'Jochen died when we crossed the Elbe. He died because he tried to warn the people still crossing. If Jochen hadn't gone back on the ice, many more people would have died.'

'How long did your relationship last?'

'Relationship? He and two others joined us several weeks after we left Krummhübel. He was an army engineer. Without his help we wouldn't have made it. We only had one night together.' Elli felt her eyes burning but fought back the tears.

Claus looked at her, his fear replaced by tenderness. There was nothing else to say. They were silent.

Claus cleared his throat. 'I was away for a long time,' he said gently.

'Yes, eight years 'Missing in Action'. Two years ago, I had to declare you officially dead so that I could get a pension.'

'Eight years. Two of them dead.' He took Elli's hands in his. 'My dear Elli, we have a lot of catching up to do, all six of us. Now let them in.'

COMING NEXT: THE VENTRILOQUIST

If *And Silently Falls the Snow* stirred your heart, then *The Ventriloquist* will keep it racing.

In this gripping follow-up, Klaus M. Schwarzenholz shifts the lens to 1960s Germany, where the Berlin Wall has carved the country in two and fear lurks behind every door. Teenage Niklas lives with his grandparents in Hamburg, where he finds refuge and excitement in the smoke and shadows of the city's variety theatres. There, he watches in awe as his grandfather Rolf, a daring ventriloquist with a sharp tongue and a handmade cockatoo puppet, mesmerises audiences and subtly defies the regime.

But in a world where freedom of expression is dangerous, Rolf's bold act soon draws the attention of the Stasi. As tensions rise, escape becomes not just a hope, but a necessity. Ruth, Rolf's headstrong daughter and a celebrated artist with international reach, is also under surveillance, refusing to be a pawn in the government's hands. As borders close and escape routes dwindle, the family faces impossible choices.

Based on real events, *The Ventriloquist* follows three generations as they navigate secrets, sacrifice, and survival in a nation ruled by silence and fear. From smuggled letters and false identities to daring escapes hidden in stage props, their story is a tribute to creativity, courage, and the power of performance.

Told through the lens of theatre and ventriloquism, this novel offers a fresh, evocative take on Cold War fiction.

Rich in historical detail and emotional depth, *The Ventriloquist* explores identity, resistance, and the unbreakable bonds of family in the face of tyranny.

The war may be over.....
but the danger has only just begun.

www.klausschwarzenholz.com

Instagram: @klausschwarzenholzauthor

Facebook: @klausschwarzenholzauthor

www.ingramcontent.com/pod-product-compliance
Lightning Source LLC
Chambersburg PA
CBHW070434170726
48291CB00002B/502

* 9 7 8 1 7 6 3 7 0 4 2 7 5 *